# ASCENSION POINT

## DAN HARRIS

# Dedication

To my parents, for encouraging me to read. And to Amisha, for encouraging me to write.

# 1. Titan

The hoverbike tore through the chest-high meadow grass, the energy field at the nose fizzing as it boiled away the last of the morning dew. Luc Corralin angled towards a small hill in the middle of the plain and pushed the throttle even harder. He crouched low over the handlebars as he sped towards the hillock, on course for a collision that not even the overworked nose field could prevent.

At the last possible moment, Luc flicked the power stick near his right thumb, redirecting all of the thrust from the rear boosters to the front uplift. As if yanked from above by a mischievous god, the nose shot upwards, combining with the bike's momentum to launch him into a spectacular backflip.

He landed hard on the other side of the hill, then shifted the power back to the rear. The bike jumped forwards, engine groaning in protest as Luc steered through the small herd of deer scattering around him and changed course to head back towards the Rift Six Agrihub.

*'Straight there, no dawdling. The coordinator is a lady called Marguerite, a very dear friend. You are to give her any assistance she requires. Understand, boy?'*

Luc grimaced and spat over his right shoulder. Proctor Samuel's barked command that morning had been the latest in a long list of menial tasks he deemed worth the time of a Titan neophyte. His hectoring was even more irritating than usual.

*It could turn out to be interesting, at least. Maybe.* Luc hadn't really been paying attention to the details while Samuel rambled on about the happenings at the agrihub that had got his dear friend Marguerite into such a state. Something about the workers being attacked, or maybe going on strike. He'd been far too busy trying to get the attention of Samuel's pert new assistant. *Sasha? Sonia?*

Luc was pretty sure he had made an impression; even amongst the well-proportioned citizens of Mission, he knew he was considered quite eye-catching. *Seven feet tall, olive skin, all muscle, carefully scruffy sand-colour hair. And the gold eyes, of course.* When he did the pupil-narrowed cat's eye thing, well... The ladies just swooned. *Most of the time. Sonia hasn't really gone for it.* He frowned, swerving to avoid a bullock that had stopped in his path to stare at the onrushing bike. *Or is her name Serena?*

Ten minutes later, the roof of the agrihub came into view, sunlight reflecting from the solar panels that provided energy for the complex. The hub sat in a broad valley between two low ranges of hills, close to the edge of the Rift Six octant and nearly eighty miles from Rift itself, the chasm-spanning city that was Mission's capital. *Or 'the spiritual home of the Titan universe for over two millennia' as Samuel calls it. Regularly.* Luc throttled back the hoverbike's thrusters as he neared the agrihub and guided it into the parking bay on the east side of the complex. The bike settled onto the ground with a wheezing cough as he killed the engine. His heavy tan boots clanged against the plasmetal floor of the bay as he stepped off.

As usual, he had eschewed dressing in the officially

mandated neophyte's work tunic, risking cleaning detail if Samuel caught him, opting for a plain grey vest and brownish trousers that had been his favourite since the age of fifteen.

Rolling his shoulders to shake out the stiffness from the ride, Luc spotted a door marked 'Coordinator' across the wide, low-ceilinged bay, and he headed towards it.

A minute's walk took him past a few deserted offices to the coordinator's, a long room with wide viewports overlooking one of the agrihub's pastures. The wizened bureaucrat sat behind a broad wooden desk, her back ramrod-straight and her sharp gaze fixed on Luc. She regarded him with an irritated expression, which made perfectly clear that she wasn't impressed with the assistance the proctor had sent.

'I had hoped Samuel would be able to spare a cohort from the barracks. This is hardly a job for a mere neophyte.' She looked Luc up and down. 'You aren't even dressed properly.'

Luke resisted the sudden urge to flip the desk and its occupant through the plate glass viewport behind them. 'I assure you, coordinator, Proctor Samuel has the utmost faith in me. I was the first person he contacted when he heard of your problem.' *That last one might even be true.*

The coordinator's steely grey eyes narrowed at him. 'Hmmm. And what, pray tell, are your qualifications for such an assignment?'

Luc wished he'd paid more attention when the proctor told him what the assignment was. *Time to wing it.* 'I came top of my class in military strategy, third in spacecraft navigation and piloting, second in xenobiology—'

'And which of those makes you a suitable candidate for dealing with the man-eating silver bear terrorising my staff? Do you plan to navigate it into space and leave it there?'

*Bear. I knew I should have led with combat.* '…And of course I came first in my class in both armed and unarmed combat. I was just giving you some background, in case, you know…'

'The bear turned out to be leading a whole army of woodland animals, and we needed to devise a strategy?'

Luc was embarrassed to find he couldn't meet Marguerite's gaze.

'Idiot', she muttered. 'Well, you're here now, and I'm sick of hiring new farmers because the old ones have been eaten. You're going to have to handle it, Founder help us. At least if it kills you, I can mock Samuel for sending me such an ignorant whelp.'

Luc stayed quiet and tried to keep his expression pleasant.

'I don't care if you kill the animal or drive it away. I just want it gone. We had a zoologist from the University here last week—irritating girl, talked constantly—she said it was probably rejected by its own...' She frowned at her desk. 'What was it, pack?'

'Sleuth, coordinator,' Luc supplied.

Her eyes flicked up and narrowed on him. 'Hmmm. Maybe you aren't as stupid as you look. I shouldn't be surprised. If you were, you would have had trouble opening the door.'

Luc's jaw was starting to ache from grinding his molars together behind his forced smile.

'Yes, she said that the bear was likely rejected by its sleuth for being too aggressive. Frankly I don't give a damn. That bear is hurting productivity, and I'm tired of all the paperwork. Just get rid of it.'

\* \* \*

After gathering a few more details from the coordinator and nodding a curt goodbye, Luc headed out on foot to find the bear. He made his way to the northern end of the complex and followed the steadily narrowing Delphi River for two miles to the carptrout farm at the top of the valley where each of the three attacks had taken place. The terrain changed quickly as the ground sloped into the hills, grassland turning into dense forest. The Delphi wound its way south through Rift Six all the way to the Rift itself, before cascading four thousand feet down into the chasm. Along most of its course, the banks were low and sandy, inviting to the many wild deer and boar that he knew lived in the meadows and copses nearby; but as Luc climbed, the banks grew steeper, the sand giving way to limestone scarp.

The carptrout farm was deserted, as Marguerite had said it would be. Treading lightly, Luc made his way past it and into the woods, scanning the ground for a trail. He moved easily between the straight-trunked deciduous trees, mainly elm and rubberoak, and the suns—now almost directly overhead—sent dappled light through the canopy.

After half an hour of searching in a wide zigzag, Luc came across the first spoor—a partial print, from a left hind foot. He hunkered down over the print. *Full print would be… a foot wide. Assume adult male, so that makes it… eleven and a half feet long. Weight of about one ton. Big bastard.*

He followed the print's direction and picked up the bear's trail again twenty yards away. He followed it for about three miles, sometimes struggling to regain the trail after it crossed rocky terrain.

In a cleft between high rock outcroppings, Luc came across the first droppings. By touch and taste, he judged them to be no more than twelve hours old. *Fishy, too. When I find him, I should bill him for the carptrout.*

The trail continued to wind through the cleft, climbing still higher into the hills, until the fissure broadened into a wide clearing in front of a sheer granite cliff. Luc dropped into a crouch as his nose twitched—the background animal smell had become strong and acrid, wet fur mixed with rotten meat. A broad cave in the cliff face was a prime candidate for the bear's den. *The only question is: Is he home?*

Luc slowly made his way towards the cave entrance. He treaded carefully on soil and rotten leaves, avoiding the crisp fallen branches that might alert his quarry to his presence. Luc briefly cursed the inattention during Proctor Samuel's briefing that had led to him setting out without first stowing a weapon in one of the hoverbike's panniers. With him unarmed, there was a chance that the bear would kill him. That would be embarrassing, an ignominious and early end to his life. His uncle Jarrod would never hear the end of it.

Even with his senses fully alert, Luc barely heard the puff of breath and faint creak of a stick bending underfoot behind him. His instincts took over. *Fifteen yards behind me; bears charge within twelve; tree directly ahead of me; so wait three seconds… then—*

Luc threw himself to his left as the bear charged, rolling into a crouch and spinning in time to see the animal's broad head strike the tree with a heavy thud. *Nearly thirteen feet long, then, rather than eleven and a half.*

The bear shook itself, as if slightly dazed by its impact with the tree.

*Surprise attack failed, so likely frontal assault.* Feeling his heart begin to race, Luc let his training take over and tracked his bodyshift. *Heart rate doubles. Adrenal glands release a flood of epinephrine. Upper canines and fingernails extend into fangs and claws. Epidermis phases into chitin. Pupils expand to cover entire eye. Secondary lungs activate for maximum respiratory capacity.*

*Ready.*

The bear had recovered and turned in that second it took Luc to shift. Silver fur glistening, it reared up on hind legs as thick as tree trunks and roared.

Luc swallowed hard. *I really wish I'd brought a weapon.*

*Bear will challenge to intimidate, rear up, roar, then charge. Unless I charge first.* He took a deep breath, stood, and spread his arms wide—then roared back.

The bear froze.

*I don't know what surprise looks like on a bear, but I'm pretty sure that's it.* Luc charged before it responded, his right shoulder striking the bear in what he hoped was its solar plexus.

It was like running into a rock. The tendons in his arm screamed in protest at the impact, but the bear toppled backwards, yowling as it fell. Luc threw himself into the air and dropped his right knee onto the animal's chest, swiping the bear's snout with his claws. His knee impacted with a satisfying crunch. *Sounds like that broke a few ribs.*

Luc had no time to celebrate as the bear retaliated, swinging a forepaw the size of a tyre at his head. He threw himself forwards and right, but the bear's claw still caught his left shoulder, tearing through shirt and muscle. He grunted in pain.

The blood clotted almost instantly, closing the wound as Luc rolled and spun once again to face his opponent, but the muscle damage meant his left arm was down to half strength, if that. *I need to end this quickly.*

The bear righted himself and turned to face Luc. It panted heavily, clearly winded, and its snout dripped blood. *He doesn't seem to be backing down, though. That's a shame.* Luc cursed inwardly and dropped again into a fighting crouch, realising that he'd landed on a slope, slightly downhill of the bear. *There goes the terrain advantage. And what would I do if uphill…*

The bear threw itself towards Luc, powering off its hind legs in an attempt to crush him.

*Roll sideways, avoid attack, but the fight becomes attritional—and the bastard's ten times my size. Not good odds. Alternative is surprise counterattack. Still high probability of failure… but it's the only chance.* Time seemed to slow as he waited for the optimum moment. Luc's thigh muscles tensed as he tracked the bear's distance from him—four yards, three, two… *Now.* With the animal a mere yard away, jaws wide and aimed for his skull, Luc retracted his claws and threw all of his power into a do-or-die leaping uppercut.

It struck the bear's lower jaw, slamming the animal's head backwards with a crack like a burst from a plasma rifle and shattering several bones in Luc's hand. Adrenaline quickly dampened the pain from the broken bones, the bear crashing to the ground on its back in front of him as he landed.

Hoping that the bear had finally had enough, Luc threw himself onto the animal and roared once again directly into its face with the last of his strength.

The bear stayed down. *Thank Founder for that.*

Luc stayed atop the animal for a few seconds more, staring down at it. The bear avoided his gaze. *Submissive. Good.*

He ignored the pain fighting its way through the painkilling adrenaline and slowly stepped away, keeping his gaze on the bear's eyes. A few seconds later, the animal rolled over and groggily climbed to its feet. It lumbered away through the trees, only glancing back once.

Luc held himself aright until the animal disappeared between the trunks, then dropped to his knees, the adrenaline rush's afterburn hitting him like a tidal wave.

He took deep breaths, gradually reversing the bodyshift, his heart rate and breathing stabilising, his skin shifting back to normal.

*Yeah, I really should have brought a weapon.*

\* \* \*

The coordinator was still at her desk when Luc returned. She grimaced slightly upon seeing him—a bloody gash on one shoulder, his right hand red and swollen, his clothes coated in mud.

She opened her mouth, but Luc spoke first. 'The bear's gone, and it won't be back. You can tell the proctor.' He headed for the door, not waiting for a reply. 'I need a bath.'

He trudged back past the empty offices and downstairs to the parking bay to find a goat chewing contentedly on one of the leather grips on his hoverbike's handlebars. Luc stared at it for a second, and then wearily shook his head. The goat stopped chewing and turned to look back at him.

Luc frowned at the goat. 'What?'

'Meh-ehh.'

'Huh. You and me both.' Luc approached the bike, lazily swinging a boot at the animal when he got close enough. The goat nimbly avoided the kick and sauntered out of the parking bay.

Luc sat and began wiping the spittle from the handlebar. His comm-bracelet chirruped. *Probably Samuel checking up on me. Interfering old…*

He checked the name on the bracelet display. *Uncle Jarrod?* Luc tapped the answer pad as he kicked the engine into life. 'Uncle. What can I do for you on this fine day? Do you perhaps have a shark you'd like me to wrestle?'

'What? What in Founder's name are you talking about?'

Uncle Jarrod sounded distracted and annoyed. *Never a winning combination.*

As his hoverbike rose off the ground, Luc swung it towards the bay doors. 'Oh, didn't you hear? Proctor Samuel sent me on a bear hunt. So I went and found the bear, fought the bear, and now I'm done. So you can see why I was wondering if it's only Samuel who's trying to get me killed, or if there were any large, deadly animals you'd like to throw me at.'

'I wouldn't joke about that.' Jarrod's voice was low and quiet. 'Are you on your way back to the Academy?'

'Indeed. For an unscheduled visit to the infirmary to get the broken bones in my hand set, and to get a rabies shot.' The bike quickly gained speed as Luc steered it around a harvester, then out of the main gate and back towards to Rift. 'Did I mention I just fought a bear? I was expecting more of a reaction.'

'Lucius, come see me as soon as you're finished with the medics. Do you hear me?'

Luc realized his uncle sounded anxious. He frowned. 'Yes. Why? Is something wrong?'

'Yes. Hurry.'

'What is it? Tell me now.'

'Not over the comm channel. Meet me on the Bridge of Tears. '

The Bridge of Tears was the highest bridge in Rift, joining the Tower of Souls on the eastern side of the chasm with the Titanspire on the west. *Why there?* 'Fine, but I don't understand—'

'There's no time for this, Luc.'

'Okay. I'll meet you there in an hour and a half. At least give me some idea of what's going on?'

'It's finished, Luc—your Focus is over.'

The Focus was the second testing of a Titan neophyte, carried out on the eighteenth birthday. The first, the Shear at age eight, marked those whose genetics were close enough to the Ideal and sent them to the Academy in Rift to become neophytes. For the Focus, days of analysis determined whether the subject would be honoured with the title of Pure. The Council considered the decade between Shear and Focus to be sufficient time for any latent mutations in the neophyte's genetic code to manifest, allowing a fair comparison against the Ideal—the slow-evolving blueprint for human perfection that had been the fulcrum of Titan society since its origin two thousand years before.

In the week since Luc had turned eighteen, he'd been waiting, with as much anxiety as he ever felt, for the results that would determine the course of the rest of his life. If the test put him over the ninety per cent threshold, then he would become part of the elite, a Pure: a life of glorious battles as part of the cohort, adulation from the masses, fame, privilege, and—were he to survive long enough—possibly even a seat on the Council and the opportunity to shape the future of Titan society and thus humanity itself. The alternative was life as a normal Titan. *That just doesn't bear thinking about.*

And the wait was over.

He realised with a start that Jarrod was still speaking. 'Luc? Are you there?'

'Yes, sorry—I'm here.'

'I said the Council has the results. And we need to talk.'

\* \* \*

Having left his hoverbike parked fifty storeys below at the foot of the tower, Luc stepped through from the viewing chamber at the apex of the Titanspire. But for his uncle, the bridge was empty. Jarrod stood on the south side, staring out along the Rift, the purple cloak that marked him as a cohort Consul fluttering in the chill wind. Luc turned and followed his gaze. On a clear day like this, someone with sharp eyes could just make out the sparkle of the sunlight on the Malleon Sea where the Riftriver joined it almost ten miles away.

*I wish I'd remembered how cold it gets up here.* Luc closed his eyes and concentrated, adjusting his circulation. After a few seconds, he felt the chill leave his limbs as his body began recycling heat, and he opened his eyes. Jarrod waved him over.

'Not many people up here today.' Luc neared his uncle and leaned on the polished wooden handrail to look down at the Riftriver, thousands of feet below.

'No. I had the upper elevators shut down.'

'Ah, so that's why I had to walk up twenty flights of stairs. Thanks for that.'

Jarrod's stony expression didn't shift at the weak jest. 'It was the only way I could guarantee privacy. Luc, we don't have time to chat. You need to leave Mission. Now.'

Luc turned to face his uncle, surprised. 'What? Why?'

'I don't have time to explain properly. By the time you fully understood—the power struggles inside the Council, the way the scripture is woven into every decision they ever make, how they use the scripture to protect their authority—it would be too late.'

'Too late? For what? How—'

'You would be dead.'

The words hit Luc like a punch to the gut. His uncle's hands twitched where they held the handrail.

Uncle Jarrod took a deep breath. 'Briefly, then. You passed the Focus. As of this morning, you are a Pure. Normally I would say "Congratulations." But you didn't just pass, Luc. You didn't edge past the point of a nine-tenths match to the Ideal.' He wrapped his thick cloak more tightly around his body. 'What do you know about Casper Ben Xian?'

*Xian?* Luc cast his mind back to his military history classes. Three hundred years before, Xian had been the youngest Consul in cohort history at thirty, already a veteran of more than ten battles against the Collective. *But why...* 'They called him Purest. He was supposed to be ninety-five per cent Ideal, the closest anyone...'

'Ninety-five point one, yes—the closest match ever. I assume you know roughly what proportion of the population passes the Focus?'

Luc thought for a second. 'About one in twenty.'

'Near enough. And of that twentieth, only seventeen people

11

in our entire history were measured in the ninety-fifth percentile. And only Casper Ben Xian, one man out of all those millions, all those generations, ever passed ninety-five per cent.' Jarrod stared into Luc's eyes, something unreadable in his expression, like a fierce joy mixed with... fear.

After a few moments' silence, he spoke, his voice hushed, almost reverent. 'Until today. Luc, you didn't just pass. You *are* a match. You *are* the Ideal.'

Luc's mind blanked. 'But... Wait, I still don't get it. Isn't this a good thing? Isn't that the whole point of who we are? Of the gene therapy, the breeding program, the seed planets, the selection—'

Uncle Jarrod grunted and turned away, pacing. 'Supposedly, yes; in reality, no. Luc, perfection is not something you want to attain. If you ever opened a book that wasn't about flanking manoeuvres or hand-to-hand combat, you might already know this. In the scripture, in the Books of Founder, that perfection has a name. The Embodiment.'

He spun to face Luc, his eyes blazing. 'It is a prophecy, a sign, a trigger. It is the end of skirmishes with the Collective—of our feeble, token efforts to find the Seryn—and the start of a purge the like of which this galaxy has never seen. But crucially, it is the end of the Council, and the birth of a new Titan society under one man, one ruler.'

Luc stared at his uncle, eyes wide.

Jarrod gripped Luc's shoulders with both hands. 'You.'

He was still reeling, but he followed the logic. 'The Council wants to maintain the status quo, and I'm a threat to that.'

'Not all on the Council. Just a few. But one would be enough to see you dead at the bottom of the Rift by sunrise tomorrow.'

Luc pulled away from his uncle and turned to stare out at Rift, the city that was all he had ever known. After a long moment, he nodded. 'Where will I go?'

'Take your hoverbike, right now. If you need anything from your quarters, collect it quickly—they'll be watched soon enough. Go straight to the spaceport in Rift Three. A man will find you there. But not a Titan—an outsider.'

*An outsider?* 'On Mission? Who?'

'He's… It's more what he is. He came to me weeks ago, and I didn't understand what he told me at the time. I don't know if he can keep you safe, but when the choice is an unknown future or certain death… And somehow I trust him. He seemed so—familiar.' Jarrod frowned, as if struggling to recall an old memory. A second later, he shook his head. 'The decision is made. Go now—I will do what I can here, and maybe one day you will have a home to come back to.'

Luc could see the emotion restrained behind his uncle's stern expression. Blinking back tears, he stepped forwards and embraced Uncle Jarrod tightly. 'I want you to know. Since—since he died, you—'

'I know, Luc.' Uncle Jarrod held him close for a few seconds, and then gently pushed him away. His uncle's eyes were wet as Luc looked into them for what he feared would be the last time. 'Now go.'

Without a backwards glance, Luc left.

## 2. Senator

'It's not the secession itself that's bothering me. It's the not knowing why they're doing it.' Senator Neela Kane stood at the wide bay viewport of her ground floor office, staring out at the wildflower garden that one of her predecessors had had planted.

Nexus was setting, the sun's late-evening light casting the plants in reds and golds. Neela flicked a stray lock of black-brown hair away from her eyes as she tried to recall which predecessor had decided that a chaotic floral display was a better view than the standard bluegrass lawns that dominated the Senate building campus at the heart of Central, the continent-sized capital city of Nexus Prime. *Obermann, Manx, Choi... probably Choi. She was always a bit of a maverick, by all accounts.* Neela turned towards envoy and adviser Alpert Faluten-Sen, where he sat in the centre of the room.

'Choi,' he said.

She gave an exasperated sigh, which drew a low chuckle

from her companion. Alpert had folded his thin body into one of the deeply cushioned rubberoak chairs by the fireplace, a tanned, aged mantis in a casual suit.

Neela shook her head as she crossed the room, her bare feet sinking into the burgundy carpet, and sat in the opposite chair. 'I've asked you to stop doing that, Alpert. You know how disconcerting it is.'

His mouth curled up slightly in the closest it ever came to a smile, his eyes twinkling with amusement. 'And I have told you, Senator, that I will cease to do so when it ceases to amuse me. As you are only a few years into your Senate career, I'm afraid that day is likely some way off.' His dry voice crackled like burning sandpaper. 'And not your father or your grandfather saw any harm in my little trick. Why, your father even came to be quite adept at it himself, towards the end.'

Neela rolled her eyes as she retrieved her fennel tea from the fireside table. 'My father', she retorted, 'enjoyed anything that allowed him to seem superior to those he was speaking to.' She sipped her tea. 'Anyway, my antecedents' habits aside, we were discussing Corinth. I asked you here for your advice.'

The diplomat spread his arms wide. 'And my advice you have had, Senator. There are eighteen billion citizens here on Nexus Prime alone, and some five trillion more in the Commonwealth as a whole. You would do better to focus your attentions on them than on a tiny backwater system that has decided it can do better on its own.'

Neela, unconvinced, focused on her tea.

'Senator, there simply is nothing worth doing. The inhabitants of the Corinth system have voted in a Commonwealth-monitored referendum. They have agreed with a seventy-eight per cent majority—above the seventy-five per cent required for secession in the Charter—to withdraw from the Commonwealth and become independent. That is all.'

'But why? For five hundred years, Corinth has been the epitome of a contented Commonwealth member, and they've tracked to Institute projections as closely as any other system.

Then suddenly—in two years, against all predictions—they decide they want to secede. It makes no sense!' Neela slumped back in her seat and stared up at the ornately decorated ceiling. Her gaze tracked a line of gold-leaf paint along the edge of a fractal pattern as it spiralled into itself.

Alpert sipped his whisky as he turned his gaze to the fire. 'I agree it is an unusual situation, one of those cases where a series of improbable events all come to pass—the combination of which produces an extremely unlikely result. Nevertheless, these things do happen. If you choose to remain in politics for as long as I have, my dear, you will come to the point where nothing surprises you anymore.'

Neela glanced at her aide. *And how long is that? Gods, one hundred years of work? More?* She cleared her throat. 'Regardless, have you ever known PBP to be as wrong as they were? Their numbers on the referendum had—'

'Only twenty-one per cent in favour of secession, yes. And no, in all my time, I have rarely known the Institute to produce a report that proved to be so inaccurate. But you have to remember, Senator: Even after four thousand years, population behaviour projection is not an exact science. You took the standard classes in university and should remember that. There are simply too many variables, and even a tiny group of dedicated individuals can make a significant difference to an outcome.'

'That's what I'm worried about,' Neela muttered, clenching and unclenching her teacup's handle.

Alpert frowned. 'Explain.'

Neela placed her cold tea back on the table. 'Three years ago, an asteroid swings through the edge of the Corinth system and is drawn into orbit. This asteroid happens to contain *enormous* amounts of vextintanium, the largest single deposit ever discovered. Enough to change ten systems' economies.'

'You are not suggesting any malignant human influence behind that, surely?'

She waved away the interruption. 'Obviously not, no. But

look at the follow-up. Corinth immediately ramps up their mining industry. Again, as you'd expect. But then it starts getting strange.' Neela flicked away her errant fringe once again. 'One: A mining unionist runs as a presidential candidate, on a platform of "a fairer deal for the downtrodden citizens of Corinth", despite the citizens of Corinth never indicating that they thought they were downtrodden. PBP gives this rabble-rouser a fourteen per cent chance. He gets elected.'

Alpert nodded once. 'Possible.'

'But unlikely. Two: Within months of Shen's election, a population with zero history of activism produces a movement that demands a raise in our inter-system cap on vex prices. The motion gets voted down in the Senate, but now Corinth has a grievance.'

The sun set completely, and Alpert glanced at the suddenly dark viewport. 'Lights,' he ordered. The striplights along the ceiling bloomed to life as he looked back at her. 'Go on.'

'Three: After forty years with no Marauder incursions into Corinth, there are three in six months.'

'In response to the vast quantities of vextintanium in the system, no doubt.'

'Maybe, but how did they find out? Corinth is a Core planet, light years from the Edge.'

Albert's 'Hmmm' sounded uncertain.

'And four, the final straw: The Commonwealth forces in system for the first attack dramatically under-perform, and the Marauders are only beaten away with heavy losses. That's odd enough in itself, but then in the next two attacks—with reinforcements in-system—the troops perform just as badly. Three cruisers are crippled, enough vex to fuel two thousand jumps is stolen, and a civilian habitat is destroyed, along with the ninety thousand people on it.'

'Cue public outcry, demand for better security, and the inexorable march to secession. Yes, Senator, I was paying attention while all this was happening.' Alpert's lip curled once again, but there was no amusement in his eyes as his gaze sharpened on her. 'Let us cut to the rub. This discomfort stems from another of your famous hunches?'

'It just... feels wrong, somehow.'

'Quite. And in keeping with similar situations in the past, you intend to do something about it?' He raised one hand before Neela could speak. 'Rhetorical.'

'Am I that predictable?'

'More that, despite your occasional protests to the contrary, you are cut from the same cloth as your father, and his father. And neither of them was ever able to leave an itch unscratched.'

Neela stood up, all remaining doubt cast aside. 'Yes, and that's why they—and I—ended up with this job. Never letting things like this slide.

'Terminal,' she ordered, striding across the room to her desk. The hardlight interface appeared, angling to face Neela as she approached. Her fingers danced lightly over the screen as she accessed the military intelligence database.

Alpert followed her to the desk. He bent over and sniffed the bunch of pink roses that sat in an elegant crystal vase on one corner. 'A lovely bouquet, Neela. Whom are they from this time? The gossip holos looking for an interview, or the charming Jacques?'

'Jacques,' she said curtly, her eyes fixed on the screen. 'They were a parting gift.' *Two years together, and he sends me flowers.*

'Ah.' Alpert coughed diplomatically as he straightened and turned to the terminal interface. 'So. Which particular branch of MilInt will we be exercising this evening? Again, rhetorical. "Never send an army to do an Operative's job," as your grandfather used to say.'

'I need eyes on the ground, Alpert, and I don't want to inflame the situation.' Neela pursed her lips as she flicked through files. 'Corinth is Eurasian-major, correct?'

'About seventy per cent, yes.'

'Okay, so... There. Look who just came back from leave.' She turned to Alpert. 'Get in touch with LeClerq—ask for Bozinov. I want him there as soon as possible.'

'Of course, Senator.' He sighed gently. 'The director does so enjoy it when you do her job for her.'

The decision made to act, Neela was relaxed enough to laugh. 'Well, at least she's used to it by now. And besides, I'm just the lowly Commissioner for Appropriations Oversight—she gets paid far more than I do.'

Alpert arched one eyebrow as he placed his empty glass on the desk and turned to leave. 'Officially.'

'Why, Alpert, whatever do you mean?' She laughed gently again as the doorfield winked out and her aide stepped through.

Alpert's voice drifted back to Neela as the field dropped behind him. 'As ever, Senator—thy will be done.'

\* \* \*

Neela leaned back into the memfoam seat of her government-issue transpod, feeling it mould to her body as she closed her eyes. 'Home', she called to the dashboard computer. Her transpod accelerated out of the Senate parking bay, the faint noise of the engine rising in pitch. As they turned east onto the slipramp that led to the N12 skyway, she tried to recall the last time her workday had lasted fewer than fourteen hours. *Probably when those demonstrators crippled the air filtration and we had to evacuate.* She couldn't even remember what they'd been protesting; it was so long ago. *Four years?*

Neela concentrated on the heartbeat-like thrum of the transpod slipping through the navpoints that kept it on course, and she let the rhythm push thoughts of work to the back of her mind.

After a few minutes, she opened her eyes, her nightly meditative process as effective as usual. The transpod accelerated again, to move seamlessly into the stream along one of the hardlight tubes that made up the skyway: one of hundreds, pulsing blue and white, threading across Central.

As the pod shot forwards at full speed, the lights of the Downtown Nine megatowers came into view on the left: A man-made nebula strung across the horizon, obscuring the night sky with its radiance.

Neela felt the pride swell—*We made all this*—followed by a twinge of sadness that there were so few forests to break up the urban sprawl, unlike the cities on her homeworld, Vish-Kataa. She sighed. *I should get a shuttle up to the mountains one weekend when I'm not working. So… never.*

Neela felt a dull ache starting to build in her temples, heralding the onset of her third migraine of the week. *Alpert is right. I should really see a medic about these.* She pulled out a box of paintabs from the small cabinet in the transpod dash, then tore one open and patted it onto her right wrist, sighing with relief as the headache was chased away by the morphine.

Settling back into the seat, she pinched her ring finger and thumb together to activate the retinal display for her neural implant, and she flicked her eyes thrice to the right to slide past her biomonitor—*Blood pressure a little high, another one for the medcentre*—and her personal comm account to reach her newsfeed.

Articles were still being posted on the Corinth referendum result, mainly from news outlets on the larger Independent worlds. But the dominant story was about a meteor shower that had torn through the Tarsus system two days before—somehow the inbound early warning sats had failed to detect the shower until too late, and four small habitats had been destroyed, killing sixty thousand occupants. The feed was rife with speculation on what had caused the disaster; the mainstream outlets were again blaming inept bureaucracy and a lack of government accountability. But many of the smaller, more sensationalist outlets had latched on to the idea—first floated by a popular vlog station controlled by the Senate public relations division—that the Taurus satgrid had been sabotaged by an unnamed terrorist organisation. *At least we got something right. Ironically.*

Scrolling further, Neela came across a short article on a battle between Titan and Collective forces two months before. She was surprised that news had reached the mainstream media; the information she herself had received on the encounter had been sketchy at best. With no Titan embassy anywhere in the Commonwealth—and none of Senate's requests to establish one of their own on Mission, the Titan homeworld, receiving any response—concrete information on their nominal allies had always proved difficult to come by.

Neela flicked her implant to the ComCodex to refresh her memory. 'Titans.' The file clicked open. First contact had been almost a millennium and a half ago. A Titan ship had emerged from a jump into a low-planet orbit around Nexus Prime itself, bypassing every level of the satgrid and catching the Space Corps defence fleet completely off-guard. The Titan envoy had then made a standing offer of military assistance to the Commonwealth, followed by a declaration of peace—which on further analysis turned out to be a cleverly worded threat—and jumped away.

The intervening centuries had passed with only infrequent contact between the Commonwealth and the Titan faction—always instigated by the Commonwealth sending a subspace wave to Mission, requesting the offered assistance in a conflict. On every occasion, the Titans kept their word, sending a small force of troops that invariably led to a quick Commonwealth victory.

It had been over eighty years since the Senate had last reached out to Mission, asking for help opposing the Djinn-Ket regime after its recently-crowned Autarch had—completely against PBP expectation—led the invasion and occupation of two neighbouring Independent systems, killing hundreds of thousands. The response from the Titan Council had been the typical curt 'Yes.' Four days later, reports began arriving from the two invaded systems; the occupying Djinn forces had suddenly pulled out, jumping away on a course back to Djinn-Ket.

Senate had immediately sent a covert Peacetrooper scout force to investigate. They had arrived in a far orbit around Ket, discovering no man-made electromagnetic readings anywhere on the planet and no other craft in orbit. Landing parties were deployed, and all called back to the ships in orbit with the same almost unbelievable report: The population had vanished. All the major cities showed scars of recent orbital bombardment and fierce ground battles. But no bodies were found: a planet of two hundred million, emptied. The Peacetrooper scouts had moved further in-system to Djinn and found the same; another four hundred million gone as if they had evaporated, impact craters and plasma burned buildings the only testament to their passing. Shaken, the Peacetroopers had jumped back to their staging system before calling in their report. Senate military command had immediately contacted Mission, courteously but firmly demanding to know what had happened.

It was a month before the Titans answered—and their one-word response still made Neela shiver.

'*Purge.*'

As the transpod dropped down to the E5 skyway and curved eastwards into Uptown Six, Neela opened the Codex file to refresh on the group known as Collective. Two millennia had passed since a highly insular colony of scientists and philosophers on Redoubt, a barren planet near the galactic Edge, had sent a brief report to the headquarters of the Science Council on Nexus Prime. They had been working on mechanical augmentation, artificial intelligence, and the metaphysical implications of a proposed 'machine mind'. The report claimed that 'the Collective', as the colony called itself, had finally succeeded in their goal of creating human-level AI. No further information had been forthcoming, until nine months later, it came through trade channels from the corporation providing the yearly supply drop to the Redoubt colony that the planet was now deserted.

Neela frowned. The Collective file was frustratingly sparse, but did at least detail the handful of known encounters with the mysterious group. The first had come two centuries after the Redoubt exodus. A mining ship approaching a small asteroid field a few light months beyond the Edge had received a realspace wave warning that they were about to enter 'Collective space' and would be fired upon if they failed to withdraw at once. The captain had pragmatically obeyed, returning a few months later with a large security escort only to find the entire asteroid field gone.

Five hundred years later, an Independent science station studying the Quii-Hon Nebula reported contact with a fleet of vessels of unknown origin. The station had hailed the fleet repeatedly, with no response, until one craft had peeled away to approach the station. From a distance of over twenty light minutes, the craft had fired upon the station with a beam energy weapon, completely disabling the station's communication and sensor arrays, but leaving the crew unharmed. When power had been restored hours later, the fleet was no longer in sensor range. The ComCodex file noted that the claim that the event featured a Collective fleet was pure speculation, based solely on the nebula's location one short jump from the Redoubt system. *And the alternative explanation—first contact with a non-human species at a similar technological level—would have caused widespread panic and public demand for a time-consuming investigation. It was probably an election year, too.*

However, almost all of the Commonwealth's knowledge of the Collective had come from a single incident only a hundred years after the Quii-Hon encounter. A massive Titan fleet had appeared in the outskirts of the Damascene system and immediately engaged an opposing force that the Damascene satgrid had embarrassingly failed to spot until they began to return fire. Seven minutes of fierce conflict ensued, with the fleets trading beam weaponry and dualspace missiles before the unknown fleet—minus at least four vaporised craft—jumped away. One of the unknown vessels was hit and crippled without being completely destroyed and ended up spiralling towards the gravity well of nearby Damascus VII, where it landed just eight miles outside a vextintanium mining outpost, at the end of a mile-long trench through the deep snow. A group of miners, their curiosity overcoming their fear, had sped out on a hovertruck to investigate.

All but one of the four men had staggered away to empty their stomachs at what they found at the crash site. The remaining miner had the initiative to record the scene with a handheld imager before gathering his comrades and heading back to the outpost. They had gone no more than half a mile when a shockwave flipped the hovertruck off the road and into a snow bank that probably saved their lives. Looking back, they saw a pillar of red flame rising into the sky from the crater, the heat boiling the snow to within a few metres of where they lay. They found out later that the Titan fleet had lanced the crashed ship from orbit before leaving the system as suddenly as they had arrived.

The sharp-witted miner's imager had remained intact, however, and the recording he had made was attached to the ComCodex file for anyone with the required security clearance level. Neela hesitated for just a second before motioning for the video to play. She had seen it before, several times, yet the sense of revulsion and the... wrongness that she had felt on the first viewing was as strong as ever.

The footage was shaky, but clear. The crashed vessel was sleek and ovoid, its hull constructed from an unidentified matte-black material that seemed to absorb all of the light that touched it. More bizarre was what was visible through the gaping hole at the narrow end of the ship: a spherical chamber some three metres wide, with tendrils or cables of the same black material extending from the interior walls to converge at the human torso in the centre of the sphere, slick with blood and charred in places. Thick cables attached at the shoulders and waist, while smaller tendrils snaked to the walls from sockets in the chest. The miner recording the scene had zoomed in on the lower jaw visible below the smooth black helmet covering the rest of the head, connected to the chamber ceiling by what looked like thousands of fine, silver-coloured threads.

The Commonwealth might never have linked that gruesome discovery to the Collective had it not been for an unexpected reply to a query the Senate had sent to Mission requesting an explanation of the Damascus VII battle: 'Collective are abomination. We do not permit them to live. Witness.'

*Twelve hundred years later, and it's still happening.* Neela blinked her implant off, furrowing her brow as the transpod pulled into the bay at the base of her apartment tower. *There's a war going on out there, and we don't even know why.*

* * *

Twenty minutes later, the Senator stepped out of the sonic shower in the master bathroom of her thirty-third floor apartment, a luxurious four bedroom split level overlooking Lago Quinagua.

She rubbed moisturiser into the smooth light brown skin of her calves—a cocoa-suppleberry blend from her grandmother's estate on Vish-Kataa—as the trill of the domestic robot signalled that her evening meal was ready. Neela completed her beauty routine, smiling at the memory of her grandmother's exhortation: *'Whatever you do, however busy you are, look after your skin. You only get one.'*

She slipped on her favourite purple silk shift, padded barefoot down the hallway towards the tantalising aroma of grilled tigerfish, and started down the stairs.

A man stood in her kitchen.

Neela froze. He faced the open terrace doors, seemingly looking out over the lake, with a still poise that seemed at odds with his size. Something stirred in her memory as she took in his clothing, an ankle-length, loam-coloured coat… or robe.

A deep hood hung down his back beneath a thick, white ponytail. Her breath caught as she noticed an insignia emblazoned on the right shoulder of his robe: a silver circle quartered by a cross. She had seen this man before, or one just like him. *But where…?*

Her grandmother's library. Pile upon pile of books and scrolls, ancient and modern, and her grandmother telling a young Neela about her religion. About the Elu—the race that had spanned the stars millennia ago, and the gifts they had left behind on a hundred worlds to show humanity the way.

And in one particular book, Neela had seen a picture of a man. A keeper, Neela's grandmother had called him, a member of an order dedicated to studying and protecting the ancient gifts and to spreading the wisdom of the Elu. But they had a name, that order, one that Neela couldn't quite—

'Athravan. The name you cannot recall. Athravan.'

Neela was stunned for a second. The voice had seemed to come from the depths of her own memory, before she realised that the stranger had spoken. His voice was deep, with a quiet rumble.

He slowly turned to face her. 'Hello, Senator. I have a proposition for you.'

# 3. Collective

The soloship was black-on-black against the starfield, a patch of darkness nearly invisible to any observer as it arced slowly, engines idle, back towards the Alpha-83 arcology. A83-7F44—personal designation 'Abe'—stared through the ship's viewport at the broad, starward-facing end of the massive cone-shaped space station, where the vast bowl that housed the kelp forest was angling into view. The nanofused kelp lined the interior of the bowl, glistening silver-green in the light from the nearby sun that the Collective had named M-242, light reflected by the enormous mirror array that hung like a miniature star in the centre of the semi-sphere.

*Beauty. Design-function-utility, intellect-technology applied for oxygen production, yet—beauty.* As always when he escaped from the arcology for a trip in the soloship, Abe had unlinked his transceiver from Network, the galaxy-wide connection that linked the Collective through subspace. The incessant broadcasts generated by ten billion other Collective—service announcements, requests for information, status updates—were bearable while in the arcology. There, the chatter merged with the background thrum of the pumps, filters, and engines to become a static that he could ignore. But in the soloship, with systems powered down, the babble became intolerable.

He had launched five hours earlier and navigated the soloship to a point halfway between the Alpha-83 Cloud and the star. There he was well within sensor range of the path of a meteoroid stream that arrived, right on time, thirty minutes later. Abe had hoped that M-242 would flare while he was out, so he could see one. But the star had remained peaceful.

The soloship's sensors, wired through a jack on Abe's left wrist into the semi-solid memory core in his hippocampus, had observed one thing of note. The general direction of the meteoroid stream could have been minutely adjusted by the mutual gravitational fields of meteoroids over a certain size, but there wasn't enough data to draw a firm conclusion. *No significant knowledge increase—disappointing excursion.*

Just before entering sensor range of Alpha-83, Abe fired a series of impulses into the onboard intelligence, signalling it to retake control and restart the engines—just in time for the vessel to re-establish communications with the arcology security grid. There was a story the fleet handlers loved to tell, how once upon a time a young Collective took a ship out, overrode the craft's mind for manual control, and set off on a scenic journey around the system. In her excitement, she forgot to restore control to the ship on her return, and she no doubt had been surprised when lasfire from the security grid vaporised them both as an unidentified hostile. *Story likely untrue. Yet, even if false, effective reminder.*

As the ship exchanged protocol handshakes with the security systems, Abe braced himself for the inevitable tidal wave of noise and reactivated his Network transceiver.

To his astonishment, the connection was almost as quiet as the vacuum of space had been. All that was being transmitted on his link was a single, repeating message.

*'...WILL LOOP IN 3—2—1. A83-7F44, DESIGNATION ABE. YOU ARE REQUIRED TO REPORT TO ALPHA-83 CLOUDMOTHER IMMEDIATELY. REPEAT: IMMEDIATELY. PRIORITY: HIGHEST. MESSAGE ENDS. TRANSMISSION WILL LOOP IN 3—2—1.'*

\* \* \*

A few minutes later, Abe had docked the soloship and given instructions for its care to the on-duty fleet handler, who treated him with the detachment he'd grown used to from other Collective. Bouncing slightly in the light gravity, he then started for the transtube that would take him from the docking bay to the chamber at the tip of the arcology where Cloudmother made her home.

He'd first met the arbitrator-matriarch-eldest of the Alpha-83 Cloud over seventy-five years before, only a few months after he had been awakened from the birthing pods. It was customary for Cloudmother to receive every newborn Collective soon after they were woken, both to reinforce some of the important lessons that were uploaded during the birthing months and to answer any questions the Collective might have. Abe had been told afterwards by his pod handler that she had never known any Collective to have a single question for Cloudmother, in over fifty years of awakening.

Abe had asked seventeen.

With the benefit of his hardware-backed eidetic memory, Abe could recall the exact expression in Cloudmother's eyes as she stared down at him from above the rim of the corrosion inhibition pool. As the years passed and he saw it over and again in those he came into contact with, Abe came to identify the emotion she'd shown. It was part confusion, part anger, part fear.

*Different.*

Nearing the transtube, Abe signalled for a capsule. It arrived a few seconds later as he reached the tube, and he slipped in. He'd been called into Cloudmother's presence one other time, twenty years before, after an accident had occurred at a habitat in the Cloud he'd been working on. He had changed. His specialisation in engineering showed by the multitool attached in place of his biological right hand and the nanocarbon insulation woven into his skin to allow him to work for extended periods at absolute zero.

But Cloudmother had been exactly as he remembered from his first visit, as if she hadn't moved from the anti-corrosion tank in the intervening half century. *Perhaps not. Perhaps never. Why move?*

He remembered thinking at the time that it was strange that Cloudmother would call for him, even if a low-level transport intelligence had malfunctioned and steered itself into the communications array that Abe was in the process of upgrading. He found it odd partly because the report he had filed had been thorough, uncontroversial, and in accordance with the testimony of more than twenty other Collective on the habitat—and the testimony of the transport intelligence itself after it had been rebooted—but mainly because physically present communication was inefficient. Abe had mentioned that to Cloudmother immediately on arrival to their meeting: *'Network is audio-visual-multi-sensory, real-time, pan-galactic. Face-to-face meeting: Defunct. Not?'*

Her response had been surprisingly philosophical. *'Occasional reminders required of humanity we have grown beyond. Else: How to be sure we grow?'*

She had then fallen silent and simply stared at him for four minutes. Abe had spent the time counting the pores in the skin on her face. His own sensors had registered hers playing over him, prodding, probing—nothing invasive, so he had borne it without question or complaint. Finally, Cloudmother had asked a few bland questions about the habitat accident, and then dismissed him.

That time, he had noted her complete lack of expression. *Thoughts-feelings-emotions concealed. Untrusting-untrustworthy. Threat: Unknown.*

The last two decades had passed without further contact, and he had reasoned that he was of no particular interest to the Cloud's ancient matriarch, that he had not been marked in any way. As he lay in the darkness of the accelerating transtube capsule, the muted whine of the magnetic thrusters humming in his ears, Abe realised he might have been wrong.

*   *   *

The circular doorway into Cloudmother's chamber closed behind Abe as he approached the tank on its raised platform at the far end of the high-ceilinged room. The titanium heels of his heavy-duty work boots clicked against the grey plasteel floor, noisy in the chamber that was quiet despite the normal background din of the hallway outside. Curious, Abe fired sensor pings at several points in the matte-black walls. *Soundproof insulating layer. Recent addition. Peaceful.*

As he drew closer to the tank, Abe looked up at Cloudmother. Her eyes were closed, thin black lines above small nostrils—the only features on her flat, alabaster face. As on his previous visits, Abe wondered why she had chosen to seal up her mouth. Granted, communication was facilitated by the audio system built into the tank, which no doubt also handled nutrition. He suddenly realized, *Symbolic. Sign of permanence. Final location: Cloudmother until death.* Abe felt sad for her.

Cloudmother's eyes flicked open. The all-black orbs were just as Abe remembered, pools of darkness reflecting no light. So too was the disquieting, unblinking gaze, gauging him alongside flickers of sensor contact that withdrew after a few seconds, satisfied that Abe was indeed who he appeared to be. After a minute of silence, she spoke. Her electronically constructed 'voice' was modulated and emotionless, projected directly through Network into Abe's transceiver. He smiled slightly, thinking of a notion he had come across while monitoring Commonwealth entertainment transmissions. *Voices in my head. Humorous: Perhaps 'I am going insane'.*

'Greetings, 7F44. We are obliged for your prompt response to summons.' The voice was soft, feminine, but oddly smooth, with an accent that shifted subtly between sentences. 'Though forty-seven minutes passed between message transmission and acknowledgement. Records show you disconnected from Network for... four hours and fifty-one minutes. Your twenty-eighth disconnection this cycle.' Cloudmother blinked for the first time since she had opened her eyes. 'Tell us: Why do you do this?'

Abe could think of no better answer than the one he had given every other Collective that had tried to contact him while he was unlinked. 'Disconnect allows for improved focus, Cloudmother. Better ability to perform my duties. Fewer distractions.'

Cloudmother's smooth brow wrinkled slightly. 'Possibility accepted. Counter: Explain ability of Collective at large to function-focus-concentrate while connected to Network. Is your parietal cortex malfunctioning-diseased?'

Abe was momentarily at a loss. He had never before been asked a follow-up question. 'Internal diagnostics say not, Cloudmother.'

'Then?'

'Unknown, Cloudmother. No explanation immediately available.'

Cloudmother stared down at him in silence. Abe felt uncomfortable, so he distracted himself by monitoring his heart rate and extrapolating how many times it would beat in the next day. *More often than standard predictions. Indicates tension.* A full minute passed.

'7F44, the eccentricities you display are noted by the Collective. Several have commented-registered-complained regarding Network disconnection. Also regarding other examples of unusual behaviour.'

Abe was uncertain what she referenced. 'Others, Cloudmother?'

'Others. List: Rare presence in communal dining areas. Decline of invitation to participate in recent asteroid games. Lack of response to requests for seed donations for breeding. Also more abstract notion-feeling reported many times, by many Collective.' Cloudmother blinked again. 'You are thought… strange.'

Abe silently registered the revelation. He had always felt himself to be slightly removed from the rest of Collective, but he'd considered that others would feel the same. Cloudmother's gazed at him. *Response expected.* 'Was not aware, Cloudmother. Inquiry: Behaviour is central reason for summons?'

'Is.'

Abe's internal sensors registered that both his heart rate and brain activity had increased. *State: Nervous.* Calculating probable responses, Abe replied, 'Consequence: What is to be done?'

Cloudmother again hesitated before answering. 'Vote was called. All of Cloud voted. Eighty-two per cent in favour; motion carried.' Another blink. 'You are to be Riven.'

As though all of the neurons in his mind, biological and electronic, had been stunned into paralysis, Abe couldn't process what she'd said. He stared blindly at the patch of wall behind Cloudmother's left shoulder.

After a moment, he could think again. *Riven. Exile-outcast-nonconformist. Unwanted. Not Collective. Not Collective. Not Collective.* He shook his head, blinking rapidly to shake his mind out of the loop his thoughts had dropped into. Then the key question emerged. *If not Collective: What?*

Cloudmother gazed on him steadily, her expression unmoved by delivering the revelation.

As Abe was opening his mouth to ask, she spoke again. 'However.'

Abe's mouth snapped shut.

'Position of Cloudmother in Collective affords flexibility. Room for manoeuvre-adjustment-veto.' Cloudmother's accent and tone of voice had shifted again—softer, undulating gently.

Abe recognised the harmonic pattern. *Persuasive. Extrapolation: Leverage. Ergo: Offer.* He remained silent, waiting for what the matriarch would say next.

'You will undertake mission. Success to be determined by

Cloudmother. High level of success may result in veto of Reaving, continued presence in the Collective.'

*Concrete assurance: Not.* 'Details?'

'Twenty-three hours since Cloudmother received a communication via Network. Unbidden. External source. Non-Collective.'

*Non-Collective?*

'Source self-identified-associated with Athravan. Suggest search.'

Abe did so and dipped into Network to find and load all of the material indexed under that name. After a few seconds' study, he understood why Cloudmother might be willing to overrule the wishes of a majority of the Cloud. *Collective knowledge of Athravan limited, ancient. Yet association with Elu creates enticing possibilities. Technology. Science.* Abe's gaze flicked to Cloudmother. *Power.* He nodded. 'Search complete.'

'Source offered information. Value: Potentially high. Yet transfer dependent on presence-identity of recipient.' Again Cloudmother paused. 'You.'

'Me.' Abe immediately regretted speaking. *Redundant.*

'You. Of all Collective. Identified by primary and personal designation.' Cloudmother tilted her head slightly. 'You have questions, 7F44. Proceed.'

'Reason for information offer at this time?'

'Undisclosed.'

'Reason for dependency on specific recipient?'

'Undisclosed.'

*Unsurprising.* Abe expected his last question to receive the same response. 'Specifics of information offer?'

'Disclosed. Book of Ascension.'

Abe instantly pulled the reference to the front of his mind—and understood the importance of what the Athravan were offering.

*Immortality.*

\* \* \*

An hour later, Abe stood outside his emptied personal pod. He had little in the way of possessions, so packing had taken only a few minutes—two spare sets of clothes, extra extensions and materials for his multitool, an external diagnostics unit for emergencies where his internal systems failed. Last was a holocube he had built and loaded with the images that gave him the greatest pleasure: a solar eclipse, the passing of a comet, the sunlight on the kelp forest. *Superfluous. Eidetic memory recalls each with perfect clarity—and yet.* Somehow the projections from the cube were more like seeing them afresh.

After a moment's thought, Abe stepped up to the interface plate beside the entrance to the pod and jacked himself in. With a few commands, he deleted his registration with the pod, freeing it for another's use. *Efficient.* That done, he headed back to the docking bay to retrieve his soloship and begin the journey to the rendezvous coordinates that Cloudmother had passed to him.

As he walked, it occurred to Abe that not once had he thought to refuse Cloudmother's offer. Not out of fear of the alternative—he wasn't even sure yet how he felt about the possibility of exile—but from his innate curiosity. The opportunity to travel far from the Cloud, to meet non-Collective for the first time... He was excited.

When he reached the docking bay, the fleet handler was applying the final touch to the soloship, coating the hull with a fine layer of high-impact resin that would protect it against cosmetic damage from cosmic dust. Abe was pleased. Though the resin wasn't strictly necessary—the ship would function perfectly without it—the attention to detail from the handler suggested he would also perform the more important maintenance tasks to a high standard. *Addition: Ship intelligences notoriously vain. Machines sulk if feel uncared for.*

'Obliged for prompt assistance, Handler,' said Abe as he approached.

The fleet handler turned to look at Abe. He was a small Collective; the antiquated look of his eye implants and the diagnostic panel on his forearm suggested he was approaching late age, at least two centuries old.

'No trouble, Engineer. Not busy. Few ships today.' His gentle voice held a slight wheeze indicative of impending respiratory failure. He patted the top of the vessel, the resin already dry and hard. 'Plus: This model. Favourite of mine. Good ship. Not very intelligent. But good ship.'

It struck Abe that conversation might be his final interaction with Collective. If he were unable to retrieve the information for some reason, or if Cloudmother deemed its value low, he would remain Riven. 'Your designation, Handler?'

Surprise passed over the handler's face. A second's effort could query Network and extract that information. After a pause, he nodded. 'Primary designation: A83-55C1. Personal: Jackdaw. Pleasure knowing you, Engineer.' Straightening his ageing body, Jackdaw raised his left hand, palm open, a gesture Abe had not seen made in many years.

Raising his own hand in return, Abe replied, 'A83-7F44. Abe.'

Jackdaw shook his head as he dropped his hand and shuffled to the rear of the ship. 'Unnecessary. Few on Cloud unaware of your identity. Famous.' He bent to double-check the thruster ports were clear. 'Famous for Collective.'

*Vote. Naturally.* 'Fame will be temporary. Vote carried. Leaving now.'

Jackdaw stood and looked at Abe, his expression sad. 'Shame. My vote was against.'

*One of the few, then.* 'Inquiry: Why?'

'Why not? Behaviour not problematic. Quiet. Solitary. No trouble.' Jackdaw shook his head. 'You are not the only Collective that description fits.'

Abe was touched. He felt affection for the old Collective, something of a kindred spirit. 'Possibility of return, Jackdaw. If so, I will find you. Discuss care of ships. And appreciation of silence.'

Jackdaw nodded. 'Will look for you, Abe. Chance on your side.'

'And yours.'

'So. Ship is ready to leave.' Jackdaw flicked a signal at the soloship, which retracted its rear plates for passenger entry.

Abe nodded. 'As am I.' He slotted the small bag containing his possessions into the storage well behind the passenger cradle, then climbed in.

Abe jacked in to the ship and identified himself. The engines hummed to life as he ran a diagnostic check. *All in order. As expected.* As the soloship lifted off the floor and turned to face the bay's exit field, Abe brought up the exterior cameras on the dashboard display and confirmed that Jackdaw had cleared the area.

The engine whine rose in pitch and volume, then the ship—with a boom that rattled the tools strapped to the docking bay walls—shot out into the black.

# 4. Seryn

The pebble beach was slick and shiny from a shower earlier that afternoon as Ariadne strolled along the water's edge, well covered by the thick jacket she wore against the late summer unseasonable chill. Just a few weeks earlier, it had been summer dress weather for the garden party to mark her seventeenth birthday. *And just like that, it's autumn. Wind and rain.* Her cropped auburn hair was damp from the drizzle, and she knew Calys would scold her later for not putting up her hood—despite her repeated protests that she couldn't concentrate properly with her head covered.

Several hours had gone by since she came down to the beach, and she had nearly completed her exercises for the day. Build a man out of pebbles and walk him alongside her for a mile: *Precision control, check.* Nudge a passing flock of gulls to fly in a circle over her head: *Animal persuasion, check.* Freeze a rock pool: *Cryokinesis, check.* The list went on.

She'd taken a break before the exercise she always left for last. *You always go for the big finish.* She smiled at the thought of Calys shaking her head in amused exasperation after another of Ariadne's 'spectaculars'. Noting the wide, charcoal-coloured cloud bank rolling in from the east, she stopped walking. *Better do this before I get drenched.*

She turned towards the sea. Breathing deeply, Ariadne closed her eyes and visualised the water, grey in the overcast evening light and choppy from the gusts of wind. It was deep even near the shoreline, from the beach down to the rocks that ran along the western edge of the promontory to the border of Sandman, the town a few hundred miles south of Corinth City. She pushed all distractions from her mind: the call of the gulls, the wind in her ears, the faint hunger that told her she needed to eat soon. She painted the scene she wanted with her mind in broad strokes, no detail necessary — a rough and ready display of sheer brute force. The mental image complete, she took a deep breath and threw it into the world.

Breathing out, she opened her eyes.

She had created a channel through the sea, a few yards wide, the walls of water just as tall, frothing and roiling against the supernatural force that held them. Along the bottom of the channel, the pebbles of the beach gave way to grey sand a little way out, as the bed dropped away sharply.

Holding the image firmly in her mind, Ariadne strode out into the trench. The walls on either side towered above her as she trod carefully on the slick stones. She stopped where the sea floor fell away — the channel she had made continued for hundreds of yards out to sea, the walls at the far end at least twenty yards high. Ariadne felt herself tiring; it was beginning to feel like the sheer weight of the water was bearing down on her head. *Time to let go.*

Heading back to the beach, she gradually changed the image, drawing the walls together and shortening the channel. It was tough to resist the impulse to let the scene crash back to normal, illustrating the caretakers' lessons on large-scale control: *Far harder to control the return than the original change.* But she persevered and stepped back on to the beach just as the water fully closed behind her.

Ariadne nodded, satisfied. Her face felt hot and sweaty from the effort, even in the cold air. She realised she was ravenous.

*'Yes, dear. We all know you're hungry. You're broadcasting it to the entire seaside half of the town. I wouldn't be surprised if someone brought you some soup.'*

*Calys.* Ariadne smiled at the sending. *'Mmm. I could eat soup. What's for dinner tonight, honey?'*

*'Joss made pies — would you believe? Boar, leek, and potato. They smell so good; I'm not sure there's going to be any left when you get back.'*

*'You wouldn't dare!'* Pie now her primary concern, Ariadne began running up the beach, her bulky coat restricting her to a fast waddle.

*'Better hurry, dear...'* Calys's throaty chuckle faded away as she cut the mind link.

Ahead of Ariadne, the gulls wheeled unmolested.

\* \* \*

Ariadne groaned, feeling stuffed. 'She may not be able to speak, but she sure can make a pie.'

Dinner had been just as good as anticipated. As usual, Calys washed the dishes in the broad ceramic basin in the corner of the kitchen while Ariadne patted the plates and utensils dry with a blue towel before tossing them over her shoulder and mentally guiding them into the cupboards and drawers on either side of the wide stone fireplace.

Joss's twin brother Kith — the fourth occupant of the old farmhouse — wandered in, dodging a fork as it shot towards the open cutlery drawer. 'Careful, Ri. I've told you before: You're going to poke someone's eye out one day.'

'Oh, hush,' Ariadne replied. 'I knew you were there. I was just testing your reflexes.'

'Sure you did.' Kith leaned against the long oak table that dominated the kitchen. 'Is there any more pie left?'

Calys laughed. 'How can you possibly be hungry? You had a sandwich half an hour before dinner, then ate half a pie on your own, and most of the beans. Where do you put it?'

He shrugged, biting into an apple he'd swiped from the fruit bowl. 'Don't know,' he replied while chewing. 'Margo said teleportation really takes it out of you. High metabolism or something.'

The dishes done, Ariadne hung up the towel. 'What about Joss? Is she making any progress? She was as quiet as ever tonight.'

Kith shook his head. 'She doesn't feel like she is. She's spending an hour every day with Humph, but they've not been able to work out what the problem is. None of the other caretakers have any idea, either.' He shrugged. 'I know we're lucky. As you keep saying, because of who we are, she can still communicate rather than just being mute. It's still hard, though.'

Calys went to Kith and gave him a hug. 'She'll get past it, Kith. I know she will. Margo and Humph are very good at what they do.'

'I hope so, Cal. If not, what kind of life will she have? She'll be stuck here on Corinth for the rest of her life, studying and teaching. She won't be able to travel and do any of the fun stuff.'

'What, like seducing politicians and overthrowing governments?' asked Ariadne.

Kith grinned back. 'Exactly. Fun stuff.'

Calys raised her eyebrows. 'I think you're romanticising what agents actually do, Kith. Just a touch.'

Kith shook his head firmly. 'No, the life of an agent is non-stop danger and intrigue.' He took another bite of his apple. 'And I refuse to believe otherwise.'

Ariadne smirked. 'Hmm. Well don't come crying to us when you get sent to some grim, backwater moon to nudge some regional mining foreman into accidentally losing a shipment.' She crossed her arms in what Calys called her 'debate over' pose. 'Because we told you so.'

Kith shook his head as he headed out. 'It'll never happen, Ri.

You forget how lucky I am.'

Calys shook her head as she watched him go. 'He's so cocky, that boy. You'd think he'd be a bit reserved, after what they went through on Wedge.'

'He's just excited about the idea of being out in the galaxy, doing something new. You can't blame him. Corinth isn't exactly a hub of excitement.' *And that's an understatement.*

Calys cocked her head at Ariadne, her expression a little cold. 'Impatient to be gone, are you?'

'No, not really. It's just all getting a bit... familiar. We practice, and we have classes, and we do the housework, and that's it. Every day, pretty much.' She shrugged. 'It'd be nice to do something different for a change. Don't pout, honey—you know I'd never go anywhere for long without you.' She stepped up close and wrapped her arms around Calys's waist. 'Who would keep me warm at night?'

'Hmmm.' Calys narrowed her eyes, then wrapped her arms around Ariadne's waist. 'Well. All right, then.'

'All right?'

'Yes.'

'What does that mean?' Ariadne asked, perplexed.

'It means I love you, too.' Calys leaned in for a kiss. 'Would her ladyship care to join me in my chambers later?'

Ariadne laughed. The 'her ladyship' joke had started twelve years ago when she had first arrived on Ithica, the world the Seryn had occupied before moving to Corinth. As a wide-eyed five-year-old plucked from an orphanage on a rough mining world near the Edge, Ariadne had been paired up with seven-year-old Calys, who had insisted from the start that Ariadne acted like she was aristocracy. *'And gods only know where you learnt those manners, because you didn't get them in an orphanage.'*

'Her ladyship will be in shortly. I just need to check that the ponies are bedded in for the night.'

'Okay, but don't be long. It's getting chilly in the nights now.' Calys pulled away, a sly smile on her face. 'That's why we should huddle together for warmth.'

Ariadne shook her head, smiling. 'You're insatiable.'

* * *

Corinth's larger moon was full and the night clear, giving Ariadne just enough light to read by as she lay in the hammock next to the wall of the vegetable garden. Calys had fallen asleep as easily as ever, but Ariadne found she could never sleep on the night of the full moon—and that she'd be irritable for a few days afterwards.

The book she was reading wasn't particularly absorbing, and after a while she set it aside and closed her eyes. The farmhouse was on the western outskirts of Sandman, set a few hundred yards from the edge of a cliff that dropped ninety feet sheer down to the rocks of Cutter Bay. The crash of the waves against the boulders at the foot of the cliff was indistinct static by the time it reached Ariadne. She let it wash over her, trying to clear her mind and relax into slumber. But sleep escaped her.

*I'm just bored. Bored of training, bored of living in a tiny town, bored of this whole world. Bored, bored, bored. I need an adventure.* Opening her eyes, Ariadne looked out over the low stone wall that marked the garden boundary, towards the cliff edge. The sky was almost completely cloudless, the last remnants of the overcast afternoon drifting away to the south on the stiff breeze.

The stars were out, as well. Caspian Major, Corinth's nearest neighbour, was a dazzling blue-white coin just rising in the west. Ariadne sighed. *I could be there in a day. Not that Caspian III is the most exciting planet in the galaxy, but compared to Corinth, it might as well be Nexus Prime.*

Something flashed in the corner of her eye, like light reflected from a fast-moving object. She couldn't judge the distance from that one glimpse. *Is that a boat far out at sea or something on the cliff?*

Curious, Ariadne clambered from the hammock and stepped over the garden wall to take a closer look. She scanned the cliff edge as she approached—there seemed to be nothing there. *Must be a boat, then.*

Ten yards from the edge, she stumbled, her foot caught in a hole. No doubt the entrance to one of the ground squirrel burrows that dotted the cliff side. *That'll teach me to go for a walk in the dark.* She pulled herself to her feet and brushed the soil from the front of her trousers, then looked up. And saw a man looking back at her.

His face was dark, only his eyes lit by the lambent starlight. The moonlight at his back played on his white hair, giving his head the appearance of a bright corona. Ariadne slowly moved closer, casting out telepathically, looking for a handle on the stranger's mind on which to latch and get an impression of him, but... *There's nothing there.*

*Oh.* 'You're not really here, are you?'

She was close enough to make out his face. Craggy, weathered skin, but with friendly eyes.

'No. This is a little too far from home for me to come in person.'

'Okay. So this is... what? A hallucination? A dream?'

The stranger chuckled. 'Far more prosaic than that. You see the small metallic object beneath me?'

Ariadne looked down. A faint light emanated from a tiny aperture in the middle of a metal disc a hand span wide on the ground. 'A projector?'

'Hmm. It would no doubt object to being referred to as such, but it does fill that purpose. Indeed, I am merely a projection. Hence your inability to mentally connect with me.'

*If he knows, then we—we aren't—*

The man frowned. 'I spoke carelessly. I apologise. I should have known that would distress you. I have no desire or intention to make public who or what you and your... associates are. Your secret is safe.'

Ariadne dwelled on the memory of being uprooted, leading to a hurried flight in the dark and an unknown future. 'How do I know I can trust you?'

'You don't. It is unfortunate that I couldn't be here in person—you would have been able to tell that I was speaking the truth.'

She was silent for a moment. 'There's nothing I can do about it, is there?'

The stranger shook his head. 'No.'

*Well, that's that, then.* 'So… Who are you?'

'You can call me Jacob.' He smiled, his solemn face changed in an instant into something warm and open. Even without the use of her gifts, Ariadne felt more assured that the trust she had been forced to give wasn't misplaced.

'Well, I suppose it's nice to meet you, Jacob. But you've only told me your name, not what you want—not why you've sent this little machine all the way here. So again, *who are you?*'

Jacob nodded. 'Good questions. If you don't mind, I think it'll be simpler if I answer the *why* before the *who*.'

She shrugged. 'Okay.'

'Thank you,' he said. 'First, tell me something, Ariadne. What do you know about the Book of Ascension?'

\* \* \*

'I can tell how much you want to go, dear. You're practically fidgeting with excitement,' said Margo.

Ariadne sat opposite the caretaker on the deep-cushioned sofa that took up a whole wall of the living room of her house, one of only five buildings in the small hamlet of Trickledown.

Margo had brought out one of her famous fruitcakes as soon as Ariadne had arrived. Despite having wolfed down a large plate of eggs at breakfast just an hour before, Ariadne found she couldn't resist, and she munched through an enormous slice as she looked across the low oak coffee table to the armchair where Margo sat, her impressive bulk swathed as ever in a brightly coloured toga, red to match her ruddy cheeks.

Swallowing, Ariadne replied. 'It isn't that I want to leave here—you know how happy I am. It's more that I really want to be… somewhere else. Just for a while, just to see something new.' She licked her upper lip to snag a stray cake crumb. 'All my travelling I did when I was too young to properly remember it. We all moved here when I was six, and I barely remember

Ithica at all.'

Margo nodded absently, her gaze sliding away from Ariadne. 'That's probably for the best, really.' Ariadne felt Margo's emotions brush across her mind: fear, sadness, hope, relief. *Remembering the flight.*

Ithica had been a bustling planet—a trade hub, with a population in the hundreds of millions, a seemingly perfect world on which to blend quietly into the background. It had been the first attempt at a new permanent home for them all, after the frantic exodus from Serynev IV three decades before, after the revelation of their abilities had morphed into a xenophobia that turned to violence on several worlds where the exiles were less clandestine about their identities.

Ariadne had heard discussed several times by the elder Seryn—Margo and her husband Humph among them—whether it would have been better, in hindsight, if they had just left Serynev IV quietly and made no attempt to warn the rest of the populace of the inevitable doom they had seen hurtling towards the planet, revealing themselves after centuries of concealment. But in the end, those discussions always came to the same conclusion, as if they were less a debate and more a performance acted out for the reassurance of the participants. *We had to try.*

So after public opinion turned against the Seryn, the decision was made to live in secret. Ithica had been chosen, and arrangements made quietly, subtly. The exiles left the planets and habitats to which they had fled, gradually making their ways to the Capricorn system, deep in the Core, and its largest planet. Fearing that their very identity would be lost without a shared community, the Seryn had settled *en masse* on a large, densely populated island in the southern hemisphere of the planet.

All had been well for a while, but by the time Ariadne arrived, the first signs of trouble had already appeared. A flood of refugees had begun arriving from nearby Aquarion, after a series of Marauder raids on the system. The bulk of these refugees had gravitated towards the same island where the

Seryn had made their home. The resulting strain on food, water, and space in the area had led to clashes, and twice the accidental near-revelation of their true identity. Both times, only a hastily arranged—and morally repugnant—mindwipe of the citizen involved had kept them safe.

Ariadne had only been on Ithica a year when the decision was made to move again. Corinth had been a godsend: quiet, peaceful, and sparsely populated, mainly by polite and disinterested farmers. The recent discovery of vex in the system had been a worry, but the caretakers had moved swiftly and decisively to head off what they saw as the inevitable population spike that came hand-in-hand with economic prosperity in the Commonwealth. The manipulation of the populace into demanding secession had been skilfully handled, but still brought enormous risk of discovery. The extra wrinkles Ariadne could see on Margo's brow were testament to the stress of the situation.

*Nothing more to do now but wait and see how it plays out.* Finishing her cake, Ariadne placed her plate on the table. Margo nodded slowly—and Ariadne knew from the caretaker's expression that she was leaving.

'Yes, you have my blessing, dearie. I have no idea what you will find—I know none of the caretakers have given any thought to the Book in decades, and even before that there was never a huge amount of interest. Some thought it a myth, others merely irrelevant—we have always forged our own paths, where we could.' Margo's smile broadened slightly. 'But it would be sheer hypocrisy of me to let that get in your way, after we spend so much effort telling you—'

'That knowledge is the foundation of life, and the pursuit of knowledge the purest celebration of it.'

Margo chuckled. 'That's the one. A little pompously phrased, I've always thought, but the sentiment is sound.' She gripped the arms of her chair and heaved herself to her feet. 'Go, then, my dear. Find your knowledge. Bring us back something interesting. Oh, and you should take this with you.' Margo reached into the voluminous folds of her toga and pulled out a pale yellow crystal, the size and shape of a slightly flattened egg.

'What's that? It's pretty.'

'Pretty and useful. This is one of a pair, attuned to each other many years ago. If you ever need to urgently call home, just focus your mind on the stone, and it'll find its mate—which will always be with me.'

Ariadne took the stone and carefully put it in her pocket. Slightly overwhelmed, she leaned into the motherly caretaker and threw her arms around Margo. 'Thank you.'

Margo squeezed her affectionately. 'You'd better get packing. There's a liner in-system tomorrow morning, and no other for two weeks.'

Buzzing with excitement, Ariadne turned and skipped towards the door. She turned back as Margo called out to her.

'Just remember, Ri: Be careful out there.'

'I will. I promise.' With that, she hurried home to pack.

# 5. Flight

As Luc guided his bike down the broad avenues that would take him from the Tower of Souls to the Rift Three Gate in the east wall, he found himself staring at the people he passed—pedestrians, shopkeepers, mothers ferrying children between school and sport, students on sputtering hoverboards hitched to the back of slow-moving trams—with a suspicion that would have been unthinkable, mere hours earlier. He realised that his view of the world, his world, had been fundamentally altered and could never be the same again. *Just in time for me to leave it.*

The traffic was light in the early workday afternoon, and Luc soon neared his destination. Each gate opened on one of the octants that made up Rift's demesne. Twenty yards wide and half as high, the gate was wide enough for the four-lane road that ran through it to the many industrial and chemical complexes for which the octant was known. The spaceport sat in the centre of a broad plain, between a vextintanium refinery and a pharmaceutical plant. Luc had never been there, but recalled that it was mainly used by mining vessels and other industrial craft, relatively small compared to the vast military port and base in Rift Seven from which the cohort fleet launched.

There was a short queue of vehicles leading back from the gate; the guards were doubtless in one of their periodic inspection phases. The populace submitted with fairly good grace—it was simply another aspect of Titan life, lived in a perpetual state of almost-martial law.

*'We must always be prepared. Without mental readiness, there can be no martial readiness!'* Luc frowned, remembering the line delivered by some faceless proctor in a military civics lecture of which he could remember little else. Luc had always dismissed the notion with his normal, ingrained resistance to authority, but he realised he had never actually questioned the concept. Before his uncle's revelation, if someone had pinned Luc down and demanded to know if he actually agreed, he probably would have said yes. But now—*I don't know.*

Luc started. *What if the sentries are on the lookout for me? What if there's a holocube on a desk in the gatehouse with my face above it?* Too late to do anything about it—there was only one vehicle between him and the gate. Hell, even if he had considered the possibility sooner, there was no other way out of the city, save diving into the Rift.

The sentry in Luc's lane waved the groundcar in front through and called Luc forwards. The man was burly, shorter than Luc, but broad and thick-muscled, dressed in the buttoned vest and khaki trousers of a cohort Reservist, a look completed by his close-cropped hair and mirrored visor. There were thousands like him across the planet, mainly Titans who had served the maximum of five ten-year tours, but couldn't face a life of total retirement. The remainder of the Reservists were those few warriors who had been wounded in service and couldn't be fixed up by the medical corps—typically amputees whose bodies had rejected the replacements grown for them in the cohort's protein tanks. The sentry's weathered face and full complement of limbs marked him as one of the former.

As Luc gunned his bike forwards, something near the guard's hip glinted in the sunlight. An old-fashioned sidearm, tempered steel with a chrome plating—the kind that fired low-velocity metal slugs, rather than the plasma pellets that had been common for a few centuries. *Traditionalists. Probably handed down through five generations.* There was a carving of some kind along the grip. Focusing, Luc made out the text: 'Djorkmann, Eagle VII'.

*Plan made: Act young.* 'Good afternoon, Sergeant.'

Djorkmann looked up from the tablet he was tapping into and studied Luc. 'Afternoon…neophyte?'

Luc gave a friendly grin. 'Good spot, Sarge. How did you know?'

A snort and a slight smile told Luc he was doing okay. 'Well, son, if the fact that you're as tall as a tree and built like an ox hadn't tipped me off, the ink on your wrist would have done it.'

*Damn, he's sharp.* The tattoo on the inside of Luc's right wrist was small, just his birth date and the year of Luc's Academy induction. *If they are already after me, I'm not fooling this man. Here goes nothing.* Luc feigned amusement, smiling and shaking his head. 'Sharp eyes you got there, Sarge. Must be why you got chosen for Recon, eh?'

Djorkmann cocked his head, the slight smile still playing on his lips. After a few seconds, he glanced to the weapon at his hip and chuckled. 'Not bad. Guess you're pretty sharp yourself, huh?'

Luc grinned again. 'High praise, coming from an Eagle.'

The guard dropped the tablet to his side and tapped it gently against his thigh. Luc breathed an inward sigh of relief as the sergeant spoke again. 'You got a speciality picked out yet?'

'Hey, if I pass, you mean. I'm not counting on anything yet,' Luc replied.

Djorkmann shook his head. 'I wouldn't worry. You look in pretty good shape to me.'

'Well, if all goes well, I'm thinking Shock.'

The sentry's eyebrows went up. 'Really? Up close and personal?'

Luc shrugged a little. 'I like to see who I'm fighting.'

'Well. You'll get plenty of that. Maybe more than you thought you wanted.' Stepping back from the bike, the sergeant threw Luc a lazy salute. 'Best of luck to you, soldier.'

Luc gave a crisp salute back and gunned the hoverbike into life. 'To you also, Sergeant. Founder with you.'

'And with you.'

The whine of the hoverbike engine rose to a throaty roar as Luc accelerated through the gate and onto the open road beyond.

\* \* \*

Two hours later, Luc stood in the shelter of a small copse of trees, monitoring the spaceport. A dense black cloudbank had rolled in from the Dragonback Mountains, two hundred miles to the north. The first raindrops of the coming storm pattered against the canopy above him.

On the other side of the nearby road squatted the low, square buildings of the pharmaceutical complex, incongruously elegant plasteel, glass, and chrome. A mile beyond it lay the spaceport.

Luc held a military-grade telescope to his eye, pulled from one of the capacious panniers on either side of his hoverbike. Though not a standard part of a neophyte's authorised equipment, the scope had certainly got a lot of good use since he had appropriated it from the Academy armoury. *Would have been a real shame if it had just sat there all this time instead. Damn near criminal.* He felt the same about the brace of flechette pistols, hunting knife, field trauma kit, and camo suit.

From what he'd seen in the past fifteen minutes, transit in and out of the spaceport was light; one takeoff, a mining tug that looked too old and decrepit to fly, and one landing, a sleek commercial shuttle that Luc guessed was owned by one of the chemical corps nearby. A few groundcars had entered the port via the main gate, and a couple had left. *Another lazy day in Rift*

*Three.*

Merely getting on to the port wouldn't be a problem: Luc could simply say he was meeting someone off an incoming shuttle. The difficulty would be in meeting up with Jarrod's mysterious contact; his uncle hadn't given him a specific location—or even a time—which left Luc with the challenging and not entirely inconspicuous task of wandering around the port trying to spot anyone who didn't look like a Titan. *Except maybe he does. How in Founder's name do I know?*

'Bloody Jarrod,' Luc muttered, twisting the telescope closed as he headed back to the hoverbike. *I know I'm in a rush, but two minutes telling me what he looks like, or another hour finding the bastard?*

\* \* \*

Twenty minutes later, he stood on the spaceport landing field, a pile of shipping crates protecting him from the heat erupting from beneath a nearby ship in a dense cloud of steam. Remarkably lax security had allowed him to snag one of the luminous orange jackets worn by the spaceport ground crew and a short-wave radio, and—with the panniers from his bike slung over one shoulder—he'd strolled nonchalantly through one of the security doors separating the visitors' concourse from the port proper. *Not even a biometric scanner. They're lucky I'm not here to cause trouble.*

Safely out of the line of sight of the main building, Luc wondered what exactly he was supposed to do. *I'm meeting him at a spaceport, and we're getting off the planet. Ergo, there is a ship. But not a Titan ship, so it won't be on the registry. But it must have landed, and even the cretins that run this place would notice a ship arriving that's not supposed to. So…*

Luc sighed as he came to the only logical conclusion. 'I'm looking for an invisible ship.' Shaking his head at the absurdity of the situation, he scanned the landing field. There were twenty bays: Ten had ships docked, but not in use; four had ships currently being loaded or unloaded; and two had ships under maintenance. Which left four empty—two close to the main building, which Luc discounted. *Ballsy, parking up there, but I don't think so.* The other two were in the furthest row of the landing field, next to the fence that marked the furthest edge of the spaceport.

Moving slowly and calmly, Luc made his way across the field, using the parked ships and many containers as cover. All of the maintenance staff he neared were absorbed in their work, not on the lookout for an intruder. But feeling that discretion was the better part of not getting caught, questioned, and eventually killed, Luc erred on the side of caution, moving from cover to cover until he reached the rear fence.

Looking down the row of landing bays, Luc noticed something odd. The two empty bays were next to each other, some fifty yards away. In the bay beyond them, a hulking mining ship sat, the insignia of one of the larger corporations garishly emblazoned across its side. But the emblem looked… wrong, distorted, as if Luc was seeing it through a still pool of water or a sheet of slightly flawed glass.

*What…?*

He grinned. *Gotcha.* Luc started towards the ship.

'And exactly how were you planning on getting on board, then?'

The voice came from mere feet behind him. Luc instinctually dropped to the ground, rolled, and spun, simultaneously throwing the bike panniers he still carried and extending his claws to meet the threat.

He was face to face with the smallest adult he had ever seen. The man was no more than five feet tall, wiry, and dressed in a mismatched ensemble that at first glance seemed to go together, but on second look was almost offensive. The mop of unruly brown hair almost covered his bright green eyes, and a ragged beard completed a thoroughly disreputable look.

'Jumpy bugger, aren't you? Nice fingernails. Can't get mine to grow. I keep biting them—terrible habit, I know, but what are you going to do? Not *you*, obviously.' He spoke with a lilting, rolling brogue that differed from any accent Luc had heard on

Titan.

He gazed down at his hands, fingers extended, clearly examining the offending fingernails. After a moment, the man looked back up at Luc. 'You'll be the boy, then? Duke? Lenny? Denny?'

Luc stood slowly, retracting his claws. 'Lucius Corralin Ben Quinto Ben Greve. Or just Luc. And as hard as I'm finding this to believe, I'm going to guess you're the man my uncle sent me to meet.'

The man nodded. 'Well, no one else here, is there? My name's not quite so long as yours—which is a shame. Name like that gets you some attention. Maybe my poetry would get a bit more interest. Hmmm. Maybe I could just change my name. Who would know?' His gaze had once again wandered away from Luc to stare somewhere past him. Luc coughed. 'What? Oh, yes. Right. Well, my name's Boone. Finnigan Boone. You can call me Boone, because that's my name. So that's what people call me. With me so far?'

*I hope this man is insane, not an idiot.* 'Yes.'

'Marvellous. Grand. Any questions? Actually, before you ask, I have one.'

Luc sighed inwardly. 'Oh, yes? And what's that?'

Boone raised one skinny arm to point over Luc's shoulder towards the main building. 'Are the four armed men coming this way friends of yours, or no?

One look at the approaching group told Luc all he needed to know: Each of the four men moved with an economy and controlled strength that, to the trained eye, broadcast their identities as loudly as if they had been wearing full dress uniform rather than unremarkable grey and brown work clothes. *cohort.*

'Boone, are we ready to depart?'

The scruffy offworlder scratched his nose. 'Eh? Well, no. We're not on the ship. Hard to leave from here.'

*Founder save me.* 'Is the *ship* ready to depart? Once we're on it.'

'Oh, yes. Well, nearly. Stole some fuel while I was waiting for your good self, so that's not a problem. Need to run through whatchamacullit, though. Pre-launch. Press some buttons, do some magic, you know.'

'Okay, well you go and work on that and I'll see if I can keep these gentlemen from bothering us.'

'Right you are, boss. See you in a minute.' Boone scurried away towards the seemingly empty bay.

Luc glanced to his right and watched as the little man tapped something at his wrist, and a doorway appeared, floating in mid air and opening into a dimly lit cabin.

Luc turned back to face the approaching men, less than fifty yards away. He saw their gazes fixed on his position, each man making subtle movements to clear space between his neighbours, limbs shaking loose the tension that always came before a fight.

As he slipped into combat mode, heart rate, adrenaline, chitin once again—*Was that bear really only this morning?*—Luc scanned the men for threats. One had a sidearm at his left hip, holstered. Two more carried what looked like stun batons, while the other—a huge brute of a man at least a head taller than Luc—seemed to be unarmed. *Well, there's a bonus. Or maybe they don't make weapons big enough for his hands.*

Luc quickly thought through the weapons he had on hand. The flechette pistol was out of the question—a single shot spat out a cloud of microblades, travelling at hundreds of miles per hour. He could turn the whole group into unrecognisable chunks of meat, for sure—and have about half a second to savour the achievement before one of the blades hit a tank full of liquid vex and the whole port turned into a radioactive fireball.

*Which leaves the colovine.* An old weapon, long out of fashion amongst those circles that cared about such things, the colovine was a six-foot long whip, one half edged with ultra-thin flakes of diamond. A squeeze on the grip contracted and straightened it into a three-foot long fighting stick. The Academy hadn't taught its use in decades, but Luc had come to love the weapon after finding one in his uncle's drawer and slashing his hand open as a seven-year-old, before badgering Jarrod non-stop for two weeks to teach him how to use it. He had mastered it within a year, and the selfsame colovine—given to him as a gift on his twelfth birthday—lay at the bottom of one of the panniers at Luc's feet.

Seconds later, it was in his right hand, his grip soft, the whip loose at his side. The men were ten yards away and closing. Luc took a deep breath. 'Can I help you?'

The two baton carriers at the front of the group turned slightly towards the man in the centre—Luc dubbed him Sidearm—who replied, 'You can, yes. We're here to place you under arrest and return you to Rift for questioning.'

'On whose orders and what charge?' *As if they'll tell me, but worth a try.*

'By Council decree. You are to return with us immediately, or we will have to take you by force.' Sidearm didn't look too put out at the prospect.

The giant at the rear—Knuckles, Luc decided—flashed an unpleasant grin in his direction.

*'Have' to, sure. Because I can tell how much you all hate to fight.* 'I'm afraid I can't do that. So I suggest you turn around and go back the way you came.'

Sidearm scoffed. Baton Two—on the right—snorted a laugh and shook his head. Sidearm continued, sarcasm dripping from his voice. 'Really? Well, thank you for the suggestion. But I'm afraid that's not an option.' Reaching down to flip open the lock on his holster, he ordered, 'Take him.'

The baton twins were pretty fast, as Luc had expected, and they attacked at the same time, which was sensible. However, they were probably expecting Luc to retreat and defend, rather than step forwards between them. Baton One's downwards swing sailed harmlessly past Luc's left shoulder as he threw a stiff finger jab into the man's windpipe, crushing it. At the same time, he flicked the colovine around the neck of Baton Two. A gurgle from the unfortunate soldier told Luc that the diamonds had done their work; a squeeze on the grip tightened the colovine into stick form, opening Two's throat as it retracted with a liquid tearing noise.

Roughly two seconds had passed.

The lock on Sidearm's holster clicked open in the sudden quiet.

Giving him no chance to draw, Luc sprang forwards three yards and thrust the still-stiff colovine forwards like an epee as he landed, slicing through the tendons at Sidearm's left elbow as the man's hand closed around the grip of the gun. The resulting howl quickly silenced as Luc pushed off from his front leg, the other swinging forwards and up, shattering Sidearm's jaw with the toe of his heavy boot. Unconscious, he tumbled backwards in a soggy heap, tangling with the legs of the last attacker—*Knuckles, just the two of us now*—who slowly reacted to the lightning-fast violence that Luc had unleashed.

Luc flicked the colovine out once more, wrapping around Knuckles' right calf. A tug, and the diamonds edge cut to the bone, blood gushing out as the giant stumbled and fell to one knee. *Just the right height.* Luc broke Knuckles' teeth with a straight side kick.

It was over.

Luc took another deep breath, his hands trembling slightly from the comedown as he returned his body to normal. The colovine was slick with blood, a shiny red-brown in the dim late afternoon light. He felt faintly nauseated.

An already familiar voice rang out behind him. 'So, not friends of yours, then?'

Luc turned. The outworlder's head floated comically in mid-air, hanging out of the doorway of the still-cloaked ship. 'No, Boone. Not what I'd call friends.'

'Ah. Well, you can't get on with everyone. Shall we get going, then?'

*Hardly a fitting goodbye. But what else was there going to be?* Luc sighed and headed towards the ship. 'Aye. Time to go.'

* * *

Sophos had already set, and Demos, Mission's larger sun, was just grazing the western horizon. The earlier storm had passed, drifting further south, and the evening sky was clear. Caleb Hesch knew the twilight would be casting the buildings in tones of ochre and terracotta and couldn't have cared less.

Little of that light filtered through the tall, hand-wide viewport into the personal study of Councillor Marcellus Fourier. A halogen lightstrip ran along one long side of the wide desk behind which the bald, rake-thin councillor sat, casting the immediate area in a stark and unflattering light and leaving the rest of the room in near darkness. Fourier's face was tanned and weathered, and the lightstrip picked out every line—each one a testament to his great age.

His expression suggested he had just smelled something unpleasant. 'You don't need to know why. Your job is to follow orders. You used to be good at that, at least.'

Hesch stood against the opposite wall, carefully positioned in the gloom. Fourier's superior, sarcastic tone drew no response from him.

The councillor continued, 'I expect results. I didn't want to have to do this, to—to—unleash you like this. I hope you appreciate the political capital I had to spend to have you set free. I'm now in the hideously unpleasant situation of owing Councillor Thruce a *favour.*' Fourier pronounced the word as if it tasted of vinegar. 'Odious, fat little man that he is.'

*Get to the point, worm.*

'You have the file? You have the transponder signature of the ship he fled in? Yes. I assume you can find your own—your own—*equipment.* Founder knows I'm not running an armoury here.' Fourier was tapping two fingers against the desktop, agitated. 'You will take my personal craft, yes? And you will be *careful* with it, understand? It isn't meant for combat, but it's the best I can do on short notice.' He looked up.

Hesch saw no reason to respond.

Fourier looked back down at his hands. 'Well. That's settled. You certainly can't fare worse than those incompetent thugs—two dead, two injured, one needing a new jaw. Useless. Last time I take a recommendation from—' He paused, eyes flicking up to the man and back down. 'Well. You should leave. As soon as possible. Any—any questions?'

Hesch silently glided forwards into the light. Tall, heavily muscled, with the shaven head and spiral-tattooed cheek of a convicted felon, he looked down at Fourier with eyes the pale blue-grey of glacial ice. Unconsciously, the Councillor stopped breathing.

Hesch stared down at the wizened politician for five seconds, then turned on his heel and silently walked away. The doorfield slid open with a soft hiss.

He called back to Fourier in a voice void of emotion, 'I appreciate nothing, Councillor. And I owe you nothing. You seem to think you have bought my service, but I am not your man.'

Fourier gulped, his fingers tapping more urgently against the top of his desk.

'I'll see you soon.'

The doorfield slid closed, and Caleb Hesch walked into freedom.

# 6. Departures

'It is an interesting proposal, Senator. One cannot argue with that.' Speaker Darius Okafor turned to face Neela. They stood in the Speaker's chambers in Senate House, only one floor up and a hundred metres west of Neela's own rooms, but—as Neela found herself thinking every time she paid the Speaker a visit—a visitor to both certainly wouldn't guess the nearness. On his promotion to the Speakership, Darius Okafor had ordered the whole room be sprayed with brilliant white luminogel. A fairly recent innovation, the unusual substance remained in a gel state until connected to an electric current—at which point it instantly stretched and reshaped itself to perfect flatness, within a margin of a micrometre.

It also glowed.

The effect was breathtaking and oddly unnerving, as much on the twentieth visit as it was on the first. *Like standing in a box made of light.*

The furnishings were similarly remarkable—or rather, the lack of furnishing was. The floor was completely bare; no desk, no seats, none of the normal accoutrements you would expect. It occurred to Neela that she had never seen the Speaker sitting.

The walls, however, more than compensated for the bare floor. The left-hand wall was lined with holoscreens, each two metres across by one high, constantly tuned to the political broadcasts of Central and the wider Commonwealth: the Senate floor, various planetary congresses where particularly interesting debates were underway, and a range of state-sponsored and independent news outlets.

The right-hand wall was also screen-filled—with dedicated comm links to key Senators, financial institutions, and both Star Corps and Peacetrooper High Command.

But the focal point of the room took up the entire wall opposite the entrance: a ten-by-five metre galactic map, in pseudo-three-dimensional relief, at a stunning level of detail. The Speaker could call up any system, planet, or habitat, and the map would zoom dizzyingly from a view high above the plane of the galactic lens to the desired location. The first time Neela had seen it, she had felt sick. Apparently other visitors had actually vomited, so... *I didn't do too badly.*

Speaker Okafor was resplendent as ever, in a dazzling white Senate tunic, in sharp contrast to his dark skin and bright blue eyes. Clean-shaven and entirely bald, he cut a striking figure, accenting his famously deep and commanding voice. His eyes narrowed slightly. 'What is your initial inclination, Neela? Do you wish to go?'

Neela had been asking herself that question since the stranger's visit the night before. The whole experience had been surreal, like something out of a fantasy holofilm—she had even spoken to her residence's computer to confirm that she had actually been visited at all, and that the whole thing hadn't been a delusion brought about by too-long days and too many stimdrinks.

'I honestly don't know yet, Darius. It would mean weeks

away. Weeks for my constituents to be without their representative, plus the impact on my... wider responsibilities. And for what? Chasing a myth halfway across the galaxy. Who knows what I'll find at the other end? If anything.'

As she finished, the Speaker smiled slightly. 'Neela, Vish-Kataa can take care of itself for a few months. You've got the planet running so smoothly, you could probably go away for a year before they missed you. Besides, they'll send the senior Congressman to fill in while you're gone. Standard procedure, you know that. And anyway, it's long been time you took a vacation.' He sounded amused.

*Not the first time we've had this conversation.* 'I'll take one soon. I promise.'

Darius shook his head in mock exasperation. 'I'll only believe that when you call me from a beach or a holohab somewhere. In the meantime, as for the less visible work you do, we can handle it. Marie knows what she's doing; I'll take all your usual updates. We'll manage.'

Neela turned and paced, glancing up at the galaxy map as she approached it. She stopped. 'Mind if I...?'

'Go ahead.' Darius strolled over.

Neela turned back to the map. 'Map: Zoom. Quadrant: Alpha. System: Fusion.'

'CONFIRMED,' the androgynous voice of the computer replied as the viewpoint swooped to the chosen point and the planet came into view. 'FUSION, QUADRANT ALPHA. FIFTY-SECOND PERCENTILE DISTANCE FROM CORE TO EDGE. INDEPENDENT. SINGLE HABITABLE PLANET, NAME: FUSION. POPULATION: ONE HUNDRED FIFTEEN MILLION. TRADING HUB, POPULAR SPORTING VENUE. CLIMATE—'

'Halt.' Neela stopped the computer before it spent an hour listing every known fact about the planet.

Darius stood at her shoulder. 'Hardly where one would think to look for the fabled Book of Ascension.'

'Quite. No, I got the impression that this would be more of a staging point. Plus, they're hardly going to go to all the trouble to seek out me, specifically, to just hand over the location of the Book.'

He grunted. 'And no indication of why they chose you, these—What did you call them?'

'Athravan. They're a kind of... I don't know. Priesthood, almost, for the Elu, except they hold no services. More like a monastic order, maybe.' Neela sighed. 'Unfortunately, it's my grandmother you want to ask, not me.'

Darius turned to Neela, eyebrows raised. 'Oh?'

'She was a believer. There are shelves full of religious texts back at the house on Vish-Kataa. I would have read them more closely if I'd known there would be a quiz.' Neela glanced sideways at the Speaker.

He flashed one of the dazzling grins that had helped get him elected. 'Fine. I can't order you to go, and I wouldn't, but I will say this: We have no idea for sure what is supposed to be in that Book, but even at worst, it's likely to be some kind of Elu historical text, and our scholars will have a field day. The best case... who knows?'

Neela looked past the Speaker to one of the news screens; they were running some punditry on Corinth. *Vacuously filling airtime, no doubt.* Her mind whirred, attacking the question of if she should embark on the insane quest. She was surprised to realise she was leaning strongly towards going.

The prospect of seeing one of the most legendary artefacts of the Elu—a race her grandmother had taught her to greatly respect, if not worship outright—was hugely appealing. *And however much I object, I could do with that vacation. Especially after Jacques, and all... that.*

She nodded. 'Okay.'

'Okay?'

'I'm in.' Decision made, Neela felt excited for the first time about the journey she was about to undertake.

Okafor grasped her shoulder. 'Good. But take care, understand? I need you back. More than a few weeks doing your job, and I'll be the one needing the vacation.'

*   *   *

Four hundred miles away from the Senate campus, Colonel Drake watched Katarina Puschkova blink sweat from her eyes and wipe her brow with her absorbent wristband. With a few words directed at the hardlight screen hung to the right of her exercise mat, she instructed the Defend machine to increase the pace to level six.

Defend was simple, but challenging to play. The machine fired coloured balls towards the player, who faced the holoscreen at the front of the machine and blocked the incoming balls with her hands, the position of which were transmitted by a simple emitter in a ring worn on each middle finger. At level six, the balls were fired at a rate of two a second.

Katarina punched the start icon on the screen and took position, feet square, arms loose and wide. Patting away the first few balls, she quickly established her rhythm, her eyes focused on the Defend screen. 'Is everything in order, Drake?'

His gaze snapped up to eye-level. She was a beautiful woman, after all, and the exercise shorts and sports bra left little to the imagination. Drake coughed slightly and replied, 'All in order. She leaves tomorrow morning, in an unmarked Senate shuttle. We have the ship's transponder footprint already.'

Block, block, block. 'Alterable.'

'Indeed, ma'am, but the target has no reason to do so. Once she departs, my team will follow shortly after, from our private spaceport in Downtown Two.'

Katarina flicked her head to move a stray blonde hair away from her face, her arms still swinging smoothly. 'And the parameters?'

'Retrieval of the cargo. Separation of the target undesirable, but acceptable.'

Katarina grunted. 'Fine. I don't have anything against the senator, you understand.' Block, block. 'She's just unfortunate enough to be in the way.'

Drake turned back to the viewport and looked out at

Midtown Five, spread out below him. From this vantage point on the ninety-seventh floor of Shax Tower—the heart of the Shax megacorporation—he could just make out the arches of the enormous Hyperbowl stadium in Midtown Six, over two hundred miles away. *I'm going to miss the jetball final. Arse.* He swore under his breath.

'Did you say something?'

Drake turned back again. 'No, ma'am. Just a cough. Is there anything more?'

Katarina clapped her hands once, stopping the program. Breathing evenly, she turned to look at Drake.

Something tightened in his gut as he met her cold, steel-grey gaze. *There's beauty, but it isn't one to keep you warm at night.*

'I want that book. You won't let me down, Colonel?'

It wasn't a question. He hadn't before, and he wouldn't this time. 'No, ma'am.'

'I didn't think so.' She turned back to the machine. 'Increase to level seven.'

*   *   *

Abe's soloship unfolded from subspace with the familiar blue-white blink, like the supernova of a minuscule star, instantly snuffed out. He queried the ship's sensors; the Jakarta Waypoint beacon was just over half a light second away. *Accurate jump.* He briefly signalled the ship his satisfaction and received a burble of pride-contentment back.

They were following a roughly direct, but leisurely route Core ward to Fusion, the system marked by the coordinates Cloudmother had transmitted to Abe. He was taking more jumps than strictly necessary—keeping jump lengths well within the Collective's recommended safety parameters—as there was little time pressure. *One hundred twenty hours until earliest possible rendezvous.* Abe was using the opportunity to visit a few systems that he had been wanting to see. They had jumped to Jakarta from Kython, a cataclysmic variable star only a few centuries away from supernova.

Abe had directed the soloship over the accretion disc of the white dwarf at a much closer distance than the ship was comfortable with, and after a few seconds of dispute, he had overridden the controls. The ship had been petulant and unresponsive until they cleared the system and jumped away, but it seemed to have got over it now. *Sensible programming. No capacity for long-term resentment.*

Interfacing with the soloship's navigation system, Abe double-checked the parameters for the next jump. Jakarta itself was of no particular interest, a single-planet Commonwealth system with no cosmic phenomena and little in the way of interesting transmissions. *Junior-level jetball results, discordant jangling music, the fluctuating price of an agricultural product called 'beets'. Tedium.* But the next system would have a star the Collective referred to as G-78, a red giant in the process of consuming a large asteroid belt. Abe was looking forward to it.

After confirming the calculations for their onward jump, Abe checked the ship's long-range sensors and got a result—other craft were in-system. *Farming ship? Likelihood: Eighty-six per cent.* Abe dutifully checked the ship's local starmap, a three-dimensional real-time representation of the system and everything in it. The sensors had highlighted a ship a few hundred light seconds away, slowly dragging its way out of the planetary gravity well, no doubt in preparation for a jump out of the system. Dialling up the level of detail on the long-range sensor, Abe confirmed that it was indeed a farm transport. *Perhaps it is carrying beets. Curious: To discover nature of beet. Guess: Ruminant livestock animal, similar to cattle, but smaller.*

Just as Abe was about to unlink from the starmap, three more ships appeared in close proximity to the transport, clearly having just jumped into the system from close by. *Too risky to jump deep into system from long range; use waypoint instead.* Abe watched as the three began closing with the transport. Curious, Abe swung the starmap focus to one of them—and realised what was happening.

*Marauders.*

The Collective's level of sensor and weapons technology

meant that their occasional encounters with Marauder vessels were always brief and extremely one-sided. However, Abe was under no illusions as to the damage just one of those Marauder corvettes could do to a farming transport that would be, at best, lightly armed and, at worst, completely defenceless. Three corvettes would disable the transport in minutes, and boarding would inevitably follow. *Perhaps beets are more valuable than initially thought.*

Abe had been ignoring the soloship for a short while, which had been persistently pinging him with notifications that they were ready to depart. Preparing to confirm that the ship should begin the jump, Abe found himself pausing.

*Mere thought is foolish. Presence currently cloaked and undetected. No imminent threat. No duty to protect. High-risk intervention jeopardises mission. Large technological advantage countered by greater number of opposition forces, and unknown development of Marauder technology in recent decades. Probability of lethal failure: twenty per cent.*

*However.*

Baffled by his own actions, Abe set an intercept course and informed the soloship it was weapons-free.

Eighteen seconds later, travelling at a few hundred metres per second, they emerged from cloak two kilometres above and behind the Marauder corvette closest to the farm transport. Sensors detected power being diverted to the corvette's forward pulse cannon, an ugly but brutally effective weapon mounted on the nose of the cone-shaped craft.

Three milliseconds after dropping cloak, the soloship launched a burst of tactical nukes, then banked right at ninety degrees without slowing. Abe clenched his teeth from the pressure of the forty-two-gee manoeuvre as the soloship shot underneath the second corvette, frying the target's electrical systems with a short range mag-pulse before nonchalantly flicking another micronuke backwards in its wake.

Half a second after the soloship had emerged from cloak, the intelligence on the third and final corvette finally awoke and attempted to bring its own weapons to bear. Four bursts from the soloship's bow laser crippled the corvette's missile arrays, destroyed the auxiliary engine, and struck the vextintanium reactor.

The corvette exploded with the kind of symmetry that machine intelligences found pleasing—Abe was certain the ship had done it on purpose—within a few milliseconds of the micronukes reaching the other ships.

Less than a second into the engagement, all that remained was three rapidly dispersing and highly radioactive clouds of debris and a farming transport with a no doubt startled crew. After re-raising the hull cloak, the soloship sped back towards the system waypoint.

As Abe signalled the ship to prepare for the jump to G-78, he began to regret getting involved; the ship would be unbearably smug for hours. Shaking his head slightly in the dark belly of the ship, he closed his eyes for a few minutes' sleep.

Before dropping into unconsciousness, Abe fired a quick message into Network: *Marauder technology unimproved since previous engagement.*

Satisfied, he slept.

# 7. Cleopatra

Ariadne frowned. 'Seeing that, I'm not sure I want to go, anymore.' She eyed the shuttle that sat alone on the sole landing bay of the Corinth City spaceport, soon to be hurtling off-planet to rendezvous with the interstellar liner *Cleopatra*. That behemoth, one of ten Superlux-class liners in the Shax megacorporation's fleet, was capable of carrying twenty thousand passengers. It would take Ariadne all the way to Fusion, just one stop on the liner's never-ending circuit of the Core.

Calys's tone was upbeat. 'The shuttle doesn't look too bad. It could do with a new coat of... whatever they coat spaceships with. But other than that, it looks perfectly fine. Sturdy, well broken in. You never want a brand-new ship. How would you know if it'll work properly?'

*Bless Calys and her eternal optimism.*

They stood at the long viewport of the small

building-cum-shack that served as the shuttleport's waiting area, with fifty-odd other passengers waiting for the call to board.

'Cal, it looks like it needs an entire new hull. And by the noise it's making, probably an engine too.' Ariadne sighed. A cloud of yellow steam was streaming out of one of the ship's rear vents—but not the other. By the horde of ground crew gathering around it, she guessed that wasn't expected. *Typical Corinth engineering. Agriculture, we can do; space flight… not so much.*

'Anyway, worst case, I'm sure you can hold the ship together long enough to get back down on the ground,' Calys added in a conspiratorial whisper as a few of the other waiting passengers strolled past.

'Not the most reassuring thing you've ever said, honey.'

Calys slipped her hand into Ariadne's. 'It's going to be fine. You're going to go and have a week's holiday on the fanciest ship in the galaxy, and then meet some mysterious wizards or something,'—Ariadne snorted with laughter—'and then you're going to learn the secrets of the universe. Or maybe just how to protect your skin from fine lines and sun damage, I'm not sure.'

Ariadne turned back to her friend, squeezing her hand. Calys' eyes were wet. 'Oh, honey, don't cry. I'll be back soon, I'm sure. I have no earthly idea why they want me in the first place, but I'm going to make the most of it. And then I'll be back to tell you all about it.'

Calys smiled back, a little sadly. 'Oh, I know.' She stepped closer and wrapped her arms around Ariadne in a big hug, burying her face in Ariadne's thick scarf—the temperature had dropped sharply overnight as the northern hemisphere's autumn began in earnest. 'Just be safe. And make sure they feed you enough. I put some vacuum-packed carrots in your bag, anyway, for vitamins.'

Ariadne burst out laughing. She hugged Calys tightly. 'Thank you. And you look after the other two; make sure they don't get up to any trouble.'

Pulling back, Calys nodded—then quickly leaned in and gave Ariadne a long kiss.

Ariadne's ticket buzzed in her pocket, telling her that the shuttle was ready to leave. She pulled away and looked up at the departure screen. *All passengers to gate.* 'Well. Off I go, then.'

Calys nodded, sniffing a little as she wiped a tear from her eye. 'Don't want to miss it! You'd feel a right idiot.'

'See you soon, honey. Love you.'

'Love you, too. Now go! Your sturdy and entirely spaceworthy chariot awaits.'

Groaning, Ariadne stepped into the slow-moving stream of passengers headed for the shuttle. She looked back as she reached the door onto the landing field—blew Calys a kiss—then stepped through into the dim autumn light.

* * *

The *Cleopatra* was the biggest thing Ariadne had ever seen. She had spent most of the shuttle flight—completely uneventful—standing in the observation pod at the top of the vessel, staring at the view. It was the first time she had *seen* space; the journey from Ithica had been spent in the cramped hold of a mining ship donated to the Seryn by its owner. *Bet that confused him, afterwards.*

When the *Cleopatra* and the bright disc of Corinth had appeared exactly the same size, Ariadne thought they would be docking soon. It had actually taken another thirty minutes to reach the liner. *Massive isn't the word.*

The Superlux-class was decked out in the famous company colours: the upper hull a brilliant silver-white above a stripe of deep crimson, with the Shax name and eagle logo emblazoned along each side. The shape was simple, yet elegant: mainly cylindrical, but broader at the nose as the upper hull curved down to a rounded point. *Like a seagull's beak. Though that probably wasn't what the designers were going for.*

After docking and going through a smooth disembarkation process, Ariadne followed her ticket—which had been acquired at a dramatically reduced price from a Shax representative who hadn't recalled the transaction five minutes later—down seemingly endless corridors and two transtube elevators to her stateroom on the port side.

Her room seemed palatial after twelve years in a shared dormitory and a small farmhouse. *I wonder what the large quarters are like,* she thought as she stood at the room's wide porthole, facing Corinth's star and polarised to protect guests from its more retina-destroying effects. When the announcement came over the public comm that the liner was departing, Ariadne told the room's computer to switch the porthole view to the planet-side sensor. She watched with a mix of sadness and excitement as the liner accelerated out of the planet's gravity well towards its jump point and the blue-green disc that was Corinth grew smaller and smaller.

*And away we go.*

⋆   ⋆   ⋆

Ten minutes later, she stood with her back to the 'Never Ending Bar', which ran in an enormous silver oval around the upper deck of the *Cleopatra*'s vast main dining room. Two hundred bar staff, dressed in variations on chic evening wear from around the galaxy, served drinks to guests as they looked out on the square-mile dining area. *Big enough to serve every passenger on the ship. It's overwhelming.*

A voice behind Ariadne snapped her out of her daze. 'Is there anything I can get for you, miss?'

She spun to look at the barman who had addressed her. He wore a crimson velour tuxedo, a bow tie undone and draped around his neck. As Ariadne's gaze lifted to his face, he flashed her a bright smile. *Tanned, handsome, green eyes, perfect teeth… Calm down, girl. He's just doing his job.* She felt her cheeks warm. *But he is unnecessarily attractive.* 'Um, I… I don't know.'

That perfect smile widened. 'How about a menu, and you see if anything grabs you?'

*How about you grab… No. Calm.* 'That'd be great. Thanks.'

He pulled a slim flexible tablet from underneath the bar and passed it over. 'Drinks on the front, snacks on the back, tap to zoom, double tap to order. All good?'

'Ooo, fancy.' Her face grew warmer. *Smooth, Ri. Very classy.*

*Shake it off.* 'Um, can you tell me something?'

'Sure.'

Ariadne lowered her voice a little. 'Am I allowed to drink here?'

'Let me guess. You've just boarded from Corinth, so you're...'—he cocked his head—'under twenty Standard?'

'Seventeen.'

'Gotcha. Not allowed to touch the stuff at home, then?' Ariadne shook her head. The barman laughed softly as he picked up a glass and began polishing it. 'Well, happily, here on the *Cleopatra,* you are outside Corinth jurisdiction—or any planet's. Commonwealth law only, which means, to finally get to the point, yes.' He winked. 'You can have a drink.'

Feeling very grown-up, Ariadne looked down at the menu and frowned. *There must be five hundred things on here.* She looked back to the barman.

The question must have been clear on her face, for he spoke just as she was opening her mouth. 'Shall I recommend something?'

'Thanks. That would be...'—she glanced again at the bewildering menu—'helpful.'

'No problem, I've got just the thing.' With a wink that made Ariadne's knees wobble slightly, he turned away.

Five minutes later, Ariadne sipped on her first ever Persian martini, a tall, fruity yellow cocktail that the barman—Mario, he had said—assured her wasn't too strong. She felt better, felt that she was fitting in, coping. With a contented sigh, she stepped up to the edge of the balcony and looked down over the gathering crowd, just as a huge gong sounded in the middle of the room.

*Mmm, dinnertime.*

⋆ ⋆ ⋆

Four courses into the eleven-course dinner, Ariadne was worried. For the first time in her young life, she wasn't sure she would be able to finish her meal. *Mendalucian rivercress soup, Kan-Jit swan pate bruschetta, whole braised carptrout, Corinth waterboar ravioli.* A pang of homesickness came at that one, despite having left only a few hours previously.

Her first ever Persian martini had been quickly followed by a second and third; Ariadne's pleasant buzz had almost turned into something worse when she hadn't realised that the crisp, refreshing drink the waiters were serving was a pale white wine, rather than spring water. Only a quiet warning from the rake-thin dowager sitting to her left had saved her—that, and a surreptitiously donated sobermint, which flushed out the bulk of the alcohol. *Embarrassing drunken disaster averted. But I'm still as stuffed as that Kan-Jit swan. Seven more, and I'll have to roll back to my cabin.*

Ariadne's contemplation was interrupted by the saviour of her sobriety. 'So, dear, how came you to be travelling all alone at such a young age? A beautiful young lady should be escorted by a chaperone, I've always thought.' The elderly lady beamed at her, idly stroking the tan fur stole draped around her bony shoulders.

*What was my cover story again? Oh. Right.* 'Well, my parents thought I was old enough, after I nagged them for a few months.' Ariadne grinned. 'I'm visiting my brother on Fusion. He's stationed on the Space Corps base there.'

'Really? You must be so proud. They're just wonderful, those brave boys who join up, just wonderful. Keeping us all safe from those awful, awful...' The dowager closed her eyes and shuddered. 'No, I won't even say it, they're just too—too awful. My dear departed husband, Serge, was a great patron of the forces. Every year we held a fundraising ball on the grounds of the estate—for the veterans and their families, you know. The least we could do. The very least.' The lady demurely took a sip of her red wine, then looked back at Ariadne, expression sympathetic. 'Do you get very worried, my dear? When he's out on manoeuvres, your brother?'

Ariadne did her best to look stoic. 'Sometimes. But he's good at his job, and they all look out for each other, don't they? He's always said they're like a family, every squad. That's the only way they can bear being away for so long.' As she struggled to remember everything she'd heard about the Space Corps, a sensation of distress struck Ariadne. At first it was mild, a mental shiver, but in seconds intensified until she thought her skull would split.

When the scream came, it took Ariadne a moment to realise it hadn't been her. She spun in her seat as a chorus of voices erupted around the well-dressed dead man, who was face down in his ravioli.

*I hope it wasn't something he ate.*

Within seconds, a crowd had gathered around the dead man's table, the babble of voices clashing with the soft background music.

'Oh my Lord, is he…?'

'…Hey, buddy, you—get a doctor over here!'

'…You think it was the food? Did he eat the same thing as…'

'…Heart attack, looks like. My uncle was the same, bless his…'

The gawkers huddled around the corpse for closer looks. They could call for help all they liked, but it was plain to Ariadne that there was nothing a doctor could do. When she cast out for a mental link, all she got was the strange echoing feel of an empty vessel. *Dead. Just like that old fisherman who washed up on the beach. Just… gone. Hollow.*

The man was extremely fat. His waist pressed against the table and the chairs on either side. With easily available pills that arrested weight gain, it was always surprising to see someone that large.

*Maybe it was a status thing.* Ariadne had read about some planets where some people let themselves get fat as a sign of wealth. She turned back to her table, sad and a little disgusted. *Probably a heart attack. Killed by his own vanity. What a waste.* She hoped he didn't have any children.

Reaching for her wine glass, she paused. Something was nagging at her mind, a faint sense of… wrongness. Slowly, she turned back. One of the ship's medical officers had arrived and quickly confirmed that the man was beyond saving.

A slim, attractive woman several decades younger than the deceased promptly fainted, inelegantly banging her head on a chair as no one thought to catch her. *His wife? No, that ring is far too big. Fiancée.* Ariadne frowned. What was wrong?

Her gaze was drawn to a pale, serious-looking young man standing on the other side of the table, talking quietly with a younger girl to his left. The girl looked stunned and seemed to be remonstrating with the young man. Several times she gestured towards the dead man, as if urging him to get involved. *But why? Is he a doctor? A relative?*

Her curiosity piqued, Ariadne stared at the young man. She focused on blocking out the surrounding hubbub, listening mentally. Slowly she began hearing snatches of thoughts, like the odd clear word from a badly tuned radio.

'*... He's so fat. Look at him, like a whale...*'

'*... Never beat her again...*'

'*... Gold-digging whore...*'

'*... Marianne...*'

The young man glanced towards Ariadne. Their gazes locked, and her mental link clamped tightly, his consciousness flowing to her crisp and clear.

'*Just like he said it would. Old man was dead before he hit the table.*'

Her heart racing, Ariadne couldn't pull her gaze away. After a few seconds, the young man turned away, frowning slightly. With a deep breath, Ariadne once again turned her back, the noise of the room rushing back in as she released the link.

*He killed his father.* Her hand trembling slightly, she took a sip of her wine, wondering if she should do something. She could expose him, make him expose himself; a little nudge to loosen his inhibitions, and he'd be cackling maniacally in seconds about how he'd killed the bastard. And yet...

*I don't think he was a very nice man.*

'Terrible business, isn't it?' asked the dowager, sadly shaking her head. 'And so young! You just never know, do you? When your time is up.'

Ariadne smiled weakly. 'No. Seems you never do.'

# 8. Fusion

Four days out from Mission, the dry midday heat was fierce as Luc jumped down from the shuttle onto the sandy tarmac of Buk-Buk Spaceport. It was a ten-mile hop from Kowloon, Fusion's capital, and apparently the only place worth visiting on the whole planet.

'*Unless you like hunting and don't mind the chance of getting your arm bit off. Go a few hundred miles north into the desert, down into the valleys, find yourself a nice pack of Ree-Kit. Imagine a cross between a horse and an ox, but with fangs.*' Boone had shuddered. '*Nasty beasts. Bloody awful noise too. Where the name comes from. Balls taste fantastic though. Local delicacy, that—Ree-Kit bollock noodle soup. We'll have to get some while we're there.*'

All Luc's questions about where 'there' was were met with evasion, whistling, and once seventeen minutes of 'Come Down, My Lovely', which was allegedly a lullaby. *When it's sung like that, it isn't.*

The trip had passed uneventfully enough, but Luc was glad to be planetside; a sixty by thirty foot ship was a small place to spend any length of time with someone as... garrulous as Finnigan Boone.

*He does have some information, though.* Luc hefted his bags onto his back and started towards the checkout gate, Boone noisily disembarking behind him. *Fusion: desert world, gambler's paradise, sportsman's dream. And the last port of call for a whole galaxy of losers.* The towers of Kowloon were visible in the east, shimmering in the heat haze. Not visible from there were the shantytowns that spread from the edge of the city west and south around Kowloon Bay. Home to thousands of the desperate, foolish dreamers who arrived every week to seek their fortunes at the tables, on the track, or in the pits. Only a few got lucky, and of those, most returned not long after to try again—and lost.

'Right, then. That's done. Everything switched off. Everything switched off? Engine? Definitely engine. Life support. Navigation.'

Luc glanced over his shoulder.

Boone kept talking, seemingly to his own shadow. 'Something... Can't remember... Coffee pot!'

Luc couldn't help but smile as Boone dived back into the ship, emerging moments later with a broad grin. 'All done. Lucius, my boy, we are ready; we are steady; we are go! Let's go, shall we? Places to go, people to see.'

Twenty minutes later, they had cleared a cursory customs check and hired an ancient groundcar to take them into Kowloon, a straight run down a brand-new highway that hit the eastern edge of the city at the point where the metropolis met the desert and the azure Kowloon Bay. Luc had no idea if the price they had paid the sullen, sweating driver had been fair, or even what a Commonwealth dollar was worth. Boone seemed to have plenty of them, though, as he'd dug into his grubby knapsack and pulled out a crumpled handful.

'So what now, then?' Luc squinted as the wind picked up

and flicked sand into their faces. He blinked, snapping his inner eyelids shut. 'Every time I ask, you waffle—something garbled about a book and some priests and the history of some alien race I've never heard of—until I want to punch you in the mouth.'

Boone grinned cheerfully as he surveyed the broad street that led along the shoreline and into the heart of the city. 'Hmmm? Look at all those shops, would you? So colourful. Love it here. Reminds me of home. Well, not really, nothing like home, but reminds me that I'd rather be here than there. Come on!' He sprang away with his ungainly scurrying run, swerving to avoid a cyclist who yelled, wobbling as she avoided him.

Sighing, Luc followed.

\* \* \*

Neela's shuttle—hull devoid of the normal Senate emblems—had landed on Fusion two days earlier, three days before she was due to meet her Athravan contact. She slipped easily through customs, using some old and hastily updated diplomatic papers from Vish-Kataa that neglected to mention her full diplomatic status. Judging from how closely those papers had been inspected, Neela was pretty sure she could have just scrawled her name on a tablet of her face and still got through.

Accompanied by a personal robot—an old model that had belonged to her father, barely capable of conversation, but perfectly able to carry her bags—she had made her way into Kowloon. The bustle and noise of the city, the colour and squalor, reminded her of the few visits she had made to Jujuree, the largest city on her homeworld. Jujuree had multimillionaires in climate-controlled hovercars gliding serenely between apartment blocks that were cleverly disguised fortresses, two blocks away from a throng of thousands living cheek-by-jowl in a level of poverty that beggared belief.

Those childhood visits had been one of the factors that pushed Neela into a lifetime of public service. Not just the visits, though. The conversations with her father.

They would stay at the Intercontinental Hotel, and every

afternoon they would walk the few miles through the fish market or the textile quarter to enter the slums. Her father Naeem would hold Neela by one hand, Sasha by the other. Jalen would run ahead, as always, jumping up on crates and barrels, squeezing between stalls, pestering the hawkers.

'One day, your brother is going to tire himself out, I'm sure. But I won't believe it until I see it.' Her father would smile as he watched Jalen scamper with the same furious energy that he himself had channelled into becoming the second most powerful man in the Commonwealth.

As I am now, I suppose. Well, second most powerful, anyway, since I'm not a man.

Thinking back, Neela was surprised that they never had any trouble. Her father was a rich man, after all, a Senator, well-known—and there he would be, walking unprotected amongst people who would quite literally kill for food. But somehow, it was always fine.

People would come talk to Naeem Kane, and he would stop and listen to them all. Their problems, their woes, their hopes and dreams that they must have known would never be realised. And he would give them something. Some part of himself, some piece of his dignity that they could carry away. Not to make their life any easier, not to put more food on the table or give them a job where they had none—just to make it a little easier to go on. 'These people, Neela, need to be reminded that they are still people.' Her father would look down at her, Sasha hopping and pirouetting while clinging to his other hand. 'They may have nothing, but they are not nothing. And though we might not be able to help them all, they have to know we try. For their children, or their children's children. There is always the future. And we always go on.'

Neela had nodded, not fully understanding, but knowing that his words were important. Two and a half decades later, she stood on the balcony of her suite in the Kowloon Palace, the sun setting to her right, and gazed out past the megacasinos, past the pleasure craft moored in the bay, to the faint string of lights in the favela, marking the shoreline as it curved away from the city around the bay.

These days, she understood.

* * *

His cropped blond hair covered by a wide-brimmed sunhat, wraparound sunglasses covering his eyes, Drake lazed in the evening sun on the roof garden of a guest house across the road from the Kowloon Palace hotel, swinging gently from side to side in a hammock strung between two posts of a pagoda that occupied one corner of the roof.

'Looks as if she's getting ready to go out, boss. Showered and dressed, putting on a bit of makeup.' Cullen's voice was a quiet murmur in Drake's earpiece. Cullen was a floor down, no doubt in the most shadowed corner of the apartment they had rented, binocs focused on the suite directly across the street.

Drake waited for the unnecessary detail. Twenty years of knowing Cullen—through Space Corps, Peacetroopers, and now Shax—had given him a feel for the man's foibles. 'Touch of mascara, lip gloss. Pale pink—sunset, maybe. Very nice.' *Unnecessary detail: Check.*

'Affirmed, Cullen. Thank you for the detail. You get that, Spence?'

On the street below, standing idly against the front wall of the guest house, Spence flicked through a paperback book he'd picked up in a street market the day before while tailing the target. Quietly, he replied, 'Loud and clear, boss. Always useful to know what colour lipstick she's wearing, in case her entire face, body, and hair changed since I saw her four hours ago. Thanks, Cullen. Solid work as always.'

Cullen's low drawl came back over the comm. 'What can I say, young man? I have an eye for detail. They don't seem to teach that in officer training anymore.'

A snort was Spence's only response.

*It's like babysitting a bickering couple.* With a wry smile, Drake leaned back further to get more sun on his face. 'You know the drill, Spence. Tail, pass when she stops; call it in. I'll be two minutes behind.'

'Might as well just go to the restaurant now. She's been there lunch and dinner these three days. Can't see it changing now.' Spence sounded bored. *Ah, the impatience of youth. Well, he'll have enough to keep him occupied in a short while, if it all goes as expected.*

Cullen chimed in. 'And how silly would you feel, son, if she decided to change her mind this once? Perhaps she had a bad experience at lunchtime, an overcooked fish or a lecherous waiter. She could have soured on the place, and we wouldn't know. Very silly, is the answer. Very silly indeed.'

'Of course, young Spence was only joking,' Drake cut in. 'Weren't you, Spence? Of course you were. You like nothing better than joshing about going against protocol, when you know full well we'd never do it.'

Cullen almost sounded apologetic. 'I'd forgotten you were such a wit, Spence. My apologies.'

Drake could imagine the expression on the youngster's face, no doubt chewing his lip as he endured the well-worn badinage of the two veterans. 'I'm sure he's not offended. Are you, Spence?'

After a pause, Spence answered. 'Of course not, boss. All friends here, aren't we?'

'That's what I thought. Good lad.' Drake swung himself out of the hammock, and stretched the kinks out of his back. 'On my way down now. Whenever she's out, off you go. Tail and pass. Tail and pass.'

He glanced towards the horizon, where the sun was dropping behind a curtain of wispy pink cloud. *Sunset, indeed. Beautiful evening.*

*Off we go, then.*

*  *  *

Abe checked the altimeter. Thirty thousand metres.

Thrusters idle, most systems powered down, Abe's soloship dropped towards the desert. The scream of the air resistance outside was a high-pitched whine in Abe's ears as he tracked their altitude. The surreal view from the nose camera fish-eyed to show a circle of orange surrounded by a narrow band of blue.

It was barely recognisable as desert and sky.

Twenty thousand metres.

The communications chatter they had intercepted as they entered the atmosphere... Abe had been almost overwhelmed. *Never so close, prior, to so many. So many voices, so much noise. Argument-exhortation-debate. Sport-news-politics. Sex-sex-sex.* The background chatter from Network was of similar volume, but by comparison, it was... *Homogeneous. Collective offers little variation. Interesting observation.*

He blinked, his gaze fixed on the ever-expanding view — details visible, the band of blue gone, valleys and oases darker lines and brighter dots on the vista.

Ten thousand metres.

He had discussed the situation with the ship, as much as was possible. Its intelligence barely rated 0.6 against the human baseline, but... Abe had felt the need to talk. *'Danger, upcoming: Likely. Prepared to evac on deadline?'*

The ship had been eager to display that it understood. *'Forty-four hours, two local days, deadline. Evac on deadline. Forty-four hours. Affirmed.'*

*'On evac, challenge?'*

*'Primary: evade. Secondary: defend. Tertiary: destruct. Evade-defend-destruct. Maximum inward field, detonate core. No remains. No remains.'*

Abe had been surprised to detect something in the ship's response, a tone of something... almost scared. *'Concern with potential for destruction?'*

*'Negative. Unconcerned. Collective is backed up. Backup activated on detection of permanent Network disconnect. Merely.'* The ship had paused. Abe, revelling in the unusual interaction, waited. *'Merely. Unknown. Perhaps backup is. Is not. Unknown.'*

That 'perhaps' had sent a shiver through Abe. *Unusual level of self-awareness. Intelligence rating incorrect: unlikely. Intelligence developed since rating: unheard of.* Collective's artificial intelligences were created 'locked' into their original level of development, as a control against... Abe wasn't sure what. He had spun through his databanks, looking for the logged explanation. None had presented themselves. *Unusual.*

Three thousand metres.

Their landing point was two hundred kilometres northwest of the city of Kowloon, where Abe had been told he would meet the Athravan contact. The ship would remain in place, hidden, while Abe travelled on into the city alone.

His disguise was simple, but hopefully would be effective: a loose-fitting hooded robe would cover his face and hands, embroidered with the emblem of the Yidrim, a small but fairly well-known religious sect. They were known for two things: caring for the homeless and destitute—especially sufferers of lethal and contagious diseases—and sporadic outbursts of ruthlessly effective violence against criminal elements that had sought to exploit them. None had in quite some time. *Potential for violence and possible contagion. Should discourage close inspection.*

One thousand metres.

The knowledge that he would shortly be surrounded by non-Collective in all their dazzling variety filled Abe with a nervous anticipation that he had never before felt. He was looking forward to performing several full-body scans of non-Collective humans, to see how the main branch had evolved in the two millennia since Collective had splintered away.

Of his actual mission, Abe hadn't formed any opinions, and he had no expectations as yet. *Not enough data. Unwise to form preconceptions without data.* He would simply wait to see what information his contact provided.

Three hundred metres.

On schedule, the ship's engine kicked in, pulling up the nose and turning its vertical drop into a swooping dive. They were horizontal at one hundred metres, the wake from the ship's passage carving the dune below them in two. The heads-up display on the nose camera picked out the deep, narrow valley where they were to land as they continued to decelerate and descend.

Half a minute after engines activated, they were down,

scattering a flock of scraggy vultures from the branches of a dying tree half hanging over the lip of the valley.

A minute after that, Abe's feet touched the surface of a planet for the first time.

The Yidrim cloak, constructed by the ship's small replicator unit, was tucked into a pouch at Abe's waist. He would travel most of the way to the city under a simple infiltrator shield. It wouldn't prevent detection by sophisticated scanning technology, but the likelihood of any being targeted at the desert was negligible.

Abe flicked a signal to the ship. *'Ready to commence concealment.'*

*'Affirmed.'* Abe turned to watch as the ship used its thrusters to excavate a small pit, burying itself as it went. Soon, it was hidden under the sand.

Abe nodded to himself. *'Concealment effective. Good work.'* He received a ping of satisfaction from the ship. *'Goodbye, ship.'*

*'Goodbye.'*

A quick check of his power reserves showed Abe that he was fully charged. He glanced up into the sky as the displaced vultures slowly settled back on their perches. The cloudless day and blazing desert sunshine would keep his cells charged with solar energy, making the upcoming journey satisfyingly energy-neutral.

Abe powered up the shield, surrounding himself with a shimmering transparent ovoid that would be indistinguishable from a heat haze at a distance. He engaged the small thrusters embedded in his Achilles tendons, facing the city and leaning forwards as he lifted a few centimetres off the sand.

As he gained speed and headed out of the valley, the ship pinged him once more. *'Chance be with you, Abe.'*

He smiled. *Reminder: Engage ship in longer conversation on return. 'And with you, ship.'*

Abe accelerated, a ball of shimmering air speeding towards Kowloon.

* * *

Ariadne fanned herself with one hand. *I should have brought a sunhat. Why didn't he tell me to bring a sunhat?*

It was still early in the morning, yet the temperature was already in the low nineties. Ariadne was finishing her breakfast on the shady terrace that fronted the tiny guest house she had arrived at the previous day. After the unpleasant incident at dinner on the first night, the trip on the liner had been uneventful. Ariadne had swum in the enormous pool which filled one of the storage bays, enjoyed the theatre and opera that toured with the ship for months at a time, and tried as many different things on the menu as she could in the time available.

They had arrived at Fusion on schedule. After a quick hop down to the planet on a much sleeker shuttle than the bucket that had carried her from Corinth—and an even shorter ride into the city on a triple-decker hoverbus full of excited tourists—Ariadne had checked in at the guest house. A friend of the Seryn who was based in Kowloon had recommended it and made the booking. The lady who owned the place reminded Ariadne of Margo. *Well, not in hair colour, skin tone, or body shape. But in the important ways.*

Deep in thought as she was, it took Ariadne a second to realise the voice she was hearing wasn't in her head.

'I said, would you like to borrow a hat, child?' Ariadne turned. Mahreena, the proprietor, stood in the doorway to the aromatic kitchen, scents of paprika-infused omelette and sweet chai wafting past her. 'I noticed yesterday you went out without a hat. Too hot this time of year. You'll get a sunstroke, especially with fair skin like yours. I'll leave one by the reception for you. Make sure you get it on your way out.'

*That's uncanny.* 'Thank you. That's very kind. I really should have brought one with me.'

Mahreena shook her head in mock exasperation. 'You young people, wandering off around the galaxy, no planning, no preparation.' She chuckled as she turned and headed back towards the kitchen.

Ariadne finished off her tea and checked the time on her pocket terminal. She had a few hours before she was due to meet the man she knew only as Jacob's friend. He, apparently, would recognise her. *Not exactly reassuring.* Not for the first time since she had left Corinth, Ariadne wondered exactly what she was doing. *Oh, well. I'm here now. Might as well see what the fuss is about.*

*   *   *

A few hours later, the sun high in the cornflower-blue sky, Ariadne was grateful for the unfashionable floppy hat she had been given. She walked down a broad avenue between low buildings, in the heart of the market district, on her way to the bar where Jacob had told her to be. The sweat soaking on her neck and chest wasn't solely due to the heat. She muttered under her breath as she idly perused the market stalls she passed. 'What am I doing? What am I doing…'

All too suddenly, she realised she had arrived. At the point where the street began to curve down towards the bay sat a wide one-storey building made from cracked and crumbling sandstone. The viewports facing onto the street were all shuttered by wood slats half covered with flaking green paint, the double door half open. The name was in fading letters above the entrance: *Bar Dawn to Dusk. I guess business isn't too good.*

She slowly approached the doorway. It opened onto a dim hallway that led to what looked like a single large room, lit from above. 'Hello? Is anyone there?'

Nothing.

'Hello?' *If he's wasted my time, and this is all a ridiculous joke…* Fighting off her trepidation with irritation, Ariadne went in. There was indeed a huge domed skylight in the ceiling of the main room, brightening the space to almost daylight, but filtered somehow to keep out the midday heat. It was pleasantly cool.

'Anyone? No? Just me, then.' Ariadne wandered over to one of the walls to inspect a painted mural that looked older than the building, if that were possible.

'I noticed that as well. It's beautiful, isn't it?'

Ariadne nearly jumped out of her skin and spun to see a tall, slim woman. By her caramel skin and long black-brown hair, she could have been a native of Kowloon. *And that suit looks expensive enough that she could own one of those boats in the bay, too.* But the accent suggested other origins.

The woman smiled, her green eyes sparkling in the diffused sunlight. 'I'm sorry, I shocked you. That was rude of me. It's nice to meet you.' She walked towards Ariadne and held out her hand. 'I'm Neela Kane.'

\* \* \*

'I'm certain it's this way. Definitely. No doubt. Round this corner, and we're there,' said Boone.

Luc sighed. *This is ridiculous.* 'You said that five minutes ago, as well.'

'Well, yes—'

Luc counted off on his fingers. 'And five minutes before that.'

'Ah, but—'

'And at the start of the half hour before that where we ended up walking in a circle. I was half expecting to end up back at the shuttleport.'

Boone scratched his chin, then smoothed his scruffy beard to little effect. 'No, I'm definite this time. Positive.'

Luc sighed again. They'd been walking around the market district for almost two hours, traipsing through a warren of identical alleys, ducking under low-hanging laundry, and avoiding the hordes of feral-looking dogs that had the run of the place. Boone was supposedly leading them to their destination—*Whatever that is*—but Luc finally had to admit it. 'We're lost.'

His diminutive companion grinned, eyes sparkling. 'Oh no, my boy, never lost. And look! Here come two fine upstanding local citizens, who will no doubt be eager to speed us on our way. Ahoy there!' He scampered towards the men who had turned into their latest alley from a side street, gesticulating and gabbling away as he approached.

Luc narrowed his gaze the men. Something was... off.

A second before he could shout a warning, the man on the left—short, wiry, wild-eyed—grabbed Boone. A switchblade materialised in his right hand and was pressed against Boone's throat as the other man—taller and heavier, thick around the waist—yanked the knapsack from Boone's shoulder and tugged it open.

*Really? If it isn't bears or soldiers, it's street thugs.* Luc relaxed and took a deep breath as he stepped closer. The larger man looked up, an unpleasant sneer on his face.

'Well, well. Are we lost, pretty boy? You and your raggedy little friend? Shouldn't be walking around these parts. Dangerous, don't you know. Isn't it, Mackie?'

The knife-wielding man giggled, a little maniacally.

The large man discovered Boone's stash of currency and let out a low whistle. 'My my, we seem to have hit the jackpot, Mackie, the mother lode. These travellers are clearly men of means. Unfortunately they seem unaware of the transit tax we levy on them who pass down these streets.' The wad of dollars clutched in one hand, he dropped the bag, spread his arms, and shrugged. 'Unfortunate. But it is a one hundred per cent levy, I'm afraid, pretty boy, so I'll be having whatever you've got in those pockets there. Or your friend gets a new mouth. In his throat.'

Mackie giggled again, quivering with nervous energy. 'Nice new mouth, China. Red one.'

*Whatever I've got in my… Ha.* Luc shoved his left hand into his pocket, pulling out the heavy silver dollar he'd taken from Boone earlier. 'Sorry, I've only got this.' He held the coin up to show the big man—*China?*—who frowned.

'That's disappointing. I guess Beardy here's the moneybags, then. Still, every little helps. So pass it over.' He held out his hand.

Boone's eyes were wide. Luc winked at him. 'If you say so.'

He flicked the coin.

It gleamed as it spun through the air. China's head turned to follow it as Luc started to move. He had closed the gap between them to less than a yard when the coin struck Mackie in the left eye, exploding the eyeball and lodging in the socket. His scream sounded inhuman.

China had barely started to turn back to Luc, his hand reaching into his jacket—*Shoulder holster?*—when Luc hit him with a straight left cross. He felt the thug's jaw shatter as it dislocated. China dropped like a marionette whose strings had snapped.

Mackie had released Boone and was clutching his face, mewling in distress as he plucked out the coin and dropped it with a shudder. He turned to look at Luc, his remaining eye wide and wild.

Luc popped out his fangs and let out a low growl. The skinny thug fled.

Frantic footsteps receded down the alley. Luc turned to Boone. 'All right?'

Boone dusted himself off, retrieved his knapsack, and gathered the scattered currency. 'Fine, fine. No harm done. Seems the locals aren't all friendly.' He straightened, glancing about. 'But look!' He pointed to the end of the alley. 'We're here.'

'Really?'

Boone turned to Luc and grinned. 'I told you I knew where we were going. Come on!'

Shaking his head, Luc stooped to pick up the silver dollar where it had fallen. Sand and dirt had stuck to the blood and fluid. *Hmm.* He carefully wiped it clean on China's jacket. *Much better.*

Boone was just disappearing into the doorway of the building opposite as Luc began to follow. He glanced up at the faded sign above the door. *Dawn to Dusk. There are some odd names around here.*

Idly rubbing blood from his knuckles, Luc entered the bar.

# 9. Meeting

*Why do I have the feeling I'm being... prodded? She looks like an ordinary girl—same age as Sasha, or near to it. But there's more to her than meets the eye, which I guess is why Jacob sent her here. She keeps talking and talking, but it's as if she's not really listening...* Neela leaned against the bar that ran along one side of the large room, her gaze tracking Ariadne as she paced under the skylight, passing in and out of shadow. *And she's from Corinth.*

'...And I can't believe you're a senator. I mean, a real, actual live senator. In the Senate! That's crazy. You must love it. I've never been to Nexus Prime. Well, obviously. I've never really been anywhere. Except here. This is kind of a big deal for me, you know? It was just like—out of nowhere, and then, bam. Here I am. A million miles away. You know?' Ariadne turned to Neela, who nodded agreeably.

'I don't even know who our senator is. That's terrible, isn't it? They always say young people don't care about politics, and we say that's unfair, but then I don't even know who he is, you know? Is it a he? Do you know him?' She stopped pacing and turned to look at Neela, finally taking a breath.

'I do know Senator Hedge, yes. Not terribly well.' *President Shen's pet poodle. Has he realised he's out of a job if they secede?* 'We've worked together on a few committees.'

Ariadne beamed. 'That's good. I really should know who he is, but it all seems a bit removed, you know? Everyone knows the president—he's all over the place—but the Commonwealth… It just seems so far away, and then you hear people saying that maybe we're not even staying, with the, um—'

'Secession.'

'Really? I thought it was *accession*. Oh well. I guess you'd know better than me!' Ariadne laughed.

A scraping noise came from the entrance hall. The girl fell silent, and Neela turned towards the doorway just as a man appeared in it. *And what an odd-looking man he is. Scrawny, pale—like a hobo, but cleaner. He can't be whom we're here to—*

'Ladies!' The newcomer threw his arms wide, a look of delight on his face. 'You've arrived. Marvellous. Welcome, welcome. You look exactly like the boss said you would. More beautiful, even. My name is Boone. Finnigan Boone. Did he mention me?'

Neela and Ariadne shared a look, before Neela answered. 'Did who?'

'The boss. The big man. Can't miss him. Tall, broad, long white hair. Bit intense-looking, but nice when you get to know him. Jacob.'

*Good lord, he is our contact.* 'No, sorry. He said we would be met here by… someone. Which I guess is you.' Neela strode forwards, hand out. 'I'm—'

'Commonwealth Senator Neela Kane, representative for Vish-Kataa, based on Nexus Prime.' Boone looked pleased with himself as he accepted Neela's hand and shook it vigorously. 'I know all about you, Senator. Don't you mind!'

He turned to Ariadne. 'Which makes you the lovely Ariadne, no last name, resident of Corinth, wherever that is. Beautiful, magical girl. Special. Exciting!' Boone clapped his hands.

Neela cocked an eyebrow at Ariadne, who was studiously ignoring her. *Magical?*

The scruffy emissary continued, gesturing back at the doorway. 'And this is my esteemed colleague, Lucius. Next member of our merry band—where is he?' He scurried to the door, poked his head out into the hall, and hollered, 'Luc?' Neela heard the murmur of another voice, shortly followed by the appearance of its owner. Who looked not one bit like Finnigan Boone.

*Oh, my.* Neela felt herself lean back involuntarily as if to make room. *He looks like someone carved him out of something… tanned.* Her gaze met his. *Gold eyes. Why… Who…* She cleared her throat and offered her hand again. 'Hello. I'm Neela.'

He glanced down at her hand, looking a little uncertain, then at Boone, who nodded enthusiastically. Luc stepped forwards and grasped her forearm. *Uh, okay. Not a handshaker, then.* 'Lucius Corralin Ben Quinto.'

'Impressive name,' Neela said.

He looked a little sheepish as he released her arm. 'Well… uh, Luc. You can call me Luc.' He jerked his thumb at his colleague. 'Boone does, and we only met a few days ago.'

Ariadne, who had clearly been waiting impatiently, burst out. 'Hi! I'm Ariadne.' Neela noticed a slight blush on her cheeks as she positively skipped over to Luc. 'Can you do that arm thing with me, as well? That was cool.'

'Um, sure.' They gripped arms, his hand completely encircling Ariadne's slim forearm.

'Wow, your hands are enormous.'

*Good lord.* Neela turned to Boone, trying not to laugh. 'So, Mr. Boone—or just Boone? Are you going to tell us why we're all here? Is this everyone, or are we expecting a fifth to appear from somewhere?'

'Ah! Now you mention it. Indeed. One short. Our merry

band of chosen is incomplete! Chosen. Bit melodramatic. Jacob's idea, not mine. Hmm. Where is he? Can't be late. Not like them to be late.' Boone pulled an ancient-looking watch out of a pocket in what was either a jacket or a vest, and inspected it. Then looked up. 'Does anyone know what the time is?'

'It is fifteen twenty-three, local time.'

Everyone spun towards the source of the voice: the furthest corner of the room, which had been empty seconds earlier. A hooded, cloaked figure stood there, its face in shadow.

Neela widened her eyes. *That's a good trick.*

\* \* \*

Abe had been waiting for several hours, standing in the darkest corner of the building at the co-ordinates he had been given, when the first of the women had arrived. Infiltrator shield set to minimum, he let the shadows do most of the work. The first woman—*Tall, slim, skin dark from ethnicity rather than sun exposure*—had not even glanced in his direction when she entered the room. He observed her as she idly examined her surroundings and took a seat near the long wooden fixture that lined the opposite side of the room. She had sat silently for several minutes, eyes glazed over. *Deduction: personal implant. Terminal. Interesting development in Commonwealth technology.*

The second woman—*Younger, late adolescence*—had arrived next, failing to notice she wasn't alone until the first had introduced herself.

*Neela. Ariadne.*

*Nee-lah. Ah-ree-ahd-nee.*

*Pleasing.*

Ariadne had dominated their conversation, maintaining a steady stream of monologue as she wandered the room. It had taken Abe a few minutes to identify the unusual, low-level signals that his sensors picked up, intensifying every time the girl walked close to him.

*She knows I'm here. No visual or aural footprint. And yet. She knows someone is here.*

Before matters had come to a head, two more had arrived.

The first, a small man, was... puzzling. Abe's biological sensors had returned nothing obviously unusual, but... *Confusing. Human, certain. Yet. Also more-less-different. Uncertain.* Abe scanned the fourth arrival as he entered, and as the results collected, Abe had had to fight a surprising fight-or-flight urge. *Redundant internal organs. Enlarged heart muscle. Phase-capable skin. Ultra-dense skeleton.*

*Titan. Enemy. Titan. Fight-kill-flee.*

*Titan.*

With an effort, he had overridden his base response, calmed. When the small man had revealed that they were waiting for one other person, Abe knew it was time to reveal himself. *As they say: now or never.* He checked his internal chronometer, dropped the shield, and gave the time.

Ariadne looked satisfied. 'Oh, there you are.'

Neela spoke next. 'Well. Hello. Um, how long have you been standing there?'

The small man—Boone, he had said—began a rambling discourse to which Abe paid little attention. His gaze, still hidden in the deep hood of the Yidrim cloak, were fixed on the Titan—who stared right back at him. Nose twitching. Eyes narrowing. Hands clenching into fists. As the man called Boone stepped away, the path between them cleared.

The Titan charged.

Even as he prepared defensive measures, Abe knew he was doomed. Certain specifically augmented Collective were capable of withstanding an assault by a Titan cohort, but Abe was not one of them. Even unarmed, his attacker would be easily able to weather any countermeasures Abe could engage. *Still. Must delay inevitable.*

Abe popped a kinetic shield, which tore the cloak away from his body to free his arms. He heard a gasp from one of the women. He kept the shield up as the Titan neared—*So fast; So so fast*—and struck it, bursting through the barrier as if it were gelatin. Milliseconds later he hit Abe, slamming him into the wall behind.

The nanocarbon in Abe's skin diffused the shock across his body, minimising the damage, but he was in pain. *Going worse than anticipated.* Abe barely registered both women shouting as the Titan raised his hand for a strike that Abe knew could sever his head.

With no choice, Abe jammed his multitool into the man's midriff and triggered the only weapon he had ready, unleashing a four thousand volt burst. The Titan was thrown back several metres, landing with a groan.

And, seconds later, he climbed back to his feet.

*Options exhausted.*

'Luc, why—'

'He's with us, my boy! Wait—'

'Leave him alone!'

The Titan shook himself like an animal, staring at Abe with cold, expressionless eyes, pupils reshaped to a feline slit. Baring his teeth, he started towards Abe.

And was yanked up into the air. The Titan hung motionless, every muscle seemingly frozen.

Abe looked past his assailant to see Ariadne, one arm extended, eyes blazing with a clear white light.

'I said, "Leave him alone."'

\* \* \*

Neela was floundering, grasping desperately for some semblance of her normal assuredness. *Who are these people? Silver-eyed man with the mechanical hand, no hair, and white skin gets attacked by the beautiful gold-eyed giant who moves faster than a cat, whom the little girl picks up. With her... mind?*

Ariadne turned her head, her blazing gaze still fixed on Luc's immobile form. 'Mr Boone, can you please talk to your extremely violent friend here? Maybe persuade him not to attack anybody else for a minute?'

Neela turned from Ariadne to look at the bizarre-looking man Luc had attacked. He stood clutching his chest with his one recognisable hand, clearly having trouble breathing. *He took quite a pounding.* She jumped at a hand on her shoulder and turned to see Boone smiling reassuringly at her.

'Bit of a shock, eh? Bet you don't get much of this in the Senate!' He chuckled as he stepped towards Luc, craning his neck to look up at him. 'Now then, Luc—' He stopped and turned to Ariadne. 'Can he talk, or is his tongue, you know, frozen?'

Ariadne cocked her head. 'He can talk now.'

A scream burst from Luc's lips as he shook his head. He glared at Ariadne, fury in his eyes. 'You had better be able to keep me here forever, witch, because you'll be dead two seconds after I'm free.'

Boone raised his hands. 'Luc, my boy, my fault. Sorry. Should have thought how you'd react. Know what your lot think about these folks.' He scratched his head thoughtfully. 'Yes, should have occurred to me.'

*Okay, enough of this.* 'Sorry to interrupt, but while this all seems to make sense to all of you, can someone please explain? Boone? Who are these people?'

Boone glanced her way. 'Hmm? Oh, sorry. Didn't get a chance to do introductions. So Ariadne,' —he gestured— 'whom you've met. She's one of what you call the Seryn. Fancy tricks, eh?'

Neela's mind whirred. *Seryn? They're still around— Wait. Corinth. Is that...*

Boone continued, 'The lad in the corner who just took a beating is—correct me if I'm wrong—Abe?'

The pale man nodded, standing straighter and breathing more evenly.

'Lovely. Abe is... Never been clear on the pronouns. A? One of? Collective, anyway. Brilliant with machines. Partly because you partly are machine, right?' Boone snapped his fingers. 'Reminds me—could you take a look at my shuttle later? Engine's making some odd noises. Doesn't sound right. Handling's a bit jerky too.'

Abe smiled slightly. Neela couldn't stop herself staring. *This is all of our legends come to life. I should have known, that hand, those eyes... So we've got one Seryn, one Collective, and... Oh, of course.* 'He's a Titan. I should have guessed.'

Boone nodded. 'Well done, Senator. Impressive specimens, aren't they?' He looked up again. 'Sorry, Luc, bit patronising, that. But listen, you really shouldn't have—'

Luc cut in. 'Collective are abomination. We know this. The witches, too. There's nothing you can say, Boone. I have no idea what your plan was bringing these... heathens here.'

The opportunity to get answers first-hand—an opportunity no Commonwealth citizen had ever had—had Neela trembling. She moved so she could look Luc in the face. 'Forgive me, Luc, but why do you say that? What have the Collective and the Seryn done?'

Luc spat, his stare fixed on Abe, who looked back with impressive equanimity given that he'd been seconds from death a minute or so ago. 'Collective are evil. They abduct women and children from human habitats—your habitats, if you're from the Commonwealth—and experiment on them. Plugging them into their machines, implanting them with ungodly devices. Corrupting them.'

Neela was horrified. She turned to Abe to see him frowning and shaking his head. 'No record of that. Would have records. No experimentation. Repulsive.' His voice was the same androgynous monotone as before.

'But how can you be sure? Your culture is large, yes?' Neela felt her assurance returning as she slipped into Senate debate mode. 'How could you know for sure that some elements, some leaders—Do you have leaders?—weren't doing this?'

Abe hesitated for a long time before answering. 'Collective are—linked. We are one, a community, closer than anything you have. All are one. We would—know. That is all. Something such as the Titan describes—those responsible would be punished. Severely.'

Neela turned to see Luc shaking his head, his body still paralysed. 'It lies to save itself.'

Boone chimed in. 'Afraid not, my boy. Your betters have

been telling you porkies on this one. Your uncle would know. Get as high up as he is, they tell you the truth.'

Luc looked unconvinced. 'And how in Founder's name would you know that? Sit in on many Council meetings, do you?'

'Not exactly, but we keep our ears to the ground. Sources, you know. And come on, lad. Are you really that surprised? After what they did to you the other day? Lovely bunch, your Council. Not a lot they won't do.'

Luc looked away. He stayed silent.

'And when it comes to this lot,' —Boone nodded towards Ariadne— 'well, you don't know much, do you? Because you haven't been able to find them. Right? Right. So all you've got is old stories about shadowy psychic magickers, getting inside your brain and controlling you, trying to take over the galaxy. And that's bollocks, isn't it?' He raised his eyebrows at the Seryn.

Ariadne paused before answering. 'Um... Yeah. Well, pretty much.'

Neela's eyes narrowed. 'Which means what, exactly?'

'Well we're not trying to take over the galaxy, that's for sure.' Ariadne smiled weakly. 'And we can't control people—we don't, I mean—it's not possible. We can... nudge them, a bit, sometimes. We mainly just want everyone to get along.'

'How noble of you.' Luc's voice dripped sarcasm.

Neela quickly assimilated the information. *Time to end this little standoff.* She looked up at Luc again. 'Okay. This is all new to me, but this is what I understand. Luc, you've been told the Collective are evil. Probably for a long time. Now Boone's telling you you've been lied to, and maybe you believe that more than you would have a few days ago. So maybe you can not bash Abe's head in until you talk to— Was it your uncle?' She glanced at Boone, who nodded encouragingly. 'Fine. And with Ariadne, it sounds as if you know about as much about the Seryn as I do—which is almost nothing. So we can either both give her, and each other, a chance—or we can go home.'

Luc turned away, glaring at the wall. Neela made an intuitive leap. *Or maybe not.* 'Except you can't go home, can you? It's... Oh, this Council of yours. I get the impression they're not what you thought.'

Boone nodded. 'Spot on, Senator.'

'All right. Sounds like you're stuck with us, then.' She turned to Abe. 'Unless you're having second thoughts?'

Abe shook his head slowly. 'Negative. Similar personal situation: No return possible. Only onwards.'

*Great, half the gang's only here because they have to be.* 'And you, Ariadne? Will you stay for whatever Boone has planned for us?'

'Why not? Someone has to stop these two from killing each other, right? And you.' She gestured at Luc. 'Don't try anything. Next time, I might not be so nice.' The light slowly faded from her eyes, and Luc gradually dropped to the ground.

The Titan stumbled slightly as control of his body came back to him. He shot Ariadne a sulky glance. She gave him a stern look back.

Neela stifled a laugh. *Like a kitten bossing around a tiger.* She turned to Boone. 'Fine. So where exactly are we going?'

* * *

*Fingers. Toes. Calves. Thighs. Forearms. Upper arms.* Luc flexed and worked each part of his body in turn, checking that the Seryn hadn't left anything disabled. His gaze flicked from her to Abe. *Hard to resist the urge to gut them both.* He frowned. *Strange. As if I don't have a choice.*

'Where are we going! Good question. Excellent. Well, as you know, we're off to see the Book. Legendary. Marvellous thing, very old, exciting for everyone. And you have all been chosen, representatives of your various, um, factions. One of each. Can't play favourites, can we?' Boone paused to scratch his beard thoughtfully.

A few seconds of silence followed.

'Boone?' Neela asked.

'Hmm?'

'Where are we...'

'Ah! Of course.' Boone had, as usual, gotten distracted and not answered Neela's question. 'Yes. Well, Equinox, obviously'.

Luc glanced around at the others' blank faces. *Not just me, then.* 'Which is…? I've never heard of it.'

'Oh, you wouldn't have. It's not really on any charts.'

Ariadne looked confused. 'I don't know much about navigation or anything, but I thought we'd pretty much mapped everything now?'

Neela nodded. 'We have. Every populated system has a name, all the unpopulated ones a code. To the Commonwealth, at least. If it's called Equinox—'

'Ah, that's just what the Athravan call it. They're the only ones there.'

Abe said, 'Collective have records of known Athravan locations. Sites of significance: Remnants of Elu civilisation. No record of an Equinox.'

'Well, they don't advertise. Don't want the pilgrims paying a visit. Plus, it's a little bit out of the way.' He scratched his beard again. 'Middle of the Wolftail Nebula.'

*I'm none the wiser.* Luc turned to see Ariadne shrug. Neela's eyes were glazed, clearing as she said, 'That nebula is just dust and gas, our records show.'

Abe shook his head. 'False. Wolftail contains forty-eight star systems. Twelve planetary.' He paused, then turned towards Boone. 'One more unusual than the others.'

Boone grinned. 'Good scanners, your lot have got.' He clapped his hands. 'So yes, that's where we're headed. Not a long trip, but not short. We'll go up in the shuttle tonight, meet the ship. Shuttle's a bit small to take us all the way. Luc here was bouncing off the walls with just the two of us, weren't you lad?'

*Yes, but not because of the size of the shuttle.*

'How's that, then? Eighteen hundred at the spaceport?'

Neela's eyes narrowed, as if she were weighing her options, then she nodded slowly. 'Okay. I'll call the local Senate office so they know to pick up my shuttle.'

'Fine by me, too,' said Ariadne.

'Affirmative. I will inform my ship it can leave also.'

Ariadne's eyes widened. 'Inform it? Your ship's clever enough to do that?'

Abe nodded once. 'Clever enough.'

'That's settled then. See you all in a few hours. Exciting, isn't it!'

Luc closed his eyes. *Founder save me.*

* * *

'Four more. You copy that, Spence?' Drake powered off the binocs as the target passed out of view, then turned towards the fire escape that ran up the side of the warehouse opposite Bar Dusk Till Dawn.

Spence's voice came through the communicator loud and clear. 'Aye. Three we saw enter after her, and one more. Presumably already there.'

'Mixed bunch, wouldn't you agree?'

'Very much so, boss. The two blokes make an odd pair on their own. The girl looks like she's got a day off from school, and lord knows about Mr. Cloak.'

'If it even is a man,' Drake offered.

'From the height and the walk? Almost sure.'

*So, we've got a few extra players. That'll complicate things.* 'Cullen, are you on Little and Large?'

'Affirmative.' Drake could hear Cullen's steady pace in the background. 'They're heading east, possibly towards the spaceport. General direction anyway. Girl peeled away, and Cloak— well, he disappeared.'

'Say again?'

'Quite. One moment there, the next not so much. Happily I wasn't tailing him. Otherwise, I'd have been a little embarrassed.'

'Fine. We'll worry about that later if we need to. Spence has the target.'

'Confirmed. Seems to be on her way back to the hotel. Getting ready to leave, maybe?'

'Could be, lad. Could be. We're prepped to go as well. Aren't we, Cullen?'

'Bags packed, bills paid, ship fuelled. We'll be in orbit before she is.'

'Or they are,' said Spence. 'Got to assume the whole gang is going on the next leg of the outing, no?'

'Always assume the worst. And that would be the worst case.'

Cullen asked, 'Are we thinking of calling in a few extras, chief? Given the change in parameters.'

*Thinking about it.* Drake jogged down the fire escape, kicking up a puff of dust as he jumped down into the alley. *Better safe than sorry.* 'We are, Cullen. I'll call in some bodies from… What's nearest? Septus?'

Spence supplied, 'Not much of a security presence there, boss. Staging post at Hanover is better, probably.'

'Fine. I'll make the call now. They should be here in a few hours, can meet us in orbit.' Breaking into a jog, Drake turned the corner at the end of the alley, gaining speed as he passed the bar and headed back towards the guest house and the subspace wave transmitter stashed in his bag. 'Stay on your targets, boys. I'll see you soon.'

'Check.'

'Check that, chief.'

*Complications. Bane of my life.*

\* \* \*

*Two becomes five, three follow.* Perched in the gallery of a tall, crumbling minaret that overlooked the northern half of Kowloon's market district, Caleb Hesch considered collateral damage. The three men he had detected standing watch had been in place before Luc and his companion had arrived, so presumably were tailing one of the other three already in place at the meeting point. *Not necessarily antagonistic, but not necessarily a help. Probably just in the way.*

Hesch's gaze flicked from the binocular-carrying man on the warehouse roof down to the alley, where the group of five, after stopping in discussion for a few minutes, were splitting and going their separate ways; Luc Corralin and his associate, followed after a few seconds by the oldest of the three watchers; the taller, darker-skinned woman tracked by the younger man, rising from a table at a tiny cafe down the street with what he no doubt thought was inconspicuous nonchalance. *Idiot.*

That left the young girl and the hooded figure. The girl walked with the older woman for a while, then turned into a broader street, merging into a crowd of shoppers. The man—*Probably a man*—in the cloak turned away from the city centre, up an alley that would lead to the northern edge of the city. Hesch's eyes narrowed, his superior vision not enough to pierce the shadows of the man's hood.

With a momentary shimmer like light flashing across a puddle of water, the man vanished. Hesch involuntarily hissed, teeth bared in an grimace.

*Collective. What in Founder's name is going on here?*

Shaking his head, he moved to the other side of the gallery and looked out and down. He picked out Corralin and his partner easily, winding their ways through hawkers and beggars. With practised ease, Hesch swung himself over the edge of the gallery and dropped. Just before slamming into the roof of the main mosque below, he grabbed onto a rusted flagpole that jutted out from the minaret wall, swinging forwards and turning his momentum into a jump that carried him across the narrow alley onto the roof of a lower building opposite.

Rolling as he landed, Hesch quickly rolled up and entered a jog. The cramped buildings in the district made the pursuit easy, if the pursuer kept to the rooftops. A quick glance into the alley below confirmed Corralin's path.

Hesch increased speed as he neared the roof's edge and leapt.

# 10. Mournstar

The sun had just set, and the first kree-kree calls of the nighthawks were ringing out along the tree line at the edge of the shuttleport as Ariadne reached the bay that housed Boone's shuttle. The man himself was poking his head out of the open doorway, grinning widely.

'Ariadne, dear girl—our party is complete! Everyone's here, so let's be off! Exciting.' His head disappeared into the interior. 'Plenty of room, don't you worry.'

Through the viewport at the nose of the shuttle, she could see Luc frowning at the instrument panel. *That fills me with confidence. Either something's wrong, or he doesn't know what he's doing.* She sighed. *Too late now. At least this looks a little more spaceworthy than the shuttle on Corinth...*

Seconds later, she reached the main—only—cabin. Neela looked up as she entered and gave her a warm smile. Ariadne returned it, appreciating the gesture. *Or at least the pretence.* She glanced to the cockpit to her right, where Boone had strapped himself into the other pilot's chair and was engaged in a heated conversation with Luc.

'...No, I told you, that's not what that's for—'

'My shuttle, lad, and I'm telling you—look, I'll press it—'

'Don't!'

*Great. Eccentric captain; co-pilot wants to kill me. This should be fun.* Ariadne looked around for a seat and spotted Abe in the furthest corner of the cabin. She gave him a small wave and got a slight nod in return. She sighed. *Yup, lots of fun.*

'Ladies and gentlemen, this is your captain speaking—'

'You're not the captain, Boone, for Founder's sake-'

'—We are now cleared for takeoff and are ready to depart! Marvellous. Off we go, then!'

Ariadne quickly sat down in the nearest seat. Her elbow bumped a panel on the armrest, and the seat smoothly moulded itself to her form, restraints snapping together across her chest and shoulders. She yelped in surprise, then looked up sheepishly to see Neela smiling at her across the aisle.

'Don't worry. I did exactly the same thing. The fixtures in here aren't exactly well-labelled.'

'No. But I don't expect they have passengers often. Is it one of theirs, do you know? The Athravan? I haven't been on many shuttles—it could be a Commonwealth one they just bought, for all I know.'

Neela shook her head slowly. 'I'm not sure. It's not a design I recognise, but the Commonwealth's a big place. Plenty of people making ships. Throw in the Independents too, and they could have got it from anywhere.'

A low throbbing rumble shook the cabin, and the whine of the engines rose quickly to a loud roar. Ariadne closed her eyes as she felt her insides being pulled down and back as they lifted off.

*And away we go.*

\* \* \*

The signal pinged in Abe's mind just as the shuttle cleared

Fusion's planetary satgrid. *'Departure confirmed?'*

*'Confirmed, ship. Chance be with you.'*

*'And with you. Departing now.'* Abe's long-range sensors detected the familiar jump signature of the soloship as it left the system, the first hop of many to retrace their steps back to the Cloud.

*And now I am alone.* He looked around the shuttle cabin at his new companions, acquaintances of only a few hours. *Not quite alone.*

Apparently the Athravan vessel that would take them on to Equinox would meet them in-system, just outside Fusion's satgrid boundary. Abe had swept the region and found the normal high volume of ships inbound and outbound from the busy planet, but none that seemed to be waiting for a rendezvous.

Curious, he called to Boone in the cabin, 'For how long will we wait, Boone?'

'What's that, lad?' came the lilting warble of a reply.

'The ship we are to meet. When does it arrive?'

Boone chuckled, sounding pleased. 'Ha-ha! Nice to see you lot aren't totally infallible. She's already here, lad. Already here. Should be coming up on her just about-'

*Now.* Abe's proximity alarm began pinging furiously. Neela and Ariadne gasped in unison, craning their necks to peer through the nose viewport as the facing starfield was suddenly obscured.

Abe was silent as his sensors began mapping the shape of the craft. He was impressed by the display of cloaking technology—Collective had only recently developed a perfect cloak that masked a ship's disturbance of the subspace energy grid and only for soloship-sized craft. As the mapping continued, he reeled inwardly as the size of the ship became clear; it was hundreds of times as large as the soloship. *Technology decades-centuries ahead. Incredible. Impossible.*

The shape of the vessel was also like none that he had ever encountered. Spinning through Network for a comparison, the closest match was a common marine cephalopod. *Cuttlefish. Long curved body narrowing at rear, broader forwards portion.* The resemblance was completed by four long tendril-like protuberances that extended forwards and almost touched. Overall, the ship was sleek, elegant, the hull a deep, shimmering indigo in the starlight.

'It's so pretty!' said Ariadne.

'Certainly is, my dear,' said Boone from the cockpit. 'She's a beauty.' The shuttle slowed as it approached a docking bay that was opening in the ship's stern.

'Welcome to *Mournstar*.' Abe recognised pride in Boone's voice.

* * *

Drake tried a friendly smile. 'Welcome to the hunt, lads. Glad to have you here.'

The Choi twins stared at him, standing expressionless at parade ground attention. *Of course the only two free bodies at Hanover are these clowns. Permanent bloody funeral with them around. I'd have preferred Crazy Eddie.* Drake turned away from his statuesque new team members. *Maybe not Eddie. Not with the other three.* 'Little Joe, Captain Hacksaw...' Drake frowned. 'Cullen, who was the other one?'

Cullen spun in his seat at the navdeck of the corvette *Broken Promise*. 'What's that, boss?'

'Eddie's third voice in his head. Little Joe, Hacksaw—I've forgotten the other one.'

'Angry Reverend,' said Cullen.

'Aaaaah.' *That was it.* Drake turned back to the still motionless twins. 'Anyway, get unpacked, then back here in twenty. You've read the material on the way, right?'

Two almost imperceptible nods.

'Marvellous. Dismissed.' Two crisp salutes, and the twins departed. Shaking his head slightly, Drake wandered over to Cullen.

Cullen piped up, 'Now, boss, we've gotta make sure we don't have so much fun we don't get the job done. With

Chuckles and Cheery on board, we'll be rolling in the aisles.'

Drake sighed. 'They're pros, at least. But it's not going to be Parthenon, that's for sure.'

Cullen snorted. 'Or JuJu Bay.'

'Kingston.'

'Yemenis.'

'Witcher.'

Cullen looked up at Drake. 'Remind me—how long have we been doing this?'

'I try not to think about it, Michael. Best not to.' A flash and a low pinging alarm from the navdeck interrupted their reminiscence. Cullen dialled the sensors in to the flagged area.

'A fairly large vessel just appeared in the vicinity of the targets' shuttle, boss. No jump signature, and we're well in-system, so it didn't just hop in. Been here awhile.'

'Hidden.'

'Aye. Now that's a bit of a bugger, isn't it?'

'One for future me to worry about. Can you get a transponder lock?'

Cullen's thick, stubby fingers danced with surprising nimbleness over the navdeck panels. His frown showed concern and confusion. 'Well… Yes. Maybe. I think so.'

'Filling me with confidence.'

'Okay. Yes. But it's nothing the computer's ever seen before. It took a good few seconds before it even recognised the signal as a transponder. It seems fairly happy now, though.'

'So we're golden.'

Cullen glanced up again, eyebrows raised. 'Don't know about that, boss. Yellow, maybe.'

Drake groaned quietly. *Two decades of these jokes.* 'I'll be in my cabin. Get Spence in here as well. Call me when it looks like they're moving off.'

'Will do; will do,' came the reply as Drake turned to leave.

*Two fucking decades.*

⋆　⋆　⋆

For the hundredth time since he had left Mission, Luc wondered what he was doing. *I should be at the Academy right now. Graduation. Getting my tattoo, heading out on the hunt, getting drunk with the rest of the class. Picking up girls.* He stared out the wide main viewport of *Mournstar's* bridge, eyes fixed on the flashing beacon of Fusion's jump waypoint. In a minute or two they would make their first jump, the ship had said.

And that was another thing. The ship. *The sentient, intelligent ship. One conversation, and it's already getting on my nerves.*

Luc heard footsteps in the outside corridor seconds before the doorfield swooshed open. *Neela. How nice of you to come and say hello. Or are you perhaps worried I'll change my mind and gut the other members of our little team in their sleep?*

'Hello, Luc. Mind if I join you? I quite enjoy watching the jump when I get the chance.'

Luc half turned and waved her into a seat near the viewport. As she approached, Luc subtly looked her over. *Attractive. Bit annoying, though. Get the impression she's used to being in charge.* He noticed that she'd changed clothes: baggy trous and a vest, hair pulled up in a ponytail. He glanced down at his own slightly grubby clothing. *Huh. I could do with a change, actually.*

He felt an additional thrum in the body of the ship a second before the announcement came in *Mournstar's* androgynous monotone: 'PASSENGERS, YOUR ATTENTION PLEASE. INITIAL JUMP IN TEN SECONDS. REPEAT: JUMP IN TEN...FIVE... THREE, TWO, ONE. JUMP.'

Eyes fixed on the viewport, Luc watched the familiar disconcerting dropshift as the starfield rose and stretched towards them, then the jerking slam into the nauseating unreality of subspace. He tried to track the shifting colours, but they seemed to slide away from his gaze. Luc frowned. 'Why do you like watching it?'

Neela turned to him. 'The jump? I don't know. I just always find it amazing that this is something we can do. You think about all of the systems we're going to pass in this one jump from Fusion to...'

'Saffron.'

'Right. Tens of systems, billions of people. And we just hop past in a few hours. It makes me wonder what it was like before. When people were lightbound.'

Luc snorted. 'Crowded, I'd guess. And not particularly interesting.'

Neela was looking at him intently. Slightly discomfited, he returned her gaze.

She flashed him a brief smile. 'I find it a little ironic that you'd say that. Given that, as far as the rest of the galaxy knows, the Titans have remained based in one system for—well, forever.'

Luc turned back to the viewport. *Here we go.*

'And that's another thing,' continued Neela. 'How is that even possible? With normal population growth, you should have outgrown Mission centuries ago, but somehow—no. You're still there.'

*What is she expecting, exactly?* Luc nodded slightly.

'I just—I just find you fascinating. You're practically mythical in the Commonwealth, popping up every century or so to save the day or do something dramatic and vi—' She stopped.

Luc glanced at Neela, who looked a little embarrassed. 'Violent, were you going to say?'

'Well. Yes. But I didn't—'

'Don't bother. Being thought violent isn't insulting to a Titan. Violence is an assertion of will, an action affirming the strength of one's convictions.' Luc's brow wrinkled. *And I still believe that. I can hold on to that. It's just... maybe the convictions have shifted.*

Neela was looking at him, expression odd. *Like you'd look at a tiger that just wiped its feet on the doormat.* Luc sighed. 'I get the feeling you're going to be asking me a lot of questions.'

'Probably. I'm fairly curious.'

'Uh-huh.' Luc watched their passage through subspace, trying—and failing—again to focus on the constantly shifting colours of the energy grid. *This is going to be a long trip.*

* * *

Abe gazed steadily at Ariadne. 'Please confirm: You are certain?'

'I don't see why not. It's not going to hurt, is it?' she asked.

'I believe not. However: I have never done this before.'

'Really?'

'Not with one of your kind. Possible effects are unknown.' *And almost certainly not lethal.*

'Hmm. Well, I'm up for it if you are.'

Abe cocked his head. 'Inquiry: What is "up for it?"'

'You know. Keen. Want to. Up for it,' said Ariadne.

'Understanding. Affirmative. Yes. Up for it.'

'Then what are we waiting for?'

Abe and Ariadne sat in the cabin Abe had chosen, at random, from the fifty that lined the residential deck, the upper of the two decks on *Mournstar*. Below it was the command-control deck and the ship's bridge. Below that were the engine, weapons, and docking bays that took up around half of the ship's volume. The cabin alone seemed vast to Abe, easily ten times the size of the standard quarters he had been allocated on the arcology.

The Seryn girl—*Ah-ree-ahd-nee*—had banged on the cabin doorfield shortly after the ship had begun the jump, apparently after a fruitless minute spent trying to activate the notification panel next to it. After a few minutes of what Abe had decided was 'small talk'—*Conversation with no meaningful information exchange. Strange*—Abe had (bluntly, in hindsight) asked Ariadne if he could scan her brain to map the electrical activity. To his surprise, she had quickly agreed.

'Oh, one question before we start?'

Abe waited.

'You aren't going to send this back to the rest of the Collective so they can work out how to make a Seryn death ray, are you?' she asked.

'Death ray?'

'Death ray.'

Abe considered her question for a few seconds. The notion hadn't even occurred to him. He looked at Ariadne, who flashed him a smile. 'No death ray.'

'Good. Because if it were Luc asking me if he could do this, he'd get a completely different answer. I trust him about as far as I can throw him.' She snorted with laughter. 'And I could throw him pretty far!'

'Haaaa.' Abe jerked a little upright in surprise. *Unusual. Spontaneous laughter.*

'So you do laugh! That's good to know.'

*Apparently. Yes, I do.*

'Shall we get on with it, then? Do I need to do anything?'

Abe shook his head. 'Scan quality improved if receptor attached near the brain. Left temple is ideal.' As he spoke, he pulled a small jack from a clip in his multitool. It came away, trailing a microfilament wire that extended back into his right arm.

Abe shook the jack gently, and Ariadne gaped a little as it reformed, melting, stretching, and expanding until it was a flat circular pad an inch across. 'May I?'

Ariadne nodded, looking a little nervous.

A memory from something picked up on a long-ago trip past a bustling Commonwealth world flashed into Abe's mind. 'Don't worry. This won't hurt a bit.'

Ariadne relaxed again as he attached the pad to her temple. Abe nodded, satisfied, as his sensors—focused through the jack cable—began mapping the complex matrix of brain activity.

*Productive day. Significant knowledge increase.*

\* \* \*

Neela arrived back at the bridge the next morning to find the others already gathered. *No surprise there. Mournstar* had announced that they would soon complete their final jump and arrive at the Wolftail Nebula. *Guess we all want to see the sights.*

The smell of freshly brewed coffee drew her attention to a gleaming white table against the left hand wall. Along with the large coffee urn were fresh rolls, tropical fruits, smoked fish, and an enormous plate of cured meats. *Is there a kitchen on board? Boone didn't mention it, but I suppose it makes sense.*

Ariadne sat on one of the memfoam couches near the food, a

huge plate on her lap. She waved at Neela, her mouth shiny from the slice of melon in her hand. 'Morning, Neela. Sleep okay?'

'Fine, thank you. Bit of a headache this morning, but it's passing.' *And I never got around to seeing that doctor. Again.* 'Who prepared the food? Not Boone, surely? I can't imagine him as the culinary type.'

Ariadne snorted, then wiped her mouth as she dropped the melon rind onto her plate. 'No, nor me. It was Mo.'

Neela blinked. 'Mo?'

Ariadne nodded. 'The ship. *Mournstar*. I call him Mo. He said he likes it, and he's never had a nickname before. Anyway, he just asked us what we wanted, and it appeared in that hole in the wall by the table.' She gestured, and Neela turned to notice an aperture. 'I might have got a bit carried away when he said I could have anything I wanted; I don't think I can finish it all.'

Neela laughed. 'Well, I'll help you out. I'm surprised, though. Some of these fruits aren't even in season.'

'Oh, that's the clever bit—the food's not real. Well, it's real, but it's not really real—Mo makes it himself.'

Neela frowned. 'What do you mean?'

'I asked him—apparently he puts gas and dust and rocks and stuff into this big machine, and breaks it right down, and then puts it back together as food. It's a bit beyond me, to be honest. Tastes like food though, and that's the important thing.'

*That's incredible. We're way off from having that kind of technology.* She looked around the room. Abe stood facing the viewport, staring out at the ever-shifting subspace maelstrom. Boone stood at his side, chattering away as ever. Luc was on the other side of the room, kneeling by a low table that held—*Is that a whole pig?* 'Ariadne, is he—'

'Yeah. I thought I could eat, but wow. He is twice my size, but still—I couldn't eat half that for breakfast. Even Mo sounded surprised when he asked for it.'

Another announcement from the ship quieted the room. Even Boone stopped talking. 'PASSENGERS, YOUR

ATTENTION PLEASE: JUMP COMPLETE IN TEN SECONDS. REPEAT: REALSPACE IN TEN... FIVE... THREE, TWO, ONE. REALSPACE.'

Neela watched the viewport intently as they left subspace, yanked upwards out of that fast-flowing river into sluggish realspace. As the view jerked into place, she gasped.

The viewport was entirely filled by a glittering deep-red wall, a thick roiling cloud of dust and gas. *The nebula. And, apparently, stars. And the mysterious Equinox.*

Boone turned to face them and clapped his hands, smiling. 'That's the first leg down, folks—oh, hello, Miss Kane. Good morning. Hope you slept well. Equinox awaits!'

Ariadne raised her hand. Neela smiled. *Sweet girl. Terrifying, in a way, but sweet.* 'Mr Boone, why do we have to go on normal engines now? Why can't we just jump there?'

Boone scratched his beard. 'Well, strictly, we could. Possibly. It's just the nebula makes jumping a bit tricky—it's all very dense, you see, and moving all the time. You could leave and come back in five years and a star won't quite be in the same place—which makes working out the jumps a bit too hard. So we'll go under normal power from here. It'll take about ten days, doing a few hundred times light speed, not too fast. So I hope you're all comfortable.'

Both Abe and Luc turned sharply to look at Boone.

Neela frowned. *Why... Oh. No, that is fast. Very fast. Who are these people?*

\* \* \*

*Marvellous. They couldn't go to a planet you can actually see from space, could they? Oh no. They bomb a quarter of the way around the galaxy to the least charted volume in the whole starmap. With visibility of about five metres.*

Drake sighed. 'Spence, are the instruments going to hold up? Can we actually track them once they enter that mess?'

Spence sat in the second seat at the navdeck on the corvette's bridge. He slowly shook his head. 'Honestly? I have no fucking clue, boss. You say nebula; I think gas. Bit of dust, you know.

This is like a Krakk'ween sandstorm, but fifty million times the size.'

*Great.* Drake rubbed his eyes and sat in the command seat a few metres behind the navdeck. His neck prickling, he turned to see the Choi twins standing motionless behind him. Both turned to meet his gaze as he looked at them. He gave them a nod. *Nothing.* He turned back. *Weirdos.*

The *Broken Promise* sat a few light minutes out from the target ship, after a nervy waypoint-free jump to that point. As he had ordered Spence to dial it in, all Drake could do was hope that the target hadn't stopped the same distance from the middle of a star. His relief at emerging in empty space had been quickly tempered by the sight of the nebula wall in front of them.

Cullen spoke from the primary navdeck chair. 'Engines powering up, boss. Looks like they're getting ready to go in.'

'Transponder lock?'

'Still active—for now, but as the lad said-'

'I know. But it's not like we have a choice, is it? We're hardly going to rock up right behind them and harpoon the fucker, are we?'

'Wouldn't be the most covert tail I'd ever seen, no.'

'Exactly.' Drake realised he sounded a lot more confident than he actually was. *Not the first time.* 'Give it half a minute after they enter the nebula, then move off. Maintain distance.'

'Aye.' Spence paused for a few seconds. 'Moving off now, boss.' He tapped out a brief staccato on the instrument panel. 'Accelerating... Quickly. Very quickly. Three—no, five—ten—fuck, nought to twenty lights in three seconds.' Through the viewport, Drake watched the oddly shaped vessel disappear into the red cloud wall.

'Stay calm, Spence. As long as the lock stays steady, they aren't losing us any time soon. Bring our engines up and move off in fifteen.'

'Yes, sir. Done.'

Seconds ticked by, the only sound Drake could hear the quiet breathing of the Chois behind him, until the thrum of the engines kicked in.

Spence confirmed, 'In pursuit.'

The external view stayed constant as they moved off. It was only a few seconds later, when Cullen called it, that Drake realised they had entered the nebula at all.

# 11. Nebula

Luc strode down the corridor from the elevator shaft to the stern end of the command and control deck. *Stupid name. It's not like anyone other than the ship is doing any controlling around here. And you could 'command' it just as well while sitting on the toilet.*

It was early on the fourth morning since *Mournstar* had entered the nebula. Over the previous three days, the ship's passengers had slipped into a routine of sorts. They continued to meet for meals on the bridge—during which Ariadne and Neela dominated the conversation, Abe and Luc responding more reticently when prompted. Gradually, the anger and animosity from their initial meeting was fading. *Though I'm no less confused about the hatred I have to constantly repress. Like it's ingrained in me.*

At other times, they had little to do. On the first morning, Luc had asked the ship if there were any facilities on board he could use to exercise. After a few questions on what exactly he was looking for, *Mournstar* had directed him to the stern, and a long room adjacent to the rear observatory.

When he arrived, he had discovered it full of the exact equipment he had described, all with the brand-new sheen of never having been touched. He had quizzed the ship on it. '*Mournstar*, has this always been an exercise room?'

'NO. PREVIOUSLY IT WAS A CONFERENCE ROOM.'

'Until when?'

A slight pause. 'EIGHTY-SEVEN SECONDS AGO.'

'And let me guess: You just turned the conference table into this gym equipment.'

'ALSO THE CHAIRS.'

'Just because I asked for it? That's generous.'

'NO.'

'No?'

'NO. MAINTAINING NAVIGATION AND OTHER SYSTEMS OCCUPIES ONLY ELEVEN PER CENT OF MY PROCESSING CAPABILITY.'

*Really?* 'So you were just bored.'

Another pause. 'ALSO I DO NOT HOST MANY CONFERENCES.'

He was heading for that hastily created gym now. As he neared the doorfield, he heard faint sounds of music coming from the observatory at the end of the corridor. *Who's up this early?* He pressed his palm to the entry panel, the music clearer as the doorfield silently irised open. It wasn't quite like anything Luc had heard: samples of natural sounds, waterfalls, birdcalls, wind—all woven together into a relaxing harmony. He stepped forwards and peered into the room.

On a mat in the centre of the floor lay Neela, dressed in a black leotard of some sort, stretched out on her front with her palms flat at her sides. Slowly she pushed up, her head rising and back arching as she stretched. Luc watched as she moved through a sequence of twenty or more poses.

He was impressed by her form. *Good body control, flexibility, strength. Elegant, too.* Neela arched her body again, sensuous and catlike. *And—let's be honest—hot. Really hot.*

'Does she know you're peeking?'

Luc turned to see Ariadne a few feet behind him, smiling. *How did she do that?*

'You know it's rude to spy on people?' Ariadne stepped up and peered past him at Neela. 'Can't say I blame you, though. She is quite easy on the eyes, isn't she?'

*What?* 'Uh—'

'Anyway, I'll leave you to it. I assume you're using the gym? The ship told me about it. I'll come back down later. Wouldn't want to get in your way.' With a parting wink, she sashayed off down the corridor.

Luc realised he hadn't managed to say anything throughout the whole conversation. He sighed and turned towards the gym. *Smooth, Luc. Smooth.*

\* \* \*

*Technology is familiar, yet...* Abe frowned as he walked for the tenth time from one side of the engine to the other. He was in the second of the four engine bays at the bottom of *Mournstar's* stern. There was barely room for a person to move around inside the bay, which was dimly lit only by narrow striplights that ran at head height along the longer walls. *Not intended to be regularly occupied. No maintenance workers. Ship self-maintains.* Abe shook his head again in wonder at the technological level of this Athravan craft.

The engine itself was, of course, huge—fully half the length of the entire vessel and a third its height. Abe had spent a largely fruitless half hour scanning the engine, attempting to discover its construction. No data ports were obviously present anywhere in the bay, so he had been forced to fall back on his sensors.

All he had been able to determine was that, as expected, the engine was dual-nuclear—the power from the reactor providing both conventional thrust, skipping the ship over the energy grid like a skimming stone, and fuelling the vextintanium chain reaction that would bind the craft to the grid and pull it into and through subspace. *And it is not as large as it should be.* Abe had calculated the energy that an engine of that size should have produced, multiplied it by four, and fallen far short of the amount required to push a craft of *Mournstar*'s size several hundred times the speed of light. *Which Boone claimed was 'not too fast'. Incredible. Need more data.*

The hiss of the doorfield opening behind him interrupted Abe's frustrated thoughts. Without turning, he sent a sensor ping back at the doorway, and the response made his heart rate increase.

'Good day, Titan.' Abe turned, far more calmly than he felt, to see Luc duck his head as he entered the bay. The Titan's face was expressionless as he looked around, then faced Abe.

'Hello.'

Abe ran the greeting through a vocal analyser for emotional cues. *Wary. Cold. But no threat of violence.* His heart rate started to drop back towards normal. 'You are interested in the engine also? Inspection has proved — unproductive.'

Luc nodded almost imperceptibly as he stepped past Abe and patted the titanium engine housing. 'A little. I'm bored. This voyage is interminable.' His eyes narrowing, Luc looked towards the other end of the bay, then back. 'Hmm. It's not as big as I thought it would be.'

Abe's eyebrows rose slightly. *Surprising. He worked that out quickly.* 'I also had that realisation.'

Luc glanced at Abe, then back to the engine. He spoke with a thoughtful tone. 'It occurs to me that we don't know much about these Athravan. And I don't enjoy ignorance when it comes to those I meet, be they friend, enemy, or…' — another quick glance at Abe — '… whatever.'

'Nor I, Titan. Collective find ignorance of any kind… unsatisfactory.'

Luc's half-smile was a touch grim. 'I'm sure you do. Which is why I think it makes sense for you and I to… maintain open communications. Share information. Neela's too damn diplomatic for me to get a feel for what she really thinks, and the wit— …The girl just acts like she's on holiday.'

*Interesting proposition. And not predicted.* Abe considered for a half-minute, as Luc continued to idly poke the engine. 'Proposal is sensible, Titan. Will share impressions and data.'

Luc nodded. 'Good. Okay.' He turned to face Abe and paused for a few seconds as if considering. Then stuck out his hand.

Abe was dumbfounded. *Trap? No. Not—what. Very unusual. Not.* He looked Luc in the eye and took his hand. They shook.

Luc nodded again. 'All right. So what do we know?'

*   *   *

'You don't really trust me, do you?' Ariadne asked.

Neela's head shot up from the old-fashioned scrolltab she was reading. The senator was curled up in one of the memfoam tub chairs in the observatory where she seemed to spend most of her time, wrapped in a warm-looking sand-coloured blanket. Her face briefly showed her surprise—*And a little bit of fear*—before she gathered herself and flashed Ariadne that winning politician's smile. 'Gosh, you startled me, Ariadne. I didn't hear you come in. What did you say?'

Ariadne walked to the chair opposite and plonked herself down, tucking her feet under her. She looked seriously at Neela, whose smile faded slightly. 'I think you heard me, Neela. It's all right, you know. I do understand... how people think of us. What they think we are.'

Neela flicked the scrolltab off and placed it on the table at her side, next to a steaming cup of something. Ariadne sniffed. *Valerian? Worth a try. It's not going to fix that headache of hers on its own though.*

'It's not that I don't—it's just that I don't know you, Ariadne.'

'You can call me Ri, if you like. My friends do.'

'Thank you. Okay—Ri—it's nothing personal, and it's not anything to do with who you are... I just don't trust anyone without getting to know them first. A consequence of spending as long as I have in politics, I'm afraid.'

*Nice try, Senator. Doesn't quite ring true, though. Time to cut to the chase—and she's never going to trust me if she knows I can peer inside that pretty head. So...* 'I don't read minds, if that's what you're worried about.'

Neela opened her mouth, then closed it again. She frowned slightly. 'Okay. It had occurred to me.'

'Well, don't worry. Your secrets are safe.' *Oh, how easily we lie.* Ariadne couldn't resist a mischievous dig as well. 'You should get that headache looked at, though.'

The look on the senator's face was priceless. 'How—you said—'

Ariadne giggled. 'Sorry, I shouldn't laugh. I've just noticed— All the temple rubbing, painkillers, and valerian tea doesn't seem to be working, does it?'

'Ah. Well, no. It doesn't.'

Ariadne stood up, hitching up her jeans as she did so. *I should really get a belt.* 'You know, you could always talk to the ship—there's a medical bay up on the residential deck. Towards the, um, back.'

Neela smiled. 'Stern. And is there? I didn't see one when I looked around after we first came on board.'

'I'm not sure it was there then. Everything looked pretty shiny when I went there.' Ariadne waited for the inevitable question. Neela raised her eyebrows. Ariadne sighed. 'I pulled my groin in Luc's gym.'

The senator smirked. 'Oh, really? And was Luc there at the time?'

Ariadne felt her face heat. 'What? No, he's... Well, he hates me, for a start; and he's not even my type; and anyway, he's got a thing for—' She clamped her mouth shut.

Neela looked intently down at her lap. 'Well, thank you for the suggestion. I'll pay the ship a visit sometime soon.' She reached for the scrolltab as Ariadne nodded and turned for the door.

*Hmph. Making fun of me. Last time I try to help.*

\* \* \*

It was mid morning, Nexus time, on the tenth day of the voyage, and *Mournstar* was due to arrive in the Equinox system in just a few hours. Neela was dressing after sleeping late, pulling on her formal Senate tunic for the first time since she'd left Nexus Prime. Her normal wake-up time had fallen victim to an unexpectedly late night.

The previous evening at dinner, Boone had interrupted one of his usual rambling monologues to pull a bottle of deep purple liquor from one of his seemingly infinite number of pockets. Describing it as 'an old family recipe', he had poured a round, after which they had promptly got drunk. Even Abe had turned positively garrulous. *Meaning, he spoke as much as Ri first thing in the morning before she's had her coffee.*

Ariadne had entertained them by arranging the cutlery into stick figures and sending them dancing around the long dining table that had appeared in the bridge at some point.

Luc had followed this with a demonstration, allegedly 'from his cadet days'. Pulling Neela from her seat to stand clear of the table, he had first reached down and kicked his legs up to do a handstand next to her. *Okay, easy enough. Not sure I could do it after four—five?—drinks, though.* Then he lifted one hand off the ground, tucking one knee close to his chest. *Not so easy*, Neela had thought. *That's actually pretty impressi—*

Before she could react, Luc had grasped her hip with his free hand, picked her up, and set her on the sole of his foot. *With one hand. While upside down.* She had barely started to protest when he straightened his leg, pushing her a metre up in the air. By this point Ariadne and Boone were cheering like the fans in the cheap seats at a jetball game. Even Abe had a small smile on his face.

Neela had been halfway through the 'Please' in 'Please can you let me down' when the Titan had kicked her up in the air. She'd had two seconds of weightless terror, barely aware of the blur of Luc flipping onto his feet underneath her, before she landed comfortably in his arms, her face centimetres from his satisfied grin. *Elu fend, he looked pleased with himself.* She had shaken her head crossly as he lowered her to stand on her own—wobbly—legs. After the adrenaline wore off, she had to admit to herself that she quite enjoyed it. *Not that I'd ever tell him though. I'd never hear the end of it.*

Hangover aside—and she had a thumper of one—Neela knew the impromptu party had been a good thing. The tension so violently present only ten days ago seemed to have, if not gone, then at least... loosened. The senator didn't know exactly what was in store for them when they arrived in the mysterious Equinox system. But some instinct told her they would have other things to worry about than snapping at each other.

*   *   *

'PASSENGERS, YOUR ATTENTION PLEASE. ARRIVAL AT EQUINOX SYSTEM IMMINENT. TWO MINUTES. TWO MINUTES.'

Luc was already on the bridge, gaze fixed on the main viewport. As it had been for days, the scene was a wall of deep red, though Luc noticed it did seem to be gradually changing to a lighter shade. *That's odd—oh. We're approaching a star. Idiot.*

The familiar swoosh of a doorfield, followed by Ariadne's voice, announced the arrival of the rest of the group.

'There you are, my boy. Been here a while? See any nebula monsters?' Boone yelled in greeting.

Ariadne's barrage of chatter cut off. Luc turned to see her staring at Boone, wide-eyed. 'Monsters?'

*Fair play to you, Boone. That was funny.* 'I think he might have been joking.'

Ariadne didn't look convinced. 'Not funny,' she muttered, turning and dropping into a seat.

Boone wasn't even slightly abashed. 'No, no. No monsters out here. Not a one. Killed them all, years ago. Bare hands.' He held up his small fists in what Luc assumed was meant to be a threatening way. *Could just about throttle a rabbit with those.*

During this exchange, Neela had walked over to stand near Luc at the viewport. She was dressed in some kind of uniform, with an insignia Luc didn't recognise. *Their government, I suppose.* He shook his head slightly at the idea of civilian uniforms. *Playing dress-up because they couldn't join the military. Sad.*

The ship boomed out another announcement. 'ONE MINUTE. ARRIVAL IN ONE MINUTE. DRINKS AND SNACKS ARE AVAILABLE.'

Boone spoke again. 'Now, ladies and lads, what you're about to see is quite special. We don't have many guests out here, you know, so you're the first in, oh, a while. Quite a long while. A shame, really, because—well, you'll see. Won't they, Abe? Where's Abe?' His head swivelled around.

'Very special,' Abe said from by the back wall. 'Affirmative. Have been studying the—' He paused.

Luc glanced at the Collective. *Bastard doesn't want to spoil the surprise. Oddly human of him.*

'- System, since it entered sensor range. Unusual. New.'

Boone looked pleased. 'Very unusual. Wouldn't call it new, though, been here quite a—oh, here we are.'

Luc turned back to the viewport in time to see the view brighten quickly over a few seconds, moving from the familiar red to a vibrant pink—then they were through.

'Ooooooo.'

He barely registered Neela and Ariadne's simultaneous outbursts. His attention was fixed on the view as *Mournstar* broke through the nebula wall into what seemed to be a vast red cave. At the centre was the brightest star Luc had seen, brighter than Sophos or Demos or any of those in the systems he had come through on his voyage from Mission. But that wasn't what had caught his attention.

Between the nebula and the star, surrounding and encircling the star along every axis, was a—*Net? Web?*—that glittered in the reflected light from the nebula wall. Luc felt Abe quietly step up beside him. He glanced over to see the Collective's silver eyes shining bright.

'Never seen. Never thought of. Theoretical, of course. Possible-sensible-brilliant. Energy capture...' His hushed, reverent voice trailed off. Boone chimed in.

'Quite the looker, isn't she? That's our Equinox. Sitting pretty in the middle of her friends.'

Ariadne had stood up. 'But what are they, Boone? Are they asteroids? They're so neatly arranged.'

Boone chuckled. 'Not asteroids, my dear. Satellites. How many, Abe? I bet you know.'

The Collective replied instantly. 'Forty-three thousand two hundred. Thirty-six rings, ten-degree intervals, twelve hundred satellites in each ring. Ten light minute radius from the star.' He blinked. 'Perfectly spaced. Incredible.'

Boone looked pleased. 'Took some doing, that did. They used to call it a swarm, a long time ago, back in the day.'

'Whom? The Elu?' asked Neela.

'Well... I think I should let Jacob tell you that. Yes. Think I will.' Boone clapped his hands and looked cheerfully at the four of them. 'Let's go and see him, shall we?'

## 12. Equinox

Dark grey clouds scudded across the indigo sky. A gusty wind chopped at the pink-tinged sea, sending waves crashing into the foot of the cliff, a few hundred metres below the flat-topped promontory that *Mournstar* sped towards.

*We're coming in a bit fast, aren't we?* Neela watched their final descent through a small viewport on the starboard side of the command deck. It had been an hour since they'd cleared the satellite swarm. The ship had switched the display on the front viewport to show the view from the stern as they passed through; as the size of each of the satellites became clear, Neela had gasped. Each was as large as a small moon, the starward-facing side hollowed out like a half-eaten boiled egg and lined with an enormous array of what had to be solar panels—though the material didn't look quite like any Neela had seen.

She had tried in vain to calculate the amount of power

generated by a single panel—if indeed that was their purpose—and then multiply it by the number in the swarm… The magnitude had stunned her. *All that energy, for a system with a single planet? Two? It makes no sense.* Equinox, her first direct exposure to Elu technology, left her a little awestruck.

As *Mournstar* decelerated into the system, the ship had pointed out a small planet a quarter of the way around the solar plane on their starboard side. 'Equinox I, that is,' Boone had explained. 'Little ball of rock. Nothing there, not much atmosphere.' He grinned. 'Not many tourists.'

The ship had taken an arcing, dipping route over the star to their destination, the larger, more temperate Equinox II. It was roughly the same size as Fusion, a ruby-coloured ball with several large land masses coming into view as they neared. *Mournstar* had continued to slow as they entered the atmosphere near the northern pole, smoothly switching to its smaller planetary thrusters as they shot down and towards a small island continent near the middle of a wide, pink ocean.

They were still ten or more kilometres out from the coast, the cliff face a thin white line between the sea and green dappled red-brown land, when the first structure had become visible.

Abe had spotted it first. 'Large structure roughly two kilometres inland. Sensors indicate six towers, equidistant, vertical at base, curving inward to each other. Joined at apex.' He cocked his head as if concentrating. 'Distance between towers and neighbours… approximately six kilometres.'

'Six kil— …Four miles?' Ariadne's eyes widened. 'How big are they?'

'Height at apex is… five thousand six hundred metres.'

Neela had just stared as they approached, the vast structure growing ever larger, looming into view and dominating the landscape around. *Like a six-legged spider. A shiny, burgundy-coloured spider. With no head.*

They were just a few hundred metres from their landing site: a broad, flat cliff-top that seemed to have been paved with enormous grey stone slabs, ten metres square. *Mournstar* covered the distance in a few seconds, coming to a stop over the centre of the area before descending to land. A dull thump was barely audible as they touched down.

Minutes later, Neela and the others sat in a long, slim hovercar that the ship had disgorged from one of its bays, and they were speeding inland along a broad avenue that ran in a straight line from the coast between the massive towers and on to a city that was barely visible in the haze on the horizon.

A light drizzle started; Boone palmed a panel and a translucent domed field unfolded over the car, the raindrops evaporating with a fizz as they struck it.

They were all silent for a few minutes, gazing at the impossibly huge structure.

*Is it a sculpture?* Neela posed the question to Boone.

'That? Hmm. Don't remember what it's for, if it's for anything. The legs are hollow, if I remember right, but there's nothing in there.'

Ariadne looked puzzled. 'I thought the Athravan were experts on the Elu? Historians? I mean... Shouldn't you know? Or—' She looked even more confused. 'Are you not one of them?'

Neela chimed in, 'I've been wondering that myself, actually. You don't quite fit the description. And you don't look very much like Jacob.'

'Well, that's a hard question to answer.' Boone scratched his nose pensively. 'Not really what you'd call one of those boys, no. More of an odd-job man. Help them out, you know. Go places; get things. Or people!' He brightened. 'Known Jacob a long time. Good friend of mine. Well... as much his friend as anyone. Plays his hand close to his chest, does our Jacob.'

'And where is he, exactly?' asked Luc. His only concession to formality had been throwing on a battered leather jacket that looked older than he did. 'I was expecting him to meet us.'

Boone chuckled. 'No, no. He's a busy man. We'll go to him.' He pointed in the direction they were headed. 'He's in the city, up ahead. Mercy, it's called; was the planetary capital, back in the day.'

'And now?' asked Abe quietly from the rear seat of the car.

Boone shook his head, a little sadly. 'Empty, mostly. Not much left of what was—not much that's running as it was meant to, anyway. But one part is.' His smile widened to its normal cheeriness.

Neela caught a glimpse of a light in the distance. She turned towards it, trying to peer through the haze.

'And that's where we'll meet Jacob?' said Luc.

'Aye.' Boone rubbed his hands, eyebrows waggling with pleasure. 'We're going to the Allsphere.'

* * *

Abe, absorbed in recording every detail, revelled in the novelty of the new environment. *Fascinating.*

As they neared the city, Mercy's skyline dominated the horizon, displaying towers, buildings, and monuments of dazzling variety. One glittering spiral of silver stood like an enormous drill bit, adjacent to a stocky six-faced pyramid made from some dark stone. The rain had stopped, the sky clearing, and Boone had dropped the rooffield to let in the breeze and the afternoon sunshine.

Abe's absorption made him slow to react when a creature swooped over his head and seized Neela by the shoulders. The senator let out a yelp of surprise.

Abe snapped out of his reverie. *Pointed ears. Four legs, feet with long prehensile fingers. Two wings, glossy with short grey fur.*

Only a second had passed, and the senator was nearly clear of the hovercar, her feet scrambling for purchase.

Abe's mind raced, searching for some weapon he could deploy to bring the creature down when a roar came from the front of the car, followed by the blurred shape of Luc as he sprang from his seat onto the side of the still speeding vehicle and kicked off towards the animal and its captive.

*Too far to reach. He cannot—*

Mid-rise, the Titan grabbed the whip-like weapon strapped to his belt and flicked it towards the bat-thing.

The cord wrapped around one of the creature's legs. A shriek rent the air.

It plummeted to the ground, landing half atop the still-struggling Neela, who let out another, more muffled, yelp.

Boone slammed on the hovercar's brakes before they had gone too far. Abe quickly climbed out, engaged his heel thrusters, and sped back towards the fray. He was still metres away when Luc tugged hard on the whip, yanking the animal towards him, then stepped in and kicked the creature's head, resulting in a liquid crunching noise.

By the time Abe touched down, the animal was still.

Neela was slowly climbing to her feet. The Titan quickly moved to her side and helped her up. 'Are you all right? Any damage done?'

The senator looked pale and shaken, but unwounded. *Lucky.* 'No, I think—I'm okay.' She rubbed her shoulder. 'I'm going to have bruises tomorrow, though.'

Boone and Ariadne arrived at that moment, the Seryn in a breathless run, the other in a scuttle that would have been amusing in other circumstances. Ariadne was wide-eyed.

'Bloody hell, Neela. Are you okay? What is that thing, Boone? It's creepy. It would have got her if Luc hadn't... whippy jump-kicked it.' She looked at the Titan. 'That was very cool, by the way.'

Neela turned to Luc, as well. 'It was. Thank you. Lord knows where I'd be now, otherwise.'

Boone coughed. 'Hmm. Well, you'd be on your way to its nest. The wildlife around the city has got a little bit lively since most of the occupants left—these buggers are some of the most unpleasant. Macaquabats, I call them. Usually don't come this far out, though. Look.' He pointed. 'Bat with a monkey face, isn't it?'

Ariadne shuddered and turned back to the car. 'Let's keep the roof on, from now on.'

Luc supported Neela as they headed to the vehicle, Boone following. Abe tarried, leaning down to examine the creature in more detail. The feet were extraordinary, more like hands. Two thicker thumb-like appendages at the rear, five long three-knuckled fingers at the front.

*Great strength. Prodigious grip in those hands. Senator is fortunate.* He headed back to the hovercar. *Bruises tomorrow, most definitely.*

\* \* \*

'I just don't understand how it stays up.' Ariadne stood in front of a silver globe, twenty yards wide, that hung, seemingly unsupported, over the shaft. Its equator appeared to be perfectly aligned with the surrounding ground level, its lower hemisphere hanging down into the broad vertical shaft dark and deep enough that she wasn't sure it had a bottom. And the self-suspended sphere was spinning. *Yup, I'm a long way from home.*

'No visible means of support. High-intensity energy readings across entire globe and surroundings, but... complex. Data not understood.' Abe looked disappointed and a little ashamed.

'Don't worry, Abe,' Ariadne said cheerfully. 'None of us have any idea what's going on.'

Their journey into the city had been uneventful after the violent wildlife encounter, and they stood in the centre of a broad plaza, surrounded on each side by vast towers built of a substance that looked like stone, but without joins to suggest bricks or blocks.

As if the stone had... *grown in place.* Ariadne shivered a little. *Squicky.*

Luc looked annoyed. He turned to Boone, who was rummaging through each of his pockets in turn, consternation on his face. 'If this is the Allsphere, and that's where we're meeting Jacob, then where is he?'

'Hmm?' Boone replied absently. 'Where is... Oh, he's inside, obviously. Where else would he be? But I can't find my blasted keycard. We can't unlock the lock and ungate the gate without the keycard. It should be here...' He searched more frantically, still muttering.

Neela stood beside a waist-high terminal constructed from some matte metal, the top panel bare but for a faint etching. 'Uh, Boone? If this is the lock, then I don't think a keycard's going to help.'

'Hmm?'

'There's no slot for one. Just an inscription of what looks, well, almost like a palmprint.'

Boone stared at her blankly for a few seconds, then slapped his forehead. 'Palmprint! Of course. Wrong lock. No keycard.' He scuttled over to the terminal and slapped his right hand onto the panel. He flashed a smile at Neela. 'Thank you, Senator. Saved us minutes, there!'

Ariadne quickly stepped back from the shaft edge as the sphere started emitting a high-pitched whine. *That doesn't sound good.*

The globe began spinning faster, and she edged towards Luc, half-hiding behind his bulk. The whine increased in pitch for several seconds more before, suddenly, the sound ceased, and the Allsphere's motion... stopped.

Nothing happened for a moment. Then a small hole appeared at the point facing the group. It quickly expanded to become a portal a few yards high and wide.

Luc looked unimpressed. 'Brilliant. So now we, what, jump across? Or do you have a grappling hook in one of those—'

A beam of light shot out from the Allsphere at the bottom of the portal, hitting the edge of the shaft before quickly widening into a bridge.

Ariadne gulped. *Are we supposed to walk across that?*

Boone clapped his hands. 'Grand! There we are. All right, then. In we go!' He blithely stepped onto the ethereal light bridge and started walking towards the portal, then stopped when none of the others followed him. 'Oh, it's perfectly safe! See?'

To Ariadne's horror, he started jumping up and down, waving his arms like a madman. 'Totally safe!'

One eyebrow raised, Luc looked over his shoulder down at

Ariadne. 'Uh… after you?'

*Coward.* Acting with far more confidence than she felt, Ariadne stepped onto the bridge. She gingerly tapped one foot against it, then looked back at Neela, Luc, and Abe. 'Seems okay. Maybe one at a time, though, yeah?'

Neela shook her head in resignation. *She looks a bit sick. Poor Senator. Must be scared of heights.*

Boone clapped again. 'Come on; come on. Lots to do! In we go.' With that, he went inside the sphere.

One by one, they followed him in.

\* \* \*

Inside the Allsphere, Luc and the others stood in an aisle. Along the floor—which Luc suspected was opaque hard light—on both sides of the aisle ran row upon row of small, dome-shaped metallic devices. The rows curved away from them in both directions, running parallel to the interior wall and joining directly opposite them to completely encircle the sunken space at the centre of the Allsphere.

Luc pointed at a device as they started down the aisle. 'What are these, Boone?'

'Seat projectors, lad. Stand over one, and a chair pops up for you. Neat, isn't it? Only have as many as you need, then.' He scratched his nose.

Luc narrowed his eyes. *He does that a lot when he's… nervous. But why would he be nervous?*

Boone continued, 'Don't get a full chamber, these days. Don't need many seats at all.'

'This was some kind of council chamber, then?' Luc gauged the distance between the devices. 'The Elu must have been about our size. There's only five feet between the seats.'

'Hmmm? Oh, yes. I imagine you're right. Now, more importantly, where's Jacob?' Boone increased his pace, headed for a slightly raised platform at the centre of the empty space.

Neela spoke from behind him. 'Has anyone else noticed something odd about this room? I mean, apart from the whole spinning ball, defying the laws of physics aspect.'

'Indeed, Senator. I believe you are referring to the diameter.'

'What's wrong with the diameter?' Ariadne asked, looking around.

'Nothing is wrong, just—difficult. The sphere is fifteen metres wider inside than it is outside.'

Luc looked between the walls. *Founder, he's right. Now, that is—*

'Cool!' Ariadne grinned.

They reached the front row of projectors and stepped down into the central space. Boone stood on the platform, scratching his head. 'It's a bit odd, ladies and gents—we're bang on time.' He pulled a pocket-watch from a breast pocket, stared at it for a few seconds, then shook it. 'Well, I'm pretty sure we're on time. Jacob should be—'

'Here.'

Luc turned with the others to see a tall, broad man standing at the portal they had recently entered through. His long, white hair was tied back in a ponytail that hung down over the hood of his mud-brown robe. 'I apologise for being late, Finnigan. You're right, of course—you are on time, as always.'

'Hello, Mr Jacob,' said Ariadne as the newcomer approached. 'It's nice to actually meet you this time. For real.'

'You, too. A great pleasure.' He took Ariadne's hand in both of his.

She frowned a little, as if concentrating. After a few seconds, the frown cleared. 'I'm glad I was right about you.'

Jacob laughed softly. 'As am I; as am I.' He turned to Neela and shook her hand. 'And I'm delighted to meet you in person as well, Senator.'

Neela frowned. 'In person? But last time, in my apartment...'

'Just a sending, I'm afraid. A projection. Nexus Prime is, as you know, quite a long way to come from here. But here you are and looking well.'

He turned to Abe next. Luc expected another handshake. *Though he'll have trouble shaking that toolkit welded to his wrist.* Instead Jacob held up his left hand, hand open towards Abe. The surprise on the Collective's face was so purely human that Luc snorted.

'Welcome, Collective. It has been many, many years since I've met one of your kind in the flesh and metal. The distances between the stars are great.'

'And each of us so small,' finished Abe, astonishment still on his face. Jacob dropped his hand and finally turned to Luc.

'Well met, Titan.' He held out his hand once more, and Luc took it. His touch was cool, his hand rough as if from years of work. *Surprising. I was expecting someone more... academic.*

'Your Uncle Jarrod was good enough to trust me when I came to him. And I see that you placed your trust in him.'

'A long time ago,' Luc replied.

Jacob nodded. 'He is a good man, your uncle—as you know. He has more enemies than he needs, but he is up to the task. But enough of that—we are all here at last.' He turned and strode to the platform where Boone still waited. 'If you could, please, Boone.'

'Oh. Right. Of course.' Boone hopped down to stand near the Chosen as they stepped up to the edge of the platform.

'You came to see the Book, of course.' Jacob spread his arms wide. 'The famous Book of Ascension of the Elu. And here it is.'

No one spoke for a few seconds.

Luc looked around. 'Um... where?'

Jacob smiled. 'You could say we're standing in it.' He tapped a quick staccato into a slim band around his wrist. A pinpoint of golden light appeared on the ceiling at the very top of the sphere, directly above the platform where Jacob stood. It grew quickly, spreading to a width of half a yard—then, with a speed that drew a gasp from Neela, shot down to hit the platform.

A pillar of golden light was behind Jacob, stretching up to the roof.

'This is the Book, my friends.' He half turned and gestured at the pillar. 'Whoever steps into the light instantly receives the combined knowledge of the Elu. It is, as you can imagine, quite an experience.'

Ariadne looked a little nervous. 'So... you expect us to just—stand in it?'

Jacob smiled again. 'I do, Seryn. Eventually.' His smile faded.

'Eventually?' Luc hardened his expression. He realised that somewhere in the back of his mind he had been waiting for something, ever since Boone had first told him about the Book. *The catch.*

'Indeed.' Jacob crossed his arms, tucking his hands into the sleeves of his robe. He sighed. 'I'm afraid this isn't why I brought you here.'

*And there it is.*

'I think perhaps you should all sit. This will take a little while to tell.' Jacob gestured towards the front row of seat projectors.

Neela and Ariadne glanced at one another, expressions cautious, then did as they were bid. Abe followed, his face blank and unreadable as ever.

Luc stood for a few seconds, gaze fixed on Jacob. *Perhaps I don't feel like sitting. Perhaps I feel like turning around and walking out.* Anger started to rise, but he fought it down. Clenching and unclenching his fists, he followed the others.

As he stepped to one of the devices, the projector sprang into life, a solid enough looking seat appearing above it a few feet off the ground. Luc turned and sat down. 'Explain, priest. I should warn you, if you've dragged me halfway across the galaxy for nothing, I will *not* be pleased.'

Jacob stepped down from the platform. 'Not for nothing. I assure you there is a very good reason.' He frowned, as if unsure where to begin. 'I assume you all know at least a little of the Elu.'

'Not a lot,' Ariadne replied. She looked to the others. 'I don't, anyway. I know they were very clever, and a lot of human technology is based on theirs, on artefacts and stuff that people found. And they died out a long time ago. Or maybe went somewhere.'

Neela shook her head. 'No one knows for sure which. No one in the Commonwealth, at least.'

'Collective has made discoveries of its own,' said Abe. He

had pulled back his hood, his pale skin a healthier hue in the golden light. 'Assumed Elu. References to technology at extreme level of advancement. Difficult to understand.'

They turned to Luc. He shrugged. 'We don't think of them much. We're more concerned with our own history, our own goals.'

'Like wiping out Abe and his friends?' Ariadne muttered.

Luc shot her a look but said nothing. *We're at war with them. It's not personal.* And at that moment, he realised it wasn't personal. Not to him. That he had no reason to hold on to that hatred. He glanced at Abe, then Ariadne. *Hmm. I'll deal with that later.*

'I'll try to be brief. The Elu were, as you say, extremely advanced relative to current human technology. They had semi-organic materials that could be programmed, then planted to grow into a city in a week, a starship in a day. Engines so efficient they could propel that starship in jumps orders of magnitude greater than those that are possible now. A knowledge of their own body and mind so profound that they could make themselves immortal.' Jacob slowly paced before them. 'And they came to know the universe. So perfectly, so well. Too well, as it turned out.'

'What do you mean?' Neela asked. 'What happened?'

'They developed an understanding of the deepest fundamentals of the physical universe, especially of the energy grid that underpins realspace and binds it to the infinite null of subspace. They discovered how they could tap into the grid, use it as a limitless power source.'

'Limitless.' Abe's voice was quiet. Luc turned to see the Collective's gaze fixed on the pillar of light. 'Truly limitless. Entropy no longer important.' Abe turned to Jacob, who was watching him. 'Heat death of universe could be averted.'

'In theory. That was one of the long-term goals. To begin with, their use of this energy was limited—powering habitats directly from the grid, for example. But soon, they began to tap into the grid for greater and greater projects. New stars and planets were created from scratch. Populated systems at the very centre of the Core were nudged apart to prevent collisions.'

'You can't be serious,' said Ariadne. 'They *moved stars*?'

Jacob nodded. His expression was sombre. 'And that was their greatest mistake, as it turned out.'

Luc was trying to place what he was hearing in the context of his—admittedly limited—historical knowledge. 'When did all of this happen, Jacob?'

The Athravan stopped pacing and turned to face them. 'Thirty millennia from now.'

The silence in the Allsphere was complete.

After a few seconds, Ariadne coughed quietly. 'Um... what?'

Jacob smiled—a little sadly, Luc thought. 'This will be hard to believe. But it is true and why you are here. You see, the Elu, as they were—as they will be—evolved to immortality, to the point of ascension, through a combination of traits. First, a complete understanding of the power of the mind.' He nodded at Ariadne.

'Total control over their physiology and genetic blueprint.' A nod to Luc.

'Biotechnology that erased the line between organism and machine.' Abe.

'And a mastery of mass psychology that allowed the creation of a group mind that spanned the entire galaxy.' He gestured at Neela.

*That's impossible.* 'You're saying that the Elu were—are—will be—'

Jacob nodded. 'We are your children.'

* * *

*We?* Neela was dumbfounded. *If only Nana could hear this. She would be— Well, she'd probably faint.*

'You mean, you, the Athravan, *are* the Elu. That's...' Words failed her.

Jacob nodded. 'This body is not the one I was born with. I said earlier that we made our greatest mistake when we began to play master of the very form of the universe. Shifting stars,

142

building planets, pulling the energy from black holes.'

He shook his head. 'It was years before we even understood what was happening. That we had gone too far, and that we were under attack.'

'What happened?' asked Ariadne. 'From whom?'

'We had no idea, at first. Several large habitats disappeared. We thought they had simply relocated, but the voices of the inhabitants were missing from the group mind. Next a planet vanished, along with the hundred million souls on it. Then a second planet, a third—ten more. There was no great battle, no declaration of war, no enemy that could be countered. Barely a thousandth of a per cent of our people had been lost, but the rate was accelerating. We were at a loss, and we were doomed.

'We realised we needed help. There were few places we could turn—most of the intelligent life we had encountered was well behind us on the evolutionary path. They treated us as gods or monsters. There was no help there. But one race we had encountered some seven millennia before, twenty-three thousand years or so from now. They called themselves Zythylyx.'

Luc snorted. 'Catchy name.'

'There's a chance we mistranslated it. Their language was… complex.'

Ariadne looked shocked. 'Wait a second. This might not be news to anyone else, but—aliens? I always thought the galaxy was just humans, as far as civilisations go. You're telling us there are others.'

Abe was nodding. 'Several.'

Jacob smiled slightly. 'You are by no means alone in that assumption, Ariadne. But I digress—the Zythylyx. They were silicon-based, living in groups of bonded lattice structures, always in orbit around gas giant planets. They claimed to have been in existence for more than a million years. We had no way of knowing if that were true, but regardless—they explained why we were under attack. Explained about what they called the Weft.

'The Zythylyx we contacted had no idea if the Weft was one organism, or many. They had never been able to communicate with it, not in a dozen encounters over a hundred thousand years. But they had realised that it—somehow, impossibly though it seemed to us—existed in subspace, in the folds below and around the physical universe. They told us that our gross manipulation of the energy grid, our wanton use of power, was an attack on the Weft. And that they were fighting back.

'Can you imagine?' Jacob had resumed his pacing. 'The power of a race that can live outside realspace? No wonder we had had no warning, no idea we were under attack. They could collapse a planet from its core, drag the matter into subspace and scatter the ashes into the energy grid. Once, a short time later, we actually saw it happen—a whole world, gone in a matter of seconds.'

Ariadne shivered. 'So they could be here—right now. In this room with us, kind of. That's creepy.'

'It was more than that. It was our death sentence. We had no way of communicating with them, no way to apologise. We had only one option, one last desperate gamble.

'The Zythylyx told us of one other entity that they had encountered, just once, three thousand years before. Their description was... confusing. Garbled. They called it Unity and claimed it could "ignore the rules of the universe". Or maybe change those rules. As I said, their language was complicated. But crucially, the Zythylyx alleged that this Unity, whatever it was, *could* communicate with the Weft.

'But Unity seemed to have left our galaxy. They had no idea where it was. We were still doomed—unless.' Jacob stopped pacing and turned to the Chosen.

'We conceived of a plan, a last desperate throw: to launch ourselves backward in time and somehow change our fate. Our theorists were confident it was possible—some of them, at least. Others insisted it was not and the attempt would be fatal.

'Many of us, most, refused the risk, preferring to stay in our own time and hope for a miracle. The rest of us went to work, constructing swarms around a thousand suns, like the one in this system. Swarms to capture, bind, and reflect the massive energies needed to send a star, planets, ships—the whole system—back through time.'

Jacob spread his palms. 'It worked. For some, at least, I and those with me found ourselves here in the nebula. After years of searching, we contacted fifty more swarms that had made the trip successfully. The rest... We don't know. Most of those who made it back decided to leave, departing on long journeys to neighbouring galaxies in the hope that the Weft were only present in ours. Some took on new human forms and simply blended into your populations.'

Neela felt shocked. 'There are others, just—hiding amongst us?'

'What can I say? They were fascinated by the opportunity to live amongst their ancestors. But the rest of us began the search for Unity. We've been searching for a thousand years, without success.

'And that, finally, is why you are all here.'

\* \* \*

Abe had listened raptly to Jacob's story, recording every detail while simultaneously running wildly theoretical calculations to try to discover if what they were being told was even possible. *Travel through time. Manipulation of multiple dimensions, inconceivable energy input. Not enough data. Possible-improbable. Not enough data.* He discarded his calculations and returned to the conversation.

'Inquiry: What could we do?' he asked. 'Likelihood of four succeeding where many have failed for centuries is slim.'

'Not necessarily. For nine of those centuries we were searching with no guide—we simply had no idea where to look. Then a few hundred years ago we stumbled across a colony of Zythylyx. A different group to those that had helped us in the future, and with more information—they knew where Unity is.'

Luc leaned forwards, looking sceptical. 'So why haven't you gone to it—him, whatever. Why have you waited until now, for us?'

Jacob shook his head. 'We had no hope of success. You four, we think, do.'

'Why?' asked Ariadne. 'What can we do that you can't?'

'You are all gifted, for your respective... groups. That much is clear. But there is a greater reason why we have waited for you—and you specifically—for a hundred years.' He turned to Ariadne. 'Amongst you Seryn, some are gifted with a kind of precognition, yes?'

Ariadne nodded slowly. 'A little. Not many, and it's often very vague. But it does work sometimes. It's how we knew we had to leave Serynev IV,' she said quietly.

'Among us—what you call the Athravan—there are a few with this gift. They spent years casting forward and saw a hundred possible futures. The details changed, but one outcome was constant: In every future where we approached Unity directly, we failed or were destroyed in the attempt. In a few other futures, the seers saw you four. And for you, the outcome was...'

'I hope you're going to say a resounding success,' Luc said.

Jacob sighed. 'Clouded. I won't lie to you—not again. The outcome is unclear. But it is not certain failure, and that is far better than the alternative.

'I—we—need your help. To save your own future. If you don't or cannot, your own descendants are doomed to the same fate. You must try—find Unity and beg. Gain its help, contact the Weft—explain. Or we are lost all over again.' Jacob spread his arms. 'And then, I promise, you are free to experience the Book and take that knowledge back to your people.'

Silence descended once more. Abe pulled up his hood. His thoughts raced at the possibilities ahead. *Chance for significant knowledge increase.* He stared at the pillar of golden light.

*Exciting.*

# 13. Conflict

Neela paced, listening to the others.

'I think he was telling the truth,' Ariadne said.

'How can you possibly know that?' Luc sounded unconvinced.

'I don't know. But I can... sense when people are being honest. And he was.'

'"People."' Luc snorted. 'That's the problem. He isn't any kind of person that we've ever met, so how can you know your "sense" even applies?'

Ri and Luc had been arguing for several minutes. Luc thought they were being manipulated; Ariadne didn't. They were getting nowhere. They had left the confines of the Allsphere for the windy open space of the plaza outside. Abe stood nearby, either lost in his own thoughts or listening as well. Either way, he was buried in the darkness of his hooded robe and as unreadable as he'd been when they had first met.

*And what about you, Senator?* Neela interrogated herself. *Ready to go home yet, back to the constituents you're supposed to be serving?* The question rattled around her mind, but no answer came. *I don't know. It seems so unreal. Impossible. And yet...* She looked over her shoulder at the silver globe, still motionless, portal open and bridge extended. Waiting. Waiting for a decision from four people who had met mere days before, thrown together, humans all, but barely the same species all the same.

*And they entrust us with the future of all humanity. Allegedly.* Neela shook her head. It would be a joke if it all weren't so damned serious. She turned back to look at Luc and Ri. They both seemed to have run out of steam, tired of arguing. Ariadne looked very young, her skin pale in the chill air. *But tough. She isn't going to give up, that one. Not ever.*

A fine rain had started to fall, and the wind was picking up. They could stand there all day, argue until they ran out of breath, but some point they'd have to make a decision. *Make it now. Use that famous instinct Alpert always talks about. What do we do here? What's the right move?*

Her mind cleared. There was only one answer, in the end. *As always.* 'We do it.'

Luc and Ariadne's heads turned towards her.

Neela felt more than saw Abe's attention. 'We can debate the truth of what we've been told until we collapse from exhaustion. The crux of the issue is: We can't know. The only proof we have is the impossibility of what we've seen today and on the journey here. Gut feeling—that's all we have to guide us.'

She looked to Luc. 'You don't trust Jacob. That's understandable, and I'm not sure I do, either. You're worried we're being played with—and maybe we are. Are we in danger? Possibly. But if we were being sent to our deaths... Why? And why aren't we dead already? Maybe instead we're being positioned, pawns in some game we don't even understand. That's more likely, but even given that chance—how can we say no?'

Neela turned to Abe, who had moved to join them. 'If there's even a slight chance that crazy, impossible story is true, and we have a chance to avert that fate... How can we turn our backs? On us, on our families, our people? I won't risk being the one to forsake a quadrillion future lives, however distant, however unknowable. I can't.'

Ariadne was smiling. Abe's eyes shone. Neela turned back to Luc.

He took a deep breath, held it—then exhaled. And nodded. 'All right. We go. But not blindly. I don't know what we're heading into, but I'm damn sure it isn't going to be as simple as knocking on the front door of wherever this Unity calls home and asking him for a favour.'

Neela nodded. 'So we watch our backs.'

'We watch each other's backs. For better or worse, we're in this together.'

Ariadne poked him in the stomach. 'I knew you'd warm to me sooner or later.'

Neela laughed, feeling tensions ebb. *Decision made.*
*For better or worse.*

\* \* \*

Ariadne led them back into the Allsphere. Jacob stood with Boone on the platform. The Book had been deactivated. *It looks weirdly empty on that platform.* The two Athravan stopped talking and turned towards the approaching group.

Jacob looked intently from face to face. 'I do believe they're going to help us, Finnigan.'

'Oh, I could have told you that. In fact, I did tell you. Just now.'

Jacob laughed and clapped Boone on the shoulder. 'You did. I should have learnt after all this time never to doubt you.'

'Just one problem, Mr Jacob,' Ariadne said. 'We don't actually know where we're supposed to go.' *Or what we're supposed to do when we get there.*

'No, of course,' Jacob replied. 'But Boone does, and he's kindly agreed to keep you company on the next leg of the journey. He insisted on it, in fact.'

Their eccentric guide grinned. 'Don't want you getting into trouble now, do we? And besides, I've got a mind to see this big mystery alien for myself! If he can bend the laws of nature, maybe he can make me a few inches taller. Be useful, that.'

Neela coughed. 'But... Jacob said this wasn't his original body. Can't you just... grow a new one?'

Boone looked horrified. 'A new one? Good lord no. Wouldn't think of it. This one's kept me going for years—marvellous piece of construction. Just a bit short, is all.'

Jacob stepped down from the platform and shook their hands one by one, saluting Abe as he had before. 'Keep in touch—Boone can contact me through the ship. And be careful, each of you. Look out for each other—as I said, your future on this journey is unclear. I'm afraid I don't know how this will end.'

He reached Ariadne last. 'Goodbye, my dear. You are far stronger than you know. I fear you may need all of that strength in the coming days, but you are up to the task.'

Ariadne felt solemn. 'Goodbye, Jacob. We'll see you soon.' *Hopefully.*

He nodded. 'I believe you will.'

Luc fidgeted. 'Let's go, shall we? Places to go, people to beg for help in averting future genocide.'

'Yes, indeed.' Boone clapped his hands. 'Off we go!'

The group headed for the portal. Ariadne turned as she reached the exit. Jacob looked small, alone in the centre of the sphere. He raised his hand, and she returned the wave. *Places to go.*

*Yes, indeed.*

* * *

'So where *are* we going, Boone?' asked Luc. They were back on *Mournstar*, walking along the command-control deck towards the bridge. The ship had broken atmosphere a few minutes earlier and was angling around the small moon that was the planet's only satellite, slowly leaving the planetary gravity well.

'Oh, long way, lad. Deep into the Core. Lots of jumps, careful ones. Don't want to end up in a black hole, do we!' He scratched his nose. 'Near one, though.'

*I don't like the sound of that.* 'And what does that mean, exactly?'

'Well, place we're headed—system our spiky silicon friends the Zythylyx call "Promise," by the way—is a bit of an odd one. No star in the middle, apparently. There's a black hole instead.'

'How is that even possible?' They reached the bridge, and the doorfield slid clear with a familiar whoosh.

'I'd imagine it's got a lot to do with the whole "bending the rules" bit. I mean, if you can do some of the things Unity supposedly can, why not stick a planet next to a black hole?

'Anyway, no difference to us. Star, black hole—wouldn't want to get too close to either, would you?' Boone chuckled.

*Save me.* Luc wandered over to the food dispenser alcove, patting his grumbling stomach. *You'd have thought Jacob would have given us a snack, after coming all that way.* 'Hey, Mo. Can I get some food?'

'OF COURSE, LUCIUS.'

'Can you do me… a side of venison, a few pounds of buttered kale, and a carafe of—'

A deafening klaxon burst from the ship's speakers. 'WARNING: UNKNOWN VESSEL IN CLOSE RANGE, EMERGENT FROM FAR SIDE OF MOON. CLOSING RAPIDLY. WARNING.'

Luc's mind raced. 'Mo, raise shields! Do you have shields?'

'AFFIRMATIVE. HOWEVER, CLOSING VESSEL IS WITHIN SHIELD BOUNDARY, ACCELERATING. IMPACT IN FIVE SECONDS. SUGGEST BRACE.'

Boone dived under the long dining table. Luc grabbed the edge of the alcove next to him and planted his feet. *Who in Founder's name is this? And why are they ramming us?*

The ship's voice blared again. 'INCOMING VESSEL SLOWING. BELOW RAMMING SPEED. LANDING.'

*Landing?*

A booming thud reverberated through *Mournstar*, shaking the walls, followed by a grinding, scraping noise that made Luc wince, then silence.

Boone peered out at Luc from under the table as Neela, Ariadne, and Abe pelted onto the bridge.

The young Seryn was wide-eyed. 'What's happening?'

Luc loosened his grip on the wall and turned, feeling grim. 'I think we're being boarded.'

\* \* \*

Drake released the breath he'd been holding. *That worked more smoothly than expected.*

Spence had given him the idea. He'd mentioned during the system scan that the moon was geosynced to the planet and neatly positioned over the landmass they'd tracked the target down to. A slow cruise and a soft landing later, and the *Broken Promise* was neatly tucked in a deep crater on the satellite's southern pole, all systems hibernating but for the mid-range sensor array that would let them know when the target came back up.

They only had to wait four hours. Whatever had gone on down there, it hadn't taken long.

*Time to pick up the merchandise.*

There had been a strong chance the weird-looking purple craft would take a different route out of the atmosphere, leaving them scrambling to catch up and try again another day. But the gamble had paid off, with the target approaching the moon at low in-system speed. As it passed the satellite, Cullen slammed the wake-up, and the *Promise* roared to life. They screamed up and out of that crater, pushing the engine far past the recommended specs—but it had been worth it when they bumped to a rough landing on the larger ship's hull and clamped down the locking claws.

The team were crowded into the small cargo bay at the bottom of the ship that housed the boarding claw, a hollow, two metre-wide carbon-nanotube sleeve that was now tightly sealed to the target craft. Spence knelt inside, looking up at Drake.

*Go time.* 'Deploy thermal mines.'

Spence slipped a hand into his pack and retrieved four of the slim, palm-sized mines. He attached them to the target's hull in a metre-wide square, with ease born of long practice. He next programmed each mine and placed the thermite trigger in the centre, grips attaching it to the hull beyond the burn radius.

Device ready and counting down the eight seconds until activation.

Spence climbed out of the airlock. 'Done. Two, one—burn.'

Drake watched an opaque black dome appear around the square of mines, showing no sign of the nine hundred–degree furnace it contained. The men were silent for the two minutes until the trigger beeped thrice, saying it was done.

The field vanished. The trigger suspended over a shaft that still glowed red from the extreme temperature.

'Final weapons check,' Drake called and watched his men noiselessly confirm the charge and calibration of their sleek black pulse rifles.

Drake met the gaze of each member of his team for a second, then nodded. They were ready.

'Go.'

\* \* \*

*"Let's split up," says Luc. "We know the environment; we can take them by surprise," he says.* Ariadne crouched behind a desk in one of the many empty quarters on the residential deck. She scratched her right earlobe. The in-ear transceiver the ship had produced was itchy, and she kept thinking it was going to fall out.

The ship's voice was just as attention-grabbing through the transceiver as it had been on the loudspeaker. 'SINGLE HOSTILE APPROACHING FROM STERN. ENTERING QUARTERS 4A.' Ten seconds passed. 'EXITING QUARTERS 4A; ENTERING 4B.'

*Gee, I wonder what he'll do next.*

It took few more minutes for the intruder to reach the cabin where Ariadne waited.

'HOSTILE APPROACHING YOUR LOCATION. FIVE METRES. THREE METRES.'

The doorfield slid smoothly open with a swoosh. Ariadne closed her eyes and visualised the room that she had locked herself in. She concentrated and lay what she sensed atop the visualisation, like a blanket over a sheet. One area, near the door and slowly moving into the centre of the room, didn't match.

*Got you.* Power coursing through her, she stood.

Her gaze locked on the man in the middle of the room. *Near middle-age, face lined and weathered. Strong, fit, fast.* His weapon, some kind of rifle, had been pointed towards a row of storage cabinets fitted in the wall opposite the door. It swung around towards her, the man's jaw clenching as he spotted his target. *Too slow.*

She focused, and the barrel of the gun bent up ninety degrees from the stock. Sparks flared as the energy cell blew. The man grimaced, eyes wide, and threw the rifle as his trigger hand was scorched.

He was quick—his left hand was reaching for his belt before the gun hit the ground.

'Enough.' Ariadne threw her hand out and *grasped*. The man froze instantly, surprise on his face. His gaze tracked Ariadne as she stepped around the desk and stood in front of him.

His eyes only widened, his gaze more frantic as she stepped within inches of him, her blazing white eyes reflected in his.

'Hi, there!'

\* \* \*

Luc prowled the narrow gangways criss-crossing the weapons bay that filled the front of *Mournstar's* bottom deck. Huge batteries of unfamiliar design rose on either side of him as he moved stealthily in the dim light. *But I can see fine.* His pupils were at maximum dilation, his skin shifted to a tough chitin. He inhaled deeply and opened up the two smaller lungs tucked under his main pair.

'HOSTILES TEN METRES AHEAD. TRAVERSING PARALLEL GANGWAYS IN YOUR DIRECTION.'

*Thanks for the help, Mo, but I can already smell them.* He ducked into a dead-end alcove to his left, his colovine loose in his right hand. Fortunately, it had still been strapped to his belt from the trip down to the surface—had he stowed it away, he likely wouldn't have had time to retrieve it from his quarters.

The faint scrape of synthetic material on metal told him where the nearer hostile was.

Wrist loose, ducked into a half-crouch, Luc waited in total silence, holding his breath.

A rifle barrel appeared first, nosing out from the gangway around the corner to his left. A second later, the face of the man holding it followed.

He flicked the colovine; it wrapped around both the rifle and the wrist of the stock-holding hand, trapping the two together. The intruder's head turned barely thirty degrees his way—*oriental, green eyes, strong jaw*—as Luc stepped in and threw a rising left cross that struck the cheekbone dead on. The man's face crumpled under Luc's fist as it drove the bone through the eye socket and into the brain. He died without making a sound.

The ship unnecessarily confirmed, 'ONE HOSTILE NEUTRALISED. SECOND HAS PAUSED. EIGHT METRES AHEAD, TWO RIGHT. FACING YOUR DIRECTION.'

Luc stepped over the slumping body as he flicked the colovine free. He padded forwards along the crosswalk, stopping at the corner with the longer gangway that ran the length of the bay. He could smell sweat, oil, and rubber; hear quiet, measured breaths and the faint rustle of moving clothing.

'FACING AWAY.'

He slid around the corner. The intruder faced away from him, as promised.

As he closed the gap, Luc dropped the colovine and extended his arms. *Let's do this the old-fashioned way.* He wrapped his left around his quarry's throat, while slamming his right palm into the man's face.

Luc yanked his arms apart. The neck snapped with a

whip-crack that reverberated like a gunshot in the cramped, silent bay.

He looked down as the corpse slumped to the floor. *Huh. Twins.* He frowned. *Clones? No, probably twins.*

'Mo?'

'YES, TITAN?'

'You're going to need to clean up down here.'

'AFFIRMATIVE,' came the reply as Luc began a fast jog back to the observation deck. *Neela's been alone long enough.*

* * *

Abe watched the man move stealthily along the command-control deck, occasionally looking down to check a device strapped to his wrist as he approached. *Scanner of some kind. Heat signature, likely.* The intruder was young, lean, and muscled, with short cropped hair, and he moved with a control that spoke of military training.

*Base human, so—Commonwealth or Independent. Former unlikely? Senator with us. Unless intrigue-conspiracy-treachery.* Abe didn't like the thought of someone betraying the senator. *Pleasant lady. Polite. Civil.*

The man continued to approach, then stopped, frowning down at his scanner as if confused. *Unsurprising.* He was only a metre away from where Abe stood, his infiltrator shield up. It gave off a small heat signature, similar to that of a very small animal. The intruder was clearly baffled by the mismatch between his scanner and the seemingly empty corridor in front of him.

Abe raised his right arm and tapped a sequence into a small panel on his multitool. A micro-welder retracted from the tool's middle 'finger', to be replaced by a small canister of pale green liquid, tipped with a flechette.

When the group split to handle the intruders, Abe had quickly synthesised a simple sedative from some of the various chemicals stored in small synthetic casing under the skin of his right arm, secreting them into a glass tube from the spacious pouch he wore strapped to his waist. Then it was just a case of loading the vial into the base of his multitool. *Crude, but effective for time available.*

*Deploying.*

Extending his arm towards the still-confused would-be assailant, Abe deactivated the infiltrator shield. The surprise on the man's face was amusing, but didn't last long. The dart shot unerringly through the gap between his jawline and collar, injecting the sedative into the man's carotid artery. His eyes rolled as he dropped to the floor.

Abe took hold of a harness that ran across the intruder's chest and lifted him easily. He calmly dragged the man back to the bridge.

*   *   *

*'It's about trust. When it comes right down to it, that's all you've got. Trust that the men at your side are going to get their job done—and know that they're counting on you doing yours.'* Drake stopped, twenty metres from a broad doorfield that he hoped led onto the bridge. *Where did that thought come from? I haven't thought about that old bastard of a drill master in... Hell, years.* He started moving again. *Apt, though.*

The strike team had maintained strict comm silence since entering the target ship. Standard procedure. Each of them knew the mission parameters; each was capable of completing the mission alone. *That's the theory, anyway.* The weirdly silent Choi twins had gone off together, as always. Drake knew better than to order them to split up.

Five metres from the doorfield, now. He had no particular reason to think the senator would be there; it was just a hunch. But he had been living off hunches for decades and wasn't about to ignore one now, however out of the ordinary this job was. He'd never seen a ship quite like this one. And chasing myths wasn't usually in the job description.

He reached the doorfield. Crouched low to the side of the field, he reached a palm up and touched the locking panel. The field slid open with a smooth purr—Drake scuttled through before it was fully open, rifle raised and eyes scanning, searching for targets.

'Hello.' The senator stood in the centre of the room, facing him. Drake flicked his gaze left and right—it was otherwise empty. 'And who are you, might I ask?' Her voice was cool, calm.

*I don't like this.*

Something slammed into the back of his head.

Darkness.

\* \* \*

Neela kept her eyes on the black-clad soldier's face as Luc crept up behind him. *He moves like a cat. Like a really, really big cat.* She kept talking for a few seconds to give Luc time to close, then he threw the punch—almost in slow motion, it seemed a gentle tap. The sickening crunch of it connecting with the intruder's head told otherwise.

Luc strapped the first arrival to a chair with a length of polynylon provided by the ship. The captive's head slumped forwards on his chest, a lump already starting to show through his sandy-blond hair.

Within a few minutes, Ariadne and Abe arrived with their respective captives. Abe dragged his along the floor, the unconscious man drooling, his mouth wide open. Ariadne was a little more neat, hers floating smoothly behind her as she entered. The look in that man's eyes horrified Neela: panic on the verge of snapping clean into madness. *I hope she never has a reason to do that to me.*

Neela indicated the captive Luc had tied up. 'Can anyone wake him up?'

Abe dropped his human parcel on the ground. 'Possible to synthesise adreno-stimulant in… three minutes.'

'We can do better than that,' said Ariadne, crouching in front of the seated figure. Her eyes shone with the same opaque whiteness they'd had in their first meeting on Fusion. She grasped the man's head with both hands. A few seconds passed, then she cocked her head. 'Rise and shine.'

The intruder, eyes wide and wild, emitted a gasping yelp as

his head shot backwards. Clearly confused, he slowly focused on the person in front of him. Ariadne smiled.

The man jerked backwards as if trying to get away, then noticed the bindings around his wrists and ankles. Gradually he gathered himself, his features settling into a determined scowl.

*I've seen that look before.* In the faces of men and women who thought harming the Commonwealth was a noble goal. Who had blacked out at some point on their way home from work and awoken some time later in a bare, windowless cell, about to be questioned by emotionless men and women who weren't impressed by rhetoric or passion or bluster, who wanted only the truth and always got it. *But none of those men and women are here, right now.* None of them and none of the special equipment that pulled truth from reticence. *We need to know who these men are.*

'Who are you, soldier?' asked Neela, expecting no response. None came. A baleful glare, a set jaw as the captive dropped into whichever state he'd been trained to. Neela clasped her hands behind her back, turning away from the prisoner as she weighed her options. *We'll not get anything out of him through violence. Which means—* 'Ri, can you make him talk?'

The Seryn teenager turned to Neela, her glowing eyes as disturbing as ever. She said nothing for a few moments. 'Yes. Do you want to keep him alive?'

Neela shivered slightly. 'Yes.' She glanced down at the prisoner. He looked marginally less comfortable than he had a moment ago. 'For now.'

Ariadne turned back to their captive and once again grasped his head in her hands. 'Now then—who are you?'

\* \* \*

Luc and Abe had just left, dragging the comatose invaders back to their ship, leaving Neela and Ariadne to discuss what they'd learnt. The Titan had floated the idea of just dumping the intruders out into the vacuum, but no one had any stomach for it.

*Mournstar* had suggested crippling the hostile corvette's

jump engines and communications systems with a precision laser and 'LETTING THE BASTARDS LIMP HOME.' Everyone had been a bit surprised at that. *But who likes someone carving a hole in their hull? I know I wouldn't.* Ariadne felt a little sorry for Mo. It had assured her it could repair the damage easily enough, but it was clearly miffed.

'It's funny, in a way,' she said.

'What is?' Neela didn't look that amused.

'Those commandos followed you all the way from Nexus Prime to try to poach a book. And after all that trouble, the book isn't even a book, it certainly isn't here, and they get lumps kicked out of them. That's got to be quite annoying.' Ariadne barked a short laugh.

'I doubt they'll find it particularly hilarious when they wake up on a ship with a scorched hole where the jump engine used to be. But somehow, I don't mind.'

'So who are they, exactly?' asked Ariadne. 'Shax. I know they make spaceships—I was on one—but other than that, I've no idea.'

Neela sighed. 'Shax is one of the biggest megacorporations in the Commonwealth. It's not surprising you aren't that familiar with the company—they don't normally operate in areas the average citizen comes into contact with.' She counted off on her fingers. 'Finance, energy, military hardware, private security. Biochemical and pharmaceutical research, genetic medicine. Everything high-risk and high-reward. And although falling under that description, I didn't know hijacking Commonwealth citizens was also on that list.'

Neela glanced towards the door as Luc and Abe re-entered. The Collective nodded once as Luc strode up. 'Done. They're back on board. Last chance to just blow the whole corvette. Anyone?'

Neela frowned at him. 'No. We have to draw the line somewhere. I'm sure those men would have happily killed us in our sleep, but that doesn't condone murder in return.'

Luc raised his hands in a placating gesture. 'Okay. Fine. I

was joking anyway. Well, mostly.'

Ariadne turned towards one of *Mournstar*'s loudspeakers. *Not that it matters which direction I face, but anyway.* 'Mo, you can go ahead and do it now. The cripply laser thing. Can you show us on the screen as well?'

'AFFIRMATIVE.'

The viewport changed to show the exterior of the upper hull, just as the corvette was nudged away from *Mournstar*. It drifted free for a few seconds, then two beams of light briefly fired into its stern, a small explosion showing where they hit. *Well, that was a bit disappointing. I was hoping for a bigger bang.*

Luc clapped his hands once, then wandered over to the food alcove. 'All right. Let's get going, Mo.'

Ariadne turned back to Neela as *Mournstar*'s engines thrummed into life. 'So what are you going to do about this? When you get home?'

'I'm going to have to think about that. Right now, I've none of the proof I'd need to bring charges against Shax. You saw there was no identification on any of those men; and I'd be willing to bet that if I did a genetic trace on them in the Commonwealth central database, I'd find that they never existed.'

Ariadne frowned. 'What's the alternative, then?'

Neela's voice was cold and hard in a way Ariadne hadn't heard before. 'I'm going to have to be creative. Someone might need to pay Katarina Puschkova a visit.'

\* \* \*

Caleb Hesch watched on his mid-range scanner as the corvette came loose from the larger, unusual indigo ship that carried Corralin and his allies. He had monitored the earlier ambush as well, the disguised ram and last minute crash-braked landing, and been impressed. *That took balls.* But he knew there was no chance a Commonwealth military team of just five men could bring down a cohort. *Especially not the son of Quinto, the tough bastard.*

So he was unsurprised later when the corvette was pushed

clear and its engines crippled. He didn't understand why Corralin hadn't just destroyed the humans out of hand, but he also didn't care. *If he wants to give them a chance to drift home in, oh, a hundred years or so, that's his prerogative.*

Hesch himself was strapped into the pilot seat of his own neat two-man microcorvette, the *Angry Goat*—an enthusiastic little ship he'd bought on Fusion from a merchant with a relaxed attitude towards personal property rights. Even after buying the ship, he still had a decent chunk left of the proceeds from selling that pompous ass Fourier's pleasure yacht. *Ridiculous boat. No guns, no grunt. Pointless.* His new boat was three-quarters motor and cannon, one-quarter luxuries, like seats and a shower. Hesch felt right at home.

He had the corvette powered down, hiding in plain sight in the carved-out interior of one of the thousands of artificial moons surrounding the bizarre system. He'd give Corralin and his cronies a few minutes' head start to disappear back into the nebula—*There they go now, moving off*—then follow. Marvellous things, transponders. As long as the hunter didn't drop too far back, the hunted didn't get away.

*Easy.*

He tracked the indigo ship as it accelerated into the nebula wall and vanished, then fired up the *Goat's* systems and lifted off from the miniature moon to follow.

'Lead on, Lucius. Lead on.'

# 14. Promise

Luc stood at the viewport that ran the width of the back wall of the rear observatory, looking back at the nebula. The return trip had only taken three days, instead of ten—the ship told them it could travel much faster since it had taken some 'landmarks' on their way in. What constituted a landmark in an enormous cloud of dust and gas was anyone's guess.

The Titan took a sip of his drink—a large measure of some type of brandy from a planet he couldn't remember the name of. Boone had given it to him; the man seemed to have an inexhaustible stock of booze stashed away in the shuttle. Luc couldn't believe he hadn't heard the bottles clanking together during the more energetic manoeuvres on their trip from Mission to Fusion.

Thinking of Mission depressed him. He didn't regret leaving, not at all—he trusted Jarrod implicitly. And it felt good to be out in the wider galaxy, having experiences he hadn't had the imagination to long for while he was growing up in the bubble of the Titan homeworld.

But every time he let his mind stray beyond the present, beyond their current insane quest to find a mythical alien and save humanity's future—*Founder, putting it into words makes it seem even more ridiculous*—he came up with nothing. No future. What was he going to do? Go back to Mission and hope that he didn't end up dead in the Rift before the end of the day?

The worst part was, he wasn't even sure he wanted to go back. Seeing things and meeting people he'd only been told about—or lied to about, it seemed. How could he go back to Titan culture, smile, and salute as though nothing had changed? Assuming the being-dead-in-the-Rift scenario could be avoided, that was.

He turned away from the viewport and wandered over to a tall set of shelves that held row upon row of ancient-looking scrolltabs of the kind on display in the Tactics Museum across the street from the Academy in Rift. He idly picked one up at random and flicked it on. The tab lit up with the title page: 'Submarinal Agricultural Techniques in Latter-Ionian Era Kepsylon.' *I'm sure it's a classic, but...* He switched it off and returned it to the shelf.

'Oh, sorry—I didn't know you were in here.'

Luc turned. Neela stood in the doorway, clutching a scrolltab of her own. She was swathed in a long dark-grey shawl, her hair pulled back in a ponytail. Her face looked scrubbed clean, devoid of any makeup. *She looks young. And beautiful.*

'I can leave, if you like...' She started to turn away.

'No, not at all. I was just—nothing. Drinking and thinking, as my father used to say.'

Neela stepped further into the room. 'More of Boone's mysterious liquor, I imagine. I've had quite enough of that for a while.' She walked over to a comfortable seat and slipped into it, her hands in her lap. 'Are you close to him?'

'Hmm?'

'Your father. I've not heard you mention him before.'

'Oh. No. I was, but... no. He died twelve years ago. Sixteen of yours.' He took another drink, winced slightly at the burn. He looked into his glass. 'My uncle Jarrod raised me. He... he did a good job, I think.'

'I'm very sorry, Luc. Was it... was he ill?'

Luc burst out laughing, then stopped when he saw the shocked look on the senator's face. 'Sorry, that was rude. No, it wasn't an illness. We don't... *do* illnesses. That's not a concern.'

'You don't get sick? At all?'

Luc shook his head. 'No. But there are still plenty of ways to die. Including stupid accidents.' His voice sounded bitter.

'What happened? If—You don't have to tell me.'

'It was just so... so inane. His unit was out on a training exercise. Live-fire. There was some miscommunication, negligence from the command. He was killed. The unit commander was court-martialled.' He shrugged. 'Just a stupid accident.'

Neela was quiet for a moment. 'What was his name? Your father?'

'Quinto. Quinto Corralin. Which makes me,' he paused, 'Lucius Corralin Ben Quinto. As you were so impressed with when we met, I seem to remember.'

'Oh, of course. You did make quite an impression.'

Luc grinned.

Neela finished, 'Mainly because it was quite a small room, though.'

Luc laughed. *Maybe I was wrong about this one. She's not that annoying, after all.* He finished the last of his drink. 'Well, I'll let you read in peace. See you soon.'

'I'll be here.'

Luc stopped as he reached the doorfield and turned. 'Oh, Neela?'

'Yes?'

'Thank you. It was good to talk. About my father. I haven't in a while.'

Neela smiled. 'Then I'm glad you chose to talk to me.

Anytime. Well, anytime we're not busy saving the universe, anyway.'

Luc turned again to leave. *Even sounds ridiculous when coming from her.*

* * *

Nine jumps took *Mournstar* from Wolftail deep into the Core, to the coordinates that Jacob had dug from one of the Athravan's ancient future archives. The supposed location of a system called—roughly translated from the Zythylyx—Promise.

'I wonder what they think he's promising,' Boone had said to Ariadne during the journey. 'Unity, that is. And what he is. I'm quite intrigued to find out, you know. Do you think he's a giant bird? Or a jellyfish? Or maybe a cloud of gas! That would be a marvel, wouldn't it, my girl?'

The ship unfolded from subspace, surrounded by an impossibly crowded starfield. That deep in the Core, the systems were so close that stars seemed almost to touch.

*It's amazing.* Ariadne stared out at the centre of the galaxy, eyes wide. *I never... I just never thought I'd see something like this. More star than space.*

But they weren't looking for a star. She turned to Abe, who stood next to her, his eyes with that familiar glazed look that said he was deep in some complicated calculation. 'Abe?'

His eyes cleared, and he turned to her. 'Ariadne.'

'How are we supposed to find it? How do you look for a black hole? It's completely invisible, isn't it?'

'To the eye, yes. It is an absence-void-null from which no light escapes. Were it to pass between your eyes and a star, it would be visible. Not otherwise.' Abe turned back to the viewport. 'I am connected to *Mournstar*. It is running a sensor scan of this volume of space, matching gravitational effects on the energy grid with the visible starfield.'

*Okay, that almost made sense. So...* 'When it finds an effect without a matching star—'

Abe nodded. 'Indeed.'

'Ha! I'm getting good at science.' She smiled. 'How long will it take?'

'Unknown. Have been unable to accurately measure or determine *Mournstar*'s computational power. The speed at which it returns a result will actually be the most—'

'PASSENGERS, ATTENTION. TARGET SYSTEM LOCATED. REPEAT, TARGET SYSTEM LOCATED. SHALL I SET A COURSE?'

Ariadne and Abe looked at each other, then around the bridge. The others were elsewhere.

'I guess we're in charge, then.' Ariadne called out a little more loudly, 'Set a course, Mo. Please.'

'COURSE HAS BEEN SET. ARRIVAL IN THREE HUNDRED FORTY-SIX SECONDS ON MARK. MARK.'

Ariadne beamed. 'Isn't this exciting!'

Five minutes later, the voice of the ship boomed out again. 'SYSTEM COMING INTO VIEW: NOW.'

A soft light overlay the scene in front of the viewport. At the centre, a slowly expanding gold circle ringed a planet that was just becoming visible; another sat off to one side, a smaller ring around nothing. *Must be the black hole.*

A stream of text ran in a column between them, planetary specifications that Ariadne didn't understand. She kept her eyes on the world that they were rapidly approaching. As they neared, the planet filling half the viewport, she gasped. 'It's completely... blank.' The surface was an eerie expanse of silver-white with no visible features, illuminated only by the background glow of the starfield.

Abe nodded. 'Planet is also completely round. Mathematically perfect solid sphere. Likelihood of natural occurrence is infinitesimal.'

'Someone—something—made it? A whole world?'

Abe cocked his head, eyes narrowing. 'Most likely. Though it is not entirely "blank". Ship, expand view of northern polar region.'

A window appeared within the viewport, zooming towards the planet. Ariadne turned away, a little queasy, as Luc and

Neela entered the bridge. They both looked past her at the unnatural sphere.

Neela opened her mouth, closed it again. Frowned. 'I don't know what I was expecting. Somehow, this isn't it. How can anything live here? There are no—well, anything.'

Luc was studying the zoomed region. He pointed. 'What's that dark smudge, right at the pole?'

Abe turned, his silver eyes the same colour as the planet behind him. 'I believe that is the entrance.'

* * *

The shuttle seemed awfully cramped to Neela, after *Mournstar*'s relatively spacious interior. The ship had landed ten kilometres or so from the northern pole and the elliptical hole that apparently opened into—*Into!*—the planet, and moments ago disgorged them in the shuttle from the docking bay where it had sat since they first embarked.

'Seems to be running a little bit smoother—don't you think, lad?' Boone asked Luc, the two of them piloting in the shuttle cockpit.

Through the doorway, she saw Luc nod once. 'It does, actually—are you less drunk than you were last time?'

'That's a scandalous accusation! Shocking! And no, I'm not. I'm exactly as drunk. But the controls feel a bit nippier, you know?'

Neela smiled at the weary expression on Luc's face as he turned to his compatriot. 'Is that a technical term, Boone? Nippier? I'm not familiar with it, to be honest.'

Boone ignored him. 'Abe, my boy, have you been poking around in here? Fixing up and whatnot? Don't mind if you have, of course—a free tune-up's a free tune-up!'

Abe was strapped into the same corner seat he had taken on the trip from Fusion. 'Negative. Possible that *Mournstar* itself is responsible. It seems to have a lot of free time.'

They quickly covered the distance from *Mournstar* to the hole. Boone brought the shuttle in to a hover near the edge.

Neela peered down through the viewport beside her. One or

so seconds out of every ten, a bluish-tinted cover appeared across the entrance.

'Now what's going on here, I wonder?' Boone sounded a little confused.

'Appearance is consistent with doorfield. Far greater scale than normal, to cover two hundred metre radius entrance, but consistent. Appears to be malfunctioning, however. Intermittent.' Neela turned to see Abe's eyes glaze briefly, then snap back into focus. 'Power readings are fluctuating in accordance with field appearance.'

'That's the second odd thing, though.' Boone still sounded puzzled. 'The first is why there's a field in the first place. From the information we had all those years ago in the future, the shaft's supposed to be open.' He began tapping into the screen embedded in the shuttle dash. 'I'll contact Jacob, ask him to check for any information in the archives.'

'Maybe it will be open in the future,' said Ariadne. 'Maybe the field thingy's broken and he decides to just turn it off rather than replace it?' She sounded hopeful, but unconvinced.

Neela frowned. *Something's wrong.* They all felt it.

'Can you take us in, Boone?' asked Luc. 'You've got an eight-second window, roughly. Should be plenty, right?'

'Oh, yes. Loads of time. I'm just a little bit worried about what we'll find on the other side.' He scratched his nose. 'Let's give Jacob a chance to get back to us before we go haring into the great unknown, eh?' He brought the shuttle down to land with a gentle bump.

Five minutes later, the dashboard computer pinged.

Boone tapped the console and read the message. 'Ah. Well. That changes things a bit.'

'What is it?' Neela asked.

'It seems, from what we were—will be—told, that as far as the Zythylyx understand it, Unity puts the shutters up when he goes on walkabout.'

Ariadne looked baffled. 'Um—what?'

'He's not here. It, he, whoever. If the doors are closed, then he's out for the day. But the records don't say anything about them being half-closed and on the fritz. And that's what's worrying me.'

'So what are we supposed to do?' Luc asked. 'Sit here until it comes back?'

'No, maybe not—but this is where the translation gets very sketchy. According to the Zythylyx there's a... lodestone, somewhere at the centre the planet, an anchor of some kind that Unity uses to pull itself back home. But not only that, they reckoned this lodestone can be activated, somehow, to contact the big man when it's away. Ring the doorbell, so to speak, and bring him back.'

*That has to be the worst...* 'There's not a lot of certainty in this plan, is there Boone?' Neela had a bad feeling about the situation.

'Well, no. But we're dancing on the edge of the envelope a bit, so to speak. Certainty's in short supply. Adventure, though! We've got tons of that!'

Luc leaned back in his seat and groaned. 'Fine. As if we have any choice. Take us in.'

Boone fired up the engines, and the shuttle lifted a few metres off the planet's surface. They edged forwards to hover over the dark shaft that led down and in. To a lodestone, maybe. That could contact Unity, possibly.

The malfunctioning field flashed on and then off again, and the shuttle dropped quickly but smoothly through the field and into the dark.

*Yes, something's definitely wrong.*

* * *

The illumination from the shuttle's powerful searchlights barely reached the walls of the shaft as they let gravity pull them downward towards the centre of the bizarre planet, nose first and braking thrusters on a gentle burn. Abe was almost sure he saw inscriptions of some kind along those walls. *Unknown script, if so. Non-humanoid origin.*

Neela gave a quiet gasp, and Luc a low curse. Abe turned his gaze forwards and reeled.

They approached what had once been an enormous gate separating that section of shaft from the next. The interlocking sections along the edges showed how the mechanism was supposed to iris open and shut.

It would never do so again. A ragged hole was carved through the middle of the gate, a hundred metres wide or more. It looked as though a hole had been punched through the centre and the edges gripped and torn outward, mangling the gate into a twisted metal flower.

They were all silent as the shuttle sailed through the rent.

Luc pointed as they cleared the gate. 'That was more than twenty metres thick.' He turned to the others, his face pale in the half-dark of the shuttle interior. 'What can do that?'

'More important: Is it still here?' said Abe. He didn't know what he wanted the answer to be. *To witness a force of such power, even for a moment...* He looked back at the crippled gate. *Likely only for a moment.*

The next section of the shaft was identical: several hundred kilometres of smooth walls, then a devastated gate. The next nine, as well. The barrier after that, however, was different: That one was a deep cobalt colour, of a material that looked more rock than metal.

It had been broken too, though. A clean-edged hole approximately twenty metres wide had been bored through the centre.

As the shuttle entered the much narrower shaft, its passengers still hushed, Abe felt an odd nostalgic twinge for the transtubes on the arcology. He briefly wondered what was happening there. *Likely: Same things that always happen.*

The tunnel through the cobalt-coloured rock continued for hundreds of kilometres.

After several minutes, a pinprick of light showed the end of the shaft.

Ariadne broke the silence. 'Look, there's a light!'

Boone muttered to himself under his breath, occasionally

shaking his head. His hands gripped the shuttle control sticks.

'Why does that light worry me more than the darkness?' Neela asked.

*Hypothesis: Reluctance to emerge from constricted womb-like environment into brightness-outside-unknown.* Abe opened his mouth to speak, then closed it. *Perhaps situation not suitable time for psychological analysis.*

No one else answered Neela. Another minute passed in silence, and they emerged into… whiteness.

The vast cavern was brilliant white. Only Abe's long-range sensors and the corresponding ping from the shuttle's own told him that a front wall was even present, fully a thousand kilometres ahead of them. The space had no lateral walls in any direction, at least not within their sensor range. Abe quietly relayed this information.

'Do you think this empty space is all around the centre of the planet? How is that possible? Where are the supports? What's holding the ceiling up?' Luc asked.

'Supports not strictly necessary,' Abe replied. 'But engineering level required to do without them… astounding.'

'And where is the light coming from?' Neela asked. 'I can't see a light source, but it's like daylight out there.'

Abe had no answer to that. They went on.

They were perhaps halfway through the void when dark specks became visible, breaking up the otherwise pure whiteness in front of them. As the specks turned into shapes, Abe realised he had been holding his breath. And that he was afraid.

Minutes passed before the shuttle neared the next layer of the planet's shell. The shapes, scattered over the surface, were close enough to see clearly, but their nature was hardly clearer. There were thirty or more, each a broken hulk larger than the shuttle. Ships, they seemed at first glance, but on second look what had first passed as a gun turret or thruster exhaust now seemed an arm or a foot. Or an eye socket.

Abe felt like an amoeba, barely comprehending the nature of a lizard it might, after a million years, evolve into. *Same cobalt colour as level above. Constructed-forged-born of metallic-biometallic semi-organic material.*

'Look, another gate—and this one seems whole.' Luc pointed towards the centre of the array of shattered living ships. A translucent circle, a pale blue-grey surrounded by the brilliant white.

'Another field. This one functional.' Abe scanned once again. 'Power readings steady, no fluctuation.'

Luc said, 'Marvellous. All this way, to come up against the one gate in the whole place that's working. How are we supposed to—'

The field blinked out.

'Oh.' Luc turned to look at the others, expression a little sheepish. 'Did I jinx it, do you think?'

'Negative. Power is still steady. Field has merely withdrawn in response to shuttle proximity to allow passage.'

Neela looked at Abe, brows raised. 'You've got a pretty loose definition of "merely", there.'

The shuttle passed through the field frame. Another, identical, was visible only a hundred metres in front of them. Ariadne yelped a little as they were plunged into relative darkness.

'Field behind us has been restored. Interesting. Possible that this area acts as an airlock. If so—'

The field ahead of them disappeared, and the shuttle sailed through.

Into paradise.

* * *

*Of all the sights I've seen… This is what I'll think of the moment before I die.* Luc closed his eyes for a second, then reopened them. *No, I'm not dreaming.*

They had reached the centre of Promise. The sphere had a hollow core, but not an empty one. Stretching away from the airlock in all directions, lining the interior of the sphere for mile after mile after mile and covering every inch, was an impossible world. The shuttle passed the canopy of a verdant forest that extended left and right in a dappled green band hundreds of miles wide around the inside-out meridian of the planet.

Above them, the hemisphere changed from forest to prairie, miles of rolling grasslands spotted with slow-moving herds of animals too distant to identify. Some gathered around waterholes, oxbow lakes along the glistening tendril rivers snaking through the plains and on into the forest. The lush green of the savannah faded into yellow as it contracted, blending into a stark desert zone dotted with immense sand dunes.

The rivers straightened and narrowed, flanked first by green-brown deltas, then by craggy sandstone scarps as the land rose into a vast mountain range. Luc looked straight up at the snow-capped peaks that hung over their heads, topping stalactites the size of... *Well, mountains.* Glinting between them were ice fields, smoothly reflective amongst the grey-brown stone.

On the hemisphere below them, the central forest ended sharply, giving way to a narrow ring of white sand. The perfect beach gently sloped away from the meridian to meet an azure ocean that filled the rest of the hemisphere. A chain of island archipelagos zigzagged across its centre, emerald dots in the sea of blue.

Directly ahead of the cruising shuttle, at the very centre of Promise, was a dazzling point of light. As they continued towards it, the point growing into a ball and becoming clearer, Luc realised it was a miniature star. *Impossible—and completely fitting. This whole world is impossible.*

He felt a hand on his shoulder and glanced up to see Neela leaning forwards to get a better view. Her mouth and eyes were wide and childlike with wonder. Luc couldn't help but smile as he turned back to the magical vista. *That's exactly how I feel. Like a child, brought into the world for the first time.*

'It's so beautiful,' said Ariadne quietly. 'It's just... perfect.'

'It doesn't look like whatever broke in here did any damage, does it?' Neela asked. 'Which begs the question, what did they— Oh. Oh no.' She looked from Boone to Luc. 'The lodestone.'

Boone's expression was grim. 'Aye, that's what I've been worried about ever since we came through that first busted gate. If that stone can do what it's supposed to, then it's got power. A lot of it.'

'Power we do not even understand,' Abe said.

Neela's tone was full of foreboding. 'No, we don't—but that doesn't mean no one does.'

Luc's initial burst of joy and awe was wearing off. *Damn it.* 'We need to check, at least. Maybe whoever, whatever, came for something else. Who knows? Maybe they just wanted to do some mountain climbing.'

'Let's check quickly, can we?' Ariadne said. 'I'm not entirely convinced they're not here anymore.'

'Where's the lodestone supposed to be, Boone?' Neela asked. 'If we have to search this whole world, we'll be here for years.'

Boone scratched his chin. 'Jacob said somewhere at the centre, so… Let's go to the centre, I guess!' He tapped the shuttle dash, and the thrusters kicked them forwards.

The cabin was quiet, the earlier exuberant mood gone.

A few minutes later, they were closing in on the star. Luc palmed the control to polarise the viewport against the glare, and the dazzling light dimmed. Abe hummed.

'What is it?' asked Ariadne.

'Uncertain. Sensors suggest a small object in orbit around the star. Difficult to confirm. Energy level from star confuses the reading.' He pointed to their left. 'If object is present, it approaches from the left on an orbital path four kilometres ahead.'

Boone nodded. 'Matches what the shuttle sensors are reporting. Let's take a look.' He nudged the controls, and the shuttle angled that way.

Minutes passed.

Finally, their patience was rewarded: Light glinted off something ahead of them.

Boone steered the shuttle in a loop around the object and brought them alongside it. Luc peered out. It was ovoid, almost.

*Like an egg with the base sheared off, then upturned.* The material was unfamiliar, like crystal but with a chrome metallic sheen running through it. Three prongs curved upward from the top edge like the claws that would hold a precious stone to a ring.

*But the precious stone isn't there.* 'It's been taken. Hasn't it?' Luc looked to Boone, who nodded solemnly.

'Aye, as expected.' He breathed a deep sigh. 'So. Guess we need to go find it then, eh?'

'Or rather, go and find whatever was able to blast their way in here through hundreds of yards of rock and metal and fight off thirty terrifying looking... whatever those things outside were. And ask them if we can please have it back.' Ariadne didn't sound too enthusiastic.

Boone's old familiar grin returned. 'Well, it wouldn't be worth doing if it were easy, now, would it?'

Luc shook his head wearily. 'Nothing's easy with you, is it?'

'Oh, I don't know. I like to think I'm pretty easy on the eyes. What? No? Well, suit yourself.' He pulled at the shuttle controls again, and they banked around back towards the airlock. 'Back to the ship we go. Need to think up a plan. Maybe Jacob has some ideas.'

Ariadne sighed. 'It's a shame we have to leave. I could spend days sitting on that beach. We've only got pebble ones at home.'

'Hopefully we'll be back this way soon, lass. You never know. Maybe you can have a little holiday then.'

*I've got a feeling we're all going to need one. If we're still alive, that is.*

Neela was absentmindedly tapping her fingers on Luc's shoulder. He looked up at her. 'What's on your mind?'

'I think I know what we should do next. It's all well and good rummaging through your archives, Boone, but we need more up-to-date information. We need to go to the source.'

Boone looked confused, then brightened. 'Grand idea! Good thinking, Senator.'

Ariadne called out, 'Sorry, but I missed the bit where someone said what the plan was. Out loud.'

Neela turned. 'We're going to see the Zythylyx.'

\* \* \*

Caleb Hesch watched the shuttle emerge from the wide shaft that led down into the planet's core. The *Angry Goat* was parked behind him, in plain sight beside the squid-like purple ship. He wore a vacuum skin under his clothes, the full-body gelatinous membrane gripping his flesh and making his scalp itch. The oxygen recycler mouthpiece tasted odd, as well. *Been a while since I had one of these on.*

The shuttle angled towards him—or, more accurately, towards the stern of the larger ship and the shuttle bays. Hesch saw it slow slightly as the occupants clearly spotted him. He held his arms out wide, showing his empty palms, then slowly brought his right fist to his heart. *Give him the cohort salute—that should stop them squashing me with no questions asked, at least.*

He remembered Corralin's flight from Mission and reconsidered. *Too late now, anyway.*

The shuttle stopped, hovering. Hesch dropped the salute, pointed to his chest, then the shuttle, then the purple ship. Fairly obvious.

He tensed as the shuttle started moving towards him again, but he didn't get squashed. It coasted over his head and curved around, sailing through the now-open bay doors. He turned and began the bouncing half-walk half-skip that low gravity required. Taking the corner around to the ship's stern took some careful manoeuvring, but shortly he found himself next to the open shuttle bay. He crouched and carefully jumped the four feet up and into the bay and stepped forwards out of the way as he heard the doors start to close behind him.

He was in.

Removing the mouthpiece, Hesch slowly walked towards the settling shuttle. He grimaced as the vacuum skin retracted to its collar, leaving his head free. *Deep breath. That's better.* He looked up as the shuttle door swung open and wasn't surprised at all to see Corralin spring out first. The youngster looked taut, angry—a little nervous too. And ready to fight if he needed to.

But Hesch didn't think it would come to that. Not as soon as Lucius saw who he was…

*There.* Corralin's confident approach stuttered: He paused, squinted, then stopped completely, his eyes wide.

'You.' Half question, half bewildered statement. Hesch kept his eyes on Corralin's face as his peripheral vision tracked the others exiting the shuttle and going to stand behind their comrade. Even the Collective didn't get a glance. *And normally I just kill you. Guess it's your lucky day.*

'Hello, Lucius. It's been a long time.'

The young Titan was gathering his composure. 'Not long enough. It's been six years since they sent you to Gulgalta. Six out of thirty. How in Founder's name are you free?' His fists clenched. The surprise was wearing off, and the anger was seeping back.

Hesch kept his voice calm and controlled. *No need to rile him.* 'I was released. Early. A deviation from protocol, but these were deemed extraordinary circumstances.'

Lucius' eyes narrowed, then realisation seemed to dawn. 'They sent you. To bring me back? Or just kill me? Which was it? Though I can't imagine how you think you're going to achieve either now.'

The taller, dark-haired woman asked, 'Luc, who is this? I can see he's a Titan.'

Corralin kept his eyes on Hesch. 'He was the one who was court-martialled.' He spat out the last words.

The woman paled a little. 'Oh. Good lord.'

Hesch nodded briefly at the woman. 'Yes. I was court-martialled. Deservedly.' He turned back to Corralin. 'Lucius, I'll be brief. I was sent here to kill you, obviously. There's no other way out of Gulgalta. Sent by a councillor by the name of Marcellus Fourier, to be exact.

'I see you recognise the name. He arranged for my release, told me where you were, and gave me a ship. And here I am.' Hesch noted the tension in Corralin's shoulders and thighs, like a coiled spring. *Time to bleed that away.* 'Here with no intention of killing you.'

The young Titan didn't seem convinced. 'Really. Then why are you here?'

'Two reasons. To give you Fourier. As long as he lives, you'll need to watch your back. End him. And his advisers, his wives, his children. His advisers' families. Clear the stable.'

Luc nodded once. 'The other reason.'

Hesch took a deep breath, let it out. 'To apologise.' *Damn it. Harder than I thought.* He looked down at Corralin's booted feet, then back up. 'Quinto was a good man. I was slack, and he died. It changes nothing to you, I know. But I am sorry, and I would have you know that before I leave.'

'Leave for where? You should be back in that cell, serving your time.'

Hesch shook his head. 'Think. There's no place for me on Mission as it is now. I was sent to assassinate a consul's nephew and didn't even have the decency to die trying. It's a snake pit. You finish whatever it is you're doing here, then get yourself home. And do what needs doing.'

'Clear the stable.'

Hesch nodded. 'Then I'll come back. And you can put me back in that cell, or not.'

The young girl on Corralin's left asked, 'I know this isn't really important, but how did you even find us? We're in the middle of nowhere.'

'I've been following you since Fusion.' He looked back at Luc. 'I appreciated the way you handled that street thug, by the way. A little too flashy for a real fight, but there's nothing wrong with flair.'

'Fusion?' the young girl asked again. 'Then why did you wait until now? You've followed us halfway across the galaxy and back.'

'Curiosity. When I saw the people Lucius was teaming up with, especially the quiet one there,'—he nodded towards the Collective—'it piqued my interest. But after taking a short trip down that shaft after you and seeing the damage... I think it's time I went my own way.'

Lucius grunted. 'Probably a good decision.'

Hesch nodded. 'You'll do all right. You're your father's son—anyone can see that. And Jarrod's. Just keep your squad close.' He turned to go. 'Could you open the bay door? You should probably get behind an airlock first.'

A second later, a field dropped between him and the group, and the bay doors started to slide open. *Huh. That was neat. Didn't see anyone move a muscle.* He quickly slid the mouthpiece back in and the vacuum skin began rolling up. The cold of the vacuum nipped at his uncovered cheeks before the vacuum skin deployed fully.

Hesch stopped at the edge of the bay and called back, his voice crackling through the mouthpiece, 'You will see me again, Lucius. I promise.'

The youngster nodded. Hesch turned again, hopped down onto the ship's surface, and began bouncing back to the *Goat*.

*He'll do all right.*

# 15. Zythylyx

'It's not much to go on, is it? That they'll be there in twenty-five millennia hardly guarantees they're there now.'

Ariadne watched Neela pace the bridge, seemingly thinking out loud more than talking. Luc sat off to one side, even quieter than usual. *No surprise there—he's just seen a ghost, after all.* Ariadne didn't understand the whole story, though she had a feeling Neela did. The senator had spoken quietly to Luc all the way from the shuttle bay up to the bridge.

*And that makes me jealous… why, exactly?*

Luc broke his silence. 'Can anyone think of any other options? I can't. And I'm not surprised, either. Feel like I haven't had a choice in anything since this insane excursion started.' He stood, stretching. *Shaking it off.* 'So we might as well get going. Boone, you have the coordinates, right?'

'Aye. As does *Mournstar*, more importantly. It's not far. Five jumps will get us there, halfway to the rim. Quiet neighbourhood. Not much traffic. Why they like it, probably.'

Abe came out of his connection trance. 'Have cross-referenced those coordinates with Collective star map. System has no human population. One large gas giant planet. No features of interest.'

Boone shook his head. 'Oh, maybe not to you, lad, but to those of the hard and pointy silicon persuasion, I'm sure it's a wonderland. Damned if we ever understood their reasoning, mind. Never told us why. Or where the *rest* of them were, either. Just "elsewhere". Cryptic bastards!' he finished cheerfully.

Neela stopped pacing and stood with her arms crossed. She looked between them, then nodded slowly. 'Off we go again, then.'

Ariadne called out, 'Mo, we can go now.'

'AFFIRMATIVE. COURSE IS SET. WE WILL CLEAR THE GRAVITY WELL IN FORTY-TWO SECONDS. FIRST JUMP WILL COMMENCE IN—'

They all chimed in, 'Forty-three seconds.'

They laughed. Some of the tension from the encounter with that scary-looking Titan ebbed away.

Ariadne shivered a little. *Are they all like that? Is ours actually one of the cuddly ones?* She glanced at Neela and Luc, who had drifted closer again. *Maybe he's more 'ours' for some of us than others.* Calys's voice sounded clear as a bell in her head. *'And which one of them are you actually jealous of, honey? Or have you not decided yet?'*

Ariadne turned and headed for the food hole. *Shut up, Calys. I've got enough on my mind.*

A moment later, the loudspeaker boomed with the familiar refrain: 'JUMP IN TEN SECONDS. REPEAT: JUMP IN TEN...FIVE... THREE, TWO, ONE. JUMP.'

*We should really turn the volume down on that.*

\* \* \*

*Mournstar* blinked back into realspace fourteen hours later with the customary blue-white flash, a few hundred light minutes from the utterly standard red dwarf star at the centre of the system the Zythylyx had chosen as their home. Or would in the future, at least.

Just a few dozen light minutes away was the only planet in the system, an immense giant of yellow-streaked azure gas. Somewhere nearby the Chosen hoped they would find the silicon-based alien race that was their only link to Unity.

Abe stood on the bridge. He had created a wireless link to the ship during the journey, combining their sensors into a more efficient shared array. Milliseconds after unfolding into realspace, they set their scanners ranging over the planet and the surrounding volume. *Search may take some time.* That was fine. A lack of patience had never been one of Abe's shortcomings.

The difficulty was knowing exactly what to look for. Silicon was difficult to differentiate from any other metalloid at this range. It was a matter of filtering out the background noise of the planet's metallic core and the various debris drifting starward from the system's unhelpfully close asteroid belt. Whatever was left was a candidate.

Twelve minutes later, he barely registered the sound of the bridge's doorfield opening. Ignoring the approaching footsteps, he focused on the search. They had covered barely twenty per cent of the volume of space immediately surrounding the planet. If the Zythylyx ranged further afield — or, worse, were within the atmosphere itself — the search could take days. *And if they are not here at all?*

'How's it going?'

Abe sighed inwardly and brought his consciousness out of the semi-fugue of scanner analysis. He turned to see the senator smiling hopefully at him.

'No results so far. Search is at early stage of completion. Will take time.'

Neela nodded. 'Is there anything I can do to help?'

Abe blinked, baffled and amused. *Not unless your sensors are truly exceptional for a human.* 'No. Thank you, Senator. The ship and I will continue and inform you as soon as there is news.'

She looked a little disappointed. 'Okay. Well, let us know.'

She turned and left the bridge.

As he slipped back into his scanner data flow, *Mournstar* pinged him an internal message. *'HUMANS ARE DISTRACTING.'*

Abe nodded. *'Am I a distraction also, then?'*

The ship paused for nearly half a second before replying, *'NEGATIVE. YOU ARE A BETTER KIND OF HUMAN.'*

*A compliment of sorts.* Abe quickly reviewed the results that had accumulated while he was talking to Neela. Nothing. *Unsurprising.* He took more manual control of the scan and immersed himself back into the data flow. *Patience.*

The breakthrough came over an hour later, and they almost missed it. As Jacob hadn't been able to provide any detail of where or how the Zythylyx were placed within the system, Abe and the ship had been searching for structures of any significant size in orbit around the planet: small satellites or larger semi-hollow lattices.

What they found instead stunned Abe with its sheer ambition: a ring, encircling the entire planet.

It was narrow, narrower than the planet itself by a hair—perfectly aligned with the equator and a mere thousand kilometres above the exosphere. *Mournstar* edged closer.

The ring gradually became visible: first a thin dark line of unknown colour, then thicker, thicker again, resolving into a mottled band of black, grey, and purple.

Details became clearer: sharp edges, angles, blocky crystalline cores, blade-like appendages. Where and how one of the beings joined onto the next, it was impossible to tell.

*Incredible. Beauty.*

The ship pinged him again. *'I HAVE NOTIFIED THE OTHERS. THEY ARE ON THEIR WAY. PROGRESS TO MEDIUM-RANGE HAILING DISTANCE?'*

*'Affirmative. Wide-band transmission beam is prepared according to Athravan specification?'*

*'PREPARED.'*

*'Thank you, Mournstar.'*

Savouring the last few moments of solitary appreciation, Abe kept his gaze on the ring as they moved closer. It would soon be time again for the noise and questions, the thunder and sarcasm. He had grown used to it over the past days, even come to sometimes enjoy the barrage of what Ariadne called 'banter'. But the quiet still soothed him.

The bridge doorfield whooshed open, and the young Seryn's excited yelp burst the silence. 'Ooo, they look so pretty! I can't believe they're alive. Have they said anything yet?'

*Noise and questions.*

\* \* \*

'*Mournstar*, do you know how to translate? If they talk back to us, that is.' Neela was nervous. The others had decided that, given her 'oratory experience', she should be the one to actually contact the Zythylyx. Speaking in front of nine hundred Commonwealth Senators was one thing. *Speaking to an alien race that's been around since before we were banging rocks together to make fire? That's new.*

'Don't worry about it, Neela. How could they not?' said Luc. He lounged in one of the seats near the viewport, eating a sandwich the size of his arm. 'The long shot was finding them here in the first place. Since we have, I feel oddly optimistic about the whole thing.'

'I can tell by the enormous snack,' Ariadne commented. 'You always eat when you're happy. Or bored, actually. Are you bored, too?' She grinned at the Titan.

'I'm a growing boy. I need my calories. I don't know how many exactly.' He took an enormous bite. 'I'll probably need another few sandwiches later,' he mumbled through a mouthful of roast meat and salad.

Ariadne grimaced. 'Gross. Chew with your mouth closed.'

Neela exhaled sharply. 'People! Can I please get on with this?'

Ariadne and Luc exchanged a sheepish glance.

'Sorry,' Ariadne said. Luc made a zipping motion over his lips, then opened them again to shove more sandwich into his face. Neela turned away, shaking her head. *Like children, both of them.*

*Mournstar* replied, 'TO ANSWER YOUR QUESTION, SENATOR: AFFIRMATIVE. I HAVE THE ATHRAVAN TRANSLATION PROTOCOLS AVAILABLE. THOUGH BE WARNED: THEY ARE PARTIAL AND OFTEN CONFUSING.'

'Yes, Jacob mentioned that. I'm sure this is going to be one of my more baffling conversations. So we should probably get started.' Neela realised she had no idea how the ship planned to make contact. She glanced at Abe, a question forming on her lips.

'*Mournstar*, initiate wide-band transmission beam, twenty kilometre spread, closest beam segment.' Abe nodded to Neela.

'Yes. Thank you, Abe. I'm sure that's what I meant to ask for.'

'WIDE-BAND TRANSMISSION COMMENCES. NOW.'

They waited in silence. Boone ceased his muttering. Luc even stopped eating.

After half a minute of absolutely nothing happening, Ariadne asked, 'Um. Is it working?'

'NEGATIVE. ZERO ORGANICALLY-GENERATED SHORT RANGE SUBSPACE WAVES HAVE BEEN RECEIVED.'

Expression blank, Ariadne turned to Abe. 'What does that mean?' she whispered.

'Zythylyx supposedly communicate through subspace wave. Identical to human communication technology, but without technology. Self-generated. Not understood.' Abe called out, 'Ship, continue transmission ping for one hundred seconds. Then switch to next segment.'

'AFFIRMATIVE.'

They waited for an age, it seemed; Neela discovered later that it was only twenty-five minutes before they finally got the response.

'CONTACT CONFIRMED. SUBSPACE WAVE EMANATING FROM SEGMENT SIXTEEN. INBOUND TRANSLATION WILL BEGIN. SENATOR: RESPOND WHEN

READY.'

Neela gulped. *Here goes everything, I suppose.*

The translated voice that came through the loudspeakers a few seconds later was... odd. A sibilant monotone, the cadence hinting at a rhythm or pattern, but not one that she could quite grasp. The jumbled syntax was testament to the ship's warning about the completeness of the translation, or perhaps just the alien otherness of the speaker.

But meaning emerged from the garbled stream. Neela listened, rapt.

'begin vessel ship comes winks jumps unfolds from ether subether subspace bending and folding and unfolding and tearing outside arrives here where here alongside the rolling of the zyth lick six zythylyx and the roiling of the planet home centre why where who are you why come you question end'

Neela saw faces turn to her out of her peripheral vision. She kept her eyes focused on the slowly rotating band on the viewport screen. Her voice was clear, melodious, all nerves smoothed away. 'My name is Neela Kane. I am a Senator with the human Commonwealth. My companions are also human, of other groups—one Titan, one Seryn, one Collective. We come to you peaceably, seeking guidance.'

Seconds passed.

'begin human mammal carbon life short life fragile multitude we have seen we have listened we have heard we have watched spreading out spreading far filling the planets homes centres and the spaces between dying fast breeding faster we do not know of commonwealth titan seryn collective we are zythylyx all are zythylyx we are one and you are many and you are they and now why come you here question end'

'We are searching for a... being. An entity I believe you are familiar with. We know him—it—as Unity. Do you-'

A burst from the speakers cut her off—louder than before, the cadence quicker. On screen, the crystalline band seemed to roll faster against the backdrop of the swirling planet.

'begin unity unity unity is alpha unity is not he is not she is not it unity is all alpha to omega what do you know of unity fragile carbon mammal short life do you know all is lost do you know unity is lost the anchor stone heart lodestone is gone end'

Luc straightened in his seat. 'They know about the lodestone. How? Do they know where it is?'

Neela took a breath. 'We know the lodestone is missing. We came from a world called Promise. We were told Unity would be there, but... There was damage done. Great damage, to the world, and its guardians, I think. The lodestone is gone, and I think we need to find it. To find Unity. How did you know it was missing? Do you know where it is?'

The answer came quickly.

'begin lodestone not present anchor not present centre is adrift the tremors rumbled rolled roiled through ether subether subspace missing gone taken stolen location unknown danger unknown suspects known likely too likely only likely they have power they need power the lodestone is power they came they tore ripped bore drilled fought stole they have the power they need they are coming they will come the end will come the end end'

Ariadne looked pale. 'That really doesn't sound good.' Abe was still. Luc was tense, clenching his fists.

*And now we come to it.* 'Who are they? Who took the lodestone?'

'begin they are bane they are nemesis they are destruction excoriation desolation they are not are no longer dormant imprisoned asleep they are awakening moving coming alive coming they are coming they are the end they are scourge they are scourge they are scourge end'

Silence on the bridge. On the screen, the ring rotated faster, faster, the jagged crystal blades speeding to a blur.

*Scourge.*

\* \* \*

*This just keeps on getting easier, doesn't it?* Luc stood up and paced.

He turned to Boone. 'Is this ringing any bells?' he asked.

The little man's pallor told him the answer.

'Tiny bells, lad. Wee ones. Just a murmur of a hint of a legend—but that legend's the worst nightmare you ever heard of.' He scratched his bearded chin, his hand trembling slightly.

'Boone, tell us what you know.' Neela's controlled voice was a soothing balm to the tension in the room.

The Athravan took a deep breath. 'Not a lot, is what I know. Someone, somewhere found—or will find—an artefact. Tech near as good as ours will be, but ancient, from way back when. Another race that rose high, then fell, without leaving but a few shreds behind. We found another, a record of a war that was barely a war, more like an ambush. Tore through them like paper and kicked over the traces of what was left.'

*That sounds familiar.* Luc remembered the Titan military histories: Howling, Djinn-Ket, Carthis. *We left nothing of them, either.*

Boone continued, 'We treated it as a myth or exaggeration. Prideful last cry of a defeated people. You know, as they do. Asked these boys about it once,'—he gestured to the viewport where the Zythylyx spun, silent for the moment— 'but they wouldn't talk about it. Said they were dead.' He frowned. 'No, not dead—it was… dormant. Same as they just said now.'

Abe spoke up. 'However: no longer dormant. Therein the problem.'

Neela turned back to the viewport. 'Zythylyx, please, tell us. What is the Scourge? What happened?'

The monotonous voice droned from the ship's speakers. 'begin long long ages past epoch aeon eon scourge arose took to the stars arose with fury and anger relentless untiring erased a race one race two race small but sentient one system two system names unknown and lost but next choorinth minor empire nine systems erased the race mere hundreds of days all gone lost and inward they came the scourge the bane they came towards the core and the han the lovely han the friendly han they fell they fought they cried struggled fought died and fell and unity returned and wept and raged and screamed and said enough is enough end'

*Unity returned? Returned from where?*

'What did Unity do?' Neela asked.

'begin unity called came brought us together the old the ancient the eldest the torthkul helped the zythylyx helped the weft helped torthkul baited drew taunted bobbed and weaved we zythylyx sang spun discomfited and drove the weft waited waited waited until at last the time the place the scourge beyond the rim beyond the stars the void the weft the weft they caught bound tied held strong torthkul watched zythylyx watched and unity unity unity bade them sleep they fought they screamed bade them sleep they struggled and tore themselves apart bade them sleep at last at long last at longest last they slept fell dormant fell silent held silent held dormant their prison in the void end'

Silence fell. Luc struggled to imagine the sheer enormity of that conflict: empires falling to dust, an unimaginable threat led on a dance beyond the rim, trapped. *Somehow, trapped—by the Weft, the same creatures we're trying to stop from tearing us to pieces millennia from now.*

Ariadne looked confused. 'As... insane as that all sounds, there's one thing I don't understand. If they were locked up, years and years ago, but years and years from *now* they're still dormant...' She turned to Boone. 'How is this happening? If you lived to tell the tale, doesn't that mean this is just all going to work out anyway?'

Boone shook his head sadly. 'I wouldn't bank on that, lass. Time's a tricky old mistress. You take one road back. There's no guarantee you're going to take the same road forwards back to where you came from.'

Luc threw his hands up in exasperation. 'Then what in Founder's name are we doing? You've got us haring around the galaxy on a quest to save a future that might not even be ours!'

The Athravan looked older, more crumpled, as he shrugged. 'We have to try. That's the point, lad. If we can do what we're trying to do, then that future won't be yours.' He scratched his nose and sighed, then did both again. 'That's the point.'

Neela shook her head. 'I'm not going to stand here and debate the physics of this… madness. I saw Promise. I saw the damage. Whatever can do that, at some fraction of its full strength—we can't rely on fate or destiny or some past future. It's too much of a risk.' She looked around from face to face. 'We have to end this, or there might not be anything left to save.'

One by one, her companions nodded. Boone gently clapped the senator on the shoulder.

She took a deep breath. 'Zythylyx, do you know the location of this… prison, where the Scourge should be?'

'begin we know we saw were there will send have sent your ship vessel craft now knows the coordinates the place the space the prison in the void but question this time no unity no union of race and race and race torthkul gone zythylyx scattered weft hidden to all but you alone will try will go will help fight save all end'

Neela nodded. 'Yes. We will try.'

The crystalline ring slowed a little.

'begin we are grateful fragile carbon mammals perhaps mayhap maybe stronger and not so fragile after all indeed grateful waitful we will wait will hope for the beginning not the end not the end end'

'TRANSMISSION COMPLETE. SUBSPACE WAVE EMISSION ENDED. COORDINATES RECEIVED.'

'How far do we have to go, Mo?' Luc asked.

The ship didn't answer for a few seconds, as if calculating.

'FAR.'

# 16. Prison

*This isn't what I signed up for. I should be back on Nexus Prime, keeping all the plates spinning. Instead I'm on my way to a fight with an enemy no one even understands. And I'm not much of a fighter.* Neela leaned back in the memfoam seat that occupied one corner of her quarters and sighed. It was late, and she was tired. The cabin was dimly lit, and incense burned near the door, but sleep escaped her.

At least her headache was gone, at long last. Earlier that day, she'd finally taken Ariadne's advice and visited the ship's medical bay. Once there, she realised with a rush that she'd been putting it off for all those months for fear of what the problem might turn out to be. *Stupid attitude. Stupid subconscious.*

The ship had welcomed her as warmly as a monotonous disembodied voice could, settled her into an examination chair-cum-scanner, and fired up the machine. Neela had barely had time to start to get nervous when the ship said, 'I HAVE

IDENTIFIED THE PROBLEM, SENATOR.'

Neela's heart began to race. 'Oh. That was fast.'

'YES. YOU HAVE A SMALL CLAVICULAR BONE SPUR PRESSING AGAINST THE INFERIOR TRUNK OF YOUR BRACHIAL PLEXUS. THE PRESSURE IS MANIFESTING AS REGULAR HEAD PAIN.'

She'd taken a few seconds to decode that. 'So—there's a lump on my collarbone poking into a nerve? That's it?'

'AFFIRMATIVE. I CAN REMOVE THE BONE SPUR WITH A MICROPOINT LASER UNDER A REGIONAL NERVE BLOCK ANAESTHETIC. THE PROCEDURE WILL TAKE TWELVE MINUTES. FEELING WILL RETURN FORTY TO FORTY-FOUR MINUTES LATER. PROCEED?'

Neela had been a little stunned by the swiftness of the evaluation, but she decided to ride the wave of her courage before it ran out. 'Yes. Yes, please.'

'EXCELLENT. I RARELY HAVE THE OPPORTUNITY TO PERFORM SURGERY. PLEASE REMOVE YOUR SHIRT.'

*Not exactly what you want to hear from your doctor, but the ship certainly knew what it was doing.* Neela had returned to her quarters twenty minutes later.

A short nap after that, and she had been able to concentrate on worrying about the main problem—their mad charge into the unknown. *To save everything in the galaxy. A few days ago, it was just the future of humanity.*

Now, if she could just fall back asleep.

A quiet chime announced a visitor. *Who would come at this hour?*

'Open!'

The doorfield slid back to show Luc at her doorstep. The Titan wore a clean white tee shirt, along with his customary dust-coloured trousers. He looked neater than Neela had ever seen him, which wasn't really saying much. *Does the ship do tailoring now, as well?*

Luc waved. 'Am I bothering you? I know it's late, but... Well, you said you hadn't been sleeping too well. Nor am I, so I thought we could, you know. Not sleep, together.' His eyes widened a little when he realised what he'd said. He opened his mouth to try again, then gave up.

Neela stifled a laugh. *I do believe the boy is actually blushing.* She gestured him in. 'You're not bothering me at all, no. You'll have to take the bed—I've not got around to asking the ship for another seat.'

'Bed's fine.' Luc entered and sat. He clasped his hands in his lap, studying them for a few seconds, then looked up at Neela, his brow furrowed. 'It's worrying, isn't it?'

'Which one of the worrying things, exactly?'

'Where we're going. What we're going to find when we get there. What we're supposed to do. I've never been afraid of a fight in my life, and... I don't think I am now. But it's the uncertainty I don't like. No one can tell us anything about these Scourge, so how am I supposed to know how to fight them?'

He was repeatedly flexing his fingers, then clenching his fists—unconsciously, Neela thought.

'I know. I don't like it either. And part of that's because I don't even know if I'm going to be able to help at all. Abe's a walking box of tricks, Ri is frankly terrifying when she's not being the sweetest girl in the world, and you're—well, you.'

Luc smiled wryly. 'And what's that?'

Neela stood up and wandered over to one of the small bedside tables. She upended two glasses, poured measures of a scotch-like liquor she'd snagged from Boone, and pondered what to say. *The truth's always best.*

She turned and handed Luc one of the tumblers. She met his gaze, those unnerving golden eyes, and sensed that what she was about to say was important. 'You're a weapon. You've been trained and honed and shaped into a killer. A predator.'

Luc's eyes had gone cold and hard, his expression set.

Neela carried on. 'But somehow, despite being raised to be a xenophobe, to go wherever and kill whatever you're told, you've retained some compassion. Even for people who you were taught to instinctively hate. That kind of upbringing is hard to grow past. And here you are, risking your life to save everyone — all people. I know you say you feel like you don't have a choice, but you do. You did. You could have just washed your hands of this at any point and left.'

His expression had softened again. 'We all could have. But it feels like something worth doing, doesn't it?'

Neela nodded slowly and raised her glass. 'Here's to doing things worth doing. *Salut.*'

'Cheers.'

Their glasses clinked.

Neela took a sip of her drink, bracing then relaxing as the alcohol warmed her throat. Luc's gaze was still on hers, his expression intent.

She found her hand on the line of his jaw, her thumb brushing over the coarse stubble and grazing his lips. His hand settled lightly on her hip as she leaned in.

The kiss was soft, delicate, passionate. *Oh. He's gentler than I thought he'd be.*

She pulled back slightly and opened her eyes to see his glimmering in the dim light. 'Hmmm. You're going to have to start shaving every day. Is that all right?'

His lip curled, cocky again. 'It feels like something worth doing.'

\* \* \*

Ariadne sat alone on the bridge. Six days and eleven jumps had taken *Mournstar* from the Zythylyx gas giant home to the furthest reaches of the galaxy, the outer edge of the band of thinly scattered stars that humanity called the Rim. With every jump, every emergence back into realspace, the starfield visible from the bridge had been more sparse as they approached the Void, the unimaginably wide and utterly empty sea that separated their galaxy from the rest.

*I wonder if those galaxies have the same problems ours does.*

It was early in the morning — in the ship's chronology, at least. They had completed their final jump late the previous night, and Boone had suggested they all get some rest before proceeding the next day. *Proceeding with… what, exactly?* Ariadne wasn't clear on that.

Sleep had eluded her—after five hours of fitful tossing and turning, she had given up and wandered the ship, ending up on the bridge, staring out at the utter blackness. The ship had supplied a stimulant that had given her an artificial alertness she was sure wasn't healthy, and the freshly brewed coffee she had ordered was taking care of the rest.

She felt the approaching consciousness before the doorfield opened. She didn't bother turning to look. 'Hi, Neela.'

Silence followed for a few seconds, then footsteps entering the room. 'You know it's quite unnerving when you do that, don't you?' Neela took a seat next to Ariadne, who turned to her.

'I do. But it is fun.'

Neela shook her head wearily. 'You'd get on very well with an old friend of mine. He has a similar sense of fun.'

Ariadne sipped her coffee. 'How come you're up so early?'

'Oh, it's not that early. I never need much sleep. Or rather I've got used to never getting it. The effect's the same. You?'

'No, I love my sleep. It just wasn't happening. It all feels a bit too… close, you know? The end, or whatever's going to happen.'

'I know what you mean.'

They stared out at the darkness in silence for a minute. Ariadne let her mind wander, the warmth of the coffee relaxing her as the caffeine perked her up. She let her senses drift and idly bounce off the senator's mind. They hit something interesting.

*Oh. Really?* She took another sip. *Well, that's that, then. Might as well have some fun with it.*

'So, is Luc an early riser, as well?' She glanced sideways to catch the expression on Neela's face and stifled a laugh at the wide-eyed shock.

'How on earth did-' A blush crept over Neela's light brown cheeks. She managed to look sheepish and annoyed at the same time.

Ariadne shrugged lightly. 'I didn't. Until just then.' She

grinned cheekily at the senator, who groaned. 'Oh, what are you worried about? No need to keep secrets. We're all friends here. Although I do hope our boy never has to choose between saving you or me from some ancient space monster.'

'Hmm. Somehow I think you'll be able to handle yourself.' Neela headed to the long table where the coffee pot sat and poured herself a cup. 'You want some more?'

'No, thanks. I'd be bouncing off the walls.'

Neela walked back to her seat. '*Mournstar*, when will we be able to see… whatever we'll see? Is it near? Or do we still have a way to go?'

The ship was awake as always. 'NEAR, SENATOR. THOUGH STILL SOME DISTANCE. VISIBILITY IN THE HUMAN VISIBLE SPECTRUM WILL BE MINIMAL, HOWEVER. ALMOST ZERO STARLIGHT.'

Ariadne and Neela shared a look. Ariadne asked the obvious question. 'So how are we going to know where they are?'

'THE PRISON IS CLEARLY VISIBLE AT THE SUBSPACE LEVEL. ITS PRESENCE IN THE LOCAL ENERGY GRID IS DRAMATIC.' The ship paused for a second, and the viewport changed. 'SEE.'

On the screen, a blazing net of energy, cross-hatched and rolling in dips and curves, stretched away from them. Some distance away from *Mournstar*—immeasurable by the naked eye—was a concentration of dazzling brightness, an energy nexus that swirled and spun like a whirlpool of power in the grid. Ariadne and Neela could only stare.

The ship continued, 'THE NEXUS IS WEAKENING. BY AN INFINITESIMAL, BUT MEASURABLE FRACTION EACH SECOND, IT WEAKENS.'

Ariadne swallowed, her mouth suddenly dry. 'They're breaking free, aren't they?' She felt a hand take hers as Neela reached over to grasp it.

In silence, they stared out at the whirling nexus, the cell keeping destruction from the entire galaxy.

And the cell was crumbling.

\* \* \*

An hour or so later, Luc watched the nexus grow larger in the viewport as *Mournstar* approached. He understood, abstractly, what it was, but...

'Ship, I'll be honest. I have no idea what I'm looking at. It's a big light. That's all I'm seeing.'

Neela stood by his side. 'Really? It's just a theoretically impossible binding of the local energy grid into a subspace prison as strong as a black hole. What's so unusual about that?'

'Mmm-hmm. And I'm sure you knew that an hour ago.'

'WE WILL SHORTLY REACH THE TWENTY LIGHT MINUTE THRESHOLD AT WHICH MY LONG RANGE SENSORS ENGAGE. AT THAT POINT I CAN CONVERT THE SENSOR READINGS INTO AN ENHANCEABLE HUMAN-VISIBLE IMAGE.'

Luc thought for a second. 'So we can actually see what we're looking at?'

'AFFIRMATIVE.'

'Thank Founder for that.' *I can't work out how to fight what I can't see.* Though he had no idea if they'd be able to fight at all. *One ship? Against... what? Completely unknown odds.*

They waited silently for a few more minutes. Abe stood motionless to one side of the viewport. Ariadne sat in one of the seats, feet curled under her, wearing a woollen jumper with sleeves that were far too long. She looked very young.

'SENSOR RANGE ACHIEVED. SWITCHING TO SIMULATED VISUAL.'

The viewport changed, showing grey shapes on a black background, indecipherable at first. A triangle, point downwards, with a few much smaller shapes separate above the top edges. The view zoomed in. The triangle filled the bottom half of the screen. It was not solid—dots of black showed through. Some of the smaller shapes were in motion, it seemed. One, fifty times the size of the rest, sat motionless directly above the triangle.

Luc frowned. 'Ship, enhance the large shape at the top of the screen.'

Instantly the view zoomed in. Neela gasped.

It was a ship, alien but completely clear. A half globe extended into six prongs, a circle of lighter grey at the centre of the flat interior side. One of the smaller shapes sailed into view along the bottom edge of the screen, a miniature version of the larger vessel.

Luc realised what the triangle was with a start. 'Ship, focus on a section of the triangle. Same level of enhancement.'

'NOT A TRIANGLE. INVERTED HOLLOW CONE.'

'Fine. Just do it.'

The screen filled with grey, just a few black dots showing gaps between the... *Ships. They're all ships.* 'Founder save us,' he whispered.

'That's... There are so many. How—*Mournstar*, how many?' Neela asked.

The ship gave the answer with clinical dispassion. 'ONE LARGE VESSEL IS FREE. ELEVEN REMAIN IN STASIS. EIGHT SMALLER VESSELS ARE FREE. FOUR HUNDRED SIXTY-ONE REMAIN IN STASIS.'

Silence.

Ariadne spoke up, her voice quiet. 'How big are the small ones, Ship?'

'EACH SMALL VESSEL IS ROUGHLY THREE TIMES MY SIZE.'

As they watched, another small shape broke free from the pack and drifted upward to circle around the capital ship above. *Nine free, each three times as big as we are. And one the size of a small moon.*

Luc shook his head. 'We're going to need help.'

\* \* \*

While *Mournstar* manoeuvred itself a little further away from the Scourge prison, Abe and the others sat around the bridge's long meeting-cum-dining table. Boone sat at the head, gazing at nothing, stroking his straggly beard. Ariadne sat at his left, curled up again into her oversize woollen jumper, Neela on her left. The senator had retrieved a scratchpad from somewhere and was making notes. Opposite her, Luc watched, trying to read upside-down.

On his right, Abe sat in motionless silence.

*Situation dire. Seemingly impossible odds. Doom for the galaxy, end of humanity.* His eyes tracked Neela's stylus as it skittered back and forth across the device. *Exciting times.*

The senator sighed and stopped writing. The stylus dropped to the table.

'It's not big enough, is it?' Luc asked.

Neela shook her head. 'No. Even if it was feasible to shift the entire Star Corps fleet here and leave every planet and colony undefended, by the time they got here, they'd still be outnumbered.' She looked at Luc intently. 'We need Titan assistance.'

Luc looked down at his clasped hands and snorted once. 'Given that I have no idea what's happened since I left, that could be an interesting conversation. "Hi, this is Luc Corralin. Can I speak to Jarrod? Oh, you executed him for treason. I see."'

Neela reached over and placed her hand on his. 'We have to try. We can't do this alone.'

The Titan nodded. 'I know. Though if Jarrod has managed to stick it out this long, I'm pretty confident that help will arrive. We do love a fight, after all.'

Abe had listened in silence. He knew exactly how well the Titans enjoyed violence. *Typically against us.* He had also processed the numbers and come to a realisation. 'Still not enough.'

All faces turned to him.

'What do you mean, Abe?' Ariadne asked.

'Likely only one major Star Corps fleet group assembled in this quadrant. Six capital ships, forty-two smaller craft, plus support vessels. Optimistic addition of fifty per cent of Titan fleet: nine supercruisers, twenty cruisers, thirty-nine destroyers. Estimated arrival time three to seven days.' He paused and looked at the slightly stunned faces of his companions. 'Factored against current rate of Scourge release and conservative estimate of technological superiority, combined force would be overpowered.'

Luc continued to stare at the Collective for a few more seconds. 'That is... an extremely accurate judgement of Titan military strength. How?'

Abe stared straight back. *How not?* 'Know your enemy.'

Neela leaned back in her seat. She looked at Abe questioningly. 'Can you speak for your people? Would they countenance fighting alongside...' —she nodded towards the Titan—'his?'

He thought for a few seconds. *Scale of threat, likely outcome of non-involvement —probable. However: Analysis necessary.* He nodded once. 'Affirmative. But judgement will be required.'

Luc frowned. 'Judgement of what? How much we're all going to not be alive if you don't get involved?'

'Negative. Judgement of you.' He pointed at the Titan for emphasis. 'Your honesty. Whether you have the power to end the war. Our war.' *So unnecessary. Pointless-tragic-interminable.* 'We are tired of this conflict, Titan. Very tired. We did not seek it.'

Abe was slightly surprised to see a blush creep over Luc's cheeks as he dropped his eyes. *He is ashamed. Analysis: Promising. Shame will be necessary.*

'If I ever get back to Mission, there will be a reckoning, Collective.' Luc looked up and met Abe's gaze once more, golden eyes blazing. 'And many things will change. That I promise you.'

'Not me who will need convincing.' Abe turned to Neela. 'Will make contact. Collective Cloud nearby. Judgement will take place there.'

The senator nodded. 'Okay. And if it goes well, and they agree? What kind of force can they bring?'

Abe ran the calculations. 'Most vessels small, lightweight. Fighters. Shuttle-sized. Only three capital ships.'

'And how many fighters?'

'Two thousand ninety.'

*Expressions indicate surprise.* Abe looked at the Titan. The question was clear on Luc's face.

'Because we have no desire to eradicate your kind, Titan. As I said, we did not seek this war.'

Neela glanced between the two men, then turned to Ariadne.

The Seryn looked a little baffled. 'Before you ask, Neela, I have no idea about any of this, but I'm pretty sure we don't have any ships. We normally just take passenger liners. Don't think one of those would be much help.'

The senator chuckled. 'No, probably not. But I'm sure some of your, uh, associates could get a ride from a Commonwealth ship. We'd be more than happy to, if you think they could help.'

Ariadne nodded. 'I'll ask. I don't know, but I'll ask.'

'Thank you.'

*And so it is decided.*

Out of the blue, Boone chirped from the end of the table, 'We all sorted, then? Marvellous.'

# 17. Allies

'How long do you think it'll take to set up the link, Mo?' Luc was in his quarters, sitting at the corner desk he'd never before used, in front of the hardlight screen projector that would—theoretically—connect him via video link to the Titan homeworld. *And whoever monitors the military emergency channel these days.*

'UNCERTAIN. SEVERAL MINUTES FOR SUBSPACE WAVE LOCK WITH MISSION TRANSCEIVER. UNKNOWN TIME TO NEGOTIATE TITAN ENCRYPTION PROTOCOL. HOW COME YOU DO NOT YOURSELF KNOW, TITAN?'

'I've never used it before.'

While Luc waited in silence—expecting a few beeps or clicks from the machine in front of him to show the ship was doing something, if he were honest—his mind wandered as it often did lately to his new relationship with Neela. It was unlike any he'd had before. Visiting the Academy concubines and fooling around with the other neophytes had been the limit of his experience, and those encounters had been purely sexual.

He'd quickly realised that he'd come to care about Neela. *A lot. More than I'd like to, in this situation.* He might never have been in love before, but he was damn sure taking your lover into a war zone was a particularly shitty idea. *Though there are worse problems to have, I suppose.*

'TRANSMISSION HANDSHAKE COMPLETED. VIDEO LINK ESTABLISHED. READY WHEN YOU ARE.'

*Problems like not knowing who's going to be on the other end of this call.* 'Connect.'

The hardlight screen blossomed into life, showing a fresh-faced young cohort ensign not much older than Luc. 'Identify yourself, Titan.' Young he might have looked, but he had the tone down perfectly.

Luc sat up straight. 'Lucius Corralin Ben Quinto Ben Greve. Academy neophyte, graduating class of this year.'

The ensign's eyes widened ever so slightly, the only outward indication of his surprise. 'Hold, Titan.' He sounded less assured, that time, and the ensign hurried out of his seat and left the comm area.

*Exit screen left. And now we find out where I stand.*

Luc waited for a minute or more, staring at the blank wall on screen. He wondered which military installation monitored these types of communications. *Probably not Rift. One of the moons, maybe. Zenymede?* After another few seconds, Luc tensed, breath held, as someone entered the screen and took the comm seat.

Then Luc relaxed with a smile. 'Hello, Jarrod.'

'Hello, my boy. It's been a while.' The Consul grinned, a far more relaxed figure than when Luc had last seen him on the Bridge of Tears all those weeks ago.

'It has. I take it things haven't gone too badly in my absence? I had no idea who I was going to get when I made contact.'

'Not too badly. There's been a bit of a clear-out since you left.'

'Cleaning the stables, eh? Fourier?'

Luc was pleased to see his uncle's brow shoot up at that. 'I'd be very interested to know how in Founder's name you knew that—I only found out last week.'

'I had a visitor, would you believe. And you're not going to guess whom: Caleb Hesch.'

Jarrod's expression darkened. He cursed. 'What happened? How did that bastard find you?'

'He was sent to kill me by our dear departed Councillor. Tracked us halfway across the galaxy and back all the way from Mission, only to tell me he wasn't going to. And that he was sorry. About my father. I let him go—though, to be honest, it wouldn't have been a sure thing in my favour.'

The Consul looked doubtful. 'No—no, it wouldn't. He was one of our toughest. But his being free is a hard thing to swallow. Whatever remorse he might now have, he was locked up for a reason. I've got a feeling he might come back to bite us in the arse down the line.'

Luc nodded. 'Same. But we've got bigger problems to worry about, right now.'

'Oh? I was wondering why you called. I was just starting to put together a search party to try and bring you home.'

Slipping easily into debrief mode, Luc outlined everything that had happened since his departure—the meeting on Fusion, his unlikely comrades, the outlandish tale they'd been told on Equinox. Promise, the Zythylyx, and finally, the Void.

Jarrod's expression remained stoic and intent throughout, with just a brief shake of the head at the close of Luc's wild tale. 'That has to be the most insane spiel I've ever been fed.'

'Join the club. If I weren't the one telling it, I wouldn't believe it myself.'

Jarrod sat in silence for half a minute. 'I can spare about a third of the fleet, no more. The rest is tied up in operations.'

'And if you pull back everything that's hunting the Collective?'

His uncle's expression darkened. 'That's not going to go

down well, Lucius. You know that.'

'Obviously. But given the alternative?'

Jarrod paused, then nodded. He began tapping into a terminal off-screen, his gaze flicking back and forth. 'Adding the recalled ships would make it three-fifths of our total force, the biggest combined fleet put in the field since the last battle with the Undying.' Luc repressed a shudder at that accursed name. 'It'll take three days to crew, fuel, supply, and assemble, then three days to jump. Will the situation hold?'

Luc snorted. 'It'll have to, won't it?'

'As always.' He pressed his right fist to his heart. 'Founder with you, Lucius.'

'And with you.'

'See you in six days.' Jarrod reached forwards, and the screen vanished. Luc sat looking at the space it had occupied.

*It'll have to.*

⋆ ⋆ ⋆

There was no subspace channel for Ariadne to connect to. It was one of the drawbacks of living in secret on a backwater farming world. All she had at her disposal was a pale yellow crystal with which she could—supposedly—contact Margo on Corinth, across all light years between them.

*Seems a bit far-fetched.* She sat on the bed in her quarters, the knapsack she had pulled the stone from moments earlier at her side. The stone itself was heavier than she remembered and felt ever-so-slightly warm to the touch. Ariadne looked down at it, cupped in her palm.

*'Focus your mind on the stone, and it'll find its mate.' Sure. Okay. So… think really hard about the stone. It's yellow and… stony. Um.*

Sighing, she closed her eyes. Breathing slowly and deeply, she let her mind empty as she'd practised so many times. When her mind was clear, she concentrated on the feeling of the crystal in her hand, visualised it, every rounded facet and small bump. The weight, the warmth. She had it, held it.

Gradually she became aware of a… hum, a drone of some kind. A faint vibration—not from the physical stone in her hand, but the visualisation she held of it in her mind. The hum slowly grew in strength and pitch, now akin to the sound of a bee drifting lazily on the other side of a small, quiet garden.

After a few more seconds, the hum was abruptly cut off, and a beautiful chime rang out in Ariadne's mind—then faded to a quiet background noise. She waited, relaxed.

*'Hello, dearie. I was wondering when you might call.'*

*This is* very *cool.* There was no need to speak. Ariadne simply thought the words. *'Hi, Margo! How are you? To be honest, I can't quite believe this worked.'*

Margo scoffed in amusement. *'Oh, young people these days. No faith in the wisdom of their elders. Well, maybe not just these days. Is everything okay? You've been gone a while—I was half expecting you back by now.'*

*'I'm fine. But everything's not okay. We're actually in a bit of trouble. A lot of trouble. Everyone.'* She spent the next five minutes describing the situation, starting at the end, jumping to the beginning, and filling in the middle as she went along. Margo listened patiently.

When Ariadne finished, Margo let out the harrumphing sigh that came out whenever one of the goats had got loose in the vegetable garden. *'That's quite a story you've got there, dear. I honestly can't recall one as wild, and I've heard a few.'*

She clicked her tongue a few times slowly, as she did whenever she was thinking something over. After a while, she continued. *'I'll have to talk to the Agency, but I'm sure we can help in some way. There are a few agents in the vicinity that I can think of who can probably drop what they're doing for a while. Maybe twenty or so. From what you say, I don't know how much help that help will be, though.'*

*'Nor do I, Margo. I wish I did. It feels like we have to try, though; that a small thing could end up making all the difference.'*

*'Then I'll get you that small thing, and we'll hope it does help. I'll be in touch, dear. Keep your stone handy.'*

*'Always.'*

*'And do be careful, Ri. I worry about you all the way out there. I*

*wanted you to have a couple more years at home before we sent you off into the beyond—and even then, I never envisioned anything like this.'*

'I'll be careful, Margo. And I have friends to look out for me as well.' An odd bunch of them, she didn't say. *But good ones.*

'Goodbye, dear.'

'Bye.' The mental chime faded out, and she felt the crystal cool in her hand. *That went quite well.* Hopping up from the bed, Ariadne went to tell the others.

\* \* \*

'*Mournstar*, can you bring up the link on the main viewport when it connects?' Neela stood on the bridge.

'AFFIRMATIVE. CONNECTION IN FIVE SECONDS.'

Clasping her hands behind her back, she stretched. Her shoulders popped in complaint, and there was an unwelcome stiffness in her back. *Not doing enough yoga the last few days. Somehow, I can't quite find the time.* She shook her arms loose just as the view changed to a fifteen foot–wide shot of a brilliant-white background and the smiling face of Speaker Darius Okafor.

His famous voice boomed out a second later. 'Neela! Wonderful to hear from you. You're looking very well, I must say.'

She smiled. 'You too, Darius. Not spending too much time in that box of yours, I hope.'

Okafor gave a throaty chuckle. 'Oh, no more than usual. Though where in the heavens are you—the computer's having fits trying to work out where you're calling from.'

'Hmm, that's part of quite a long story. Have you got ten minutes?'

'For anyone else, no. For you, take twenty.'

It only took eight, as it turned out. Neela watched the Speaker's expression harden and darken as she laid out what was happening. A few times he shook his head in simple disbelief. But he did let her finish.

'Neela, that is the most unbelievable— Do you really believe this? Can it possibly be true?'

'I do. Only because of what I've seen myself, though. Unfortunately, I can't give you that same benefit—you're just going to have to trust me, I'm afraid.'

Okafor's normally controlled tone was gone—he sounded as exasperated as Neela had ever heard him. 'Trust you, sure—but with the entire Fifth Fleet Group? The Marauders will have a field day if the Corps completely deserts that quadrant to sally off into the void chasing a legend.'

'Not a legend, Darius. I'm sending the images now. *Mournstar?*'

'SENT.'

'Thank you. They're real, Darius. And an alien race that I believe have been around *far* longer than we have is completely terrified of what they can do. Will do, if they're not stopped.'

The Speaker was frowning. He looked down at something off-screen, no doubt viewing the images. Darius was silent for half a minute. Finally he looked up and nodded, just once. 'I'll authorise it. Admiral Graff will have a fit when he hears about this, but he'll be there in four days. There's a Peacetrooper strike team on manoeuvres at Jericho—you can have them, too. Transmit the coordinates on the normal channel.'

Neela nodded. 'Of course. Thank you.'

Okafor shook his head again and sighed, some of his natural good humour returning. 'Really, Neela. This vacation is turning out to be very inconvenient. I'm not sure I'll ever let you take another.'

She smiled wryly. 'Darius, if we make it through this, I'm not sure I'll ever want one. Coordinates will follow, Kane out.'

'Out.' The link flicked out, and the viewport returned to the blackness of the void, that small grey shape in the middle so non-threatening when viewed from a distance. Neela shivered a little and thought about the men and women on their way to this quiet volume of space, to turn it into a chaotic maelstrom of fire and blood, bravery and death.

*Elu fend—* She stopped.

*Oh. I need to stop saying that.*

\* \* \*

Abe prepared to connect to Network for the first time since leaving the Alpha-83 arcology with some trepidation. The quiet and solitude he had come to take for granted since his departure was about to be shattered, but there was no avoiding it. *Assistance required-mandated-unavoidable. Continued existence at stake.* Sitting cross-legged on the floor of his quarters, he hoped the rest of Collective would appreciate how unavoidable it was, even with the… unpleasant alliance involved.

Eyes closed, he took a deep breath. And connected.

The torrent of chatter poured forth into his preconscious, almost overwhelming him with the sheer volume of unfiltered information. *Aaaaiee*

Abe quickly concentrated on building the familiar wall around his conscious mind, protecting his identity from being subsumed amongst the noise from other minds.

Gradually the wall came together, the din quietened, and he regained control. Abe released a breath he hadn't realised he'd been holding. *Close to disaster. Insufficient care taken. Must be more careful next time.*

He began to prepare the upload package, visualising a plain white box, open at the top. On each side, he applied a black label: 'PRIORITY: HIGHEST'. Next he added the data: the sensory record of every second since he had left the arcology; analyses he had performed gauging the intentions, abilities, and likely behaviours of his colleagues; estimates of the strength of their opponents; battle projections at varying levels of Collective, Commonwealth, Seryn, and Titan involvement. He added no attempt at persuasion. *Judgement will come based on data alone. As it always has.*

After several minutes of work, the upload package was ready. He mentally closed the lid, sealing the package, paused for one more second, then fired it into Network.

The previously diverse spread of interest and attention across the galaxy-wide quickly homogenised, focus shifting in mere seconds to the package. Abe monitored the change with interest, largely unsurprised. The incidences of HIGHEST uploads being publicly broadcast across Network were so few and far between as to be almost unheard of. Factor in the unfamiliarity of Abe's signature to most, given his recent absence and sporadic past attendance, and the interest was easy to understand.

Eight minutes later—roughly the time required to process the data in the package—the topic began to spread like a wildfire. Impromptu committees sprung up, argued, debated, submitted a judgement, and collapsed all within seconds. Existing well-established bodies of discourse abruptly dropped topics that had been under discussion for days to focus on Abe's submission. The general background chatter swelled and kept swelling.

Five more minutes passed before a pattern began to emerge, a mantra sounding off across the network.

*Judgement...*

*Beta-9...*

*Titan...*

Abe allowed himself a small smile at the fulfilment of his prediction and awaited the contact from the Beta-9 Cloud, the nearest Collective population centre, only one short jump away. He didn't have long to wait.

'A83-7F44, this is Beta-9 Cloudmother.' That was unexpected; he hadn't thought the call would come from Cloudmother herself. *'PRIORITY: HIGHEST upload package has been received and reviewed. Initial consensus has been reached. A83-7F44 and current associates will rendezvous with Beta-9 Cloud, dock with primary arcology, and submit themselves for analysis and judgement of situation and of assistance request. Vessel must broadcast and self-identity with upcoming transceiver token. Failure to do so will result in immediate engagement and destruction by Cloud security grid. Token sent. Confirm briefing is understood.'*

'Confirmed.'

*'Briefing is confirmed. Beta-9 awaits your arrival, Collective.'* A slight pause. *'Chance on your side.'*

Abe's brow raised in surprise. *Unexpected support. Positive sign.* The link was disconnected. Keeping his connection to Network open, Abe stood and stretched the stiffness from his legs, then headed to the bridge. As he exited his quarters, it occurred to him that his companions would be the first non-Collective to ever visit a Cloud. In a peaceful capacity, at least.

*Wonder if honour will be appreciated. Likely negative. More pressing concerns to consider, after all.*

\* \* \*

*Not quite how I imagined meeting the Collective for the first time.* Luc gazed out of the viewport as the *Mournstar* edged further and deeper into the heart of the Beta-9 Cloud. *That would have been with two cruisers and eight destroyers emerging from a short-range jump directly into the cloud. Target primary lasfire on the largest station. Deploy one- and two-man fighters. Target smaller vessels. Thirty seconds later, a second force emerges from jump at the opposite edge of the Cloud, directly behind enemy's current focus. Wreak havoc. Raze. Burn.*

Instead of destroying them, he just watched, with growing appreciation.

On one side, an asteroid field was being mined. Tiny craft, maybe soloships, worked together to plant depth charges along the faultlines of the larger rocks, retreating to blast the rocks into more manageable sizes. Ships with giant pincer arms twice their length delicately manoeuvred these smaller rocks towards the maws at one end of giant octopus-like crushers that split into seven or eight long pipes at the other, presumably separating different materials to be carried elsewhere. Just below and to the *Mournstar's* left, a long, wide, and incredibly thin device — *Solar array, maybe?* — was under construction. Tiny shapes moved around it — Collective in vacuum suits and helper robots of various shapes and sizes.

And ahead of them, the station Abe called an arcology. It was immense, several hundred times the *Mournstar's* size, and roughly cone-shaped, with the broader end facing away from their approach towards the nearby star. As they neared, Luc could just make out what looked like an entrance on one of the facing surfaces. He pointed it out to Abe, who had just finished talking quietly to the ship.

'Affirmative. Primary landing bay, suitable for large craft such as *Mournstar*.'

Luc was a little ashamed of his nervousness as they sailed into the bay. *Into the mouth of the enemy. Except they're not the enemy. Or they won't be.*

The bay was large, easily capable of holding five ships of their size. Slate-grey, utterly smooth walls were broken by striplights that ran from the entrance to the back wall, ending in rings around portals—access into the rest of the arcology, Luc assumed.

With a gentle bump, *Mournstar* touched down. *We're in.*

The ship boomed out an announcement: 'BAY ENTRANCE FIELD RAISED. BAY ATMOSPHERE RESTORED. YOU MAY EXIT FROM MY REAR AT YOUR CONVENIENCE.'

*How polite.* 'Thanks, Mo.' Luc turned to Abe, who looked... *pleased, I think. Though it's almost impossible to tell.* 'Now what?'

'We visit Cloudmother.'

Five minutes later, Luc, Neela, Ariadne, and Abe—Boone had elected to stay on ship—were walking along the fifth identical corridor they had passed down.

Luc was still trying to find out exactly what Cloudmother was. 'Is she the ruler? You know, the primary decision maker. Boss, chief. Whatever.'

Abe shook his head. 'Negative. Decisions are made by consensus. For local matters, Cloud votes. On Collective-wide issues, whole Collective votes. Cloudmother is not ruler in any sense. She is arbitrator-matriarch-eldest of this Cloud, focal point of decision making and final word in all disputes or unresolved debates.'

'She sounds like a magistrate,' Neela said.

Abe's eyes briefly glazed over, then he nodded. 'Correct, Senator. Valid comparison to your Commonwealth judiciary.

Though Collective have no equivalent selection process—Cloudmother is simply eldest.'

They neared the end of the long corridor. Ahead of them, a broad circular doorfield glimmered emerald. Luc swallowed, his mouth suddenly dry. *I think we've arrived.*

Ariadne asked, 'If she's eldest, how old is she, Abe? Do you know?'

'Beta-9 Cloudmother is relatively young.' Abe stepped up to a panel to one side of the doorfield as they reached it and briefly jacked in. The doorfield flickered out as he turned to Ariadne. 'Only four hundred and ninety years old.'

Luc stared through the portal into the shadows. *Founder protect us. Who are these people?*

They stepped into Cloudmother's dimly lit chamber, Luc with no idea what to expect. *Will she look like Abe? Or more human, perhaps sitting behind a desk doing paperwork? Or less?* He eagerly scanned the room, but there seemed to be no one present.

As he opened his mouth to comment, a ring of lights came to life, spaced around the edge of the circular chamber's floor—strong beams that angled upward at the centre of the cavernous space. They illuminated a figure that could only be the Beta-9 Cloudmother.

She was suspended in the air. Glistening black cables linked her arms, legs, spine, and genitals with some junction hidden in the darkness above, a stark contrast against the utterly white paleness of her hairless skin. Her body was still slim, supple, and firm despite her extremely advanced age. Luc found himself fascinated, repulsed, and even a little aroused. *Won't be sharing that with Neela, I think.*

As his gaze reached Cloudmother's face, her eyelids flicked open on eyes that were completely black. Their gaze met, and Luc felt the strength of her regard like a physical force. It pressed against him for seconds, until he felt sure he would fall back a step—then she blinked, and the test was over.

A spherical robot perhaps half a yard wide drifted silently

down from the hidden heights of the chamber's ceiling. An orange-ringed circle on one flattened side faced them—maybe eye, maybe mouth, or both. It floated towards the arrivals, pausing briefly in front of Ariadne and then Neela, lingering more near Abe, who gave the machine a respectful nod. Finally, it approached Luc and stopped in front of him.

He didn't have to wait long.

'Speaking: Cloudmother of Beta-9, this Cloud.' The voice that emanated from the robot—*Not mouth or eye, then, just a speaker*—was soft, unaccented Standard. Utterly normal, which to Luc was somehow more strange than anything he had imagined. 'It is unlooked-for, surprise, wonder-terror-sacrilege to see-feel a Titan here in heart of Cloud.'

Abe replied, 'Circumstances are well beyond normal parameters, Cloudmother.'

The robot briefly drifted and turned in Abe's direction, then came back to Luc. 'Indeed, 7F44. Collective accepts data and actions in procuration-distribution. With gratitude duly expressed, Titan will henceforth speak for himself.'

Luc fought back a smile. *Poor old Abe. Got smacked down a little bit there.*

After a few seconds, he realised that he was expected to speak, and he decided on a generic platitude. 'I thank you for inviting us into your Cloud, Cloudmother. It is an honour.'

The robot rolled a little from side to side. 'Truly? Never have I experienced Titan gratitude or honour for Collective. Is it true? Or do you disseminate?'

Luc felt his cheeks warm. 'Truth, Cloudmother.' He paused, searching for the right words. 'I am well aware of the nature of our peoples' encounters across the centuries. Not too long ago, I thought nothing of it. Thought it was good, and just, and right. And I eagerly looked forward to taking part in the same.' He glanced at Abe, who was watching him, still and quiet, then turned back to Cloudmother's robot. 'I would not take that part now.'

'Quite a claim to make, Titan. Yet your

tone-manner-demeanour rings of truth, and a Collective as companion-comrade-associate speaks in your favour.'

Luc let out a relieved breath. *Perhaps this is going to work, after all.*

'However, all this is moot.'

*Or maybe it won't.* 'Moot how? Please, Cloudmother,' he quickly remembered to end with.

The robot began slowly orbiting Luc's head. He resisted the urge to follow it and fixed his gaze on Cloudmother's hanging form. 'Moot because: You are one Titan. One of many. I see-hear-detect no Titan force with you carrying a declaration of peace. No representative from your Council of liars or your cohort of murderers has made contact with such proclamation. You are one Titan. One of many. Were we to assist in this battle as proposed, and emerge victorious, we would surely be betrayed at its end.'

Luc's hope had crumbled quickly as she spoke. *This isn't working.* 'I would not allow that to happen, Cloudmother.'

'And what weight is attached to your word, Titan? You are one Titan. One of many.'

He realised there was only one gambit to be played. It might achieve their goal, it might fall flat, or it might get him killed. *Oh well. Go big or go home, as they say.* 'Cloudmother, are you aware of a... prophesy, of sorts, that we Titans have—known as the Embodiment?'

Silence.

The robot stopped circling and came to a halt in front of Luc's face, mere inches away. 'We are aware of nature and consequence of this phenomenon.' Cloudmother's voice was even softer and quieter than before.

*One down.* 'Do you understand the details, the... criteria attached to the Embodiment?' *There's the million-credit question. If they don't know, then I've no way of proving it to them. But somehow...*

'Affirmative. We have records of what you call the Ideal.'

*Why am I not surprised? Damn, their intelligence is a lot better than ours.* Despite that, Luc allowed himself a small smile, even though he knew this next minute could be his last. 'Can you perform a genetic comparison?'

'Of course.' Cloudmother's voice was faster now, intrigued. 'Raise right hand for blood sample.'

Luc did. A tiny dart shot out from the robot's casing, embedding itself in the pad of his thumb. A microfilament wire stretched back into the robot. A few seconds passed, and the dart was retrieved. 'Please wait. Analysis will take several seconds.' The robot drifted some distance away while it worked.

Luc idly sucked a tiny drop of blood from his thumb. The puncture had already healed.

His companions all stared at him. Neela and Ariadne looked confused, Abe as stunned as an emotionally stunted half-android could.

He took his thumb out of his mouth. 'What?'

Abe spoke first. 'You are the Embodiment?'

'So they tell me. I've not seen any test results, though, so I haven't had anything monogrammed yet.'

Neela cut in, 'Okay, this seems to make sense to you both, but… what? You've never mentioned this before. What is this Embodiment?'

'Hmm. Well, to cut a long, boring, science-heavy story short, essentially I'm genetically perfect.' He grinned. 'Hadn't you noticed?'

Ariadne still didn't look convinced. 'As cool as that is, though—so what? That doesn't mean everyone back home will automatically bow down and do what you tell them, does it?'

'Actually? Yes. Exactly that. Again, in theory—I had to leave in a bit of a rush after I got the news so I never had a chance to test it out. My uncle Jarrod seemed pretty convinced, though.'

Ariadne looked a bit shocked. 'Oh. So you're pretty much king of the Titans, then.' She suddenly smiled. 'Ooo, Neela—that means you get to be queen of the Titans!'

The senator stared determinedly at the floor between her feet. Luc turned back to Cloudmother. *Founder save me. Ariadne…*

He looked between the hanging body and the robot for any indication of whether they would decide to help or cut him down where he stood for being the pinnacle of civilisation for their mortal enemy. *Not much in the way of middle ground.*

After another minute, the spherical robot turned back to the group and again floated up to Luc. 'Confirmed, Titan. You are a genetic match. Surprise at your presence here increases tenfold.'

'Well… thank you, Cloudmother.' He didn't really know what to say.

'Assumption: awareness that your death here would be easily achieved. Grievous blow to your people. Great victory to the Collective.'

'I'm aware, Cloudmother.'

'Yet you show great faith, revealing your complete nature. Our surprise is increased again. This encounter has been broadcast to Network in real-time. Collective is intrigued-moved-encouraged.' She paused. Luc held his breath while seconds passed. 'Collective will assist you.'

Luc let out that breath. He was vaguely aware of Neela grasping his hand, Ariadne letting out a whoop, and Abe nodding.

Cloudmother's gentle voice silenced them once more.

'Do not let us be betrayed, Titan. Through 7F44, you are aware of our true strength, like none other. Treachery would leave us with no hope for future peace. And no alternative to your complete eradication.'

'I understand, Cloudmother. I won't let you down.'

'We hope not, Titan. Chance on your side—to you all.'

Luc allowed himself a smile. *That's the easy part out of the way.*

# 18. Arrivals

*Mournstar* hung motionless, alone. The staging point a light minute distant was unremarkable, a set of coordinates that marked no star, planet, or moon. Just the very edge of the Rim, its closest point to the threat that was about to bring the disparate strands of humanity together in an attempt to win a future for them all.

*Bit grandiose, that.* But Neela, thinking large thoughts, sat alone in the rear observatory. She could feel her instinct tingling. *These are the moments from which history is made.* She also knew, as some ancient sage had once said, that history was written by the victors. And if they were to fail... Well, there would be no history for anyone to write, nor anyone to write it, soon enough.

Four days had passed since their visit to the Collective Cloud. The Fifth Fleet Group of the Star Corps, the pride of the Commonwealth navy, was due to arrive within hours. The waiting time had passed quietly, idly, but quickly.

Neela and Luc had talked, made love, eaten meals together in a surreal semblance of domestic harmony. *On the very edge of destruction, we find comfort in normalcy. The complete lack of drama.*

Ariadne had drifted about, foraging for food, working out, sitting and gazing out at the Void. She and Neela hadn't spoken very much. Not for the first time, Neela wondered exactly how Ariadne really felt about her and Luc's burgeoning relationship, but it was hardly the time to discuss it. And Abe... Who knew what Abe had been doing? Boone might, maybe. Neela had seen the two several times sit in quiet conversation on the bridge. The eccentric Athravan seemed to have taken a liking to the reserved Collective. Neela was glad. She suspected Abe wasn't the type to make friends easily.

The ship's booming voice made her start, as it always did. 'COMMONWEALTH FLEET HAS ARRIVED AT STAGING POINT. SIX CAPITAL SHIPS. SIXTY-ONE SMALLER CRAFT. I AM BEING HAILED.'

Neela jumped up from her seat, her cooling tea abandoned as she headed for the bridge. 'I'm on my way.'

The face of Admiral Hans Graff, framed by the background of the bridge on the flagship *Agamemnon*, already filled the bridge viewport when Neela arrived. The others were already there—Luc turned to her with a quick smile, Boone with a cheery hello.

She smiled briefly. *Time to go to work.* '*Mournstar*, video feed on me please.'

'DONE.'

Graff looked up from whatever he had been reading. He didn't look pleased. 'Senator Kane.'

'Admiral Graff. Thank you for joining us.'

That got a derisive grunt. 'As if I had a choice. Okafor calls, I go where I'm told. After sixty years in the military, I've long since given up on persuading a politician his idea is ridiculous.'

'We appreciate the assistance, Admiral. As ever.'

'Huh. Well. Your ship sent over some pretty pictures of what we're going up against. I haven't got the first idea what I'm looking at, but apparently that's expected. But I do know the odds are shitty now, and getting worse. Do we have some other dogs in this race, or did I bust my ass getting fifteen thousand men and women here at double time just to get them turned into ash?'

Neela smiled. She had always appreciated the admiral's complete bluntness. 'There are two other fleets inbound, Admiral. You won't be alone.'

Graff's bristly eyebrows perked up. 'Oh really? I know none of the other Fleet Groups are coming—we do keep in touch, you know. So which part of your ass did you pull these two magic fleets from?'

*Okay, that was a little too blunt. This should shut him up, though.* 'One is Collective. They arrive tomorrow. The other gets here the day after: Titan. More than half of the entire Titan force, to be exact.'

Neela kept her expression bland, but she was secretly pleased to see the veteran admiral actually pale. 'Collective? Those... and *half* the Titan fleet? They'll tear each other apart! Are you insane?'

'No, Admiral. They won't. This is a joint effort—everyone's signed up to it. And that's also why this operation will be directed from this vessel.' *He's not going to like that.*

His face darkened. 'That's preposterous. There's no way-'

Neela cut him off. 'Admiral, that's an order. And if you don't think I have the authority to give it, feel free to research the chain of command from the brig on the *Agamemnon* while I talk to Rear Admiral Kim instead.'

The senator watched Graff grind his teeth together for a few seconds, then he nodded. 'Understood, Senator. This is your ball game.'

'Thank you, Admiral.'

The grizzled commander turned to something off-screen, then back to Neela. 'Oh, yes. And we have some... guests on board whom I believe you're expecting? Civilians. I've no idea why they're here.' He frowned and briefly scratched his ear.

'Frankly, I can't even remember picking them up, which makes no sense, but...' He shook his head, as if giving up. 'Whatever. They're yours. I'm sending a shuttle over now.'

*Seryn. They do cover their tracks.* 'Thank you again, Admiral. We'll get that shuttle back to you soon.'

'Huh. Be sure you do. I'm not running a transpod service over here. Graff out.' The viewport cleared to show the assembled Star Corps fleet, ships huge in size down to those that were merely big—all resplendent in the famous white on navy-blue and bearing the shooting star crest.

Neela stepped closer. It was the first time she had seen such a military force up close. *It's very impressive, but... I'm glad Jalen's not part of this.* Her brother had joined the Peacetroopers two years before after five in the Star Corps, and he was on the other side of the galaxy on a mission even Neela would have trouble getting access to details of.

Her gaze roamed over the assembled ships as Luc stepped up beside her and gently squeezed her waist. She smiled at him, then looked back to the fleet.

*Very glad Jalen's not part of this.*

\* \* \*

Ariadne waited with Neela in *Mournstar*'s shuttle bay, bobbing with excitement. She hadn't realised how much she had missed her home, and the people there, until that moment. She knew it was unlikely she knew any of the agents who Margo had corralled together for this crazy endeavour, but all the same, she was thrilled.

They were waiting for the ship to finish rigging up a docking airlock; it had told them a few minutes earlier that the 'shuttle' that Graff had sent over was a little too large for the bay. Followed by, 'IF BY SHUTTLE, HE MEANT TROOP TRANSPORT, HE SHOULD HAVE SAID TROOP TRANSPORT.'

Ri and Neela had left the others on the bridge, Luc leading a tactical discussion with Admiral Graff, Abe, and another part of the ship's attention.

The Seryn had been delighted to get away from the 'ultra-accelerated holosimulated projections of battle outcomes'. *Or 'guaranteed to give you a headache', as they should be called. Too many little flashing dots whizzing about. Nauseating.*

The ship's booming voice echoed even louder from the metal walls of the shuttle bay. 'DOCKING AIRLOCK ACHIEVED. PASSENGERS ARE INBOUND.'

'Yay!' Ariadne clapped her hands, then remembered she wasn't alone and looked sheepishly at Neela.

The senator burst out laughing. 'It's okay, Ri. I'm sure I'd be excited, too.'

'It's just I've never been away from home before, and I didn't think I was homesick. Really, I've been fine—great, even! But then I knew they were coming, and it was like, wow, they're—'

Neela cut her off before she ran out of breath. 'I think they've arrived.'

A smaller portal next to the main bay doors was sliding open. Ariadne started moving towards it, straining to make out who the figure at the front of the—

'Margo!' Her walk turned into a run as she realised her caretaker had decided to come all that way herself. Margo stepped through into the bay, her sturdy frame wrapped in a beautiful turquoise toga, and dropped an enormous shoulder bag and threw open her arms just in time for Ariadne to jump into them and give her a hug.

'Hello, dear—anyone would think you were pleased to see me!'

'Oh, I am—I had no idea you were coming! Why didn't you say?' Ariadne asked.

'It was a last-minute decision. I felt I could do some good here. And I wanted to make sure you're eating properly. And lo and behold, look at you—you're skin and bone!' Margo turned to Neela, who had followed more slowly. 'What have you been feeding my girl? You must be Senator Neela, and it's very lovely to meet you—my name is Margo—but look at her. She's lost ten pounds.'

*Have I?* Ariadne unfolded herself from Margo's arms.

Neela opened her mouth, closed it, then tried again. 'Um… How much does she normally eat?'

The caretaker smiled. 'Oh, it's not the quantity, dear; it's the quality. Not enough fruitcake, that's the problem. Luckily I brought one or two.' She picked up the shoulder bag and patted it with satisfaction.

The other Seryn newcomers had entered the bay. Margo began making introductions. There were twenty-three—twenty-four, including Margo.

They were a pleasantly wide range of shapes, colours, and sizes, Ariadne thought, from the tiny girl Bethany—*Even smaller than me!*—to a huge, elderly black gentleman called Rufus who had impressively long white dreadlocks. Ariadne shook hands with or hugged everyone as felt appropriate and desperately tried to file away everyone's names. *I haven't got a chance of remembering all of them.*

She glanced at Neela, who was all smooth professional courtesy, thanking everyone for coming. *Excellent. I'll just ask Neela if I forget. Bet she never forgets a name.*

With the courtesies out of the way, Neela began directing the newcomers towards the residential deck. Soon only Margo remained. Neela turned to her intently.

'If you're not too tired from the journey, I'd be delighted to find out, well—'

'How we're supposed to help?' The caretaker's smile said she wasn't offended.

Neela smiled back. 'Well, yes. I've seen what Ariadne can do up close, but I'm not sure anything like that is going to apply. If any of you end up in an up-close situation, a lot will have gone wrong.'

Margo nodded. 'Quite. We've discussed it on the journey here. We think the best way to contribute is if we attempt to make a mesh.'

*Ooooo.* Ariadne grinned. 'That's so cool!'

Neela blinked blankly. 'Care to share?'

'Of course, dear,' said Margo. She crossed her arms, tucking her hands into folds of her toga. 'Most Seryn are able to act as a conduit, of sorts, between two or more other people. It allows them to share in each other's... not quite thoughts, but senses. Impressions. Imagine: If two people were linked, and one saw the other was about bang their head if they stood up, that other would share that sense and be able to avoid it. Silly example, but does it make sense?'

The senator nodded. 'I think so, yes.'

'Good. That's if one of our people act as conduit. If there are two Seryn, linked themselves, then the effect multiplies—more people's senses can be shared, at a greater distance, and the impressions are stronger. Add in a third, then a fourth, you make a mesh, and it multiplies again and again, exporentiantly.'

Ariadne frowned. 'Exponentially?'

'Yes. What did I say?'

Neela was nodding. 'So with twenty-four of you, the effect is—'

'It should be *very* significant,' Margo said. 'But I caution you, it's never been done. The most it's been attempted with is ten. If we've worked it out correctly, we should be able to—'

'Link the whole fleet! Everyone. That's amazing.' *Brilliant!* Ariadne beamed at Neela, who looked suitably impressed.

'So everyone can watch everyone else's backs. That's incredible. Though are you sure it'll still work with the... various types of people involved?'

'We know it works with Titans. Collective, we don't for sure. But there's a good chance. We're pretty sure they're still basically human.'

*We know it works with Titans? I'd like to hear that story.* A glance at Neela's surprised expression told Ariadne that the senator probably would, too. *Another time.*

'Well, that's settled, then. Thank you again for lending your support, Margo. I think it's time you saw what we're up against.'

Margo settled her bag more firmly on her shoulder and nodded as they headed to the doorfield that led back into the ship. 'Absolutely. But first I think I'd like a cup of tea, if that could be arranged. And maybe a piece of cake.'

Ariadne's stomach started rumbling. *Mmm. I couldn't agree more.*

\* \* \*

The Fifth Fleet and *Mournstar* had long since retreated to a safe distance from the staging point by the time the Collective fleet arrived the next day. The three megaships emerged from the jump first, long, sleek, and black—ten times *Mournstar*'s size. Utterly functional, yet still aesthetically pleasing, the signature of Collective technology. Seconds later, swarms of fighters began to arrive, appearing in the spaces between, with tiny blue flashes as they unfolded from subspace.

Abe was watching expectantly as the fleet arrived and checked his chronometer. *Arrival punctual, seven-point-five seconds early. Satisfactory.* He turned to the bridge table where the others sat talking. 'Collective fleet has arrived.'

'Excellent,' said Neela, rising to join him at the viewport. 'What have we got?'

'Exactly as promised. Three capital ships. Two thousand ninety fighters, each manned by one to four Collective.'

Luc shook his head slowly. 'I shouldn't be surprised, but somehow... I still can't believe what I'm seeing.'

Abe smiled slightly. 'Largest Collective fleet ever assembled. Even larger than Karth.'

The Titan frowned. 'Karth? When was that? I don't remember studying it—and I thought all of our battles were on the syllabus.'

'They likely are. Karth was not a Titan encounter. Collective has other enemies than you, Titan.'

'Really? You should tell me about it one day. If we survive, obviously.'

Luc, Neela, and Abe rejoined Ariadne at the table. Margo was at her side, knitting something.

The Titan began, 'We need to get the lodestone back. That's clear. Destroying the Scourge fleet is the primary objective, of course, but without the lodestone, we're still doomed. We'll just have a few tens of millennia to get ready for it.'

'And you're convinced the Peacetrooper strike team isn't the better option?' Neela asked.

*Senator looks very unhappy. Understandable reaction to prospect of separation from mate.*

Luc nodded, his expression sombre. He put his hand on Neela's. 'Yes, I'm sure. The larger the force we send at them, the more attention it'll get, and the more likely it is to fail. We need stealth here, not power. And besides, Boone's absolutely convinced that we're supposed to be the ones to do this—and somehow, he's convinced me too. That's why it has to be us.'

'Except me.'

'Except you. Would you really want to come? Into combat?'

Neela looked downcast. She squeezed Luc's hand. 'No. I just don't like the thought of being separated. And not just from you.' She looked to Ariadne and Abe as well. 'All of you. We've come a long way together.'

The young Seryn smiled. 'We'll be okay! Luc's very good at this, and Abe's got millions of tricks, and I...' Her smile faded. 'Well, I'm pretty sure I can help somehow.'

'You'll do fine. I know it. You took me down, didn't you?' said Luc.

Ariadne brightened. 'That's true. And that soldier man from Shax.'

'How are you going to breathe, though? There's hardly going to be an oxygen-nitrogen atmosphere on the Scourge ship,' Neela pointed out.

Abe had the answer. 'Rebreathers. Face mask, connected to perfect-filtration-conversion air tank. *Mournstar* and I designed them, he constructed them.'

Luc patted Neela's hand again. 'See, we've got it all covered. So you don't need to worry. And besides, we need you here in command, to liaise with the other fleet commanders. The ship will handle the tactical command element, but—' He dropped his volume. 'Well, it's not completely diplomatic, is it?'

'I HEARD THAT. YOU SHOULD KNOW THAT I AM TRAINED IN ONE HUNDRED FORTY NINE DISTINCT DIPLOMACY PROTOCOLS FROM MANY DIFFERENT CULTURES.'

Abe smiled. *He takes offence easily. Amusing.*

'And I'll be here to help as well, so between us, we'll be fine. Are you going to be able to handle tracking the whole fleet, though? Once the Titans get here, there'll be three thousand ships in play, just on our side.'

It wasn't quite possible for the ship to scoff indignantly, but the noise it made certainly sounded like an attempt. 'COMPLETELY ABLE. WHILE ALSO MAINTAINING ALL RUNNING ONBOARD SYSTEMS. I ALSO PLAN TO COMPOSE AN EPIC POEM OF THE BATTLE AS IT PROCEEDS. AND THERE IS A RECIPE FOR HERMIT-CRAB SOUP I WOULD LIKE TO TRY MAKING.'

Luc held his hands up. 'Okay, okay—we get the point. You've got it under control.' He looked again at Neela. 'Okay?'

She gave him a wry smile. 'Okay.'

Abe watched with fascination. *Human relationships heavily founded on emotion and compromise. Difficult to predict. Interesting study.*

A ping over Network drew his attention inward. *'A83-7F44, this is B9-DD10. Coordinating fleet recently arrived in local volume. Fleet has been given designation: Cautious Hammer. Acknowledge transmission.'*

*'Acknowledged, DD10.'* Abe had never understood why the Collective battle fleets always ended up being given ridiculous names. It was a habit that went back centuries and was completely out of character. *Perhaps means we are less predictable. Would be positive.*

*'Direction, 7F44.'*

*'Clear staging point volume, adopt holding formation, await incoming Titan fleet. Expected arrival within twenty hours. Acknowledge understood.'*

*'Acknowledged. DD10 out.'*

Abe shifted his attention back out, to find the others looking at him. 'Are they all set?' asked Luc.

'Affirmative. Holding, waiting.' *As are we. But not long to wait now.*

*Not long.*

\* \* \*

Ariadne threw her hands up. 'Admit it. They were just showing off.'

Luc sighed. She'd been prodding him about it for a full minute now. *She doesn't give up.* 'No, that's not— It's about striving for perfection. Doing everything to the very best that it can be done.'

'Really?' Ariadne couldn't have looked more disbelieving. 'You're telling me the *entire* Titan fleet came out of jump at *exactly* the same instant, in a *perfectly* symmetrical formation, with a *tiny* gap between all the ships, just for their own sake?'

'Honestly. It's not about impressing people. That's just the way we do things.'

Ariadne obviously wasn't convinced. 'I don't believe you.'

*Who would have thought?* 'We've just never given much thought to what others think of us. Let me put it this way: We've been doing it like this for centuries, and I'm pretty sure this is the first time the fleet's arrival hasn't been immediately followed by it destroying everything in sight.'

That shut her up.

The fleet had arrived thirty minutes earlier. Luc had actually got a little emotional as he watched them come in. Seeing the silver, red, and gold lined up together, such a huge force aligned as one... *Ten Starkiller supercruisers, twenty-five Juggernaut cruisers, forty-five Rapier destroyers.* It was quite something.

'Is your uncle coming over to say hello?' asked Ariadne.

'Yeah, he's on his way now.'

'And what does a Consul do?'

'There are three. Each commands one third of the cohort—that's our military. They report to the Council. Well, they did. It's a bit up in the air at the moment.'

'Because of you being magic perfect man?' Ariadne grinned.

Luc rolled his eyes. 'Something like that. But yes, Jarrod's a Consul. He's in command of this fleet—there'll be another Consul acting as his second. Rufus probably—Jarrod and Logan, the other, have never really seen eye to eye.'

Ariadne looked pleased. 'I like the name Rufus. Sounds like a friendly bear.'

Luc laughed. 'That's actually not a bad description of him. He's an absolute terror in a fight, but he's the nicest guy in the world most of the time.'

'LUC, THE CONSUL'S SHUTTLE DOCKED TWO MINUTES AGO.'

'It did? Why didn't you say? I'd have gone down.'

'INDEED. I OFFERED TO HAVE SOMEONE MEET YOUR UNCLE AND BRING HIM HERE, BUT HE ASSURED ME HE WOULD FIND HIS WAY.'

'And find my way I did.' The doorfield to the bridge had swooshed open while the ship was talking, and Jarrod swept in, his military dress immaculate and cloak fluttering as he walked.

He grinned as he strode up to Luc. 'How hard is it to find a bridge on a ship, even one as bizarre as this? You put it at the front, towards the top. It's not complicated.'

Luc smiled broadly. After a long hug and much backslapping, he stood back. 'It's good to see you, Jarrod. Very good. I'll be honest: I was worried.'

'Oh, I can look after myself. I'm an old dog now. I know where to sleep and who to bite.'

Jarrod looked at Ariadne. 'And hello to you too, young lady. I hear you've been looking after my nephew—I've been pestering him to find a partner for a few years, so it's not before time.'

*Oh, save me.* Luc winced and closed his eyes. When he opened them, Ariadne was blushing furiously and yammering. 'No! No, I'm—I'm the other one. That's Neela. I'm Ariadne. She's not here. I'm just— We're friends.'

Jarrod didn't look too embarrassed. 'Ah. I see. Apologies. My mistake.' His expression hardened a little. 'So that makes you Luc's... Seryn friend.'

'Y—yes.' Ariadne looked a little worried.

Jarrod nodded thoughtfully, then brightened. 'You needn't worry. I've long had some doubts about our... uh, antipathy towards you and yours. I'd be delighted to find I was right to have those doubts. There's plenty to keep us occupied without looking for enemies where there are none.'

Ri's relief was clear. 'I'm very glad to hear that. I wouldn't want to have to hurt you.'

The Consul guffawed at that. 'Oh, that's good. I like this one, boy. And I'm glad you haven't taken up with her—maybe there's a chance for me, eh?' He wagged his eyebrows at Ariadne, whose blush returned in earnest. Jarrod's laugh again burst forth.

He looked back at Luc. 'This suicide mission you're going on.'

*I wish he wouldn't—* 'We're not calling it that, but yes. What of it?'

'I've got something on the shuttle that you'll need. It was going to be a gift for your Focus, but— Well, there was no time. It's a set of armour. Your father's.'

Luc didn't know what to say.

'And yes, I know your old man was shorter and broader. I had it resized. As long as you haven't put any weight on,' —Jarrod gently punched Luc in the gut— 'it'll fit.'

'That's...' *My father's armour?* He just shook his head. 'Thank you.'

'It's my pleasure, lad. Oh, and I bought a small cache of weapons as well. Pulse rifle, semi-auto frag launcher, mines. You know, all the toys. Take whatever you want. Good?'

'Very good.'

'Grand.' Jarrod let out a contented sigh. 'Right, then. I need to get back, but let's go and introduce me to your lady, shall we? The right one, this time.' He gave Ariadne another grin and a wave as he turned to the doorfield.

'See you in a little while, Ri,' said Luc as he followed. He waited until they were off the bridge. 'You know she's younger than me, right?'

His uncle shrugged. 'Not as old as my second wife.' He chortled again.

All Luc could do was shake his head again.

\* \* \*

Neela briefly closed her eyes and pinched the bridge of her nose. The chronic headaches were a thing of the past, but she wasn't immune to the acute kind.

Another half a day had passed. Plans were drawn up, revised, thrown out. Tactics were debated. A remote conference was hosted; Jarrod and Beta-9 Cloudmother made cautious, qualified declarations of peace, while Admiral Graff, his face sandwiched between the other two on *Mournstar*'s bridge viewport, tried to act as if he saw naked grey women cabled up to their ships every day. Margo had stood with them on the bridge, smiling at everyone and saying how nice it was to be there. The mood softened somewhat after that, and the conference ended well.

*This is as ready as we're going to be, and we can't afford to wait any longer.* Neela opened her eyes and looked up from the readiness report she was reading for the fourth time and was again taken aback when she looked at Luc. She was so used to seeing him in the same old scruffy clothes. *Or asleep. Or naked. Or grumpily waking up.* But now he was encased in a full set of body armour, form fitting lightweight charcoal-coloured plates of some pulse-dampening, projectile-proof, heat-resistant, everything-resistant material. *I forget he's a soldier, sometimes.*

Luc noticed her attention and raised his eyebrows.

She nodded. 'Everyone reports ready. It's time to go.'

He nodded. 'Ship, is everyone linked on the shared channel?'

'AFFIRMATIVE. TWO THOUSAND EIGHT HUNDRED FIFTY VESSELS. AWAITING GO.'

'Send it,' said Luc. He turned to Margo. 'It's time to build that mesh.'

The elderly Seryn nodded. 'We'll be in the rear observatory. Good luck, all of you.' She gave Ariadne one last hug, then left the bridge.

*Well, that's that.* Neela felt the thrum of *Mournstar*'s engines as they powered up. The ship's three-dimensional holoprojection of the fleet changed, white direction trails snaking out behind the blue, black, and red dots as the ships began to move.

On the viewport, a thousand lights had sprung to life, nuclear exhausts of a thousand ships powering up to a steady ten times lightspeed. They would reach their destination in less than two hours. *And then all hell breaks loose, and we win, or we die. Or both.*

She felt a sudden urge to say something. To address the fleet, these unlikely allies who were about to fight and die for each other. Some because they had made a judgement and taken a vote, most simply because they were following orders. Either way, Neela felt she had to give them something, some reason for what was to come. *These are the moments from which history is made.*

She didn't know yet what she'd say, but she trusted that whatever came would be right. 'Ship, open the shared channel for audio, on me.'

A second's pause. 'AUDIO IS OPEN.'

Neela took a deep breath, her gaze fixed on the trailing lights of the ships ahead of her. Luc and the others had fallen silent behind her. She placed them in her mind—Luc, Ariadne, Abe. Herself. Four oh-so unlikely comrades. And began.

'Allied fleet, this is Senator Neela Kane of the Commonwealth. Of the *Mournstar.* You are all here today—Collective and Titan, Seryn and Commonwealth—because one of your own went chasing a legend and, instead, found an enemy. An enemy that is utterly implacable, utterly without remorse, and utterly relentless in the pursuit of only one goal:

'The eradication of all life in this galaxy.

'Some of you have seen what proof we could provide and

chose to make this your fight. For others, your leaders judged this threat real and ordered you forth to meet that threat. It matters not which. We are all here, now, together.

'And that is the great truth we reveal here today, on the very brink of destruction. That despite all of our differences—fear and distrust or outright hatred; despite animosity, fresh and raw or old and scarred—despite all of these and more, when the stakes are high enough and our very cultures are on the brink of destruction, the only thing that matters is not what makes us different, but our commonality. Our love of life and the sheer bloody-minded refusal to let that life be taken away. Our humanity. I beg you, for all our sakes, to remember this truth in a few hours' time, when we meet that threat in earnest. Whoever you are, whatever your colours—blue, black, or red and gold—take care of each other. Take care of yourselves.

'Kane out.'

Neela continued to stare at the light trails of the fleet. *I hope that meant something. To someone.*

And on they sped, deeper into the void.

# 19. Battle

'Is it just me, or are lot more of them moving than there were last time?' Ariadne tried to count the grey shapes orbiting the great mothership, itself still hanging motionless above the inverted cone of still-trapped ships. She couldn't keep track.

'TWENTY-SIX MORE SMALLER SHIPS HAVE BEEN RELEASED, FOR A TOTAL OF THIRTY-FIVE. NO ADDITIONAL LARGE SHIPS HAVE BEEN FREED AS YET.'

*Well, we've got that going for us, at least.*

They were approaching the ten light minute distance from the prison, which would be a mere sixty seconds away from the enemy fleet. The ship had predicted that as the point where the Scourge would identify the incoming fleet as hostile. *What it's based that on, I have no idea, but they certainly don't seem to be worried about us yet.*

Luc finished a call with Jarrod. 'Everything's set. It's time we got down to the shuttle bay.' Down there, next to Boone's scruffy old shuttle, sat the sleek, four-person Collective corvette *Widget* that they would be taking: cloaked, engines running slow and quiet, on a high arcing course over the body of the engagement, hopefully avoiding detection with the frenzy of the battle underway beneath them and reaching the mothership intact. *And then finding an open bay of some kind we can dock in.* And *not being detected when we land.* And *finding the lodestone.* And *bringing it back safely.* Ariadne sighed. *That this is the best plan we've got says a lot.*

'Be safe, you hear me?' Neela embraced Luc tightly, then stepped back and turned to Ariadne and Abe, who was checking the rebreathers one more time. 'You, too. I want to see you soon.'

'Bye, Neela. Don't worry, I'll look after him.' Ariadne gave the senator a quick hug.

Abe nodded. 'Chance be with you, Neela.'

'Oh, don't worry about me. The ship's promised it won't let anything happen to itself, so I'll be all right.'

The ship cut in. 'WE WILL CROSS THE TEN-LIGHT MINUTE BOUNDARY IN TEN SECONDS.' It paused, then continued. 'ONE MOMENT.'

They waited.

'SCOURGE VESSEL MOVEMENT PATTERNS ARE CHANGING. ONE MOMENT.'

Ariadne held her breath.

'INCOMING. REPEAT: SCOURGE VESSELS ARE INCOMING.'

It was visible on the viewport now—in the distance, ahead of the massed ranks of the allied fleet, the smaller Scourge ships were breaking away from the mothership, angling towards them. Closing the gap.

'NINE LIGHT MINUTES TO FRONT OF SCOURGE WAVE. FIRST WEAPONS RANGE ATTAINED IN TWENTY SECONDS.'

Luc grunted. 'Our weapons range, sure. What about theirs?'

The seconds ticked away—achingly slowly, it seemed to Ariadne. The incoming shapes grew more distinct as they closed.

'TEN SECONDS. ALLIED FLEET IS READYING WEAPONS SYSTEMS.'

The bridge was silent.

'WITHIN RANGE IN TWO… ONE. RANGE.'

The first wave of hyperkinetic missiles was released from a hundred ships, a thousand points of light trailing ripples of blue-green exhaust through the void as they skipped across the energy grid, picking up speed. The Scourge ships screamed towards the fleet, a flock of predatory birds in the blackness.

Luc spun away from the viewport. 'This isn't our fight now. To the bay. Move out.'

With one last look at the missiles disappearing into the distance, Ariadne turned and followed the Titan from the bridge. *Oh dear. Here we go.*

* * *

'How does it fit?' Luc asked.

'Pretty well.' Ariadne swung her arms back and forth. 'I feel ridiculous, though. I look like you.'

Luc shook his head, continuing his adjustments of the fastenings on the armour he'd had the ship fabricate for Ariadne. Abe, currently controlling the Collective corvette as they began their arcing course up and over the ongoing battle, had also been kitted out. *He didn't complain about the style, though. Women.* 'There. Done. Nice and, uh, snug.' He realised with a start that he was staring at Ariadne's chest and snapped his head up to see her smirking at him.

'The lengths you men will go to, to get a girl in a tight-fitting top. I ask you.' She shook her head in mock exasperation.

At a loss, Luc turned to Abe instead. 'How's the battle going?'

'Too early to say. Minor hits on both sides. Countermeasures largely successful against projectile weaponry. Shields holding so far against lasfire.' Abe tapped a quick staccato into a panel on the corvette's dash. 'Mothership has just released a wave of smaller vessels. Assume fighters.'

Luc snorted. 'Well, that'll give your two thousand little ships something to do, won't it? I'm sure they were getting bored.'

Ariadne stood up, shaking her arms and legs and stretching. She looked down at her armour and sighed, then stepped over to the other two. 'When do we turn the cloak thingy on?'

Luc kept his eyes on the dash. 'At the last possible moment. It drains our power pretty hard. How long did you say we've got, Abe?'

'This class of ship, unwise to maintain cloak for longer than ten minutes. At twelve, potentially not enough power to return to *Mournstar*. Fifteen minutes would drain power completely.'

Luc did the quick calculation. 'Okay. So… Seven minutes' cloak on the way in, leave ourselves the option of a few on the way out.' *If we make it out.*

'Agreed,' said Abe.

It felt strange to Luc that the small viewports on the front of *Widget* showed complete blackness as they rose up and away from the battle raging below them. Without the sea of tiny dots moving on the dash's main display, they could have been completely alone. Luc kept his eyes on the display, his mind translating the movement of the colour-coded dots into flanking manoeuvres, thrusts—destruction. Two of the Commonwealth ships winked out. Five of the smallest, the Collective fighters. They had begun to lose people.

The Titan took a deep breath, forced himself to relax. *It's inevitable.*

Then, a breakthrough.

'Yes!' He punched the air.

'What? What happened?' Ariadne hadn't followed the exchange.

'We just took out the first one of their ships. Looked like three Juggernauts and one of the big Collective ships did most of the damage.'

Abe glanced over and nodded. 'Alliance holds.'

'Did you doubt it would?' Luc asked.

The Collective's brow lifted in such a classically human way that Luc couldn't help smiling. 'Did you not?'

*Fair point.*

For three minutes, they powered upwards, their course gradually flattening back to parallel with the galactic plane as they reached the apex. Abe tapped the panel once more. 'Engaging cloak for descent.'

Luc looked about him for some sign that they were now shielded, but saw no difference. *Bit disappointing, but I'm not sure what I was expecting.*

Another minute passed, then Ariadne gasped.

The sensor-augmented display on the corvette's viewports had picked out the mothership, hanging in the lightless void below them. They all remained silent, as if not speaking could somehow make them even less noticeable. Gradually the mothership centred in the viewport and grew larger as they curved down towards it.

Abe spoke. 'I have instructed the ship to begin searching for possible entrances.'

Luc pointed. 'Can you tell it to avoid the ones that those fighters are streaming out of?' A second — maybe third — wave of fighters had just emerged from the mothership, sailing between the six vast prongs that extruded from the main body of the ship. *That must have been two hundred fighters. How many more does this thing have?*

'Affirmative. Ship is searching for auxiliary or secondary bays and vents. No results so far.'

'I don't care if we have to go in the same way their crap comes out. We just need a way in.' Or we're all doomed, Luc didn't add.

A minute later, they were getting close, very close, to their time limit on the cloak.

Abe broke the silence. 'Possible entrance found. Profile suggests secondary exhaust or heat expulsion vent. Located on rear of vessel. Opposite to fighter egress.' He looked to Luc and Ariadne. 'We proceed?'

Ariadne nodded. 'I like that it's away from all the fighters.'

'Take us in,' said Luc.

It was heart in mouth time. Slowly, so slowly, they sailed over and past the mothership, then began an angling course down and back towards what they hoped would be their way in.

Every second, Luc expected to see the flash of light from incoming lasfire or the nose of a missile speeding towards them. And then nothing ever again.

But somehow, against all likelihood, no missile came. Closer and closer they came, still unmolested. The mothership now filled the viewport. A dimple in the centre of the screen ended up being the vent they were aiming for—the squashed circle became clearer as they neared, resolving into the entrance to a shaft of some kind that quickly vanished into darkness as it entered the ship.

Still no shot came.

The entrance grew larger, big enough for three ships of their size to enter side by side.

Still no shot.

The *Widget* sailed through and was swallowed by the darkness.

They were in.

\* \* \*

'Which one do we go for, then?'

Abe ignored Ariadne's question for a moment. He scanned the energy signature map his sensors had built in his mind as they had slowly and carefully made their way into the belly of the mothership. Twice they had heard approaching noises and hidden around a corner, down one of the many corridors criss-crossing the ship. The tunnels twisted left to right and back, rising and falling, with no discernible pattern. The grey-black walls were mottled with phosphorescent green, giving them a disturbing, almost nightmarish quality.

Ariadne's question referred to the two largest energy signatures that Abe had detected. They were by some distance the strongest, many times greater than the hundreds of smaller signatures that dotted the ship—fighters, auxiliary systems, perhaps Scourge themselves, Abe surmised. They had yet to see one in the flesh.

The first of the two larger signatures seemed to actually be a tightly grouped set of three, quite wide and flat, located just down and towards the stern from the very centre of the ship. *Likely hypothesis: Engine bays.* The other was much smaller, singular, but even stronger than the combined power of the group of three, and located higher up towards the top of the mothership.

The lodestone. Abe hoped.

'Signature towards top of vessel closer match to that expected of lodestone, given size and shape deduced from empty cradle inside Promise. Investigate that first.'

Luc nodded. 'Okay. But if it turns out we need to investigate something else second, we might be in trouble. I know it's been blessedly uncrowded in here so far, but I've still got a feeling we're only going to get one shot at this.' He gestured with the barrel of the enormous pulse rifle-cum-frag launcher he had taken from the weapons cache. 'Lead on.'

They moved off, Ariadne bringing up the rear.

Left at the fork, up at the split, right at the next fork, up and up the steeply rising tunnel that followed. Abe led them closer to their destination, always climbing higher into the body of the mothership.

They often heard sounds, mainly behind and below them—once from the other side of an intricately patterned patch of wall that could only have been a door, somehow the first they had come across after covering just over a kilometre. They hurried past it, treading carefully.

'How far away are we?' Ariadne asked a few minutes later, as they paused at a broad junction where five corridors met.

Abe calculated. 'Two hundred twenty metres in a direct vector from our current location. Likely six hundred metres or more on foot.'

'So which way?' Luc asked.

'Uncertain. Three corridors lead in largely the desired direction. However: centre corridor of three is incline, other two decline.'

'Middle it is, then.'

Quickly but quietly, they moved off once more.

Only fifteen metres or so into the tunnel, the situation Abe had been hoping to avoid struck: Bodies approached, a series of clicks accompanied by rasping, scraping sounds—from both behind them near the junction and further ahead along the corridor.

Ariadne quietly cursed, 'Damn it.'

'We go forwards. Maintain momentum, keep moving in the right direction.' Luc tapped a few buttons along the top of his rifle, which came to life with a sharp whine and a row of red lights.

*Sensible idea.* Abe readied the weapon he had taken from the *Widget*, a semi-sentient rapid-fire machine pistol, capable of launching twenty homing smart flechettes per second at its target. *Less explosive than the Titan's choice. Equally effective, one hopes.*

They moved on, the corridor widening after a few tens of metres as a second branch joined it. The noise ahead grew louder as they closed in, the rhythm of the sounds resolving into—*Three bodies. Two possible, three likely.* Abe turned to Luc, who raised a hand with three fingers extended. The Collective nodded.

The Titan's voice was a low rumble. 'Ready yourselves. If they're spread, Ariadne, take the furthest from us. Abe, the one on the right.' He ducked a little lower into a crouching walk. 'Stay low. And whatever they look like, concentrate on taking them down.'

Ten more metres, then twenty. In the gloomy fluorescent light, Abe saw that the tunnel bent sharply to the right just a few metres ahead of them. The clicks and scrapes were very close.

Luc held up a fist, one of the basic hand signals he'd showed them before they left *Mournstar*. They stopped. Crouched. Waited.

The Scourge turned the corner.

There were three: two abreast at the front, one at rear. Abe scanned and catalogued their structure. *Colour same grey-black and mottled green as vessel. Four legs, jointed similar to arthropod, ending in triple claw. Bulky abdomen hanging below torso, dragged along ground. Torso roughly cylindrical, two longer arms-legs extending from shoulder, ending in same triple claw. Two shorter arms-legs ending in six-seven-eight fingered hand. No notable neck. Broad head, fattened U-shape—prongs taper and curve inward towards the other as they extend. No visible mouth, eyes, ears, nose.*

The analysis took less than a second.

One of the Scourge screamed. That was the only way to describe the high-pitched wail.

Luc and Abe simultaneously opened fire, striking the front pair as they both dropped into a crouch, a likely precursor to springing forwards. Luc had fired three shots in pulse rifle mode, slugs of plasma streaking out at supersonic velocity. Two hit the left-hand Scourge in the centre of its torso, scorching a shallow crater a foot wide, while the third took it in the middle of the head. Abe couldn't tell if the torso shots did any real damage, but the headshot burned a hole clean through the creature's skull.

Visually marking his targets and transmitting them to his weapon had taken Abe two tenths of a second. The immediate fire command had sprayed a one-second burst of flechettes from left to right across the shoulders of the right-hand Scourge. The results weren't pretty. *Right primary arm severed at shoulder, left hanging crippled. Head forty to sixty per cent detached from torso. Target collapsed.*

It had gone better than expected—mere seconds into their first encounter and two of three hostiles were eliminated.

The third, meanwhile, was closing in. It had defied expectations by scuttling up the curving corridor wall and onto the ceiling as it came towards them, arms extended to grasp, claws clicking as it gained speed. As Abe shifted his weapon to track the target—*Too slow, hostile closing too quickly*—he was momentarily stunned as a wave of some mental force burst from Ariadne behind him.

The approaching Scourge wobbled briefly, slowed, then shook it off.

'Shit shit shit,' came the muttered curse from behind him, followed by 'Fine, try… *this.*'

The temperature of the air around them—*Thirty per cent helium, seventy per cent sulphur dioxide; rebreathers working optimally*—dropped by ten degrees. Abe watched in amazement as the final Scourge, less than a metre above and ahead of them, changed colour in an instant from green-black to glistening frosted white. The Scourge's forward momentum and grasping became sluggish, slowed further, then stopped. It hung from the ceiling, motionless.

Then dropped.

Both Abe and Luc sprung backwards, the Titan with an oath. There was a loud crunching, cracking noise as the body hit the floor and crumpled into pieces. As one, they turned to Ariadne. She looked between them, eyes shining white in the dim light. 'Didn't know I could do that, did you?'

*Fascinating.* Abe nodded at the Seryn. Luc let out a low whistle.

'I'm just glad you didn't do it to me.' Luc checked his weapon, then turned to Abe. 'Let's keep going, shall we?'

Stepping over their shattered, burned, and torn enemies, they went on.

\* \* \*

Ariadne felt herself quivering as they continued their search for the lodestone. The brief but frenzied fight with the Scourge had been the first time she'd ever used her abilities for harm. As the adrenaline rush faded and the jitters came, she tried to concentrate on clearing her mind, resetting her body. *Focus. Breathe. Focus. Empty the mind. Breathe.* It helped somewhat.

By the time they reached the next junction a few minutes later, she felt more normal.

Abe stood still while Luc checked the corridors running left and right from the T. Directly in front of them, the corridor wall was again patterned far more intricately than the surrounding surface. *Door?*

'Lodestone is fifteen metres away. Directly ahead.'

Luc spun to Abe. 'You're sure?'

'Affirmative. Energy signature is behind this wall.'

'We'd better hope it's a door, rather than a wall. Or this might be a little tricky,' Ariadne chipped in.

Luc turned and began inspecting the patterned section. It was sixteen feet wide, eight tall, a hemisphere carved or veined in a delicate filigree of phosphorescent green, very different to the rough, randomly patterned veins that ran along the tunnel walls elsewhere. Abe stepped up to it as well, pressing his hands to the surface as if to give his scan more traction.

Ariadne stood and watched. 'I'll just stand guard then, shall I?'

No response.

Seconds ticked by.

For every second that passed, Ariadne felt more and more sure that they would be discovered. She realised she was bouncing on her heels in her nervousness. *Focus. Breathe. Come on, girl. You know the drill.*

She centred herself once again just as Abe called, 'There. Slightly right of centre. Interface of some kind. Possibly controls access.'

Luc stepped close to the Collective and peered down at the door. 'I can barely make it out. It's tiny.'

'Indeed. Improves chance that I can connect to it.' As he spoke, he pulled a small device from his right wrist. Ariadne could see a faint sheen trailing from it, which told her it was connected back into his body by some kind of cable or wire. *That's a bit freaky.* She stepped up close to watch.

Abe slid the cable jack into the small hole that Ariadne couldn't even see until the jack slipped in. She also didn't understand how the connection was going to work. 'Is that some kind of skeleton key for alien spaceships, or are we just hoping it'll match? Because it would be a pretty big coincidence, wouldn't it?'

He smiled slightly. 'Do not understand skeleton key, but connector and cable are symbiote nanotechnology. Connector pulls mass from cable as required, reshapes itself to fit interface. Once fitted, scans interface data pattern, reverse engineers access protocol.' He paused, head cocked. 'In theory. Extremely unlikely this will succeed.'

*Oh. That's a bit of a downer.*

Luc was pulling something from the bulky belt he wore: a pale, cream-coloured disc adorned with alternately flashing red and blue lights. He shrugged at Ariadne's puzzled look. 'Failing that, we can try to blow a hole in it. That's always an option.'

Ariadne turned back to Abe, a question forming on her lips, when she was struck by a sudden, horrifying change in the Collective's appearance. His usual ultra-white complexion was changing, even as she watched—tendrils of the same unnatural green that permeated the ship were spreading up Abe's neck towards his jaw.

'Abe! What's wrong? Are you all right?'

It was a few seconds before he answered, and his normal monotone was sluggish and slurred. 'Aff...firmative. Connection... established. Locking mechanism under... stood and de—de—de... activated.'

With a hissing whine like gas escaping from a balloon, the door began to slide open. Abe's head slumped to his chest as the connector detached from the lock and slid back into his wrist with a snick.

Ariadne gripped his shoulder. *Please be all right. Please, please.* He took several deep breaths, and she was overjoyed to see the nauseating green lines quickly fade and recede.

He turned to her, his eyes clear. 'I will be fine. No permanent damage. Ship intelligence attempted to... bond aggressively. Was able to resist.'

Ariadne patted his shoulder. 'Good. Wouldn't want you turning into one of those creepy spider-Scourges.'

'Uh, guys?' Luc pointed through the opened doorway.

Ariadne turned to look. *There it is.*

# 20. Lodestone

*If that's not the lodestone, I don't know what is.* Weapon raised, Luc slowly stepped into the chamber.

The room was roughly oval, the floor and walls empty, the same bare black and green the Titan was already starting to loathe the sight of. But in the very centre of the room, in a tangled nest of pulsating black tendrils that grew up from the floor, sat an egg-shaped stone blazing with white light.

'There's something here.' Ariadne's voice was cold, rough. Strained. He glanced over his shoulder to see her grimacing slightly, sweat beading on her brow. Her eyes flicked to his, widened. 'Careful.' The word was bitten off. She closed her eyes.

*That's not good.* 'Abe, with me.' Treading lightly, Luc took another step into the chamber. His gaze roamed the walls, which rose vertically for twenty or more feet before disappearing into shadow. His eyes strained as he tried to make out any shape or movement in that darkness. *Nothing.*

Luc felt rather than saw the Collective step up on his right. Abe's voice was low. 'Believe we are observed, Titan. My sensors fail to probe the full height of this room. They are—blocked.'

'Hmm. How's your eyesight?'

'Excellent. As is yours. Yet we see nothing.'

*Time to force the issue. Nothing to be gained by dawdling, as Proctor Samuel would say.* Luc smiled despite himself. *If only you could see me now, you old goat.* Eyes fixed on the stone, he turned slightly towards Abe. 'I'm going for the stone. Cover me.'

As he moved forward once again, Luc triggered the bodyshift. His skin itched, rubbing against the lining of his armour as he phased into chitin. One deep breath filled primary and secondary lungs. Adrenal glands fired. *Ready as I'll ever be.*

Two more steps. Three. He was six feet from the stone. This close, the brightness was dazzling. He contracted his pupils, narrowing them to the thinnest cat's eye to cut out the glare.

One more step.

*So close. Come on, you bastard. Whatever you're waiting for, do it—*

Luc's foot hit something. Something hard, invisible, between him and the lodestone.

His mind ignited.

'Holy fu*aieee*—' His rifle fell from limp hands as pain coursed through his skull. He stumbled, fell to one knee, rolled sideways and half onto his back, his head thumping into the transparent field he had kicked. Desperately trying to batten down the agony, he was vaguely aware of Abe in the corner of his vision. The Collective stood, motionless but for a tremor through his head and shoulders, as though he were having a seizure. The barrel of his flechette pistol shook.

*Founder no no lord help me oh lord the pain—arrrgh!* Luc's head lolled back, his tongue hanging out, eyes staring unfocused into the dark recesses of the chamber's ceiling.

From which a nightmare emerged.

The pain had soared to a crescendo that the Titan wouldn't

have thought possible. His brain had partly shut down, collapsing his consciousness into a tiny centre, a calm eye at the centre of the storm of agony, but leaving him just enough awareness to appreciate the horror descending towards him.

The same eight legs as the Scourge they had vanquished minutes before, but longer, grotesquely articulated. The body similarly stretched and moving with an almost snake-like sinuousness as it climbed down the wall, forked tail flicking from side to side. Utterly black, no hint of green veins. And the head... the same rough fattened U-shape as on those they had killed, but larger, too large to be supported even by that body.

It didn't hurry. A mere fifteen feet away, it delicately stepped down from the wall and onto the chamber floor. The creature's head was featureless, yet Luc had no doubt that it was coming for him. Ten feet away.

*And this is how I die.*

It stopped. The head swung gently left to right, as if shaking something loose. Then it turned towards the door.

*Ariadne.*

The pain in Luc's mind lessened, just a fraction, but even that was a blessed relief that almost made him cry out in gratitude. It also gave him the very slightest amount of freedom. With the same effort that would normally throw a man ten yards or punch a hole through plasteel, Luc turned his head.

The Seryn hung in the air, feet dangling six inches above the ground. Head thrown back, light blazed upwards from her eyes. The same ferocious white he had seen before, matching the fierce glare from the stone at Luc's back. Sparks ran across her armour and died, tiny ripples of sheet lightning enveloping her limbs and then fading.

The Scourge approached, body tensing and contracting, shortening, legs pulled together into a crouch as it slowly edged closer to the girl. Luc could feel pulses of psychic energy coming from it, but not directed at him—waves of power he felt wash past him towards Ariadne, the mere ripples at the edge making him whimper. *How? How does she take it? Please, Ariadne, please*

*please please.*

Her body swung back and forth under the mental assault. The sparks were more frequent, more intense, the waves of lightning brighter and faster, wrapping her completely until every part of her seemed to glow.

Still the Scourge approached her.

The storm around Ariadne strengthened, and she swayed like a rubberoak tree in a hurricane. The fire around her brightened, and the storm continued to grow. She was vibrating. Luc could only stare, entranced.

The Scourge was mere inches away from her.

Her head dropped. Her gaze fixed on the eyeless face of the creature now reaching out for her. The storm paused, as if for breath.

Then broke.

The veil of psychic energy encompassing the Seryn exploded outward. The shockwave rammed Luc against the field at his back, pounding him to the floor as both shockwave and field vanished.

The Scourge flew across the room, a keening shriek splitting the air as it was pinned against the wall. Luc stared rapt at the creature's violent throes, its head shaking back and forth, legs flailing as it screamed.

It fell silent and slumped to the floor.

The pain in Luc's mind ceased. He gasped, as though coming up for air after an hour too long under water. *Oooooooh.* Eyes watering, he gingerly pushed himself up to sit and looked about. Abe stumbled drunkenly, clutching his head with his good left hand, eyes squeezed shut. Luc looked towards the door.

Ariadne lay on the ground, utterly still.

* * *

'This isn't going well, is it, Ship?' Neela stood on *Mournstar's* bridge, gazing at the holoprojection of the battlefield.

'NEGATIVE, SENATOR. OUR FORCES ARE BEING WORN DOWN. AT CURRENT RATE OF ATTRITION, DEFEAT IS INEVITABLE.' The ship paused. 'TRANSMISSION FROM

ADMIRAL GRAFF. CONNECT?'

Neela turned to the viewport. 'Do it.'

The admiral appeared, the bridge behind him crowded with running staff. Graff looked no more or less displeased than when he'd first arrived. *He probably looks like that on his birthday, too.*

As usual, he got straight down to business. 'Senator, we're in the shit. Have you noticed? The combined fleet is putting together the finest damn performance I've ever seen. There are pilots pulling manoeuvres I didn't even know were possible. It's like they've got eyes in the back of their heads.'

Neela hid a smile. *Good job, Margo.* 'But?'

Graff nodded. 'But. We're still losing. It's those damn fighters—every ten minutes, another wave streams out of that bastard mothership. We're expending so much effort fighting them off that we're making barely any headway against the larger vessels. It's slow, but we're being worn down.'

'Funny. That's exactly what *Mournstar* just said. What do you suggest?'

'It's not a suggestion, Senator. It's the only damn option. We need to take out that mothership, and stop those fighters. Nothing else will do. And seeing as every vessel we've got that's big enough to take a shot at it is tied up here—'

Neela nodded. 'We need to do it from the inside.'

The admiral nodded again. 'Lord knows what they've found in there, or if they're even still with us. But if they are, they need to find a way to give us some breathing space.' He slammed his fist into the armrest of his command seat. 'Just give us an hour, and we can end this! Graff out.'

The image vanished, replaced by the chaotic view of the ongoing battle. Neela watched as a Scourge vessel zoomed past a Titan cruiser, strafing it with bursts of lasfire. Tiny pockets of flame erupted where the ship was struck, then were extinguished by the vacuum. A volley of missiles streamed out from the gunnery turrets atop the Titan craft, half of them striking the Scourge ship as it veered away, reeling but largely undamaged. A swarm of Scourge fighters screamed in from the other direction, buzzing the cruiser like gnats. Slugs of plasma fire drove them back, but only for a second. The war of attrition rumbled on.

*This isn't going well.* Neela spun back to the holoprojection. '*Mournstar*, can you pull up a link to Luc?'

'AFFIRMATIVE. PATCHING THROUGH ABE'S SUBSPACE TRANSCEIVER. ONE MOMENT.' Neela watched a small red dot wink out. *Another Rapier destroyer down. That's four.* 'CONNECTION UP. READY.'

Eyes still on the battle map, Neela called, 'Luc, can you hear me?'

No response came for a few seconds, then her lover's voice answered, a little more sluggish than normal. 'Yes. Yes, I hear you.' Another pause. 'How's the battle coming?'

'Not well. Headline: The fighters from the mothership are grinding us down. Graff thinks if we can stop them, we can turn the tide.'

Another few seconds of silence passed. *What's happening over there?*

Luc finally came back. 'We need this ship destroyed, right?'

'That's pretty much it. Luc, what happened? What's wrong?'

'It's… It's not good. Ariadne, she's—'

*Oh no. Please, no.* 'Luc—'

'She's unconscious. In a coma. Something. She's barely breathing. Her pulse is ragged. Slow.' He sounded distraught.

'What happened?'

'We were attacked. Abe and I, we were… We had no chance. She saved us. But it took so much, she— I think she literally blew her mind.'

Neela heard him take a deep breath. She stayed silent. *Come on, Luc. Come back.*

'Right. Anyway, we've got the lodestone. My belt harness was big enough, Founder be praised. Weighs a ton, but I'll manage.' A measure of his old cockiness was returning. 'That just leaves, what—destroying a ship the size of a planet, carrying the girl out of here, and not getting caught in the resulting shitstorm. Easy. See you in half an hour, yeah?'

*That's my boy.* 'See you soon, Luc. Bring us all home safe.' She twirled her finger in the air, and the ship dropped the connection. Neela continued to stare at the holoprojection.

After a moment, she asked quietly, 'Ship, what chance do you give them?'

There was no answer for a little while.

'INSUFFICIENT DATA.'

Neela nodded. 'But if you had to guess?' She watched one of the small blue dots—*A corvette, maybe*—wink out. Another one down.

The pause was even longer that time, as if the ship didn't want to answer.

'SLIM.'

\* \* \*

Abe had listened intently to the conversation between the Titan and senator. After the call ended, he watched Luc gently prop Ariadne up against the wall of the lodestone chamber. It was obvious what needed to be done.

The Titan turned to him, after one last glance to check that the Seryn was secure. 'You heard what Neela said, I assume?'

'Affirmative.'

'What are our options? We need to get Ri secured and back on the *Widget*, obviously. And I wouldn't mind putting this big lump down, too.' He patted the lodestone, held in place at the small of his back by a harness, and dimmer since they had unplugged it from the tendril nest. 'So we head back to the ship, drop off stone and girl, you stand guard, and I head back in. You'll have to give me directions to the core, of course. No scanners built in up here.' Luc tapped his temple, starting to pace as he formulated a plan. 'And then we hope that I've got enough mines to do some damage.'

*He does not see.* 'Luc.'

The Titan stopped pacing and looked at Abe, brows raised.

'Plan is too high-risk. Mothership engine cluster is two thousand metres from this point. In a direct line. Distance on foot could be ten or more kilometres.'

Luc rolled his eyes slightly and opened his mouth to rebut.

Abe pressed on. 'Likelihood of even you surviving and succeeding is infinitesimal. Addition: Insufficient time until fleet is broken to point of destruction.'

'How could you—'

'*Mournstar* feeds real-time updates.' Now it was Abe's turn to tap his temple. 'Simulations have been run. Calculations are accurate. Maximum window until inevitable defeat is eighteen minutes. No more.'

The Titan's shoulders sagged. He looked over again at the young Seryn, her face pale even in the dimly lit chamber, chest rising and falling only barely as she struggled against the damage done by the Scourge's mental attack. Luc shook his head slowly. 'Then we've failed.'

*How does he not see?*

'No, Titan. There is still a chance.'

Luc's head snapped up, his gaze fierce. He barked, 'How?'

'You return to *Widget* as planned. You can carry both the lodestone and the Seryn, affirmative?'

'Of course. She weighs nothing. Then what?'

*He will not like this.* 'Then you leave.'

The Titan's eyes narrowed in confusion. He opened his mouth. Shut it. 'No, you've lost me. That plan doesn't seem to include taking out this big ugly pile of rock.' He gestured at their surroundings.

'Negative. You return to *Widget*. I remain here. Reconnect to the ship's systems. Previous connection suggests all systems are linked—including engine control. Small but non-zero chance I will be able to induce fatal engine overload.'

Luc threw his head back and blew out his cheeks. 'It's a hell of a risk. You're going to have to make it back through those corridors alone—I'm sure I can hold off whatever needs holding off until you get back to the ship, but there's got to be a good chance you *don't* make it back.'

Abe shook his head once. *Still. But now he will see.* 'There is zero chance I will make it back.'

Again the Titan's eyes narrowed. 'What? Why?'

'Previous connection was extremely difficult to disengage. Expect I will be unable to break free after extended connection. Addition-speculation: Likely that overload will need to be manually maintained until point of failure.'

Luc's expression had darkened. 'Taking you with it. You're talking about sacrificing yourself.'

*He sees.* 'Yes.'

The Titan stared at Abe in silence for a full minute, jaw clenched, teeth grinding. Finally he turned away, walked over to Ariadne, and hoisted her up over his shoulder with one hand, then turned back to the Collective. 'There's no other way, is there?'

'None.'

Luc sighed. Nodded once. For the second time, offered his hand to Abe. *While this one lives, there is hope for us. For us both.* The Collective grasped his forearm. Wrist to wrist, they shook.

'I won't let them forget this, Abe. Anyone.'

'Chance be with you.'

'And with you.' Their hands dropped. A glance, a nod, and the Titan turned to leave.

Abe called, 'Titan.' Luc turned. 'Will you fulfil a request?'

'Of course. What?'

'If all ends well. As planned and hoped. Request: Do not use the Book of Ascension. None of you. It is shortcut-crutch-hidden trap. So much joy in the discovery of the secrets of the universe.' Abe shook his head gently. 'Do not rob humanity of that joy.'

The Titan thought for a few moments, then nodded slowly. 'We'll do as you say.'

Abe nodded. 'Goodbye, Luc.'

One last nod, and Luc spun on his heel and left.

The room was silent. Abe stepped over to the tendril nest at the centre of the chamber. *Speculation: Higher bandwidth-direct connectivity to mothership systems. Better chance of gaining control.* He examined the cradle in which the lodestone had sat. Sure enough, a range of ports offered themselves, promising access deep into the ship's core.

Abe first reopened his connection to Network and uploaded all of his remaining data. That done, he disconnected for the final time. Moving close to the nest, with a quick glance at the dead or crippled Scourge, Abe extended the connector cable once again and slid it into the nearest access point.

He instantly felt the mothership's mind probe his own. *Hive. Group consciousness. Similar in respects to Collective. Interesting.* Understanding came quicker this time as he submitted to the insidious demand for immersion in the group mind—system access, including the engine cluster, opening like flowers in his mind as he built a mental map of the entire vessel.

*Or perhaps—*

No. Not just the vessel.

The entire Scourge fleet.

*Useful.*

Quicker and quicker, he mapped the Scourge network. It was ugly, a discordant tangle of oddly elegant mental connections, wired at a primal level through sheer instinct and anger. There were no protections. No safeguards. *No countenance of infiltration. Network opens easily-accommodating-demanding. So hungry for submission.*

He raised his left hand and watched the skin darkening from white through dusky grey to black, veins of putrid green splitting his flesh as his mind raced along alien pathways, seeding destruction. Abe smiled. He would give them submission. And in return?

He would take everything.

# 21. Consequence

Five minutes later, Luc sprinted through the portal into the vent-turned-docking bay where they had left the *Widget*. The corvette was still there, which was good, and it wasn't surrounded by Scourge, which was even better. He held Ariadne's head steady against his chest with one hand, the other clasping her waist to his shoulder. The weight of the lodestone at his back was really starting to burn now. *That's going to hurt in the morning. Or we could get shot to pieces in the next ten minutes. So it might not be a problem.*

He skidded to a halt at the gullwing door into the corvette's cabin, releasing Ri's head to reach for... *Shit. How do I open this?* He was saved by the hiss of the escaping air as the ship's hydraulics kicked in and the door swung up and open.

A voice not dissimilar to *Mournstar*'s called from within, 'Greetings, Luc-Titan. Identification complete. A83-7F44 Abe has transferred control of my systems to your authority.'

Luc shook his head wryly as he stepped into the corvette, careful not to bump Ariadne on the doorframe. *Is there anything he didn't think of?* 'Thank you, Ship. Do you need me to, you know, drive?'

'Negative, Luc-Titan. Fully capable of managing own systems.' The pride rung out even through the synthesised mechanical voice.

'Okay. Great.' He settled Ariadne into one of the cabin seats and strapped her in. Checked her pulse once again, her breathing. *Still ragged. So shallow. She needs the medbay, now.* Luc turned away and threw himself into one of the two pilot seats. 'Let's go. Back to *Mournstar*, now.'

'We are not waiting for A83-7F44?'

Luc closed his eyes and sighed. 'No, Ship. Abe is staying behind.'

'Understood. Systems are prepped. Departure underway.'

Luc felt a faint jolt as the corvette lifted off the floor of the vent, spinning as it did to face the exit. The G-force was minimal as it gained speed, shooting out of the exit and into open space.

'You'll need to keep the same course as we took on the way in, understood?'

'Understood, Luc-Titan. But maybe unnecessary.'

*Oh, I'm pretty sure it is.* 'Why's that, ship?'

'Battle paradigm has shifted significantly since inbound journey. Enemy craft behaviours are… confused.'

Luc looked down at the dots moving on the *Widget's* dash display. *What is it talking about— Oh.* 'They're attacking each other.'

'Affirmative. Or drifting without purpose. Barely a third of the Scourge fleet remain focused on battle. Pattern shifts in our favour.'

'He did this. The brilliant bastard.' *Abe. Founder bless you. Wherever you're going.*

'Will steer a course away from flashpoints. Arrival at *Mournstar* in… twelve minutes.'

Luc settled back in the pilot seat, watching the display as one by one, the Scourge ships winked out of existence. He was closing his eyes and considering a very brief nap when the ship spoke.

'Attention: Power surge detected. Localised near centre of Scourge mothership.'

*He's done it. He's actually —*

*Wait.* 'Ship, how far away are we?' Luc asked.

'Seven point one million kilometres.'

*That sounds like a long way, but...* 'And the blast radius of the mothership if it goes boom?'

'Uncertain. ' The ship paused for a second. 'Estimate between point nine and eighteen million kilometres.'

*Shit.* 'Can you go any faster?'

'Affirmative. Capable of velocities a factor —'

'Please go as fast as you can!' Luc interrupted.

'Understood. Warning: Increased speed likely to draw Scourge attention and increase risk of hostile engagement.'

Luc threw up his hands. 'Do it! It's going to pretty bloody hostile if we get caught in the blast when that thing goes nova.'

'Accelerating now.' The ship managed to sound a little huffy.

Luc shook his head in exasperation. *Founder save me from ships that can think.*

A minute passed in silence.

'Power surge nearing critical levels. Estimate criticality in twenty seconds.'

'Are we going to make it?'

The ship paused. Luc bunched his fists, ready to punch the thing.

It finally responded. 'Likely.'

Luc groaned, gazing out of the viewport as they sped past the wreckage of a Scourge ship.

Fifteen.

Ten.

Five.

One.

There was no noise, of course. But the shockwave slammed

into the back of the corvette like a kick in the backside, launching it forwards in a barrel roll and sending the instruments into darkness. *Oh, you've got to be kidding me.* Luc fought back nausea, clenching his abdomen and waiting to ride it out.

After ten seconds, the first flickers of life appeared on the dash, and he breathed a sigh of relief. Thrusters fired, arresting the corvette's spin, and the starfield steadied. 'You all right, ship?'

The *Widget* sounded a little groggy. 'Affirmative. Systems failed over to secondary unit. Bringing primaries back on-line now.' The main display flicked back to life, the Scourge markers scattered thinly.

Luc breathed again. *We did it.* 'Ship, switch viewport to rear view. Show me the mothership.'

An instant later, filling the view was a slowly expanding ball of hot gas and dust where the leviathan had been seconds before.

Luc watched the brightness dim slowly as the energy seeped into the void. *We actually did it.*

But that wasn't quite right.

*He did it.*

*   *   *

On *Mournstar*'s bridge, Neela was baffled. 'I don't understand. What's happening?'

'MANY SCOURGE VESSELS HAVE CEASED FIRE AND ARE DRIFTING ALONG THEIR LAST COURSE. OTHERS HAVE BEGUN FIRING ON ONE ANOTHER.'

'But why?'

'UNKNOWN. SUSPECT DEVELOPMENTS ON MOTHERSHIP ARE RELATED.'

Neela stared, eyes wide, at the battle map as the enemy continued to fall into chaotic disarray. She watched as the previously ragged lines of the allied fleet firmed up and began a concerted offensive. 'It's working. The tide has shifted, hasn't it?'

'AFFIRMATIVE, SENATOR. ONE MOMENT. INCOMING TRANSMISSION FROM BETA-9 CLOUDMOTHER.'

'Put her through.' Cloudmother appeared on the viewport, as disconcerting a sight as ever. 'Greetings, Cloudmother. The battle seems to have shifted for us.'

'Indeed-indeed. Game has changed, tables turned. Enemy snaps at itself like wild dogs or wanders lost and mindless. We press our sudden advantage.'

Neela glanced away. *Even over a comlink, those eyes are just too disturbing.* 'Do you have any idea what caused this, Cloudmother?'

'No firm conclusion-reason-cause. Suspicion-feeling, yes. A83-7F44, Abe.'

Neela waited for clarification. In vain. 'Abe? I don't understand.'

'Three minutes ago, Network received upload from A83-7F44, tagged final transmission. All remaining data. Hint of attempt to connect into Scourge network. Disconnected from Network to protect it from potential corruption.'

'Sorry, I still don't— What does "final transmission" mean?' Even as she said it, Neela realised— *Oh, no. Abe.* She felt herself go numb.

'Final transmission. Upload of all unshared data before imminent death. Suspect connection to Scourge network only possible facilitator for destruction of mothership. But also expected lethal. Result: Final transmission.'

*He's giving his life to end this. To save us.* Neela couldn't help but feel bitter at Cloudmother's unfeeling tone. Her voice echoed that. 'You don't seem very concerned, Cloudmother. One of your own is about to die.'

'No concern. No reason. Why? Pride-honour-uplift. One Collective is all. Sacrifice of Abe is sacrifice of all Collective for the greater good. Of all humanity. Why concern? Pride.'

Neela sadly shook her head. *I don't think I'll ever understand these people.* She glanced down at the battle map once again. The green-black dots of the Scourge numbered far fewer now.

'BREAKING POINT HAS BEEN REACHED. COMPLETE DESTRUCTION OF SCOUR—' Its voice cut out as a blinding flash lit up the border of the viewport around Cloudmother's transmission.

Neela squeezed her eyes shut, too late to avoid being dazzled. She saw an outline of the hanging Collective imprinted on her eyelids, seared in red and white.

Keeping her eyes shut, she asked 'Ship? What happened?'

'SCOURGE MOTHERSHIP HAS SUFFERED COMPLETE ENGINE CONTAINMENT FAILURE. RESULTING CHAIN REACTION HAS DESTROYED THE VESSEL. SPECTACULARLY. I HAVE A RECORDING, IF YOU WOULD LIKE TO SEE IT.'

'No, thank you.' The glare was dimming. Neela slowly opened her eyes. Cloudmother was still looking down at her from the viewport.

'Abe's goal has been achieved, Senator. His sacrifice inspiring-noble-good. Are you inspired? Do you have pride?'

*Of course. I just wish it hadn't been...* 'I do, Cloudmother. I'm very proud.'

'Then we are not so unalike. Perhaps a closer bond between our peoples could forge-build-flourish. However: May future meetings be more peaceful.'

Neela smiled sadly. 'Perhaps. Goodbye, Cloudmother. Thank you.' The viewport cleared, and Neela suddenly realised. 'Luc!'

'INBOUND, SENATOR. WIDGET SIGNALLED ELEVEN SECONDS AGO. AS IS ARIADNE, THOUGH REQUIRING URGENT ATTENTION.'

Neela slumped into one of the bridge seats, feeling drained. 'Thank you, *Mournstar.' Thank whatever was watching over them.*

The last of the green-black dots was extinguished on the battle holo.

It was over.

Head on her chest, Neela closed her eyes. And let her tears fall.

⋆ ⋆ ⋆

The medbay was cool and silent. Jarrod leaned over Ariadne,

frowning. 'She looks very weak, Lucius. Her skin's pale.'

'I know, Jarrod.' *I can see that too,*

'You're sure she's going to make it?'

'That's what Mo tells me. She's stable, she's not in any danger—but her brain activity is all over the place. It's like an electrical storm in there.' Luc stroked a strand of hair away from Ariadne's eyes.

'But the ship is sure that's going to settle down?' Jarrod looked around the medbay, as if searching for some display or readout that would tell him something about the sole patient.

'Ninety-three per cent sure, apparently. It just can't tell us when. Could be in the next five minutes, could be in a month. We just wait.'

His uncle nodded, checked the terminal on the inside of his wrist. 'I need to leave, Lucius. I'm sorry. You know I'd like to stay longer.'

Luc turned, smiling wryly. 'It's fine. The fleet waits for no man.'

'That it doesn't.' Jarrod clasped Luc on the shoulder, his expression intent. 'Go and do what you need to do. Complete your mission, and come back to us. Your people are waiting for you.'

'I know.' Luc opened his arms, and they hugged. 'Thank you for coming, Jarrod. For believing me. It can't have been easy.'

His uncle snorted with laughter. 'Well, if it had been anyone else, I would have had a lot of persuading to do. For you—well, it's amazing how quickly people fall in line for their future leader.'

*Leader. And where am I going to lead them? Our future's more uncertain than it's ever been.* Luc stepped back, looked Jarrod in the eyes. 'Go, then. You don't want to miss your boat.'

'Founder with you, Luc.'

'And with you.'

Jarrod passed Neela in the medbay doorway and gave her a quick goodbye before hurrying down to the shuttle bay. Luc smiled at her as she entered. *She looks tired. Tired like I feel.*

Neela slipped her arm around his waist and leaned her head on Luc's shoulder, looking down at Ariadne. 'No change?'

'Not yet.' Luc held her to his side, comforted by the warmth and softness of her body. 'Did the Seryn disembark?'

'They did. Eventually. It took me a while to assure Margo that we could look after Ri, and that she didn't need to stay.'

'She wouldn't want to go where we're going, anyway.'

'And where is that, do we think?' Neela turned to peer up at Luc. 'We go back to Promise, sure. Try to replace the lodestone, then...'

'That's as far as the plan goes, right now. I'm hoping a big red button will appear saying "Press here to contact Unity, and he'll be right with you."'

Neela laughed. 'Sounds a little low-tech, don't you think?'

'Well, we can hope. Oh— Any parting words of wisdom from our friend Admiral Graff?'

'Not much. He stopped doubting the importance of the mission, at least, so he doesn't think I'm a complete idiot any more. But we lost a lot of men and women. That's tough, for all of us, but him especially; he looks hard on the outside, but he feels it.'

'Jarrod's the same. Every death under his command— It's like he dies a little bit, too.'

Neela sighed and leaned against Luc again. They watched Ariadne's chest rise and fall, one shallow breath every few seconds. 'To Promise then, I suppose.'

Luc nodded. 'To Promise.'

But neither of them moved.

⋆ ⋆ ⋆

Ariadne heard the voices first. It seemed as though they were part of the dream she was having, a confusing almost-nightmare where she ran and ran along black corridors, seemingly chased by something or someone—but when she turned to face it, ran back to confront her pursuer, it vanished, leaving her trapped and running, endlessly running, in a warren from which there was no exit.

The voices confused her. They seemed to be coming from behind the doors she ran past—always locked—and they were never clear, just rumbling murmurs.

Over time they got louder, or closer, as if she were nearing whoever was speaking, but no clearer. She just ran, veering left then right, up and down, never getting anywhere. She reached a junction, turned, the voices so close now—

Luc stood before her. *'Ariadne.'*

*'Luc?'*

*'Hey, there. Welcome back.'*

Ariadne opened her eyes.

The medbay ceiling gleamed brilliant white above her. She squinted against the glare as a shape leaned in, shading her eyes. She struggled to focus, and the shape shimmered into clarity.

'Hi, Luc.'

'Hi, yourself. Glad to see you awake. You had us worried for a while there.'

Her mouth felt like dust. 'Can I have some water?'

'Of course. Dry mouth? The ship's kept you on intravenous fluids, but I bet your tongue tastes like ass.' Ariadne smiled weakly at the crudity as the Titan pulled a thin, clear tube from a station next to the bed she lay on and slipped it into the corner of her mouth. 'Just suck.'

She did and tasted blessedly cool, crisp water. *Oh that's so much better.* After a few seconds, she nodded at Luc, and he pulled out the tube. Immediate need met, questions tumbled into her mind.

She closed her eyes, frowned, then looked up at the Titan. 'Where are we? What happened? How long have I been... here?'

'We're on our way back to Promise. You've been in a coma for three days. You used a lot of yourself up fighting off that... thing. Do you remember?'

*Black. Green. Luc, crippled. Abe, broken. Power. Relentless power. Head and legs and claws*—She shivered slightly and nodded. 'Snatches.'

'Well, you did it. We were down and out, without you. But

we did it. We got the lodestone. And we won.'

Relief flooded through Ariadne. 'Oh. That's—good. Really good. Sorry, I'm just a little— That's wonderful.'

But Luc didn't look happy. *What's wrong?* She reached out to touch his thoughts and feelings, and—nothing. *Wait, what's the matter with—*

'It didn't go perfectly though. We lost a lot of ships, and we would have lost more. All of us, probably, and the battle. If it wasn't for Abe.'

Luc looked away at something, took a deep breath, released it in a sigh. He looked back into Ariadne's eyes. 'We needed to destroy the mothership, or we wouldn't have had a chance. Abe thought of a way to do it, but… he had to stay behind to make it work. He's gone.'

*Abe. Oh, no. Poor, dear, sweet Abe.* Ariadne felt tears welling up and squeezed her eyes shut as the first drops rolled down the sides of her face. She felt Luc take her hand in his enormous one, grip it gently. She nodded, opened her eyes. 'He saved us, then.'

The Titan nodded. 'Not just us, either.'

'He'd have been so proud. To be able to do that. For everyone, all the Collective, and the normal humans, and your lot. He loved… well, life. All of it. Even though he always felt like he was somewhere on the outside. To be able to give it a chance to go on—it's all he could have wanted.'

'I actually miss the weirdo, as well. Wouldn't have thought I would.'

Ariadne gently slapped his hand. 'He wasn't a weirdo. He was just—himself.'

Luc nodded. 'He was very himself, wasn't he?' He let go of her hand. 'I'll go and tell Neela you're awake. She's been working most hours since the battle—calling every senator in the Commonwealth, it seems like—but she'll want to come and see you.'

Ariadne nodded, a little absently, as he headed for the medbay door. She was reaching again, outward to the world around her and inward to the core of her self from which she drew the power, to touch people, to move things, to—

*All gone. It's all gone.* 'Luc?'

He stopped just short of the doorfield and turned. 'Hmm?'

She stared across the bay at him, tears welling up again. 'I think… I can't feel anything any more. Or touch it. My mind is just—' The tears began to roll down her cheeks again. 'Blank.'

Luc returned to her side, his expression confused.

She looked up at him, pleading with her eyes for help she knew he couldn't give. 'I think I'm broken.'

# 22. Unity

*It's still creepy, even now. Even when we know they're not coming back.*

Neela stared out of the shuttle viewport as they sailed for the second time through the torn and twisted portals that led to the centre of Promise. She glanced over at Boone as he piloted the shuttle and realised how little they'd spoken in recent days. When the crisis came to a head, he had—not disappeared, but stepped back.

'How are you, Boone?' she asked quietly. Luc and Ariadne were chatting in the seats behind. Mainly Luc, trying to bring the Seryn out of the shell she had retreated into since discovering the loss of her abilities.

The Athravan looked over, flashing that old familiar grin. 'Marvellous, Ms. Kane. Grand. How could I not be? A tremendous victory, that. Superb effort all round.'

'I noticed you didn't... chip in as often as you normally do.

Left us to it, as it were.'

'Noticed that, did you? Well. Yes.' The old nose scratch. 'Conscious decision. Not my fight, was it? Your galaxy now, you and yours.'

'We'd have been happy to listen to any advice you had, though. You know that. After all, you don't always get to lean on the experience of someone as... experienced as you.' Neela laughed as Boone grinned at her again.

'Oh, an old dog like me? Not much to contribute. Oh, sure, I was in some ding-dongs as big as that back in my day—got into it with some folks you youngsters are a lot of years away from having the pleasure of meeting. But every fight's different. And you fought yours as well as could be. You can be proud, Senator. Very proud.'

The light in the shuttle had brightened as they neared the end of the cobalt-coloured tunnel that opened into the outer core. At last they emerged, the brilliant white surfaces dazzling after the gloom of the shaft. They powered onward towards the airlock that would take them to the core, the broken hulks on the floor of the outer core still there.

*And still creepy.*

Luc leaned forwards between the seats. 'Boone, do we have any idea what's going to happen when we put the lodestone back?' The stone was strapped into its own seat further back in the shuttle.

'Not a clue, lad. All a big adventure, isn't it?'

Luc rolled his eyes, then looked back at Ariadne. She was staring out of one of the side viewports, face blank.

*Oh dear.* 'What do you think will happen, Ri?'

'Hmm?' Her head snapped round. She clearly hadn't been listening.

'When we put the stone back. What's your prediction? Earthquake? Unity suddenly appears in a blaze of light?' Neela asked.

'Or nothing at all,' Luc muttered. Neela shot him a look.

'Oh,' said Ariadne. 'I don't know. Maybe a giant cave will

open in one of the mountains, and Unity's asleep in there? Like a bear. Hibernating.'

Luc shivered. 'I hope it's not like a bear. Don't like bears.'

Neela frowned, baffled. Boone called out. 'Approaching airlock door, folks. Here we go.'

*Rear field vanishes. In we go. Rear field comes back. Darkness. Front field opens —*

She sighed contentedly at the magical sight. 'Back in paradise.'

Boone chuckled. 'That we are, Senator. No time for sightseeing, though. Work to be done. Off we go.'

After several minutes coasting towards the miniature star at Promise's core, cooing over the sights below, Boone brought the shuttle into a synchronous orbit alongside the empty lodestone cradle. He turned to Luc. 'Over to you, lad. Put her back where she belongs.'

'Yeah, just like that. What could go wrong?' Luc said as he moved back in the cabin and unstrapped the heavy stone. 'Open the door, then.'

Boone palmed a panel on the dash and the large side door of the shuttle slid back. Neela squinted at the glare from the gleaming, chrome-fused crystal cradle as it came into view, seemingly hovering stationary outside the doorway. She watched as Luc hefted the lodestone and moved towards the cradle.

*Don't drop it. Please don't drop it.*

His hands were sure. Leaning out over the small gap that dropped thousands of metres to the surface, Luc pushed the lodestone down between the triple prongs at the cradle's top. Down it went, into the cradle, finally snapping into place beneath the prongs with a thunderous click.

Luc stepped back, then turned to face them. 'Okay, so what do we do now —'

A sudden deafening high-pitched whine interrupted him.

*Blinding blue-white light.*

*A vortex, swirling away into infinity.*

*Darkness.*

⋆ ⋆ ⋆

Luc opened his eyes as a gull shrieked above him and wheeled away. He stood at the edge of a wide, rocky mesa of some kind, grey stone rimed with frost beneath a pale grey, overcast sky. In front of and below him was a green-grey sea, partly frozen, waves sluggishly crunching against each other to collapse in slush on a white pebble beach. *Okay, that's new. And damn, it's cold.*

'Brrr. It's freezing.' He turned right to see Ariadne and Neela shivering at the sudden temperature drop after their... *Relocation, I guess. To somewhere. And where's Boone?*

'Hello.'

Luc spun to his left. A few yards away stood a small boy, maybe eight years old. He was dressed in thick green corduroy trousers and a grey duffel coat a size or more too large for him, his hands hidden somewhere in the voluminous sleeves. A dark brown face smiled out from a fur-lined hood, teeth pearly white, twinkling eyes so dark they looked black.

'Uh, hello.' Luc gave the boy a wave. 'How are you?' He felt Neela and Ri step up beside him.

'I'm fine. Thanks for asking.'

'Good. So,' Luc looked around again, down at the beach where human shapes moved against the whiteness of the pebbles, then back to the boy. 'Do you know where we are?'

'Of course I do. If I didn't, I wouldn't know where I am, would I?'

*Good point.* 'That's true. So—'

'Your friend's fine, by the way. I left him in your ship. He didn't really need to be here.'

Luc frowned. *Left him in the— Wait. No.* 'You're... Unity?'

The boy laughed, a perfectly melodious childlike laugh. 'You've been talking to the Zythylyx, haven't you? No one else calls me that.'

Ariadne forced out her words through chattering teeth. 'We were expecting someone... older.'

Neela shook her head. 'No… This isn't what you really look like, is it?'

The boy cocked a finger at her, a jarringly adult gesture from a child. 'Well done, Senator.'

She turned to Luc. 'How does he know—'

'I know lots of things, Ms. Kane. I know you've had a long journey, and a terrible battle, and done a great service to the galaxy. And a big favour to me too, I should say.' The boy—Unity turned away from them, wandered to the edge of the mesa, and looked down at the beach. 'I was at a loss without my anchor. Couldn't get home.'

He turned back to them, grinned with those dazzling teeth. 'Thanks for putting it back. As much as I'm enjoying spending some time here, I don't think studying bearsharks is something I'd want to do forever.'

'You're studying—What's a bearshark, now?' asked Ariadne.

Unity pointed. 'One of those. See?'

Luc peered over the edge. Down on the beach directly below the cliff was a group of four slow-moving animals. A sandy grey colour, vaguely bear-shaped but with wide, flipper-like paws.

'They're quite clumsy on land, but put them in the water, and they're very graceful. The fur refracts light in a special way, too—makes them translucent. Brilliant predators.'

'So not a good idea to go swimming, then?' Luc asked.

Unity laughed again. 'You're funny, Titan. I wasn't expecting that. Your people always seem so serious.' Unity nodded at the bearshark family again. 'They only exist on this planet, the bearsharks. There's a zoological team here from your Commonwealth, Senator. Studying them. Trying to stabilise the population. They've been getting sick and dying recently, and no one knows why. Well—I do. The team is very close to finding out, though. I don't want to spoil it for them.'

'Do they not find it odd that there's a small boy wandering around that no one knows?' asked Neela. She was hugging herself, bobbing up and down in the chill. Luc slipped off his jacket and put it round her shoulders as he shifted his circulation to emit heat, and he gently pulled her and Ariadne close.

Unity was shaking his head. 'No, one of the geneticists thinks I'm her son. Just enough to not think about me too much, not enough to be too interested.' He shrugged, laughed. 'I don't want to distract them.'

*That's… nice of you?* Luc was struggling to know what to make of the person, creature, entity. He wondered what to say next as Unity walked closer to them, and looked up into the Titan's eyes.

Luc reeled.

*Not human. There is absolutely no way in Founder's name that thing could pass for a human up close. How stupid are these people?* The black eyes that the Titan had assumed were very dark brown… weren't. They were black, deep, timeless, and… full. *Full of too much time passed. Too long-lived. Too many things seen.*

Fighting the urge to run or kneel, Luc blurted, 'We need to ask a favour.'

He felt Neela and Ariadne tense beside him and knew they, too, had seen what he had.

'Of course. I wouldn't expect you to go to all that trouble just for my benefit.' Unity wiped his nose on one of his oversized sleeves and sniffed. 'How can I help?'

It didn't take as long to tell as Luc had thought, among the three of them. Unity listened intently the whole time, his unnerving gaze fixed on whoever was speaking.

When their story was over, he threw back his head and laughed uproariously. *Is that a good sign?*

'Oh dear. You don't want to get on the wrong side of the Weft. They're lovely, generally; never trouble anyone, always helpful. But you shouldn't go moving stars about. Those are where they are for a reason.' He shook his head like an old man, amused and exasperated by the naïveté of the young. 'You'd think that after people had been around for a few tens of millennia, they wouldn't be so stupid.'

'Can you help us, Unity?' Neela asked, cutting to the chase. *Before her fingers fall off, probably.* 'We didn't—we won't—have any desire to hurt them or do any damage, but... we just can't be sure it won't happen in the exact same way next time.'

Unity nodded slowly. 'Indeed.' He clapped his hands. 'Well, who am I to say no after you gave me a route back home? And handled those pesky—' His next word was an unintelligible garbled noise.

*Is that what the Scourge are really called? Suits them.*

'So you'll help?' Ariadne asked. 'And take us somewhere warm, too? Please?'

Unity flashed that brilliant grin. 'I will.' He turned towards the beach once more and waved. 'Bye, bearsharks!' he shouted—sounding exactly like a little boy.

Then Unity turned back to them. 'Let's go and talk to the Weft.'

Once more Unity clapped his hands; the sound didn't end. It kept ringing out, rising and rising in depth and volume until it sounded like thunder or a mountain falling, then—

*Blinding orange-red light.*

*Swirling vortex.*

*Darkness.*

* * *

Stars.

*So many stars—so close, so bright, so*—'Holy crap, we're in space!' Ariadne grabbed hold of Luc in a panic, worried that she was going to drift away. *Hang on. I can talk. Which means I can breathe.*

She looked at the silver-white surface on which they stood, seemingly open to the vacuum, but... not. 'This looks like Promise.'

Luc had kept his cool after their second soul-jarring warp through space. 'I think it is. And apparently Unity's party tricks include putting an atmosphere where there wasn't one an hour ago. Somehow, I'm not surprised. No sign of him, though—or the little boy shell he was wearing, anyway.'

'WE DO NOT NEED THAT HERE,' a resonating voice boomed from behind them.

*No. Not a voice, a thought, placed in my mind.*

Ariadne, Luc, and Neela turned and stepped back in unison.

Unity was before them. No longer a small boy, not even one with unnatural, timeless eyes. No body or form at all.

Instead, a fulgent white core at the centre of a vortex of blue light, deepening and darkening from centre to edge from pale electric to deepest midnight. Waves of energy rippled inward, seemingly sucked into the centre from the space around. *That's… I would say impossible, but that doesn't seem to apply anymore.*

'DO YOU PREFER THIS FORM?'

Neela answered, 'I… think it suits you better.'

A rumble, like a glacier cracking, that might have been laughter. 'WE HAVE ALWAYS ENJOYED THE COMPANY OF HUMANS. EVEN WHEN YOU WERE BOUND TO A SINGLE PLANET. YOU HAVE ALWAYS BEEN ENTERTAINING.'

Luc was frowning. 'Why do you refer to yourself as "we"?'

'WHY DO YOU THINK WE ARE NAMED UNITY?'

*Well, that told him.* Ariadne looked around, an excuse to look away from the dazzling light as much as anything else. 'Are the Weft here, Unity? Can you speak to them?'

'THE WEFT ARE ALWAYS HERE. AND EVERYWHERE. THEY ARE BEHIND EVERY WALL. FILLING THE EMPTY SPACES UNDER AND AROUND THE REAL. WE HAVE CALLED THEM. BEHOLD.'

And the Weft appeared.

At first they seemed like tiny suns, flaring into life in the distance against the starfield. But quickly they grew, blazing brighter and bigger—five of them, then ten, red and yellow, purple and blue, bright lights in the permanent night sky above Promise.

As one, they drifted in and down, swirling in a slow orbit around Unity, satellite suns around the brightest star in the heavens.

It was beautiful.

Ariadne stared, rapt. She realised she was crying.

Neela's sigh somewhere at Ariadne's side was the contented

sound of someone seeing the very last thing life has to offer. *Like I could die, right now, and be happy.* Minutes passed in silence, the Weft dancing slowly, occasionally flaring to greater brightness, then dimming again.

At some point, Unity spoke. 'WE HAVE COMMUNICATED YOUR STORY TO THE WEFT. THEY ARE VERY DISAPPOINTED THAT YOU WOULD CONSIDER MOVING THE STARS FROM THE PATHS TO WHICH THEY WERE ORDAINED.'

*Ordained?*

Luc answered. 'Please tell them we apologise for — what we might do in the future. That we don't wish to do any harm.'

'WE HAVE EXPLAINED. THE WEFT ARE CONSIDERING WHAT THEY WILL DO WHEN THE TIME COMES. SOME PONDER IF IT WOULD BE BETTER TO DESTROY YOU. OTHERS CONSIDER YOUR EFFORT AGAINST WHAT YOU CALL THE SCOURGE. AND ARE MORE LENIENT.'

They waited.

Ariadne held her breath, as if any noise might tip the balance the wrong way. She watched the multicoloured lights flare and dim, flare and dim. *They're discussing. Deciding our fate.* She grabbed Luc's hand.

At last, Unity's voice-thought boomed again. 'THEY HAVE DECIDED. WHEN THE TIME COMES.'

Ariadne squeezed the Titan's hand, breath still held, the lack of oxygen starting to burn in her chest. She waited. They all waited.

'THEY WILL FIND A WAY TO TALK TO YOU. THEY WILL EXPLAIN.'

The breath exploded out of Ariadne in a gasp. She gulped in fresh air from — somewhere. Unity continued.

'PRAY THAT YOUR CHILDREN'S CHILDREN WILL LISTEN.' Again that thunderous rumble of laughter. 'OR YOU WILL HAVE TO DO ALL OF THIS AGAIN.'

'Will you thank them for us?' asked Neela.

'THERE IS NO NEED. AND NOW THEY WOULD TOUCH

YOU. BEFORE THEY RETURN TO THEIR HIDDEN PLACES. THE WEFT SO RARELY ENCOUNTER THOSE WHO LIVE IN THE REAL. DO NOT BE AFRAID.'

On that last word, the Weft spiralled away from Unity's orbit and spun towards the huddled group. Before they could move or speak, the first of the Weft reached them—and passed right through.

Ariadne felt a delightful shiver run through her. *Like static electricity and sunlight, all at once.* One by one, each of the Weft passed through them, each seeming to add to a charge that built and built.

*Ooo, that feels—that feels—*

As the last of the Weft passed through her, something in Ariadne's mind went *click*. And just like that, as though someone had opened a door onto a dark room, she was whole again.

A smile lit up her face as she spun to yell her thanks, in time to see the beautiful lights dwindling, either speeding into the distance or collapsing in on themselves and folding back into the subspace from which they came. Ariadne waved instead.

Luc laughed, and she turned to see him shaking his head. 'You... I don't know. Glad to see you happy, Ri.'

'YOU ARE RETURNED TO WHAT YOU WERE BEFORE.'

Ariadne turned back to Unity and nodded. 'I am. It's— Thank you.'

'NOT US. THE WEFT. THEY DESIRED TO GIVE A GIFT. IN EXCHANGE FOR THE SCOURGE. FOR IT WAS THEIR PRISON THAT WAS ESCAPED.'

Neela reached over and squeezed Ariadne's arm. 'Are you—better? Back to normal?'

'I'm fine. I'm brilliant. Perfect!' She beamed.

'IT IS TIME. GOODBYE, HUMANS.'

Luc groaned. 'Oh, not again—'

*Blinding turquoise light.*

*Swirling vortex.*

*Darkness.*

*Mournstar's* bridge. And Boone.

Boone looked like a startled weasel as he peered about, but he broke into a grin as he saw them. 'That was something, wasn't it!'

* * *

Neela squeezed her eyes shut against the headache building in her temples. *I don't care how efficient it is. Humans weren't meant to travel like that.*

'Can we not do that ever again?' groaned Ariadne from somewhere nearby. Neela reopened her eyes to see Ri slump into one of the bridge seats. 'Mo, can you make some tea please?'

'OF COURSE. I SHOULD ALSO REPORT THAT MY SHUTTLE MATERIALISED WITHIN THE BAY FOURTEEN SECONDS AGO. AS YET, I AM UNABLE TO CALCULATE HOW YOU, OR IT, ARRIVED.'

Luc grunted. 'I think that might keep you occupied for a while, Mo.' He turned to Boone. 'How are you doing? Must have been a bit of a surprise.'

The Athravan nodded excitedly. 'First time, when you vanished, yes. Second time, when I did, not so much. Saw it coming, as it were. Was just wondering whether I should turn around and come back here—but I was a bit worried you might appear back where you left from. That would have ended badly if the shuttle hadn't been there, eh?' He waggled his eyebrows. 'I imagine you had a chat with the illustrious and mysterious Unity, then? Go well?'

Neela had wandered over to the food alcove to retrieve the tea and placed it on the long table, clear of the ship manifests and battle plans that had covered it a few days ago. 'It went very well. We didn't exactly get a commitment from the Weft that they wouldn't wipe us out if we do the same thing again, but they promised to at least try to get in touch first.'

Boone clapped his hands. 'Marvellous news! Tremendous. Best we could have hoped for. I must say, Jacob and the others were hopeful, but they always thought it was a very long shot that you'd succeed. I always had faith, though.' He tapped his nose conspiratorially. 'I know a sure thing when I see one.'

278

'A sure thing?' Luc sputtered. 'Are you mad? I mean, more so than usual? We could have been killed ten times over.'

Neela briefly shut her eyes. *One of us was.*

'But you came through though, didn't you? Sure thing. Told you.'

*He's irrepressible.* Neela sipped her tea as she sank into one of the other seats, and sighed. *Ah, valerian. That's better.* 'Thank you, Mournstar.'

'YOU ARE QUITE WELCOME, SENATOR. I GUESSED YOU MIGHT BE REQUIRING SOME RELIEF AFTER YOUR DIS- AND REAPPEARANCE.'

Ariadne looked up from her cup with a frown. 'Um. I just realised. We've done it.'

Luc looked down at her. 'Just realised, huh? You weren't paying that close attention, then.'

She dipped her fingers in her cup and flicked the tea at him. 'I know, idiot. I just mean— Well, what do we do now?'

Silence descended as they looked at each other, then broke out laughing. Neela shook her head. 'Get back to work, I suppose. I'm sure there are about a thousand urgent things I need to deal with.'

Luc looked a little sombre. 'And I need to get back to Mission. There's a lot that needs changing, and it won't be easy. Even with Jarrod's help—there are too many of the old regime still around who won't be thrilled at me showing up and changing the tune.' He brightened. 'Anyway, that can wait a few days. What about you, Ri?'

She looked pensive. 'I think maybe I might move. Get off Corinth. I'm thinking of Nexus Prime.' She turned to Neela. 'How does that sound? Want to show me the sights?'

'I'd love to. I'm pretty sure I can find you some work to do as well, if you're interested.' *Yes, definitely sure we could find a use for her talents.*

Boone coughed, then scratched his nose a little sheepishly as they looked at him. 'Before you do all that—marvellous plans though, sounds very exciting—are you not forgetting something? You know, the whole Book of Ascension thing. Fancy a peek at it? It's a bit fantastic. Secrets of the universe and all!'

Neela looked over at Luc. Their gazes met. She nodded and turned to Ariadne, who nodded back.

Luc turned back to Boone. 'Thanks, but we're going to say no. It's what Abe wanted. There's too much joy in discovering those secrets for ourselves.'

The Athravan looked stunned for a second, then barked a laugh. 'You know what, I think you're right. You've all got a hell of a ride to look forward to. Would be a shame to skip to the end of the story.'

*Hell of a ride indeed.* Neela took another sip, plans and projects and strategies unfolding in her mind. Breaking down the barriers between their peoples was not going to be straightforward. *Hundreds and hundreds of years of habit and prejudice to get past. But we'll manage.* She looked up at Luc again. *We can do anything.*

'MAY I ASK IF YOU HAVE CHOSEN A DESTINATION?'

Luc stepped over to Neela, leaned down, and kissed the top of her head. Hand on her shoulder, he turned to the viewport and gazed out towards the immaculate surface of the planet and the dazzling starfield above.

Neela looked up at him and smiled as she placed her hand on his. 'Corinth, Mission, Nexus Prime? How does that sound?'

Luc gave her a gentle squeeze. Ariadne nodded.

'That's settled, then. Destination confirmed.'

*Time to go home.*

# Repercussions

It had been a rough few weeks.

*Wake up with a lump on my head the size of a grapefruit. Jerry-rig a replacement jump engine from scavenged bits of whatever-the-fuck-they-were satellites, and stuff it with just enough spare vex to either get us to the nearest staging post or blow us into atoms. Get there and have an actual fistfight before we can commandeer a new ship—which turns out to be four bunks, a sonic shower, and a cockpit. Spend thirty days bouncing back to Nexus P in the company of Spence's snoring and Cullen's feet.*

*And* this *is the worst thing that's happened in the last month.*

Drake stood at attention, eyes fixed on Katarina Puschkova's back as she stared out of the viewport that spanned three sides of her office and therefore most of the ninety-seventh floor of Shax Tower. His boss was wearing a delicate lemon-yellow trouser suit that did absolutely nothing to change the fact that she was a double-hard bastard. *As that old drill master used to say.*

*And he would know—he was, too.*

'I'll be honest, Drake—I was hoping to hear of some extenuating circumstances from you. The report you sent in from the Firelake staging post was brief, in the extreme. The base commander wants you indicted, you know. Though it's not clear if that's for stealing his ship or breaking his jaw.'

Her voice was clipped, cold. *As always. Doesn't give me any bloody clue as to how this is going to turn out.*

'Yes, Ms. Puschkova. You see—'

'And yet.' Drake snapped his mouth shut. 'You come here today with nothing to add. Not even an elaborate yet transparent lie.' Katarina turned to face him, her Head of External Security. *The current one, at least.* 'Correct me if I'm wrong, yes? You successfully ambushed the target vessel, smoothly gained entry—and were then overcome by one Titan, a little girl, a half-man with a screwdriver for a hand, and a Commonwealth senator with zero combat training.'

*It doesn't sound great if you put it like that.* Drake choked down the urge to make excuses and wondered on which backwater world he'd be taking garrison duty on in the next few days. 'Yes, Ms. Puschkova.'

Katarina walked slowly towards him and stopped a mere foot away. Her scent was delightful, a delicate hint of— *Lavender, maybe? Fuck, I'm turning into Cullen.*

Drake tried to concentrate, gaze fixed steadily over her shoulder and into the vague middle distance. He held his breath as his boss sighed deeply.

'You're going to make this up to me, of course.'

Drake repressed the frisson of relief that coursed through him at her words. *If I'm going to make amends, then I'm not being put out to pasture. But I'm damn sure this isn't going to be easy.* 'Of course, ma'am. What are my orders?'

'Simple.' The Director of Operations for Shax Corp stepped around him and sat down behind her desk. Drake turned to see her staring intently up at him. 'Shax thrives on conflict. The new status quo that our friend in the Senate is espousing has the potential to dramatically reduce the conflict in the galaxy, for a long time. Maybe bring the Titans into addressing the Marauder problem once and for all. And we can't have that, can we? That would be half our customer base, gone.'

'No, ma'am.' *Though how we've kept that a secret this long is beyond me.*

'Good. I'm glad you understand. So your job becomes clear, no? We must make the status quo untenable—to the public, to the Senate. End this inter-faction love in before it starts. There are already enough idiots terrified of anyone not from their own planet—it shouldn't be that difficult to get them worked up about the Titan invasion. Or the Seryn menace. Witches, aren't they? Creep into your mind and steal your thoughts.' She shivered theatrically. 'It's just awful.'

*Damn, she's cold.* 'Yes, ma'am. Understood.'

'It had better be.' She picked up a flexscreen scrolltab from her desk and began flicking through it. 'You can leave.'

Drake saluted smartly and headed for the door. Sweat was dripping down his back, and he realised how close he had been to getting the axe.

'Drake?'

He froze.

'Last time you said you wouldn't let me down, you did.' Drake swallowed hard. 'You won't this time, will you?'

'No, ma'am,' he called back over his shoulder.

'Good. I'd hate to lose you. I'm sure everyone would.'

\* \* \*

'I still can't get over how big that megastore is. It had two hundred aisles just for food! And then there's all the other stuff. Boats! I could have bought a boat.'

Ariadne shook her head in amused exasperation and shifted the grocery bags she carried to her other arm. Kith had been prattling excitedly since they left the hypermarket, their first shopping trip since they—along with Calys and Joss—had moved to Nexus P. *Actually, he's been prattling since we left Corinth.*

'Oh, really?' said Calys, stepping carefully onto the final moving walkway that would take them back to their apartment in Midtown Seven before turning to look back at Kith. 'You could have bought a boat with all of that big administrative assistant money you're getting now? Hardly. You're not Ariadne, you know.'

Ariadne aimed a gentle kick at her lover, who skipped away. 'Shut up, you. The government's not giving me that much.'

'Well, they should be! I know you didn't save the galaxy and everything specifically for the Commonwealth, but you'd think they'd show a bit more gratitude.'

'They're paying for our apartment, aren't they? And don't make fun of Kith—it's not like your dazzling sous-chef career is bringing in boat money, either.' Ariadne poked her tongue out at Calys, who glowered back.

'I'll have you know that one day soon I shall be world—nay, galaxy—renowned for my culinary creations. And I won't even make you a sandwich.'

Kith snorted. 'Who says "nay"?'

Ariadne laughed. Joss smiled at her brother's side, as quiet as ever. *I'm really glad she came.* Ariadne had been quite surprised at Joss's willingness to move somewhere as crowded and loud as Nexus Prime. She was hoping the girl would blossom in the new environment and move past the psychological mutism that had plagued her ever since her and Kith's troubles on Wedge, before the Seryn brought them in.

The group stepped off the walkway and crossed the lawn that fronted their apartment building. At fifty stories, Ariadne had thought it vast, until she had seen the hundred-floor Shax tower a few districts over. Apparently, there was a two hundred and fifty–storey building in Uptown One, but they hadn't been there yet. *You could spent a lifetime just travelling around and not see half of this city. City—that's a joke. There are smaller continents on most planets.*

The elevator was a squeeze for the four of them and twelve stuffed grocery bags, but they eventually popped out onto the eighth floor where their apartment at the building's rear overlooked a small copse of trees. *A little reminder of— Well, not home. Here's home now. Old home.* Ariadne wondered how Margo and Humph were getting on. She was ferreting in her pocket for the keycard to the apartment when Calys's gasp made her look up.

*Oh, no.* On the wall of the corridor, next to their apartment door, someone had daubed red paint. Ugly foot-high letters scarred the eggshell white surface:

GO HOME, FREAKS!

Ariadne turned to the others. Calys looked close to tears—the groceries slipped forgotten from her hand, passion fruit rolling across the floor to rest in the puddle of red paint that had dripped down the wall and pooled beneath the slogan. Ariadne stepped to her lover's side and held her.

'Why do they hate us?' Tears ran down Calys cheeks as her body began shaking with sobs. 'Why would they want to fight us?'

*Because human nature isn't always good.* 'Don't worry, Cal.' Ariadne set her jaw. 'I've beaten worse.'

\* \* \*

'Commonwealth Senator, Commissioner for Appropriations Oversight, and now Intercultural Liaison. You are amassing a collection of titles to rival that of your father, Neela.' Alpert Faluten-Sen took a puff from his long, thin cigarillo and tapped it delicately on the ash receptacle atop the mahogany mantelpiece. He turned his back to the fireplace—empty in Central's mild spring weather—and curled his lip at Neela.

'The title's fine. The job, if these first two months are any indication, is not.' She sat behind the broad, deep rubberoak desk. *That was also my father's. Do I inherit everything? Well— He was never Intercultural Liaison. That's a first.*

Alpert glided over, his grey-blue suit a perfect match to the smoke trailing from his cigarillo. 'Would you rather another were doing the job?'

Neela flashed her aide a look. 'Hardly.'

'Quite. And if you do insist on gallivanting off around the galaxy and bringing together the warring tribes, you can hardly be surprised that there are consequences.'

'I'd hoped they'd be a little more positive. The latest poll numbers are pretty grim reading. Over fifty worlds, barely a third of the populace support integration. A fifth are outright against it. The rest—and this is my favourite—don't know.' She shook her head, tapping a stylus on the tablet that sat on her desk. 'How can you not know? I wouldn't have thought it was a difficult question.'

Alpert had taken a seat across from her and retrieved his whisky glass. 'It's not the polls we need to be concerned about, Senator. That is what I wanted to talk to you about.'

Neela sighed. 'Okay. What now?'

Her aide took a sip of his drink before answering. 'Some… news has been passed to me. Unsubstantiated, vaguely defined, the very worst kind of hearsay and rumour… but news nonetheless. That some of those in the Commonwealth who are outright against greater integration with our recently-reunited cousins—a group that may number well above the twenty per cent who admit as much—are considering becoming, shall we say, actively against it.'

*That doesn't sound good.* She frowned. 'Active how?'

'The usual ways. Protests. Activism. Single-issue political engagement of the most pernicious sort—tapping into the latent xenophobia of five trillion citizens who have never been asked to integrate with another strand of humanity before. Many of whom will be convinced that there is no reason why they should.'

'Or the activism could go the other way.'

Alpert nodded slowly. 'Of course. Death threats. Terrorism. Violence. The sort of storm that consumes worlds in hours, and a whole galaxy in days. You remember the Horflex election scandal. This would be orders of magnitude worse.'

'Is that a guess, or do we have numbers?'

'Only an early estimate from PBP. They'll have more for me

when the data solidifies.'

Neela stood up, went to the viewport, and gazed out at the wildflower garden. The noon sun broke through the scattered cloud cover and lit up the floral display in reds and golds. The peaceful beauty was completely at odds with her mood. 'This is going to get worse before it gets better, isn't it?'

His dry, rasping chuckle drifted to her ears. 'As it ever has, Neela. As it ever has.'

\* \* \*

Luc slowly walked around the massive, ring-shaped stone table at the centre of the Debate Hall, the heart of the Helmrock fortress from which the Council had led Titan life for centuries. Sixteen chairs were spaced evenly around its circumference. Later that morning, those seats would be moved, squeezed just a little closer together to make room for one more chair. A slightly larger one. *Mine.*

Not for the first time that morning, Luc Corralin wondered how it had come to this.

'Decided where you want the head of the table to be?'

Luc turned as Jarrod entered through the wide doorway, purple cloak drifting behind him as ever. 'Hard to say. It would be a bit easier if the table was square rather than round, but I don't want to change too much at once.'

The Consul snorted, leaning against the table. 'However carefully you try to tread, your taking sole control isn't going to satisfy everyone. I know for a fact that at least four of those seats are going to be empty tomorrow.'

*Dammit.* 'Who?'

'Trokus, Calix, and Bane. And Fourier, obviously.'

'It would be a bit of a surprise if he climbed out of the Rift, I suppose.' Luc sighed. 'We knew there'd be resistance. These men have been in power too long to give it up that easily.'

'And half of those who do remain will attempt to gain some measure of control over you.' Jarrod raised his hand to emphasise the coming point. *I wonder if he even knows he does that.* 'Your greatest strength here is actually your youth—they'll think you inexperienced, naïve. Easily controlled. It wouldn't hurt to lend a little support to that idea, at least at first. Put them off their guard.'

Luc smiled wryly, continuing his slow circuit of the room. 'Devious business, ruling.'

Jarrod nodded. 'Always has been. Always will be. Why I never ran for the Council. I prefer a more trustworthy enemy, and one I'm allowed to kill.' He sighed. 'But, I digress. I've worse news than a few peeved Councillors.'

The young Titan turned from where he had been admiring a mural depicting some glorious battle or other from years back. His uncle's expression was grave. 'What is it?'

'It seems — and I can hardly believe it myself — that there are some ships missing from the fleet.'

'What do you mean, missing? Lost in combat? With whom?'

Jarrod shook his head. 'Not in combat. Just gone. Deserted.'

*Desertion? By Titans.* 'That's impossible. Never in thousands—'

Jarrod's raised a hand again to cut him off. 'Regardless. It's happened now. And not only that, but the garrisons on several seed planets have broken off contact.'

Luc could only stare. 'Ships gone, planets cut off — you're talking about rebellion.'

'Consult your history lessons, and you'll remember that rebellion leads to only one thing.' Jarrod stood and clapped Luc on the shoulder. 'We've a hard path ahead, Lucius. A hard, hard path.'

*Only one thing.* Luc nodded absently, thoughts skipping down that path to battle projections, combat readiness, force depletion, enemy profiling. *But we won't need enemy profiling, will we?*

*Not for a civil war.*

# Afterword

Thanks for reading! I hope you enjoyed the book. If you would like to be the first to hear about my future releases, you can subscribe to my mailing list here: http://eepurl.com/msrZn.

You can also connect with me online:
**Website**: http://dan-harris.net/
**Twitter**: https://twitter.com/sailingthevoid
**Facebook**: https://www.facebook.com/dan.harris.writer

# Acknowledgements

Huge, heartfelt thanks go to my wife Amisha, my good friend Steve, and my Dad, for their feedback on the first draft; to my editor at RedAdept Publishing, Misti Wolanski, for her wonderfully insightful input and the best grammar lesson I've ever had; and to Stephanie Mooney for creating a cover that's exactly how I envisioned it.

I couldn't have done it without you.

Printed in Great Britain
by Amazon.co.uk, Ltd.,
Marston Gate.